One of the Best Books of the Year!

GOODREADS · *VOGUE* · NPR · *BOOKPAGE*

REFINERY29 · **NEW YORK PUBLIC LIBRARY** · *POPSUGAR*

BUZZFEED · *HYPABLE* · **BOOK RIOT** · *BUSTLE*

O, THE OPRAH MAGAZINE · *HELLOGIGGLES*

HARPER'S BAZAAR · *SHELF AWARENESS* · *SHE READS*

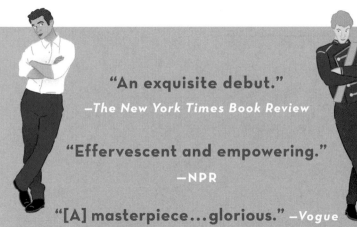

"An exquisite debut."
—*The New York Times Book Review*

"Effervescent and empowering."
—NPR

"[A] masterpiece…glorious." —*Vogue*

"Hilarious." —*Bustle*

"Destined to leave you swooning." —*Popsugar*

"Heartwarmingly romantic." —*Oprahmag.com*

"Charming." —*Us Weekly*

"Clever, romantic, sexy."
—*Kirkus Reviews* (starred review)

"Outrageously fun…romantic, sexy, witty, and thrilling." —TAYLOR JENKINS REID

RED,
WHITE &
ROYAL
BLUE

CASEY McQUISTON

RED, WHITE & ROYAL BLUE

ST. MARTIN'S GRIFFIN
NEW YORK

This is a work of fiction. All of the characters, organizations,
and events portrayed in this novel are either products of the author's
imagination or are used fictitiously.

RED, WHITE & ROYAL BLUE. Copyright © 2019 by Casey McQuiston. All
rights reserved. Printed in the United States of America. For information,
address St. Martin's Publishing Group, 120 Broadway, New York, NY 10271.

www.stmartins.com

Designed by Anna Gorovoy

Library of Congress Cataloging-in-Publication Data

Names: McQuiston, Casey, author.
Title: Red, white & royal blue : a novel / Casey McQuiston.
Other titles: Red, white and royal blue
Description: First edition. | New York : St. Martin's Griffin, 2019.
Identifiers: LCCN 2018055526 | ISBN 9781250316776
    (trade pbk.) | ISBN 9781250316783 (ebook)
Classification: LCC PS3613.C587545 R43 2019 |
    DDC 813/.6—dc23
LC record available at https://lccn.loc.gov/2018055526

Our books may be purchased in bulk for promotional, educational,
or business use. Please contact your local bookseller or the Macmillan
Corporate and Premium Sales Department at 1-800-221-7945, extension
5442, or by email at MacmillanSpecialMarkets@macmillan.com.

First Edition: May 2019

30 29 28 27 26 25

for the weirdos & the dreamers

ONE

On the White House roof, tucked into a corner of the Promenade, there's a bit of loose paneling right on the edge of the Solarium. If you tap it just right, you can peel it back enough to find a message etched underneath, with the tip of a key or maybe a stolen West Wing letter opener.

In the secret history of First Families—an insular gossip mill sworn to absolute discretion about most things on pain of death—there's no definite answer for who wrote it. The one thing people seem certain of is that only a presidential son or daughter would have been daring enough to deface the White House. Some swear it was Jack Ford, with his Hendrix records and split-level room attached to the roof for late-night smoke breaks. Others say it was a young Luci Johnson, thick ribbon in her hair. But it doesn't matter. The writing stays, a private mantra for those resourceful enough to find it.

Alex discovered it within his first week of living there. He's never told anyone how.

It says:

RULE #1: DON'T GET CAUGHT

The East and West Bedrooms on the second floor are generally reserved for the First Family. They were first designated as one giant state bedroom for visits from the Marquis de Lafayette in the Monroe administration, but eventually they were split. Alex has the East, across from the Treaty Room, and June uses the West, next to the elevator.

Growing up in Texas, their rooms were arranged in the same configuration, on either side of the hallway. Back then, you could tell June's ambition of the month by what covered the walls. At twelve, it was watercolor paintings. At fifteen, lunar calendars and charts of crystals. At sixteen, clippings from *The Atlantic*, a UT Austin pennant, Gloria Steinem, Zora Neale Hurston, and excerpts from the papers of Dolores Huerta.

His own room was forever the same, just steadily more stuffed with lacrosse trophies and piles of AP coursework. It's all gathering dust in the house they still keep back home. On a chain around his neck, always hidden from view, he's worn the key to that house since the day he left for DC.

Now, straight across the hall, June's room is all bright white and soft pink and minty green, photographed by *Vogue* and famously inspired by old '60s interior design periodicals she found in one of the White House sitting rooms. His own room was once Caroline Kennedy's nursery and, later, warranting some sage burning from June, Nancy Reagan's office. He's left up the nature field illustrations in a neat symmetrical grid above the sofa, but painted over Sasha Obama's pink walls with a deep blue.

Typically, the children of the president, at least for the past few decades, haven't lived in the Residence beyond eighteen, but Alex started at Georgetown the January his mom was sworn in, and logistically, it made sense not to split their security or costs to whatever one-bedroom apartment he'd be living in. June came that fall, fresh out of UT. She's never said it, but Alex knows she moved in to keep an eye on him. She knows better than anyone else how much he gets off on being this close to the action, and she's bodily yanked him out of the West Wing on more than one occasion.

Behind his bedroom door, he can sit and put Hall & Oates on the record player in the corner, and nobody hears him humming along like his dad to "Rich Girl." He can wear the reading glasses he always insists he doesn't need. He can make as many meticulous study guides with color-coded sticky notes as he wants. He's not going to be the youngest elected congressman in modern history without earning it, but nobody needs to know how hard he's kicking underwater. His sex-symbol stock would plummet.

"Hey," says a voice at the door, and he looks up from his laptop to see June edging into his room, two iPhones and a stack of magazines tucked under one arm, and a plate in her hand. She closes the door behind her with her foot.

"What'd you steal today?" Alex asks, pushing the pile of papers on his bed out of her way.

"Assorted donuts," June says as she climbs up. She's wearing a pencil skirt with pointy pink flats, and he can already see next week's fashion columns: a picture of her outfit today, a lead-in for some sponcon about flats for the professional gal on the go.

He wonders what she's been up to all day. She mentioned a column for *WaPo*, or was it a photoshoot for her blog? Or both? He can never keep up.

She's dumped her stack of magazines out on the bedspread and is already busying herself with them.

"Doing your part to keep the great American gossip industry alive?"

"That's what my journalism degree's for," June says.

"Anything good this week?" Alex asks, reaching for a donut.

"Let's see," June says. "*In Touch* says I'm . . . dating a French model?"

"Are you?"

"I wish." She flips a few pages. "Ooh, and they're saying you got your asshole bleached."

"That one is true," Alex says through a mouthful of chocolate with sprinkles.

"Thought so," June says without looking up. After riffling through most of the magazine, she shuffles it to the bottom of the stack and moves on to *People*. She flips through absently—*People* only ever writes what their publicists tell it to write. Boring. "Not much on us this week . . . oh, I'm a crossword puzzle clue."

Following their tabloid coverage is something of an idle hobby of hers, one that in turns amuses and annoys their mother, and Alex is narcissistic enough to let June read him the highlights. They're usually either complete fabrications or lines fed from their press team, but sometimes it's just funny.

Given the choice, he'd rather read one of the hundreds of glowing pieces of fan fiction about him on the internet, the up-to-eleven version of himself with devastating charm and unbelievable physical stamina, but June flat-out refuses to read those aloud to him, no matter how much he tries to bribe her.

"Do *Us Weekly*," Alex says.

"Hmm . . ." June digs it out of the stack. "Oh, look, we made the cover this week."

She flashes the glossy cover at him, which has a photo of the two of them inlaid in one corner, June's hair pinned on top of her head and Alex looking slightly over-served but still handsome, all jawline and dark curls. Below it in bold yellow letters, the headline reads: FIRST SIBLINGS' WILD NYC NIGHT.

"Oh yeah, that was a wild night," Alex says, reclining back against the tall leather headboard and pushing his glasses up his nose. "Two whole keynote speakers. Nothing sexier than shrimp cocktails and an hour and a half of speeches on carbon emissions."

"It says here you had some kind of tryst with a 'mystery brunette,'" June reads. "'Though the First Daughter was whisked off by limousine to a star-studded party shortly after the gala, twenty-one-year-old heartthrob Alex was snapped sneaking into the W Hotel to meet a mystery brunette in the presidential suite and leaving around four a.m. Sources inside the hotel reported hearing amorous noises from the room all night, and rumors are swirling the brunette was none other than . . . *Nora Holleran,* the twenty-two-year-old granddaughter of Vice President Mike Holleran and third member of the White House Trio. Could it be the two are rekindling their romance?'"

"Yes!" Alex crows, and June groans. "That's less than a month! You owe me fifty dollars, baby."

"Hold on. *Was* it Nora?"

Alex thinks back to the week before, showing up at Nora's room with a bottle of champagne. Their thing on the campaign trail a million years ago was brief, mostly to get the inevitable over with. They were seventeen and eighteen and doomed from the start, both convinced they were the smartest person in any room. Alex has since conceded Nora is 100 percent smarter than him and definitely too smart to have ever dated him.

It's not his fault the press won't let it go, though; that they *love* the idea of them together as if they're modern-day Kennedys. So, if he and Nora occasionally get drunk in hotel rooms together watching *The West Wing* and making loud moaning noises at the wall for the benefit of nosy tabloids, he can't be blamed, really. They're simply turning an undesirable situation into their own personal entertainment.

Scamming his sister is also a perk.

"Maybe," he says, dragging out the vowels.

June swats him with the magazine like he's an especially obnoxious cockroach. "That's cheating, you dick!"

"Bet's a bet," Alex tells her. "We said if there was a new rumor in a month, you'd owe me fifty bucks. I take Venmo."

"I'm not paying," June huffs. "I'm gonna kill her when we see her tomorrow. What are you wearing, by the way?"

"For what?"

"The wedding."

"Whose wedding?"

"Uh, the *royal wedding*," June says. "Of England. It's literally on every cover I just showed you."

She holds *Us Weekly* up again, and this time Alex notices the

main story in giant letters: PRINCE PHILIP SAYS I DO! Along
with a photograph of an extremely nondescript British heir
and his equally nondescript blond fiancée smiling blandly.

He drops his donut in a show of devastation. "That's *this*
weekend?"

"Alex, we leave in the morning," June tells him. "We've got
two appearances before we even go to the ceremony. I can't
believe Zahra hasn't climbed up your ass about this already."

"Shit," he groans. "I know I had that written down. I got
sidetracked."

"What, by conspiring with my best friend against me in the
tabloids for fifty dollars?"

"No, with my research paper, smart-ass," Alex says, gesturing dramatically at his piles of notes. "I've been working on it
for Roman Political Thought all week. And I thought we
agreed Nora is *our* best friend."

"That can't possibly be a real class you're taking," June says.
"Is it possible you willfully forgot about the biggest international event of the year because you don't want to see your archnemesis?"

"June, I'm the son of the President of the United States.
Prince Henry is a figurehead of the British Empire. You can't
just call him my 'archnemesis,'" Alex says. He returns to his
donut, chewing thoughtfully, and adds, "'Archnemesis' implies
he's actually a rival to me on any level and not, you know, a
stuck-up product of inbreeding who probably jerks off to photos of himself."

"Woof."

"I'm just saying."

"Well, you don't have to like him, you just have to put on a
happy face and not cause an international incident at his
brother's wedding."

"Bug, when do I ever not put on a happy face?" Alex says. He pulls a painfully fake grin, and June looks satisfyingly repulsed.

"Ugh. Anyway, you know what you're wearing, right?"

"Yeah, I picked it out and had Zahra approve it last month. I'm not an animal."

"I'm still not sure about my dress," June says. She leans over and steals his laptop away from him, ignoring his noise of protest. "Do you think the maroon or the one with the lace?"

"Lace, obviously. It's England. And why are you trying to make me fail this class?" he says, reaching for his laptop only to have his hand swatted away. "Go curate your Instagram or something. You're the worst."

"Shut up, I'm trying to pick something to watch. Ew, you have *Garden State* on your watch list? Wow, how's film school in 2005 going?"

"I hate you."

"Hmm, I know."

Outside his window, the wind stirs up over the lawn, rustling the linden trees down in the garden. The record on the turntable in the corner has spun out into fuzzy silence. He rolls off the bed and flips it, resetting the needle, and the second side picks up on "London Luck, & Love."

If he's honest, private aviation doesn't really get old, not even three years into his mother's term.

He doesn't get to travel this way a lot, but when he does, it's hard not to let it go to his head. He was born in the hill country of Texas to the daughter of a single mother and the son of Mexican immigrants, all of them dirt poor—luxury travel is still a luxury.

Fifteen years ago, when his mother first ran for the House, the Austin newspaper gave her a nickname: the Lometa Long-shot. She'd escaped her tiny hometown in the shadow of Fort Hood, pulled night shifts at diners to put herself through law school, and was arguing discrimination cases before the Supreme Court by thirty. She was the last thing anybody expected to rise up out of Texas in the midst of the Iraq War: a strawberry-blond, whip-smart Democrat with high heels, an unapologetic drawl, and a little biracial family.

So, it's still surreal that Alex is cruising somewhere over the Atlantic, snacking on pistachios in a high-backed leather chair with his feet up. Nora is bent over the *New York Times* cross-word opposite him, brown curls falling across her forehead. Beside her, the hulking Secret Service agent Cassius—Cash for short—holds his own copy in one giant hand, racing to finish it first. The cursor on Alex's Roman Political Thought paper blinks expectantly at him from his laptop, but something in him can't quite focus on school while they're flying trans-atlantic.

Amy, his mother's favorite Secret Service agent, a former Navy SEAL who is rumored around DC to have killed several men, sits across the aisle. She's got a bulletproof titanium case of crafting supplies open on the couch next to her and is serenely embroidering flowers onto a napkin. Alex has seen her stab someone in the kneecap with a very similar embroi-dery needle.

Which leaves June, next to him, leaning on one elbow with her nose buried in the issue of *People* she's inexplicably brought with them. She always chooses the most bizarre reading ma-terial for flights. Last time, it was a battered old Cantonese phrase book. Before that, *Death Comes for the Archbishop*.

"What are you reading in there now?" Alex asks her.

She flips the magazine around so he can see the double-page spread titled: ROYAL WEDDING MADNESS! Alex groans. This is definitely worse than Willa Cather.

"What?" she says. "I want to be prepared for my first-ever royal wedding."

"You went to prom, didn't you?" Alex says. "Just picture that, only in hell, and you have to be really nice about it."

"Can you believe they spent $75,000 just on the cake?"

"That's depressing."

"*And* apparently Prince Henry is going sans date to the wedding and everyone is freaking out about it. It says he was," she affects a comical English accent, "'rumored to be dating a Belgian heiress last month, but now followers of the prince's dating life aren't sure what to think.'"

Alex snorts. It's insane to him that there are legions of people who follow the intensely dull dating lives of the royal siblings. He understands why people care where he puts his own tongue—at least *he* has personality.

"Maybe the female population of Europe finally realized he's as compelling as a wet ball of yarn," Alex suggests.

Nora puts down her crossword puzzle, having finished it first. Cassius glances over and swears. "You gonna ask him to dance, then?"

Alex rolls his eyes, suddenly imagining twirling around a ballroom while Henry drones sweet nothings about croquet and fox hunting in his ear. The thought makes him want to gag.

"In his dreams."

"Aw," Nora says, "you're blushing."

"Listen," Alex tells her, "royal weddings are trash, the princes who have royal weddings are trash, the imperialism that allows princes to exist at all is trash. It's trash turtles all the way down."

"Is this your TED Talk?" June asks. "You do realize America is a genocidal empire too, right?"

"Yes, *June,* but at least we have the decency not to keep a monarchy around," Alex says, throwing a pistachio at her.

There are a few things about Alex and June that new White House hires are briefed on before they start. June's peanut allergy. Alex's frequent middle-of-the-night requests for coffee. June's college boyfriend, who broke up with her when he moved to California but is still the only person whose letters come to her directly. Alex's long-standing grudge against the youngest prince.

It's not a grudge, really. It's not even a rivalry. It's a prickling, unsettling annoyance. It makes his palms sweat.

The tabloids—the world—decided to cast Alex as the American equivalent of Prince Henry from day one, since the White House Trio is the closest thing America has to royalty. It has never seemed fair. Alex's image is all charisma and genius and smirking wit, thoughtful interviews and the cover of GQ at eighteen; Henry's is placid smiles and gentle chivalry and generic charity appearances, a perfectly blank Prince Charming canvas. Henry's role, Alex thinks, is much easier to play.

Maybe it is technically a rivalry. Whatever.

"All right, MIT," he says, "what are the numbers on this one?"

Nora grins. "Hmm." She pretends to think hard about it. "Risk assessment: FSOTUS failing to check himself before he wrecks himself will result in greater than five hundred civilian casualties. Ninety-eight percent probability of Prince Henry looking like a total dreamboat. Seventy-eight percent probability of Alex getting himself banned from the United Kingdom forever."

"Those are better odds than I expected," June observes.

Alex laughs, and the plane soars on.

London is an absolute spectacle, crowds cramming the streets outside Buckingham Palace and all through the city, draped in Union Jacks and waving tiny flags over their heads. There are commemorative royal wedding souvenirs everywhere; Prince Philip and his bride's face plastered on everything from chocolate bars to underwear. Alex almost can't believe this many people care so passionately about something so comprehensively dull. He's sure there won't be this kind of turnout in front of the White House when he or June get married one day, nor would he even want it.

The ceremony itself seems to last forever, but it's at least sort of nice, in a way. It's not that Alex isn't into love or can't appreciate marriage. It's just that Martha is a perfectly respectable daughter of nobility, and Philip is a prince. It's as sexy as a business transaction. There's no passion, no drama. Alex's kind of love story is much more Shakespearean.

It feels like years before he's settled at a table between June and Nora inside a Buckingham Palace ballroom for the reception banquet, and he's irritated enough to be a little reckless. Nora passes him a flute of champagne, and he takes it gladly.

"Do either of y'all know what a viscount is?" June is saying, halfway through a cucumber sandwich. "I've met, like, five of them, and I keep smiling politely as if I know what it means when they say it. Alex, you took comparative international governmental relational things. Whatever. What are they?"

"I think it's that thing when a vampire creates an army of crazed sex waifs and starts his own ruling body," he says.

"That sounds right," Nora says. She's folding her napkin into a complicated shape on the table, her shiny black manicure glinting in the chandelier light.

"I wish I were a viscount," June says. "I could have my sex waifs deal with my emails."

"Are sex waifs good with professional correspondence?" Alex asks.

Nora's napkin has begun to resemble a bird. "I think it could be an interesting approach. Their emails would be all tragic and wanton." She tries on a breathless, husky voice. "'Oh, please, I beg you, take me—take me to lunch to discuss fabric samples, you beast!'"

"Could be weirdly effective," Alex notes.

"Something is wrong with both of you," June says gently.

Alex is opening his mouth to retort when a royal attendant materializes at their table like a dense and dour-looking ghost in a bad hairpiece.

"Miss Claremont-Diaz," says the man, who looks like his name is probably Reginald or Bartholomew or something. He bows, and miraculously his hairpiece doesn't fall off into June's plate. Alex shares an incredulous glance with her behind his back. "His Royal Highness Prince Henry wonders if you would do him the honor of accompanying him for a dance."

June's mouth freezes halfway open, caught on a soft vowel sound, and Nora breaks out into a shit-eating grin.

"Oh, she'd *love* to," Nora volunteers. "She's been hoping he'd ask all evening."

"I—" June starts and stops, her mouth smiling even as her eyes slice at Nora. "Of course. That would be lovely."

"Excellent," Reginald-Bartholomew says, and he turns and gestures over his shoulder.

And there Henry is, in the flesh, as classically handsome as ever in his tailored three-piece suit, all tousled sandy hair and high cheekbones and a soft, friendly mouth. He holds himself with innately impeccable posture, as if he emerged fully formed and upright out of some beautiful Buckingham Palace posy garden one day.

His eyes lock on Alex's, and something like annoyance or adrenaline spikes in Alex's chest. He hasn't had a conversation with Henry in probably a year. His face is still infuriatingly symmetrical.

Henry deigns to give him a perfunctory nod, as if he's any other random guest, not the person he beat to a *Vogue* editorial debut in their teens. Alex blinks, seethes, and watches Henry angle his stupid chiseled jaw toward June.

"Hello, June," Henry says, and he extends a gentlemanly hand to June, who is now blushing. Nora pretends to swoon. "Do you know how to waltz?"

"I'm . . . sure I could pick it up," she says, and she takes his hand cautiously, like she thinks he might be pranking her, which Alex thinks is way too generous to Henry's sense of humor. Henry leads her off to the crowd of twirling nobles.

"So is that what's happening now?" Alex says, glaring down at Nora's napkin bird. "Has he decided to finally shut me up by wooing my sister?"

"Aw, little buddy," Nora says. She reaches over and pats his hand. "It's cute how you think everything is about you."

"It should be, honestly."

"That's the spirit."

He glances up into the crowd, where June is being rotated around the floor by Henry. She's got a neutral, polite smile on her face, and he keeps looking over her shoulder, which is even more annoying. June is amazing. The least Henry could do is pay attention to her.

"Do you think he actually likes her, though?"

Nora shrugs. "Who knows? Royals are weird. Might be a courtesy, or—oh, there it is."

A royal photographer has swooped in and is snapping a shot of them dancing, one Alex knows will be leaked to *Hello* next week. So, that's it, then? Using the First Daughter to start some idiotic dating rumor for attention? God forbid Philip gets to dominate the news cycle for one week.

"He's kind of good at this," Nora remarks.

Alex flags down a waiter and decides to spend the rest of the reception getting systematically drunk.

Alex has never told—will never tell—anyone, but he saw Henry for the first time when he was twelve years old. He only ever reflects upon it when he's drunk.

He's sure he saw his face in the news before then, but that was the first time he really *saw* him. June had just turned fifteen and used part of her birthday money to buy an issue of a blindingly colorful teen magazine. Her love of trashy tabloids started early. In the center of the magazine were miniature posters you could rip out and stick up in your locker. If you were careful and pried up the staples with your fingernails, you could get them out without tearing them. One of them, right in the middle, was a picture of a boy.

He had thick, tawny hair and big blue eyes, a warm smile, and a cricket bat over one shoulder. It must have been a candid, because there was a happy, sun-bright confidence to him that couldn't be posed. On the bottom corner of the page in pink and blue letters: PRINCE HENRY.

Alex still doesn't really know what kept drawing him back, only that he would sneak into June's room and find the page and touch his fingertips to the boy's hair, as if he could somehow feel its texture if he imagined it hard enough. The more his parents climbed the political ranks, the more he started to reckon with the fact that soon the world would know who he was. Then, sometimes, he'd think of the picture, and try to harness Prince Henry's easy confidence.

(He also thought about prying up the staples with his fingers and taking the picture out and keeping it in his room, but he never did. His fingernails were too stubby; they weren't made for it like June's, like a girl's.)

But then came the first time he met Henry—the first cool, detached words Henry said to him—and Alex guessed he had it all wrong, that the pretty, flung-open boy from the picture wasn't real. The real Henry is beautiful, distant, boring, and closed. This person the tabloids keep comparing him to, whom he compares *himself* to, thinks he's *better* than Alex and everyone like him. Alex can't believe he ever wanted to be anything like that.

Alex keeps drinking, keeps alternating between thinking about it and forcing himself not to think about it, disappears into the crowd and dances with pretty European heiresses about it.

He's pirouetting away from one when he catches sight of a lone figure hovering near the cake and the champagne fountain. It's Prince Henry yet again, glass in hand, watching Prince Philip and his bride spinning on the ballroom floor. He looks politely half-interested in that obnoxious way of his, like he has somewhere else to be. And Alex can't resist the urge to call his bluff.

He picks his way through the crowd, grabbing a glass of wine off a passing tray and downing half of it.

"When you have one of these," Alex says, sidling up to him, "you should do two champagne fountains instead of one. Really embarrassing to be at a wedding with only one champagne fountain."

"Alex," Henry says in that maddeningly posh accent. Up close, the waistcoat under his suit jacket is a lush gold and has about a million buttons on it. It's horrible. "I wondered if I'd have the pleasure."

"Looks like it's your lucky day," Alex says, smiling.

"Truly a momentous occasion," Henry agrees. His own smile is bright white and immaculate, made to be printed on money.

The most annoying thing of all is Alex *knows* Henry hates him too—he *must,* they're naturally mutual antagonists—but he refuses to outright act like it. Alex is intimately aware politics involves a lot of making nice with people you loathe, but he wishes that once, just once, Henry would act like an actual human and not some polished little windup toy sold in a palace gift shop.

He's too perfect. Alex wants to poke it.

"Do you ever get tired," Alex says, "of pretending you're above all this?"

Henry turns and stares at him. "I'm sure I don't know what you mean."

"I mean, you're out here, getting the photographers to chase you, swanning around like you hate the attention, which you clearly don't since you're dancing with my sister, of all people," Alex says. "You act like you're too important to be anywhere, ever. Doesn't that get exhausting?"

"I'm . . . a bit more complicated than that," Henry attempts.

"*Ha.*"

"Oh," Henry says, narrowing his eyes. "You're drunk."

"I'm just saying," Alex says, resting an overly friendly elbow on Henry's shoulder, which isn't as easy as he'd like it to be since Henry has about four infuriating inches of height on him. "You could try to act like you're having fun. Occasionally."

Henry laughs ruefully. "I believe perhaps you should consider switching to water, Alex."

"Should I?" Alex says. He pushes aside the thought that maybe the wine is what gave him the nerve to stomp over to Henry in the first place and makes his eyes as coy and angelic as he knows how. "Am I offending you? Sorry I'm not obsessed with you like everyone else. I know that must be confusing for you."

"Do you know what?" Henry says. "I think you are."

Alex's mouth drops open, while the corner of Henry's turns smug and almost a little mean.

"Only a thought," Henry says, tone polite. "Have you ever noticed I have never once approached you and have been *exhaustively* civil every time we've spoken? Yet here you are, seeking me out again." He takes a sip of his champagne. "Simply an observation."

"What? I'm not—" Alex stammers. "You're the—"

"Have a lovely evening, Alex," Henry says tersely, and turns to walk off.

It drives Alex *nuts* that Henry thinks he gets to have the last word, and without thinking, he reaches out and pulls Henry's shoulder back.

And then Henry turns, suddenly, and almost does push Alex off him this time, and for a brief spark of a moment, Alex is impressed at the glint in his eyes, the abrupt burst of an actual personality.

The next thing he knows, he's tripping over his own foot and stumbling backward into the table nearest him. He notices too late that the table is, to his horror, the one bearing the massive eight-tier wedding cake, and he grabs for Henry's arm to catch himself, but all it does is throw both of them off-balance and send them crashing together into the cake stand.

He watches, as if in slow motion, as the cake leans, teeters, shudders, and finally tips. There's absolutely nothing he can do to stop it. It comes crashing down onto the floor in an avalanche of white buttercream, some kind of sugary $75,000 nightmare.

The room goes heart-stoppingly silent as momentum carries him and Henry through the fall and down, down onto the wreckage of the cake on the ornate carpet, Henry's sleeve still clutched in Alex's fist. Henry's glass of champagne has spilled all over both of them and shattered, and out of the corner of his eye, Alex can see a cut across the top of Henry's cheekbone beginning to bleed.

For a second, all he can think as he stares up at the ceiling while covered in frosting and champagne is that at least Henry's dance with June won't be the biggest story to come out of the royal wedding.

His next thought is that his mother is going to murder him in cold blood.

Beside him, he hears Henry mutter slowly, "Oh my fucking Christ."

He registers dimly that it's the first time he's ever heard the prince swear, before the flash from someone's camera goes off.

TWO

With a resounding smack, Zahra slaps a stack of magazines down on the West Wing briefing room table.

"This is just what I saw on the way here this morning," she says. "I don't think I need to remind you I live two blocks away."

Alex stares down at the headlines in front of him.

THE $75,000 STUMBLE

BATTLE ROYAL: Prince Henry and FSOTUS Come to Blows at Royal Wedding

CAKEGATE:
Alex Claremont-Diaz Sparks Second English-American War

Each one is accompanied by a photo of himself and Henry flat on their backs in a pile of cake, Henry's ridiculous suit all askew and covered in smashed buttercream flowers, his wrist pinned in Alex's hand, a thin slice of red across Henry's cheek.

"Are you sure we shouldn't be in the Situation Room for this meeting?" Alex attempts.

Neither Zahra nor his mother, sitting across the table, seems to find it funny. The president gives him a withering look over the top of her reading glasses, and he clamps his mouth shut.

It's not exactly that he's afraid of Zahra, his mom's deputy chief of staff and right-hand woman. She has a spiky exterior, but Alex swears there's something soft in there somewhere. He's more afraid of what his mother might do. They grew up made to talk about their feelings a lot, and then his mother became president, and life became less about feelings and more about international relations. He's not sure which option spells a worse fate.

"'Sources inside the royal reception report the two were seen arguing minutes before the . . . *cake-tastrophe*,'" Ellen reads out loud with utter disdain from her own copy of *The Sun*. Alex doesn't even try to guess how she got her hands on today's edition of a British tabloid. President Mom works in mysterious ways. "'But royal family insiders claim the First Son's feud with Henry has raged for years. A source tells *The Sun* that Henry and the First Son have been at odds ever since their first meeting at the Rio Olympics, and the animosity has only grown—these days, they can't even be in the same room with each other. It seems it was only a matter of time before Alex took the American approach: a violent altercation.'"

"I really don't think you can call tripping over a table a 'violent'—"

"Alexander," Ellen says, her tone eerily calm. "Shut up."

He does.

"'One can't help but wonder,'" Ellen reads on, "'if the bitterness between these two powerful sons has contributed to what many have called an icy and distant relationship between President Ellen Claremont's administration and the monarchy in recent years.'"

She tosses the magazine aside, folding her arms on the table.

"Please, tell me another joke," Ellen says. "I want so badly for you to explain to me how this is funny."

Alex opens his mouth and closes it a couple of times.

"He started it," he says finally. "I barely touched him—he's the one who pushed me, and I only grabbed him to try and catch my balance, and—"

"Sugar, I cannot express to you how much the press does not give a fuck about who started what," Ellen says. "As your mother, I can appreciate that maybe this isn't your fault, but as the president, all I want is to have the CIA fake your death and ride the dead-kid sympathy into a second term."

Alex clenches his jaw. He's used to doing things that piss his mother's staff off—in his teens, he had a penchant for confronting his mother's colleagues with their voting discrepancies at friendly DC fund-raisers—and he's been in the tabloids for things more embarrassing than this. But never in quite such a cataclysmically, internationally terrible way.

"I don't have time to deal with this right now, so here's what we're gonna do," Ellen says, pulling a folder out of her padfolio. It's filled with some official-looking documents punctuated with different colors of sticky tabs, and the first one says: AGREEMENT OF TERMS.

"Um," Alex says.

"You," she says, "are going to make nice with Henry. You're leaving Saturday and spending Sunday in England."

Alex blinks. "Is it too late to take the faking-my-death option?"

"Zahra can brief you on the rest," Ellen goes on, ignoring him. "I have about five hundred meetings right now." She gets up and heads for the door, stopping to kiss her hand and press it to the top of his head. "You're a dumbass. Love you."

Then she's gone, heels clicking behind her down the hallway, and Zahra settles into her vacated chair with a look on her face like she'd prefer arranging his death for real. She's not technically the most powerful or important player in his mother's White House, but she's been working by Ellen's side since Alex was five and Zahra was fresh out of Howard. She's the only one trusted to wrangle the First Family.

"All right, here's the deal," she says. "I was up all night conferencing with a bunch of uptight royal handlers and PR pricks and the prince's fucking *equerry* to make this happen, so you are going to follow this plan to the letter and not fuck it up, got it?"

Alex still privately thinks this whole thing is completely ridiculous, but he nods. Zahra looks deeply unconvinced but presses on.

"First, the White House and the monarchy are going to release a joint statement saying what happened at the royal wedding was a complete accident and a misunderstanding—"

"Which it was."

"—and that, despite rarely having time to see each other,

you and Prince Henry have been close personal friends for the past several years."

"We're *what*?"

"Look," Zahra says, taking a drag from her massive stainless steel thermos of coffee. "Both sides need to come out of this looking good, and the only way to do that is to make it look like your little slap-fight at the wedding was some homoerotic frat bro mishap, okay? So, you can hate the heir to the throne all you want, write mean poems about him in your diary, but the minute you see a camera, you act like the sun shines out of his dick, and you make it convincing."

"Have you met Henry?" Alex says. "How am I supposed to do that? He has the personality of a cabbage."

"Are you really not understanding how much I don't care at all how you feel about this?" Zahra says. "This is what's happening so your stupid ass doesn't distract the entire country from your mother's reelection campaign. Do you want her to have to get up on the debate stage next year and explain to the world why her son is trying to destabilize America's European relationships?"

Well, no, he doesn't. And he knows, in the back of his mind, that he's a better strategist than he's been about this, and that without this stupid grudge, he probably could have come up with this plan on his own.

"So Henry's your new best friend," Zahra continues. "You will smile and nod and not piss off anyone while you and Henry spend the weekend doing charity appearances and talking to the press about how much you love each other's company. If somebody asks about him, I want to hear you gush like he's your fucking prom date."

She slides him a page of bulleted lists and tables of data so elaborately organized he could have made it himself. It's labeled: HRH PRINCE HENRY FACT SHEET.

"You're going to memorize this so if anybody tries to catch you in a lie, you know what to say," she says. Under HOBBIES, it lists polo and competitive yachting. Alex is going to set himself on fire.

"Does he get one of these for me?" Alex asks helplessly.

"Yep. And for the record, making it was one of the most depressing moments of my career." She slides another page over to him, this one detailing requirements for the weekend.

> Minimum two (2) social media posts per day highlighting England/visit thereof.
>
> One (1) on-air interview with *ITV This Morning*, lasting five (5) minutes, in accordance with determined narrative.
>
> Two (2) joint appearances with photographers present: one (1) private meeting, one (1) public charity appearance.

"Why do I have to go over there? He's the one who pushed me into the stupid cake—shouldn't he have to come here and go on *SNL* with me or something?"

"Because it was the *royal wedding* you ruined, and *they're* the ones out seventy-five grand," Zahra says. "Besides, we're arranging his presence at a state dinner in a few months. He's not any more excited about this than you are."

Alex pinches the bridge of his nose where a stress headache is already percolating. "I have class."

"You'll be back by Sunday night, DC time," Zahra tells him. "You won't miss anything."

"So there's really no way I'm getting out of this?"

"Nope."

Alex presses his lips together. He needs a list.

When he was a kid, he used to hide pages and pages of loose leaf paper covered in messy, loopy handwriting under the worn denim cushion of the window seat in the house in Austin. Rambling treatises on the role of government in America with all the Gs written backward, paragraphs translated from English to Spanish, tables of his elementary school classmates' strengths and weaknesses. And lists. Lots of lists. The lists help.

So: Reasons this is a good idea.

One. His mother needs good press.

Two. Having a shitty record on foreign relations definitely won't help his career.

Three. Free trip to Europe.

"Okay," he says, taking the file. "I'll do it. But I won't have any fun."

"God, I hope not."

The White House Trio is, officially, the nickname for Alex, June, and Nora coined by *People* shortly before the inauguration. In actuality, it was carefully tested with focus groups by the White House press team and fed directly to *People*. Politics—calculating, even in hashtags.

Before the Claremonts, the Kennedys and Clintons shielded the First Offspring from the press, giving them the privacy to go through awkward phases and organic childhood experiences and everything else. Sasha and Malia were hounded and picked apart by the press before they were out of high school. The White House Trio got ahead of the narrative before anyone could do the same.

It was a bold new plan: three attractive, bright, charismatic, marketable millennials—Alex and Nora are, technically, just past the Gen Z threshold, but the press doesn't find that nearly as catchy. Catchiness sells, coolness sells. Obama was cool. The whole First Family could be cool too; celebrities in their own right. *It's not ideal,* his mother always says, *but it works.*

They're the White House Trio, but here, in the music room on the third floor of the Residence, they're just Alex and June and Nora, naturally glued together since they were teenagers stunting their growth with espresso in the primaries. Alex pushes them. June steadies them. Nora keeps them honest.

They settle into their usual places: June, perched on her heels at the record collection, foraging for some Patsy Cline; Nora, cross-legged on the floor, uncorking a bottle of red wine; Alex, sitting upside down with his feet on the back of the couch, trying to figure out what he's going to do next.

He flips the HRH PRINCE HENRY FACT SHEET over and squints at it. He can feel the blood rushing to his head.

June and Nora are ignoring him, caught in a bubble of intimacy he can never quite penetrate. Their relationship is something enormous and incomprehensible to most people, including Alex on occasion. He knows them both down to their split ends and nasty habits, but there's a strange girl bond between them he can't, and knows he isn't supposed to, translate.

"I thought you were liking the *Post* gig?" Nora says. With a dull pop, she pulls the cork out of the wine and takes a swig directly from the bottle.

"I was," June says. "I mean, I *am.* But, it's not much of a gig. It's, like, one op-ed a month, and half my pitches get shot down for being too close to Mom's platform, and even then, the press team has to read anything political before I turn it in. So it's like, email in these fluff pieces, and know that on the other side of the screen people are doing the most important journalism of their careers, and be okay with that."

"So . . . you don't like it, then."

June sighs. She finds the record she's looking for, slides it out of the sleeve. "I don't know what else to *do,* is the thing."

"They wouldn't put you on a beat?" Nora asks her.

"You kidding? They wouldn't even let me in the building," June says. She puts the record on and sets the needle. "What would Reilly and Rebecca say?"

Nora tips her head and laughs. "My parents would say to do what they did: ditch journalism, get really into essential oils, buy a cabin in the Vermont wilderness, and own six hundred LL Bean vests that all smell like patchouli."

"You left out the investing in Apple in the nineties and getting stupid-rich part," June reminds her.

"Details."

June walks over and places her palm on the top of Nora's head, deep in her nest of curls, and leans down to kiss the back of her own fingers. "I'll figure something out."

Nora hands over the bottle, and June takes a pull. Alex heaves a dramatic sigh.

"I can't believe I have to learn this garbage," Alex says. "I *just* finished midterms."

"Look, you're the one who has to fight everything that moves," June says, wiping her mouth on the back of her hand, a move she'd only do in front of the two of them. "Including the British monarchy. So, I don't really feel bad for you. Anyway, he was totally fine when I danced with him. I don't get why you hate him so much."

"I think it's amazing," Nora says. "Sworn enemies forced to make peace to settle tensions between their countries? There's something totally Shakespearean about it."

"Shakespearean in that hopefully I'll get stabbed to death," Alex says. "This sheet says his favorite food is mutton pie. I literally cannot think of a more boring food. He's like a cardboard cutout of a person."

The sheet is filled with things Alex already knew, either from the royal siblings dominating the news cycle or hate-reading Henry's Wikipedia page. He knows about Henry's parentage, about his older siblings Philip and Beatrice, that he studied English literature at Oxford and plays classical piano. The rest is so trivial he can't imagine it'll come up in an interview, but there's no way he'll risk Henry being more prepared.

"Idea," Nora says. "Let's make it a drinking game."

"Ooh, yes," June agrees. "Drink every time Alex gets one right?"

"Drink every time the answer makes you want to puke?" Alex suggests.

"One drink for a correct answer, two drinks for a Prince Henry fact that is legitimately, objectively awful," Nora says. June has already dug two glasses out of the cabinet, and she hands them to Nora, who fills both and keeps the bottle for herself. Alex slides down from the couch to sit on the floor with her.

"Okay," she goes on, taking the sheet out of Alex's hands. "Let's start easy. Parents. Go."

Alex picks up his own glass, already pulling up a mental image of Henry's parents, Catherine's shrewd blue eyes and Arthur's movie-star jaw.

"Mother: Princess Catherine, oldest daughter of Queen

Mary, first princess to obtain a doctorate—English literature," he rattles off. "Father: Arthur Fox, beloved English film and stage actor best known for his turn as James Bond in the eighties, deceased 2015. Y'all drink."

They do, and Nora passes the list to June.

"Okay," June says, scanning the list, apparently looking for something more challenging. "Let's see. Dog's name?"

"*David,*" Alex says. "He's a beagle. I remember because, like, *who does that?* Who names a dog *David?* He sounds like a tax attorney. Like a dog tax attorney. Drink."

"Best friend's name, age, and occupation?" Nora asks. "Best friend other than *you,* of course."

Alex casually gives her the finger. "Percy Okonjo. Goes by Pez or Pezza. Heir to Okonjo Industries, Nigerian company leading Africa in biomedical advancements. Twenty-two, lives in London, met Henry at Eton. Manages the Okonjo Foundation, a humanitarian nonprofit. Drink."

"Favorite book?"

"Uh," Alex says. "Um. Fuck. Uh. What's the one—"

"I'm sorry, Mr. Claremont-Diaz, that is incorrect," June says. "Thank you for playing, but you lose."

"Come on, what's the answer?"

June peers down at the list. "This says . . . *Great Expectations?*" Both Nora and Alex groan.

"Do you see what I mean now?" Alex says. "This dude is reading Charles Dickens . . . *for pleasure.*"

"I'll give you this one," Nora says. "Two drinks!"

"Well, I think—" June says as Nora glugs away. "Guys, it's kinda nice! I mean, it's pretentious, but the themes of *Great Expectations* are all like, love is more important than status, and doing what's right beats money and power. Maybe he relates—"

Alex makes a long, loud fart noise. "Y'all are such assholes! He seems really nice!"

"That's because you are a nerd," Alex says. "You want to protect those of your own species. It's a natural instinct."

"I am helping you with this out of the goodness of my heart," June says. "I'm on *deadline* right now."

"Hey, what do you think Zahra put on my fact sheet?"

"Hmm," Nora says, sucking her teeth. "Favorite summer Olympic sport: rhythmic gymnastics—"

"I'm not ashamed of that."

"Favorite brand of khakis: Gap."

"Listen, they look best on my ass. The J. Crew ones wrinkle all weird. And they're not *khakis,* they're *chinos.* Khakis are for *white people.*"

"Allergies: dust, Tide laundry detergent, and shutting the fuck up."

"Age of first filibuster: nine, at SeaWorld San Antonio, trying to force an orca wrangler into early retirement for, quote, 'inhumane whale practices.'"

"I stood by it then, and I stand by it now."

June throws her head back and laughs, loud and unguarded, and Nora rolls her eyes, and Alex is glad, at least, that he'll have this to come back to when the nightmare is over.

Alex expects Henry's handler to be some stout storybook Englishman with tails and a top hat, probably a walrus mustache, definitely scurrying to place a velvet footstool at Henry's carriage door.

The person who awaits him and his security team on the tarmac is very much not that. He's a tall thirty-something

Indian man in an impeccably tailored suit, roguishly hand-some with a neatly trimmed beard, a steaming cup of tea, and a shiny Union Jack on his lapel. Well, okay then.

"Agent Chen," the man says, extending his free hand to Amy. "Hope the flight was smooth."

Amy nods. "As smooth as the third transatlantic flight in a week can be."

The man half-smiles, commiserative. "The Land Rover is for you and your team for the duration."

Amy nods again, releasing his hand, and the man turns his attention to Alex.

"Mr. Claremont-Diaz," he says. "Welcome back to England. Shaan Srivastava, Prince Henry's equerry."

Alex takes his hand and shakes it, feeling a bit like he's in one of Henry's dad's Bond movies. Behind him, an attendant unloads his luggage and carries it off in the direction of a sleek Aston Martin.

"Nice to meet you, Shaan. Not exactly how we thought we'd be spending our weekend, is it?"

"I'm not as surprised at this turn of events as I'd like to be, sir," Shaan says coolly, with an inscrutable smile.

He pulls a small tablet from his jacket and pivots on his heel toward the waiting car. Alex stares at his back, speechless, be-fore hastily refusing to be impressed by a grown man whose job is handling the prince's schedule, no matter how cool he is or how long and smooth his strides are. He shakes his head a little and jogs to catch up, sliding into the back seat as Shaan checks the mirrors.

"Right," Shaan says. "You'll be staying in the guest quar-ters at Kensington Palace. Tomorrow you'll do the *This Morning* interview at nine—we've arranged for a photo call at the studio. Then it's children with cancer all afternoon and off you go back to the land of the free."

"Okay," Alex says. He very politely does not add, *could be worse.*

"For now," Shaan says, "you're to come with me to chauffeur the prince from the stables. One of our photographers will be there to photograph the prince welcoming you to the country, so do try to look pleased to be here."

Of course, there are *stables* the prince needs to be *chauffeured* from. He was briefly worried he'd been wrong about what the weekend would look like, but this feels a lot more like it.

"If you'll check the seat pocket in front of you," Shaan says as he reverses, "there are a few papers for you to sign. Your lawyers have already approved them." He passes back an expensive-looking black fountain pen.

NONDISCLOSURE AGREEMENT, the top of the first page reads. Alex flips through to the last page—there are at least fifteen pages of text—and a low whistle escapes his lips.

"This is . . ." Alex says, "a thing you do often?"

"Standard protocol," Shaan says. "The reputation of the royal family is too valuable to risk."

The words "Confidential Information," as used in this Agreement, shall include the following:

1. Such information as HRH Prince Henry or any member of the Royal Family may designate to the Guest as "Confidential Information";

2. All proprietary and financial information regarding HRH Prince Henry's personal wealth and estate;

3. Any interior architectural details of Royal Residences including Buckingham Palace, Kensington Palace, etc., and personal effects found therein;

4. Any information regarding or involving HRH Prince Henry's personal or private life not previously released by official Royal documents, speeches, or approved biographers, including any personal or private relationship the Guest may have with HRH Prince Henry;

5. Any information found on HRH Prince Henry's personal electronic devices . . .

This seems . . . excessive, like the kind of paperwork you get from some perverted millionaire who wants to hunt you for sport. He wonders what the most mind-numbingly wholesome public figure on earth could possibly have to hide. He hopes it's not people-hunting.

Alex is no stranger to NDAs, though, so he signs and initials. It's not like he would have divulged all the boring details of this trip to anyone anyway, except maybe June and Nora.

They pull up to the stables after another fifteen minutes, his security close behind them. The royal stables are, of course, elaborate and well-kept and about a million miles from the old ranches he's seen out in the Texas panhandle. Shaan leads him out to the edge of the paddock, and Amy and her team regroup ten paces behind.

Alex rests his elbows on the lacquered white fence boards, fighting back the sudden, absurd feeling he's underdressed for this. On any other day, his chinos and button-down would be fine for a casual photo op, but for the first time in a long time, he's feeling distinctly out of his element. Does his hair look awful from the plane?

It's not like Henry is going to look much better after polo practice. He'll probably be sweaty and disgusting.

As if on cue, Henry comes galloping around the bend on the back of a pristine white horse.

He is definitely not sweaty or disgusting. He is, instead, bathed dramatically in a sweeping and resplendent sunset, wearing a crisp black jacket and riding pants tucked into tall leather boots, looking every inch an actual fairy-tale prince. He unhooks his helmet and takes it off with one gloved hand, and his hair underneath is just attractively tousled enough to look like it's supposed to be that way.

"I'm going to throw up on you," Alex says as soon as Henry is close enough to hear him.

"Hello, Alex," Henry says. Alex really resents the extra few inches of height Henry has on him right now. "You look . . . sober."

"Only for you, Your Royal Highness," he says with an elaborate mock-bow. He's pleased to hear a little bit of ice in Henry's voice, finally done pretending.

"You're too kind," Henry says. He swings one long leg over and dismounts from his horse gracefully, removing his glove and extending a hand to Alex. A well-dressed stable hand basically springs up out of the ground to whisk the horse away by the reins. Alex has probably never hated anything more.

"This is idiotic," Alex says, grasping Henry's hand. The skin is soft, probably exfoliated and moisturized daily by some royal manicurist. There's a royal photographer right on the other side of the fence, so he smiles winningly and says through his teeth, "Let's get it over with."

"I'd rather be waterboarded," Henry says, smiling back. The camera snaps nearby. His eyes are big and soft and blue, and he desperately needs to be punched in one of them. "Your country could probably arrange that."

Alex throws his head back and laughs handsomely, loud and false. "Go fuck yourself."

"Hardly enough time," Henry says. He releases Alex's hand as Shaan returns.

"Your Highness," Shaan greets Henry with a nod. Alex makes a concentrated effort not to roll his eyes. "The photographer should have what he needs, so if you're ready, the car is waiting."

Henry turns to him and smiles again, eyes unreadable. "Shall we?"

There's something vaguely familiar about the Kensington Palace guest quarters, even though he's never been here before.

Shaan had an attendant show him to his room, where his luggage awaited him on an ornately carved bed with spun gold bedding. Many of the rooms in the White House have a similar hauntedness, a sense of history that hangs like cobwebs no matter how pristine the rooms are kept. He's used to sleeping alongside ghosts, but that's not it.

It strikes further back in his memory, around the time his parents split up. They were the kind of married lawyer couple who could barely order Chinese takeout without legally binding documents, so Alex spent the summer before seventh grade shuttled back and forth from home to their dad's new place outside of Los Angeles until they could strike a long-term arrangement.

It was a nice house in the valley, a clear blue swimming pool and a back wall of solid glass. He never slept well there. He'd sneak out of his thrown-together bedroom in the middle of the night, stealing Helados from his dad's freezer and standing barefoot in the kitchen eating straight from the quart, washed blue in the pool light.

That's how it feels here, somehow—wide awake at midnight in a strange place, duty-bound to make it work.

He wanders into the kitchen attached to his guest wing, where the ceilings are high and the countertops are shiny marble. He was allowed to submit a list to stock the kitchen, but apparently it was too hard to get Helados on short notice—all that's in the freezer is UK-brand packaged ice cream cones.

"What's it like?" Nora's voice says, tinny over his phone's speaker. On the screen, her hair is up, and she's poking at one of her dozens of window plants.

"Weird," Alex says, pushing his glasses up his nose. "Everything looks like a museum. I don't think I'm allowed to show you, though."

"Ooh," Nora says, wiggling her eyebrows. "So secretive. So fancy."

"Please," Alex says. "If anything, it's creepy. I had to sign such a massive NDA that I'm convinced I'm gonna drop through a trapdoor into a torture dungeon any minute."

"I bet he has a secret lovechild," Nora says. "Or he's gay. Or he has a secret gay lovechild."

"It's probably in case I see his equerry putting his batteries back in," Alex says. "Anyway, this is boring. What's going on with you? Your life is so much better than mine right now."

"Well," Nora says, "Nate Silver won't stop blowing up my phone for another column. Bought some new curtains. Narrowed down the list of grad school concentrations to statistics or data science."

"Tell me those are both at GW," Alex says, hopping up to sit on one of the immaculate countertops, feet dangling. "You can't leave me in DC to go back to MIT."

"Haven't decided yet, but astonishingly, it will not be based on you," Nora tells him. "Remember how we sometimes talk about things that are not about you?"

"Yeah, weirdly. So is the plan to dethrone Nate Silver as reigning data czar of DC?"

Nora laughs. "No, what I'm gonna do is silently compile and process enough data to know exactly what's gonna happen for the next twenty-five years. Then I'm gonna buy a house on the top of a very tall hill at the edge of the city and become an eccentric recluse and sit on my veranda. Watch it all unfold through a pair of binoculars."

Alex starts to laugh, but cuts off when he hears rustling down the hall. Quiet footsteps approaching. Princess Beatrice lives in a different section of the palace, and so does Henry. The PPOs and his own security sleep on this floor, though, so maybe—

"Hold on," Alex says, covering the speaker.

A light flicks on in the hallway, and the person who comes padding into the kitchen is none other than Prince Henry.

He's rumpled and half awake, shoulders slumping as he yawns. He's standing in front of Alex wearing not a suit, but a heather-gray T-shirt and plaid pajama bottoms. He has earbuds in, and his hair is a mess. His feet are bare.

He looks, alarmingly, human.

He freezes when his eyes fall on Alex perched on the countertop. Alex stares back at him. In his hand, Nora begins a muffled, "Is that—" before Alex disconnects the call.

Henry pulls out his earbuds, and his posture has ratcheted back up straight, but his face is still bleary and confused.

"Hello," he says, hoarse. "Sorry. Er. I was just. Cornettos."

He gestures vaguely toward the refrigerator, as if he's said something of any meaning.

"What?"

He crosses to the freezer and extracts the box of ice cream cones, showing Alex the name *Cornetto* across the front. "I was out. Knew they'd stocked you up."

"Do you raid the kitchens of all your guests?" Alex asks.

"Only when I can't sleep," Henry says. "Which is always. Didn't think you'd be awake." He looks at Alex, deferring, and Alex realizes he's waiting for permission to open the box and take one. Alex thinks about telling him no, just for the thrill of denying a prince something, but he's kind of intrigued. He usually can't sleep either. He nods.

He waits for Henry to take a Cornetto and leave, but instead he looks back up at Alex

"Have you practiced what you'll say tomorrow?"

"Yes," Alex says, bristling immediately. This is why nothing about Henry has ever intrigued him before. "You're not the only professional here."

"I didn't mean—" Henry falters. "I only meant, do you think we should, er, rehearse?"

"Do you need to?"

"I thought it might help." Of course, he thinks that. Everything Henry's ever done publicly has probably been privately rehearsed in stuffy royal quarters like this one.

Alex hops down off the counter, swiping his phone unlocked. "Watch this."

He lines up a shot: the box of Cornettos on the counter, Henry's hand braced on the marble next to it, his heavy signet ring visible along with a swath of pajamas. He opens up Instagram, slaps a filter on it.

"'Nothing cures jet lag,'" Alex narrates in a monotone as he taps out a caption, "'like midnight ice cream with

@PrinceHenry.' Geotag Kensington Palace, and posted." He holds the phone for Henry to see as likes and comments immediately pour in. "There are a lot of things worth over-thinking, believe me. But this isn't one of them."

Henry frowns at him over his ice cream.

"I suppose," he says, looking doubtful.

"Are you done?" Alex asks. "I was on a call."

Henry blinks, then folds his arms over his chest, back on the defensive. "Of course. I won't keep you."

As he leaves the kitchen, he pauses in the doorframe, considering.

"I didn't know you wore glasses," he says finally.

He leaves Alex standing there alone in the kitchen, the box of Cornettos sweating on the counter.

The ride to the studio for the interview is bumpy but merci-fully quick. Alex should probably blame some of his queasi-ness on nerves but chooses to blame it all on this morning's appalling breakfast spread—what kind of garbage country eats bland beans on white toast for breakfast? He can't decide if his Mexican blood or his Texan blood is more offended.

Henry sits beside him, surrounded by a cloud of attendants and stylists. One adjusts his hair with a fine-toothed comb. One holds up a notepad of talking points. One tugs his collar straight. From the passenger seat, Shaan shakes a yellow pill out of a bottle and passes it back to Henry, who readily pops it into his mouth and swallows it dry. Alex decides he doesn't want or need to know.

The motorcade pulls up in front of the studio, and when the door slides open, there's the promised photo line and barricaded royal worshippers. Henry turns and looks at him, a little grimace around his mouth and eyes.

"Prince goes first, then you," Shaan says to Alex, leaning in and touching his earpiece. Alex takes one breath, two, and turns it on—the megawatt smile, the All-American charm.

"Go ahead, Your Royal Highness," Alex says, winking as he puts on his sunglasses. "Your subjects await."

Henry clears his throat and unfolds himself, stepping out into the morning and waving genially at the crowd. Cameras flash, photographers shout. A blue-haired girl in the crowd lifts up a homemade poster that reads in big, glittery letters, GET IN ME, PRINCE HENRY! for about five seconds until a member of the security team shoves it into a nearby trash can.

Alex steps out next, swaggering up beside Henry and throwing an arm over his shoulders.

"Act like you like me!" Alex says cheerfully. Henry looks at him like he's trying to choose between a million choice words, before tipping his head to the side and offering up a well-rehearsed laugh, putting his arm around Alex too. "There we go."

The hosts of *This Morning* are agonizingly British—a middle-aged woman named Dottie in a tea dress and a man called Stu who looks as if he spends weekends yelling at mice in his garden. Alex watches the introductions backstage as a makeup artist conceals a stress pimple on his forehead. *So, this is happening.* He tries to ignore Henry a few feet to his left, currently getting a final preening from a royal stylist. It's the last chance he'll get to ignore Henry for the rest of the day.

Soon Henry is leading the way out with Alex close behind. Alex shakes Dottie's hand first, smiling his Politics Smile at her, the one that makes a lot of congresswomen and more than a few congressmen want to tell him things they shouldn't. She giggles and kisses him on the cheek. The audience claps and claps and claps.

Henry sits on the prop couch next to him, perfect posture, and Alex smiles at him, making a show of looking comfortable in Henry's company. Which is harder than it should be, because the stage lights suddenly make him uncomfortably aware of how fresh and handsome Henry looks for the cameras. He's wearing a blue sweater over a button-down, and his hair looks soft.

Whatever, fine. Henry is annoyingly attractive. That's always been a thing, objectively. It's fine.

He realizes, almost a second too late, that Dottie is asking him a question.

"What do you think of *jolly old England,* then, Alex?" Dottie says, clearly ribbing him. Alex forces a smile.

"You know, Dottie, it's gorgeous," Alex says. "I've been here a few times since my mom got elected, and it's always incredible to see the history here, and the beer selection." The audience laughs right on cue, and Alex shakes out his shoulders a little. "And of course, it's always great to see this guy."

He turns to Henry, extending his fist. Henry hesitates before stiffly bumping his own knuckles against Alex's with the heavy air of an act of treason.

Alex's whole reason for wanting to go into politics, when he knows so many past presidential sons and daughters have run away screaming the minute they turned eighteen, is he genuinely cares about people.

The power is great, the attention fun, but the people—the

people are everything. He has a bit of a caring-too-much problem about most things, including whether people can pay their medical bills, or marry whomever they love, or not get shot at school. Or, in this case, if kids with cancer have enough books to read at the Royal Marsden NHS Foundation Trust.

He and Henry and their collective hoard of security have taken over the floor, flustering nurses and shaking hands. He's trying—really trying—not to let his hands clench into fists at his sides, but Henry's smiling robotically with a little bald boy plugged full of tubes for some bullshit photograph, and he wants to scream at this whole stupid country.

But he's legally required to be here, so he focuses on the kids, instead. Most of them have no idea who he is, but Henry gamely introduces him as the president's son, and soon they're asking him about the White House and does he know Ariana Grande, and he laughs and indulges them. He unpacks books from the heavy boxes they've brought, climbs up onto beds and reads out loud, a photographer trailing after him.

He doesn't realize he's lost track of Henry until the patient he's visiting dozes off, and he recognizes the low rumble of Henry's voice on the other side of the curtain.

A quick count of feet on the floor—no photographers. Just Henry. Hmm.

He steps quietly over to the chair against the wall, right at the edge of the curtain. If he sits at the right angle and cranes his head back, he can barely see.

Henry is talking to a little girl with leukemia named Claudette, according to the board on her wall. She's got dark skin that's turned sort of a pale gray and a bright orange scarf tied around her head, emblazoned with the Alliance Starbird.

Instead of hovering awkwardly like Alex expected, Henry is squatting at her side, smiling and holding her hand.

". . . Star Wars fan, are you?" Henry says in a low, warm voice Alex has never heard from him before, pointing at the insignia on her headscarf.

"Oh, it's my absolute favorite," Claudette gushes. "I'd like to be just like Princess Leia when I'm older because she's so tough and smart and strong, and she gets to kiss Han Solo."

She blushes a little at having mentioned kissing in front of the prince but fiercely maintains eye contact. Alex finds himself craning his neck farther, watching for Henry's reaction. He definitely does not recall Star Wars on the fact sheet.

"You know what," Henry says, leaning in conspiratorially, "I think you've got the right idea."

Claudette giggles. "Who's your favorite?"

"Hmm," Henry says, making a show of thinking hard. "I always liked Luke. He's brave and good, and he's the strongest Jedi of them all. I think Luke is proof that it doesn't matter where you come from or who your family is—you can always be great if you're true to yourself."

"All right, Miss Claudette," a nurse says brightly as she comes around the curtain. Henry jumps, and Alex almost tips his chair over, caught in the act. He clears his throat as he stands, pointedly not looking at Henry. "You two can go, it's time for her meds."

"Miss Beth, Henry said we were mates now!" Claudette practically wails. "He can stay!"

"Excuse you!" Beth the nurse tuts. "That's no way to address the prince. Terribly sorry, Your Highness."

"No need to apologize," Henry tells her. "Rebel commanders outrank royalty." He shoots Claudette a wink and a salute, and she positively melts.

"I'm impressed," Alex says as they walk out into the hallway

together. Henry cocks an eyebrow, and Alex adds, "Not impressed, just surprised."

"At what?"

"That you actually have, you know, feelings."

Henry is beginning to smile when three things happen in
rapid succession.

The first: A shout echoes from the opposite end of the hall.

The second: There's a loud pop that sounds alarmingly like
gunfire.

The third: Cash grabs both Henry and Alex by the arms
and shoves them through the nearest door.

"Stay down," Cash grunts as he slams the door behind them.

In the abrupt darkness, Alex stumbles over a mop and one
of Henry's legs, and they go crashing down together into a
clattering pile of tin bedpans. Henry hits the floor first, face-
down, and Alex lands in a heap on top of him.

"Oh God," Henry says, muffled and echoing slightly. Alex
thinks hopefully that his face might be in a bedpan.

"You know," he says into Henry's hair, "we have got to stop
ending up like this."

"Do you *mind?*"

"This is *your* fault!"

"How is this *possibly* my fault?" Henry hisses.

"Nobody ever tries to shoot me when I'm doing presidential appearances, but the minute I go out with a fucking
royal—"

"Will you shut up before you get us both killed?"

"Nobody's going to kill us. Cash is blocking the door. Besides, it's probably nothing."

"Then at least *get off me.*"

"Stop telling me what to do! You're not the prince of me!"

"Bloody hell," Henry mutters, and he pushes hard off the ground and rolls, knocking Alex onto the floor. Alex finds himself wedged between Henry's side and a shelf of what smells like industrial-strength floor cleaner.

"Can you move over, Your Highness?" Alex whispers, shoving his shoulder against Henry's. "I'd rather not be the little spoon."

"Believe me, I'm trying," Henry replies. "There's no room."

Outside, there are voices, hurried footsteps—no signs of an all-clear.

"Well," Alex says. "Guess we better make ourselves comfortable."

Henry exhales tightly. "Fantastic."

Alex feels him shifting against his side, arms crossed over his chest in an attempt at his typical closed-off stance while lying on the floor with his feet in a mop bucket.

"For the record," Henry says, "nobody's ever made an attempt on my life either."

"Well, congratulations," Alex says. "You've officially made it."

"Yes, this is exactly how I always dreamed it would be. Locked in a cupboard with your elbow inside my rib cage," Henry snipes. He sounds like he wants to punch Alex, which is probably the most Alex has ever liked him, so he follows an impulse and drives his elbow into Henry's side, hard.

Henry lets out a muffled yelp, and the next thing Alex knows, he's been yanked sideways by his shirt and Henry is halfway on top of him, pinning him down with one thigh. His head throbs where he's clocked it against the linoleum floor, but he can feel his lips split into a smile.

"So you *do* have some fight in you," Alex says. He bucks his hips, trying to shake Henry off, but he's taller and stronger and has a fistful of Alex's collar.

"Are you *quite* finished?" Henry says, sounding strangled. "Can you perhaps stop putting your sodding life in danger now?"

"Aw, you do care," Alex says. "I'm learning all your hidden depths today, sweetheart."

Henry exhales and slumps off him. "I cannot believe even mortal peril will not prevent you from being the way you are."

The weirdest part, Alex thinks, is that what he said was true.

He keeps getting these little glimpses into things he never thought Henry was. A bit of a fighter, for one. Intelligent, interested in other people. It's honestly disconcerting. He knows exactly what to say to each Democratic senator to make them dish about bills, exactly when Zahra's running low on nicotine gum, exactly which look to give Nora for the rumor mill. Reading people is what he does.

He really doesn't appreciate some inbred royal baby upending his system. But he did rather enjoy that fight.

He lies there, waits. Listens to the shuffling of feet outside the door. Lets minutes go by.

"So, uh," he tries. "Star Wars?"

He means it in a nonthreatening, offhanded way, but habit wins and it comes out accusatory.

"Yes, Alex," Henry says archly, "believe it or not, the children of the crown don't only spend their childhood going to tea parties."

"I assumed it was mostly posture coaching and junior polo league."

Henry takes a deeply unhappy pause. "That . . . may have been part of it."

"So you're into pop culture, but you act like you're not," Alex says. "Either you're not allowed to talk about it because it's unseemly for the crown, or you choose not to talk about it because you want people to think you're *cultured*. Which one?"

"Are you psychoanalyzing me?" Henry asks. "I don't think royal guests are allowed to do that."

"I'm trying to understand why you're so committed to acting like someone you're not, considering you just told that little girl in there that greatness means being true to yourself."

"I don't know what you're talking about, and if I did, I'm not sure that's any of your concern," Henry says, his voice strained at the edges.

"Really? Because I'm pretty sure I'm legally bound to pretend to be your best friend, and I don't know if you've thought this through yet, but that's not going to stop with this weekend," Alex tells him. Henry's fingers go tense against his forearm. "If we do this and we're never seen together again, people are gonna know we're full of shit. We're stuck with each other, like it or not, so I have a right to be clued in about what your deal is before it sneaks up on me and bites me in the ass."

"Why don't we start . . ." Henry says, turning his head to squint at him. This close Alex can just make out the silhouette of Henry's strong royal nose. ". . . with you telling me why exactly you hate me so much?"

"Do you really want to have that conversation?"

"Maybe I do."

Alex crosses his arms, recognizes it as a mirror to Henry's tic, and uncrosses them.

"Do you really not remember being a prick to me at the Olympics?"

Alex remembers it in vivid detail: himself at eighteen, dispatched to Rio with June and Nora, the campaign's delegation to the summer games, one weekend of photo ops and selling the "next generation of global cooperation" image. Alex spent most of it drinking caipirinhas and subsequently throwing caipirinhas up behind Olympic venues. And he remembers, down to the Union Jack on Henry's anorak, the first time they met.

Henry sighs. "Is that the time you threatened to push me into the Thames?"

"*No,*" Alex says. "It was the time you were a *condescending prick* at the diving finals. You really don't remember?"

"Remind me?"

Alex glares. "I walked up to you to introduce myself, and you stared at me like I was the most offensive thing you had ever seen. Right after you shook my hand, you turned to Shaan and said, 'Can you get rid of him?'"

A pause.

"Ah," Henry says. He clears his throat. "I didn't realize you'd heard that."

"I feel like you're missing the point," Alex says, "which is that it's a douchey thing to say either way."

"That's . . . fair."

"Yeah, so."

"That's all?" Henry asks. "Only the Olympics?"

"I mean, that was the start."

Henry pauses again. "I'm sensing an ellipsis."

"It's just . . ." Alex says, and as he's on the floor of a supply closet, waiting out a security threat with a Prince of England at the end of a weekend that has felt like some very specific ongoing nightmare, censoring himself takes too much effort. "I don't know. Doing what we do is fucking hard. But it's harder for me. I'm the son of the first female president. And

I'm not white like she is, can't even pass for it. People will *always* come down harder on me. And you're, you know, *you,* and you were born into all of this, and everyone thinks you're Prince fucking Charming. You're basically a living reminder I'll always be compared to someone else, no matter what I do, even if I work twice as hard."

Henry is quiet for a long while.

"Well," Henry says when he speaks at last. "I can't very well do much about the rest. But I can tell you I was, in fact, a prick that day. Not that it's any excuse, but my father had died fourteen months before, and I was still kind of a prick every day of my life at the time. And I am sorry."

Henry twitches one hand at his side, and Alex falls momentarily silent.

The cancer ward. Of course, Henry chose a cancer ward—it was right there on the fact sheet. *Father: Famed film star Arthur Fox, deceased 2015, pancreatic cancer.* The funeral was televised. He goes back over the last twenty-four hours in his head: the sleeplessness, the pills, the tense little grimace Henry does in public that Alex has always read as aloofness.

He knows a few things about this stuff. It's not like his parents' divorce was a pleasant time for him, or like he runs himself ragged about grades for fun. He's been aware for too long that most people don't navigate thoughts of whether they'll ever be good enough or if they're disappointing the entire world. He's never considered Henry might feel any of the same things.

Henry clears his throat again, and something like panic catches Alex. He opens his mouth and says, "Well, good to know you're not perfect."

He can almost hear Henry roll his eyes, and he's thankful for it, the familiar comfort of antagonism.

They're silent again, the dust of the conversation settling. Alex can't hear anything outside the door or any sirens on the street, but nobody has come to get them yet.

Then, unprompted, Henry says into the stretching stillness, "*Return of the Jedi.*"

A beat. "What?"

"To answer your question," Henry says. "Yes, I do like Star Wars, and my favorite is *Return of the Jedi.*"

"Oh," Alex says. "Wow, you're wrong."

Henry huffs out the tiniest, most poshly indignant puff of air. It smells minty. Alex resists the urge to throw another elbow. "How can I be wrong about my own favorite? It's a personal truth."

"It's a personal truth that is wrong and bad."

"Which do you prefer, then? Please show me the error of my ways."

"Okay, *Empire.*"

Henry sniffs. "So *dark,* though."

"Yeah, which is what makes it *good,*" Alex says. "It's the most thematically complex. It's got the Han and Leia kiss in it, you meet Yoda, Han is at the top of his game, fucking *Lando Calrissian,* and *the* best twist in cinematic history. What does *Jedi* have? Fuckin' Ewoks."

"Ewoks are *iconic.*"

"Ewoks are *stupid.*"

"But *Endor.*"

"But *Hoth.* There's a reason people always call the best, grittiest installment of a trilogy the *Empire* of the series."

"And I can appreciate that. But isn't there something to be valued in a happy ending as well?"

"Spoken like a true Prince Charming."

"I'm only saying, I like the resolution of *Jedi*. It ties everything up nicely. And the overall theme you're intended to take away from the films is hope and love and . . . er, you know, all that. Which is what *Jedi* leaves you with a sense of most of all."

Henry coughs, and Alex is turning to look at him again when the door opens and Cash's giant silhouette reappears.

"False alarm," he says, breathing heavily. "Some dumbass kids brought fireworks for their friend." He looks down at them, flat on their backs and blinking up in the sudden, harsh light of the hallway. "This looks cozy."

"Yep, we're really bonding," Alex says. He reaches a hand out and lets Cash haul him to his feet.

Outside Kensington Palace, Alex takes Henry's phone out of his hand and swiftly opens a blank contact page before he can protest or sic a PPO on him for violating royal property. The car is waiting to take him back to the royals' private airstrip.

"Here," Alex says. "That's my number. If we're gonna keep this up, it's going to get annoying to keep going through handlers. Just text me. We'll figure it out."

Henry stares at him, expression blankly bewildered, and Alex wonders how this guy has any friends.

"Right," Henry says finally. "Thank you."

"No booty calls," Alex tells him, and Henry chokes on a laugh.

THREE

FROM AMERICA, WITH LOVE: Henry and Alex Flaunt Friendship

NEW BROMANCE ALERT? Pics of FSOTUS and Prince Henry

PHOTOS: Alex's Weekend in London

For the first time in a week, Alex isn't pissed off scrolling through his Google alerts. It helps they've given *People* an exclusive—a few generic quotes about how much Alex "cherishes" his friendship with Henry and their "shared life experience" as sons of world leaders. Alex thinks their main shared life experience is probably wishing they could set that quote adrift on the ocean between them and watch it drown.

His mother doesn't want him fake-dead anymore, though, and he's stopped getting a thousand vitriolic tweets an hour, so he counts it as a win.

He dodges a starstruck freshman gawking at him and exits the hall onto the east side of campus, draining the last cold sip of his coffee. First class today was an elective he's taking out of a combination of morbid fascination and academic curiosity: The Press and the Presidency. He's currently jet-lagged to all hell from trying to keep the press from *ruining* the presidency, and the irony isn't lost on him.

Today's lecture was on presidential sex scandals through history, and he texts Nora: numbers on one of us getting involved in a sex scandal before the end of second term?

Her response comes within seconds: 94% probability of your dick becoming a recurring personality on face the nation. btw, have you seen this?

There's a link attached: a blog post full of images, animated GIFs of himself and Henry on *This Morning*. The fist bump. Shared smiles that pass for genuine. Conspiratorial glances. Underneath are hundreds of comments about how handsome they are, how nice they look together.

omfg, one commenter writes, make out already.

Alex laughs so hard he almost falls in a fountain.

As usual, the day guard at the Dirksen Building glares at him as he slides through security. She's certain he was the one who vandalized the sign outside one particular senator's office to read BITCH MCCONNELL, but she'll never prove it.

Cash tags along for some of Alex's Senate recon missions so nobody panics when he disappears for a few hours. Today,

Cash hangs back on a bench, catching up on his podcasts. He's always been the most indulgent of Alex's antics.

Alex has had the layout of the building memorized since his dad first got elected to the Senate. It's where he's picked up his encyclopedic knowledge of policy and procedure, and where he spends more afternoons than he's supposed to, charming aides and trawling for gossip. His mom pretends to be annoyed but slyly asks for intel later.

Since Senator Oscar Diaz is in California speaking at a rally for gun control today, Alex punches the button for the fifth floor instead.

His favorite senator is Rafael Luna, an Independent from Colorado and the newest kid on the block at only thirty-nine. Alex's dad took him under his wing back when he was merely a promising attorney, and now he's the darling of national politics for (A) winning a special election and a general in consecutive upsets for his Senate seat, and (B) dominating *The Hill*'s 50 Most Beautiful.

Alex spent summer 2018 in Denver on Luna's campaign, so they have their own dysfunctional relationship built on tropical-flavored Skittles from gas stations and all-nighters drafting press releases. He sometimes feels the ghost of carpal tunnel creeping back, a fond ache.

He finds Luna in his office, horn-rimmed reading glasses doing nothing to detract from his usual appearance of a movie star who tripped and fell sideways into politics. Alex has always suspected the soulful brown eyes and perfectly groomed stubble and dramatic cheekbones won back any votes Luna lost by being both Latino and openly gay.

The album playing low in the room is an old favorite Alex remembers from Denver: Muddy Waters. When Luna looks up and sees Alex in his doorway, he drops his pen on a hap-hazard pile of papers and leans back in his chair.

"Fuck you doing here, kid?" he says, watching him like a cat.

Alex reaches into his pocket and pulls out a packet of Skittles, and Luna's face immediately softens into a smile.

"Atta boy," he says, scooping the bag up as soon as Alex drops it on his blotter. He kicks the chair in front of the desk out for him.

Alex sits, watching Luna rip open the packet with his teeth. "Whatcha working on today?"

"You already know more than you're supposed to about everything on this desk." Alex does know—the same health care reform as last year, the one stalled out since they lost the Senate in midterms. "Why are you really here?"

"Hmm." Alex hooks a leg over one armrest of the chair. "I resent the idea I can't come visit a dear family friend without ulterior motives."

"Bullshit."

He clutches his chest. "You *wound* me."

"You exhaust me."

"I enchant you."

"I'll call security."

"Fair enough."

"Instead, let's talk about your little European vacation," Luna says. He fixes Alex with shrewd eyes. "Can I expect a joint Christmas present from you and the prince this year?"

"Actually," Alex swerves, "since I'm here, I do have a question for you."

Luna laughs, leaning back and lacing his hands together behind his head. Alex feels his face flash hot for half a second, a zip of good-banter adrenaline that means he's getting some-where. "Of course you do."

"I wondered if you had heard anything about Connor," Alex asks. "We could really use an endorsement from another Independent senator. Do you think he's close to making one?"

He kicks his foot innocently where it's dangling over the armrest, like he's asking something as innocuous as the weather. Stanley Connor, Delaware's kooky and beloved old Independent with a social media team stacked with millen-nials, would be a big get down the line in a race projected to be this close, and they both know it.

Luna sucks on a Skittle. "Are you asking if he's close to en-dorsing, or if I know what strings need to be pulled to get him to endorse?"

"Raf. Pal. Buddy. You know I'd never ask you anything so unseemly."

Luna sighs, swivels in his chair. "He's a free agent. Social issues would push him your way usually, but you know how he feels about your mom's economic platform. You probably know his voting record better than I do, kid. He doesn't fall on one side of the aisle. He might go for something radically differ-ent on taxes."

"And as for something you know that I don't?"

He smirks. "I know Richards is promising Independents a centrist platform with big shake-ups on non-social issues. And I know part of that platform might not line up with Connor's position on healthcare. Somewhere to start, perhaps. Hypo-thetically, if I were going to engage with your scheming."

"And you don't think there's any point in chasing down leads on Republican candidates who aren't Richards?"

"Shit," Luna says, the set of his mouth turning grim. "Chances of your mother facing off against a candidate who's not the fucking anointed messiah of right-wing populism and heir to the Richards family legacy? Highly fucking unlikely."

Alex smiles. "You complete me, Raf."

Luna rolls his eyes again. "Let's circle back to you," he says. "Don't think I didn't notice you changing the subject. For the record, I won the office pool on how long it'd take you to cause an international incident."

"*Wow,* I thought I could *trust* you." Alex gasps, mock-betrayed.

"What's the deal there?"

"There's no *deal,*" Alex says. "Henry is . . . a person I know. And we did something stupid. I had to fix it. It's fine."

"Okay, okay," Luna says, holding up both hands. "He's a looker, huh?"

Alex pulls a face. "Yeah, I mean, if you're into, like, fairy-tale princes."

"Is anyone not?"

"*I'm* not," Alex says.

Luna arches an eyebrow. "Right."

"What?"

"Just thinking about last summer," he says. "I have this really vivid memory of you basically making a Prince Henry voodoo doll on your desk."

"I did not."

"Or was it a dartboard with a photo of his face on it?"

Alex swings his foot back over the armrest so he can plant both feet on the floor and fold his arms indignantly. "I had a magazine with his face on it at my desk, once, because I was in it and he happened to be on the cover."

"You stared at it for an hour."

"Lies," Alex says. "Slander."

"It was like you were trying to set him on fire with your mind."

"What is your point?"

"I think it's interesting," he says. "How fast the times they are a-changin'."

"Come on," Alex says. "It's . . . politics."

"Uh-huh."

Alex shakes his head, doglike, as if it's going to disperse the topic from the room. "Besides, I came here to talk about endorsements, not my embarrassing public relations nightmares."

"Ah," Luna says slyly, "but I thought you were here to pay a family friend a visit?"

"Of course. That's what I meant."

"Alex, don't you have something else to do on a Friday afternoon? You're twenty-one. You should be playing beer pong or getting ready for a party or something."

"I do all of those things," he lies. "I just also do this."

"Come on. I'm trying to give you some advice, from one old man to a much younger version of himself."

"You're thirty-nine."

"My liver is ninety-three."

"That's not my fault."

"Some late nights in Denver would beg to differ."

Alex laughs. "See, this is why we're friends."

"Alex, you need other friends," Luna tells him. "Friends who *aren't in Congress*."

"I have friends! I have June and Nora."

"Yes, your sister and a girl who is also a supercomputer," Luna deadpans. "You need to take some time for yourself before you burn out, kid. You need a bigger support system."

"Stop calling me 'kid,'" Alex says.

"Ay." Luna sighs. "Are you done? I do have some actual work to do."

"Yeah, yeah," Alex says, gathering himself up from his chair. "Hey, is Maxine in town?"

"Waters?" Luna asks, crooking his head. "Shit, you really have a death wish, huh?"

As political legacies go, the Richards family is one of the most complex bits of history Alex has tried to unravel.

On one of the Post-it notes stuck to his laptop he's written: KENNEDYS + BUSHES + BIZARRO MAFIA OLD MONEY SITH POWERS = RICHARDSES? It's pretty much the thesis of what he's dug up so far. Jeffrey Richards, the current and supposedly only frontrunner to be his mother's opponent in the general, has been a senator for Utah nearly twenty years, which means plenty of voting history and legislation that his mother's team has already gone over. Alex is more interested in the things harder to sniff out. There are so many generations of Attorney General Richards and Federal Judge Richards, they'd be able to bury anything.

His phone buzzes under a stack of files on his desk. A text from June: Dinner? I miss your face. He loves June—truly, more than anything in the world—but he's kind of in the zone. He'll respond when he hits a stopping point in like thirty minutes.

He glances at the video of a Richards interview pulled up in a tab, checking the man's face for nonverbal cues. Gray hair—natural, not a piece. Shiny white teeth, like a shark's. Heavy Uncle Sam jaw. Great salesman, considering he's blatantly lying about a bill in the clip. Alex takes a note.

It's an hour and a half later before another buzz pulls him out of a deep dive into Richards's uncle's suspicious 1986 taxes. A text from his mother in the family group chat, a pizza emoji. He bookmarks his page and heads upstairs.

Family dinners are rare but less over-the-top than everything else that happens in the White House. His mother sends someone to pick up pizzas, and they take over the game room on the third floor with paper plates and bottles of Shiner shipped in from Texas. It's always amusing to catch one of the burly suits speaking in code over their earpieces: "Black Bear has requested extra banana peppers."

June's already on the chaise and sipping a beer. A stab of guilt immediately hits when he remembers her text.

"Shit, I'm an asshole," he says.

"Mm-hmm, you are."

"But, technically . . . I am having dinner with you?"

"Just bring me my pizza," she says with a sigh. After Secret Service misread an olive-based shouting match in 2017 and almost put the Residence on lockdown, they now each get their own pizzas.

"Sure thing, Bug." He finds June's—margherita—and his—pepperoni and mushroom.

"Hi, Alex," says a voice from somewhere behind the television as he settles in with his pizza.

"Hey, Leo," he answers. His stepdad is fiddling with the wiring, probably rewiring it to do something that'd make more sense in an *Iron Man* comic, like he does with most electronics—eccentric millionaire inventor habits die hard. He's about to ask for a dumbed-down explanation when his mother comes blazing in.

"Why did y'all let me run for president?" she says, tapping

too forcefully at her phone's keyboard in little staccato stabs. She kicks off her heels into the corner, throwing her phone after them.

"Because we all knew better than to try to stop you," Leo's voice says. He peeks his bearded, bespectacled head out and adds, "And because the world would fall apart without you, my radiant orchid."

His mother rolls her eyes but smiles. It's always been like that with them, ever since they first met at a charity event when Alex was fourteen. She was the Speaker of the House, and he was a genius with a dozen patents and money to burn on women's health initiatives. Now, she's the president, and he's sold his companies to spend his time fulfilling First Gentleman duties.

Ellen releases two inches of zipper on the back of her skirt, the sign she's officially done for the day, and scoops up a slice.

"All right," she says. She does a scrubbing gesture in the air in front of her face—president face off, mom face on. "Hi, babies."

"'Lo," Alex and June mumble in unison through mouthfuls of food.

Ellen sighs and looks over at Leo. "I did that, didn't I? No goddamn manners. Like a couple of little opossums. This is why they say women can't have it all."

"They are masterpieces," Leo says.

"One good thing, one bad thing," she says. "Let's do this."

It's her lifelong system for catching up on their days when she's at her busiest. Alex grew up with a mother who was a sometimes baffling combination of intensely organized and committed to lines of emotional communication, like an overly invested life coach. When he got his first girlfriend, she made a PowerPoint presentation.

"Mmm." June swallows a bite. "Good thing. Oh! Oh my God. Ronan Farrow tweeted about my essay for *New York* magazine, and we totally engaged in witty Twitter repartee. Part one of my long game to force him to be my friend is underway."

"Don't act like this isn't all part of your extra-long game of abusing your position to murder Woody Allen and make it look like an accident," Alex says.

"He's just so frail; it'd only take one good push—"

"*How many times* do I have to tell y'all not to discuss your murder plots in front of a sitting president?" their mother interrupts. "*Plausible deniability.* Come on."

"*Anyway,*" June says. "One bad thing would be, uh . . . well, Woody Allen's still alive. Your turn, Alex."

"Good thing," Alex says, "I filibustered one of my professors into agreeing a question on our last exam was misleading so I would get full credit for my answer, which was correct." He takes a swig of beer. "Bad thing—Mom, I saw the new art in the hall on the second floor, and I need to know why you allowed a George W. Bush terrier painting in our home."

"It's a bipartisan gesture," Ellen says. "People find them endearing."

"I have to walk past it whenever I go to my room," Alex says. "Its beady little eyes follow me everywhere."

"It's staying."

Alex sighs. "Fine."

Leo goes next—as usual, his bad thing is somehow also a good thing—and then Ellen's up.

"Well, my UN ambassador fucked up his *one job* and said something idiotic about Israel, and now I have to call Netanyahu and personally apologize. But the good thing is it's two in the morning in Tel Aviv, so I can put it off until tomorrow and have dinner with you two instead."

Alex smiles at her. He's still in awe, sometimes, of hearing her talk about presidential pains in the ass, even three years in. They lapse into idle conversation, little barbs and inside jokes, and these nights may be rare, but they're still nice.

"So," Ellen says, starting on another slice crust-first. "I ever tell you I used to hustle pool at my mom's bar?"

June stops short, her beer halfway to her mouth. "You did what now?"

"Yep," she tells them. Alex exchanges an incredulous look with June. "Momma managed this shitty bar when I was six-teen. The Tipsy Grackle. She'd let me come in after school and do my homework at the bar, had a bouncer friend make sure none of the old drunks hit on me. I got pretty good at pool after a few months and started betting the regulars I could beat them, except I'd play dumb. Hold the stick the wrong way, pretend to forget if I was stripes or solid. I'd lose one game, then take them double or nothing and get twice the payout."

"You've got to be kidding me," Alex says, except he can to-tally picture it. She has always been scary-good at pool and even better at strategy.

"All true," Leo says. "How do you think she learned to get what she wants from strung-out old white men? The most important skill of an effective politician."

Alex's mother accepts a kiss to the side of her square jaw from Leo as she passes by, like a queen gliding through a crowd of admirers. She sets her half-eaten slice down on a paper towel and selects a cue stick from the rack.

"Anyway," she says. "The point is, you're never too young to figure out your skills and use them to get shit accomplished."

"Okay," Alex says. He meets her eyes, and they swap appraising looks.

"Including . . ." she says thoughtfully, "a job on a presidential reelection campaign, maybe."

June puts down her slice. "Mom, he's not even out of college yet."

"Uh, yeah, that's the point," Alex says impatiently. He's been *waiting* for this offer. "No gaps in the resume."

"It's not only for Alex," their mother says. "It's for both of you."

June's expression changes from pinched apprehension to pinched dread. Alex makes a shooing motion in June's direction. A mushroom flies off his pizza and hits the side of her nose. "Tell me, tell me, tell me."

"I've been thinking," Ellen says, "this time around, y'all—the 'White House Trio.'" She puts it in air quotes, as if she didn't sign off on the name herself. "Y'all shouldn't only be faces. Y'all are more than that. You have skills. You're smart. You're talented. We could use y'all not only as surrogates, but as staffers."

"Mom . . ." June starts.

"What positions?" Alex interjects.

She pauses, drifts back over to her slice of pizza. "Alex, you're the family wonk," she says, taking a bite. "We could have you running point on policy. This means a lot of research and a lot of writing."

"Fuck yes," Alex says. "Lemme romance the hell out of some focus groups. I'm in."

"Alex—" June starts again, but their mom cuts her off.

"June, I'm thinking communications," she goes on. "Since your degree is mass comm, I was thinking you can come handle some of the day-to-day liaising with media outlets, working on messaging, analyzing the audience—"

"Mom, I have a job," she says.

"Oh, yeah. I mean, of course, sugar. But this could be full-time. Connections, upward mobility, real experience in the field doing some amazing work."

"I, um . . ." June rips a piece of crust off her pizza. "Don't remember ever saying I wanted to do anything like that. That's, uh, kind of a big assumption to make, Mom. And you realize if I go into campaign communications now, I'm basically shutting down my chances of ever being a journalist, because, like, journalistic neutrality and everything. I can barely get anyone to let me write a column as it is."

"Baby girl," their mom says. She's got that look on her face she gets when she's saying something with a fifty-fifty chance of pissing you off. "You're so talented, and I know you work hard, but at some point, you have to be realistic."

"What's *that* supposed to mean?"

"I just mean . . . I don't know if you're happy," she says, "and maybe it's time to try something different. That's all."

"I'm not y'all," June tells her. "This isn't *my* thing."

"Juuuuune," Alex says, tilting his head back to look at her upside down over the arm of his chair. "Just think about it? I'm doing it." He looks back at their mom. "Are you offering a job to Nora too?"

She nods. "Mike is talking to her tomorrow about a position in analytics. If she takes it, she'll start ASAP. You, mister, are not starting until after graduation."

"Oh man, the White House Trio, riding into battle. This is awesome." He looks over at Leo, who has abandoned his project with the TV and is now happily eating a slice of cheesy bread. "They offer you a job too, Leo?"

"No," he says. "As usual, my duties as First Gentleman are to work on my tablescapes and look pretty."

"Your tablescapes are really coming along, baby," Ellen says, giving him a sarcastic little kiss. "I really liked the burlap placemats."

"Can you believe the decorator thought velvet looked better?"

"Bless her heart."

"I don't like this," June says to Alex while their mother is distracted talking about decorative pears. "Are you sure you want this job?"

"It's gonna be fine, June," he tells her. "Hey, if you wanna keep an eye on me, you can always take the offer too."

She shakes him off, returning to her pizza with an unreadable expression. The next day there are three matching sticky notes on the whiteboard in Zahra's office. CAMPAIGN JOBS: ALEX-NORA-JUNE, the board reads. The sticky notes under his and Nora's names read YES. Under June's, in what is unmistakably her own handwriting, NO.

Alex is taking notes in a policy lecture when he gets the first text.

This bloke looks like you.

There's a picture attached, an image of a laptop screen paused on Chief Chirpa from *Return of the Jedi*: tiny, commanding, adorable, pissed off.

This is Henry, by the way.

He rolls his eyes, but adds the new contact to his phone: HRH Prince Dickhead. Poop emoji.

He's honestly not planning to respond, but a week later he sees a headline on the cover of *People*—PRINCE HENRY FLIES SOUTH FOR WINTER—complete with a photo of Henry artistically posed on an Australian beach in a pair of sensible yet miniscule navy swim trunks, and he can't stop himself.

you have a lot of moles, he texts, along with a snap of the spread. is that a result of the inbreeding?

Henry's retort comes two days later by way of a screenshot of a *Daily Mail* tweet that reads, *Is Alex Claremont-Diaz going to be a father?* The attached message says, But we were ever so careful, dear, which surprises a big enough laugh out of Alex that Zahra ejects him from her weekly debriefing with him and June.

So, it turns out Henry can be funny. Alex adds that to his mental file.

It also turns out Henry is fond of texting when he's trapped in moments of royal monotony, like being shuttled to and from appearances, or sitting through meandering briefings on his family's land holdings, or, once, begrudgingly and hilariously receiving a spray tan.

Alex wouldn't say he *likes* Henry, but he does enjoy the quick rhythm of arguments they fall into. He knows he talks too much, hopeless at moderating his feelings, which he usually hides under ten layers of charm, but he ultimately doesn't care what Henry thinks of him, so he doesn't bother. Instead, he's as weird and manic as he wants to be, and Henry jabs back in sharp flashes of startling wit.

So, when he's bored or stressed or between coffee refills, he'll check for a text bubble popping up. Henry with a dig at some weird quote from his latest interview, Henry with a random thought about English beer versus American beer, a picture of Henry's dog wearing a Slytherin scarf. (i don't know WHO you think you're kidding, you hufflepuff-ass bitch, Alex texts back, before Henry clarifies his dog, not him, is a Slytherin.)

He learns about Henry's life through a weird osmosis of text messages and social media. It's meticulously scheduled by

Shaan, with whom Alex is slightly obsessed, especially when Henry texts him things like, Did I tell you Shaan has a motorbike? or Shaan is on the phone with Portugal.

It's quickly becoming apparent the HRH Prince Henry Fact Sheet either omitted the most interesting stuff or was outright fabricated. Henry's favorite food isn't mutton pie but a cheap falafel stand ten minutes from the palace, and he's spent most of his gap year thus far working on charities around the world, half of them owned by his best friend, Pez.

Alex learns Henry's super into classical mythology and can rattle off the configurations of a few dozen constellations if you let him get going. Alex hears more about the tedious details of operating a sailboat than he would ever care to know and sends back nothing but: cool. Eight hours later. Henry hardly ever swears, but at least he doesn't seem to mind Alex's filthy fucking mouth.

Henry's sister, Beatrice—she goes by Bea, Alex finds out—pops up often, since she lives in Kensington Palace as well. From what he gathers, the two of them are closer than either are to their brother. They compare notes on the trials and tribulations of having older sisters.

did bea force you into dresses as a child too?

Has June also got a fondness for sneaking your leftover curry out of the refrigerator in the dead of night like a Dickensian street urchin?

More common are cameos by Pez, a man who cuts such an intriguing and bizarre figure that Alex wonders how someone like him ever became best friends with someone like Henry, who can drone on about Lord Byron until you threaten to block his number. He's always either doing something insane—

BASE jumping in Malaysia, eating plantains with someone who might be Jay-Z, showing up to lunch wearing a studded, hot-pink Gucci jacket—or launching a new nonprofit. It's kind of incredible.

He realizes that he's shared June and Nora too, when Henry remembers June's Secret Service codename is Bluebonnet or jokes about how eerie Nora's photographic memory is. It's weird, considering how fiercely protective Alex is of them, that he never even noticed until Henry's Twitter exchange with June about their mutual love of the 2005 *Pride & Prejudice* movie goes viral.

"That's not your emails-from-Zahra face," Nora says, nosing her way over his shoulder. He elbows her away. "You keep doing that stupid smile every time you look at your phone. Who are you texting?"

"I don't know what you're talking about, and literally no one," Alex tells her. From the screen in his hand, Henry's message reads, In world's most boring meeting with Philip. Don't let the papers print lies about me after I've garroted myself with my tie.

"Wait," she says, reaching for his phone again, "are you watching videos of Justin Trudeau speaking French again?"

"That's not a thing I do!"

"That is a thing I have caught you doing at least twice since you met him at the state dinner last year, so yeah, it is," she says. Alex flips her off. "Wait, oh my God, is it fan fiction about yourself? And you didn't *invite me*? Who do they have you boning now? Did you read the one I sent you with Macron? I *died*."

"If you don't stop, I'm gonna call Taylor Swift and tell her you changed your mind and want to go to her Fourth of July party after all."

"That is *not* a proportional response."

Later that night, once he's alone at his desk, he replies: was it a meeting about which of your cousins have to marry each other to take back casterly rock?

Ha. It was about royal finances. I'll be hearing Philip's voice saying the words "return on investment" in my nightmares for the rest of time.

Alex rolls his eyes and sends back, the harrowing struggle of managing the empire's blood money.

Henry's response comes a minute later.

That was actually the crux of the meeting—I've tried to refuse my share of the crown's money. Dad left us each more than enough, and I'd rather cover my expenses with that than the spoils of, you know, centuries of genocide. Philip thinks I'm being ridiculous.

Alex scans the message twice to make sure he's read it correctly.

i am low-key impressed.

He stares at the screen, at his own message, for a few seconds too long, suddenly afraid it was a stupid thing to say. He shakes his head, puts the phone down. Locks it. Changes his mind, picks it up again. Unlocks it. Sees the little typing bubble on Henry's side of the conversation. Puts the phone down. Looks away. Looks back.

One does not foster a lifelong love of Star Wars without knowing an "empire" isn't a good thing.

He would really appreciate it if Henry would stop proving him wrong.

————

HRH Prince Dickhead 💩

Oct 30, 2019, 1:07 PM

i hate that tie

HRH Prince Dickhead 💩
What tie?

the one in that instagram you
just posted

HRH Prince Dickhead 💩
What's wrong with it? It's only grey.

exactly. try patterns sometime,
and stop frowning at your phone
like i know you're doing rn

HRH Prince Dickhead 💩
Patterns are considered a
"statement." Royals aren't
supposed to make statements with
what we wear.

do it for the gram

HRH Prince Dickhead 💩
You are the thistle in the tender and
sensitive arse crack of my life.

thanks!

Nov 17, 2019, 11:04 AM

HRH Prince Dickhead 💩

I've just received a 5-kilo parcel of
Ellen Claremont campaign buttons
with your face on them. Is this your
idea of a prank?

just trying to brighten up that
wardrobe, sunshine

HRH Prince Dickhead 💩

I hope this gross miscarriage of
campaign funds is worth it to you.
My security thought it was a bomb.
Shaan almost called in the sniffer
dogs.

oh, definitely worth it. even more
worth it now. tell shaan i say hi
and i miss that sweet sweet ass
xoxoxo

HRH Prince Dickhead 💩

I will not.

FOUR

"It's public knowledge. It's not my problem you just found out," his mother is saying, pacing double-time down a West Wing corridor.

"You mean to tell me," Alex half shouts, jogging to keep up, "every Thanksgiving, those stupid turkeys have been staying in a luxury suite at the Willard on the taxpayers' dime?"

"Yes, Alex, they do—"

"Gross government waste!"

"—and there are two forty-pound turkeys named Cornbread and Stuffing in a motorcade on Pennsylvania Avenue right now. There is no time to reallocate the turkeys."

Without missing a beat, he blurts out, "Bring them to the house."

"Where? Are you hiding a turkey habitat up your ass, son? Where, in our historically protected house, am I going to put a couple of turkeys until I pardon them tomorrow?"

"Put them in my room. I don't care."

She outright laughs. "No."

"How is it different from a hotel room? Put the turkeys in my room, Mom."

"I'm not putting the turkeys in your room."

"Put the turkeys in my room."

"No."

"Put them in my room, put them in my room, put them in my room—"

That night, as Alex stares into the cold, pitiless eyes of a prehistoric beast of prey, he has a few regrets.

THEY KNOW, he texts Henry. THEY KNOW I HAVE ROBBED THEM OF FIVE-STAR ACCOMMODATIONS TO SIT IN A CAGE IN MY ROOM, AND THE MINUTE I TURN MY BACK THEY ARE GOING TO FEAST ON MY FLESH.

Cornbread stares emptily back at him from inside a huge crate next to Alex's couch. A farm vet comes by once every few hours to check on them. Alex keeps asking if she can detect a lust for blood.

From the en suite, Stuffing releases another ominous gobble.

Alex was going to get things accomplished tonight. He really was. Before he learned of exorbitant turkey expenditures from CNN, he was watching the highlights of last night's Republican primary debate. He was going to finish an outline for an exam, then study the demographic engagement binder he convinced his mother to give him for the campaign job.

Instead, he is in a prison of his own creation, sworn to babysit these turkeys until the pardoning ceremony, and is just now realizing his deep-seated fear of large birds. He considers finding a couch to sleep on, but what if these demons from hell break out of their cages and murder each other during the night when he's supposed to be watching them? BREAKING: BOTH TURKEYS FOUND DEAD IN BEDROOM OF FSOTUS, TURKEY PARDON CANCELED IN DISGRACE, FSOTUS A SATANIC TURKEY RITUAL KILLER.

Please send photos, is Henry's idea of a comforting response.

He drops onto the edge of his bed. He's grown accustomed to texting with Henry almost every day; the time difference doesn't matter, since they're both awake at all ungodly hours of the day and night. Henry will send a snap from a seven a.m. polo practice and promptly receive one of Alex at two a.m., glasses on and coffee in hand, in bed with a pile of notes. Alex doesn't know why Henry never responds to his selfies from bed. His selfies from bed are always hilarious.

He snaps a shot of Cornbread and presses send, flinching when the bird flaps at him threateningly.

I think he's cute, Henry responds.

that's because you can't hear all the menacing gobbling

Yes, famously the most sinister of all animal sounds, the gobble.

"You know what, you little shit," Alex says the second the call connects, "you can hear it for yourself and then tell me how you would handle this—"

"Alex?" Henry's voice sounds scratchy and bewildered across the line. "Have you really rung me at three o'clock in the morning to make me listen to a turkey?"

"Yes, obviously," Alex says. He glances at Cornbread and cringes. "Jesus Christ, it's like they can see into your *soul.* Cornbread knows my sins, Henry. Cornbread knows what I have done, and he is here to make me atone."

He hears a rustling over the phone, and he pictures Henry in his heather-gray pajama shirt, rolling over in bed and maybe switching on a lamp. "Let's hear the cursed gobble, then."

"Okay, brace yourself," he says, and he switches to speaker and gravely holds out the phone.

Nothing. Ten long seconds of nothing.

"Truly harrowing," Henry's voice says tinnily over the speaker.

"It—okay, this is not representative," Alex says hotly. "They've been gobbling all fucking night, I swear."

"Sure they were," Henry says, mock-gently.

"No, hang on," Alex says. "I'm gonna . . . I'm gonna get one to gobble."

He hops off the bed and edges up to Cornbread's cage, feeling very much like he is taking his life into his own hands and also very much like he has a point to prove, which is an intersection at which he finds himself often.

"Um," he says. "How do you get a turkey to gobble?"

"Try gobbling," Henry says, "and see if he gobbles back."

Alex blinks. "Are you serious?"

"We hunt loads of wild turkeys in the spring," Henry says sagely. "The trick is to get into the mind of the turkey."

"How the hell do I do that?"

"So," Henry instructs. "Do as I say. You have to get quite close to the turkey, like, physically."

Carefully, still cradling the phone close, Alex leans toward the wire bars. "Okay."

"Make eye contact with the turkey. Do you have it?"

Alex follows Henry's instructions in his ear, planting his feet and bending his knees so he's at Cornbread's eye level, a chill running down his spine when his own eyes lock on the beady, black little murder eyes. "Yeah."

"Right, now hold it," Henry says. "Connect with the turkey, earn the turkey's trust . . . befriend the turkey . . ."

"Okay . . ."

"Buy a summer home in Majorca with the turkey . . ."

"Oh, I *fucking* hate you!" Alex shouts as Henry laughs at his own idiotic prank, and his indignant flailing startles a loud gobble out of Cornbread, which in turn startles a very unmanly scream out of Alex. "*Goddammit!* Did you hear that?"

"Sorry, what?" Henry says. "I've been stricken deaf."

"You're such a *dick,*" Alex says. "Have you ever even *been* turkey hunting?"

"Alex, you can't even hunt them in Britain."

Alex returns to his bed and face-plants into a pillow. "I hope Cornbread does kill me."

"No, all right, I did hear it, and it was . . . proper frightening," Henry says. "So, I understand. Where's June for all this?"

"She's having some kind of girls' night with Nora, and when I texted them for backup, they sent back," he reads out in a monotone, "'hahahahahahahaha good luck with that,' and then a turkey emoji and a poop emoji."

"That's fair," Henry says. Alex can picture him nodding solemnly. "So what are you going to do now? Are you going to stay up all night with them?"

"I don't know! I guess! I don't know what else to do!"

"You couldn't just go sleep somewhere else? Aren't there a thousand rooms in that house?"

"Okay, but, uh, what if they escape? I've seen *Jurassic Park.* Did you know birds are directly descended from raptors? That's a scientific fact. Raptors in my bedroom, Henry. And you want me to go to sleep like they're not gonna bust out of their enclosures and take over the island the minute I close my eyes? Okay. Maybe your white ass."

"I'm really going to have you offed," Henry tells him. "You'll never see it coming. Our assassins are trained in discretion. They will come in the night, and it will look like a humiliating accident."

"Autoerotic asphyxiation?"

"Toilet heart attack."

"Jesus."

"You've been warned."

"I thought you'd kill me in a more personal way. Silk pillow over my face, slow and gentle suffocation. Just you and me. Sensual."

"Ha. Well." Henry coughs.

"Anyway," Alex says, climbing fully up onto the bed now. "It doesn't matter because one of these goddamn turkeys is gonna kill me first."

"I really don't think— *Oh, hello there.*" There's rustling over the phone, the crinkling of a wrapper, and some heavy snuffling that sounds distinctly doglike. "*Who'za good lad, then?* David says hello."

"Hi, David."

"He— Oi! *Not* for you, Mr. Wobbles! Those are *mine!*" More rustling, a distant, offended meow. "*No,* Mr. Wobbles, you bastard!"

"What in the fuck is a Mr. Wobbles?"

"My sister's idiot cat," Henry tells him. "The thing weighs a ton and is still trying to steal my Jaffa Cakes. He and David are mates."

"What are you even doing right now?"

"What am *I* doing? I was trying to *sleep.*"

"Okay, but you're eating Jabba Cakes, so."

"*Jaffa* Cakes, my *God*," Henry says. "I'm having my entire life haunted by a deranged American Neanderthal and a pair of turkeys, apparently."

"And?"

Henry heaves another almighty sigh. He's always sighing when Alex is involved. It's amazing he has any air left. "And . . . don't laugh."

"Oh, yay," Alex says readily.

"I was watching *Great British Bake Off.*"

"Cute. Not embarrassing, though. What else?"

"I, er, might be . . . wearing one of those peely face masks," he says in a rush.

"Oh my God, I knew it!"

"*Instant* regret."

"I knew you had one of those crazy expensive Scandinavian skin care regimens. Do you have that, like, eye cream with diamonds in it?"

"No!" Henry pouts, and Alex has to press the back of his hand against his lips to stifle his laugh. "Look, I have an appearance tomorrow, all right? I didn't know I'd be *scrutinized.*"

"I'm not scrutinizing. We all gotta keep those pores in check," Alex says. "So you like *Bake Off*, huh?"

"It's just so soothing," Henry says. "Everything's all pastel-colored and the music is so relaxing and everyone's so lovely to one another. And you learn so much about different types of biscuits, Alex. So much. When the world seems awful, such as when you're trapped in a Great Turkey Calamity, you can put it on and vanish into biscuit land."

"American cooking competition shows are nothing like that. They're all sweaty and, like, dramatic death music and intense camera cuts," Alex says. "*Bake Off* makes *Chopped* look like the fucking Manson tapes."

"I feel like this explains loads about our differences," Henry says, and Alex gives a small laugh.

"You know," Alex says. "You're kind of surprising."

Henry pauses. "In what way?"

"In that you're not a totally boring asshole."

"Wow," Henry says with a laugh. "I'm honored."

"I guess you have your depths."

"You thought I was a dumb blond, didn't you?"

"Not exactly, just, *boring*," Alex says. "I mean, your dog is named David, which is pretty boring."

"After Bowie."

"I—" Alex's head spins, recalibrating. "Are you serious? What the hell? Why not call him Bowie, then?"

"Bit on the nose, isn't it?" Henry says. "A man should have some element of mystery."

"I guess," Alex says. Then, because he can't stop it in time, lets out a tremendous yawn. He's been up since seven for a run before class. If these turkeys don't end him, exhaustion will.

"Alex," Henry says firmly.

"What?"

"The turkeys are not going to *Jurassic Park* you," he says. "You're not the bloke from *Seinfeld*. You're Jeff Goldblum. Go to sleep."

Alex bites down a smile that feels bigger than the sentence has truly earned. "You go to sleep."

"I will," Henry says, and Alex thinks he hears the weird

smile returned in Henry's voice, and honestly, this whole night is really, really weird, "as soon as you get off the phone, won't I?"

"Okay," Alex says, "but, like, what if they gobble again?"

"Go sleep in June's room, you numpty."

"Okay," Alex says.

"Okay," Henry agrees.

"Okay," Alex says again. He's suddenly very aware they've never spoken on the phone before, and so he's never had to figure out how to hang up the phone with Henry before. He's at a loss. But he's still smiling. Cornbread is staring at him like he doesn't get it. *Me fuckin' too, buddy.*

"Okay," Henry repeats. "So. Good night."

"Cool," Alex says lamely. "Good night."

He hangs up and stares at the phone in his hand, as if it should explain the static electricity in the air around him.

He shakes it off, gathers up his pillow and a bundle of clothes, and crosses the hall to June's room, climbing up into her tall bed. But he can't stop thinking there's some end left loose.

He takes his phone back out. i sent pics of turkeys so i deserve pics of your animals too.

A minute and a half later: Henry, in a massive, palatial, hideous bed of white and gold linens, his face looking slightly pink and recently scrubbed, with a beagle's head on one side of his pillow and an obese Siamese cat curled up on the other around a Jaffa Cake wrapper. He's got faint circles under his eyes, but his face is soft and amused, one hand resting above his head on the pillow while the other holds up the phone for the selfie.

This is what I must endure, he says, followed by, Good night, honestly.

HRH Prince Dickhead 💩

Dec 8, 2019, 8:53 PM

> yo there's a bond marathon on
> and did you know your dad was
> a total babe

HRH Prince Dickhead 💩
I BEG YOU TO NOT

Even before Alex's parents split, they both had a habit of calling him by the other's last name when he exhibited particular traits. They still do. When he runs his mouth off to the press, his mom calls him into her office and says, "Get your shit together, Diaz." When his hard-headedness gets him stuck, his dad texts him, "Let it go, Claremont."

Alex's mother sighs as she sets her copy of the *Post* down on her desk, open to an inside page article: SENATOR OSCAR DIAZ RETURNS TO DC FOR HOLIDAYS WITH EX-WIFE PRESIDENT CLAREMONT. It's almost weird how much it isn't weird anymore. His dad is flying in from California for Christmas, and it's fine, but it's also in the *Post*.

She's doing the thing she always does when she's about to spend time with his father: pursing her lips and twitching two fingers of her right hand.

"You know," Alex says from where he's kicked back on an Oval Office couch with a book, "somebody can go get you a cigarette."

"Hush, Diaz."

She's had the Lincoln Bedroom prepared for his dad, and she keeps changing her mind, having housekeeping undecorate and redecorate. Leo, for his part, is unfazed and mollifies her with compliments between fits of tinsel. Alex doesn't think anyone but Leo could ever stay married to his mother. His father certainly couldn't.

June is in a state, the perpetual mediator. His family is pretty much the only situation where Alex prefers to sit back and let it all unfold, occasionally poking when it's necessary or interesting, but June takes personal responsibility for making sure nobody breaks any more priceless White House antiques like last year.

His dad finally arrives in a flurry of Secret Service agents, his beard impeccably groomed and his suit impeccably tailored. For all June's anxious preparations, she almost breaks an antique vase herself catapulting into his arms. They disappear immediately to the chocolate shop on the ground floor, the sound of Oscar raving about June's latest blog post for *The Atlantic* fading around the corner. Alex and his mother share a look. Their family is so predictable sometimes.

The next day, Oscar gives Alex the follow-me-and-don't-tell-your-mother look and pulls him out to the Truman Balcony.

"Merry fuckin' Christmas, mijo," his dad says, grinning, and Alex laughs and lets himself be hauled into a one-armed hug. He smells the same as ever, salty and smoky and like well-treated leather. His mom used to complain that she felt like she lived in a cigar bar.

"Merry Christmas, Pa," Alex says back.

He drags a chair close to the railing, putting his shiny boots up. Oscar Diaz loves a view.

Alex considers the sprawling, snowy lawn in front of them,

the sure line of the Washington Monument stretching up, the jagged French mansard roofs of the Eisenhower Building to the west, the same one Truman hated. His dad pulls a cigar from his pocket, clipping it and lighting up in the careful ritual he's done for years. He takes a puff and passes it over.

"It ever make you laugh to think how much this pisses assholes off?" he says, gesturing to encompass the whole scene: two Mexican men putting their feet up on the railing where heads of state eat croissants.

"Constantly."

Oscar does laugh, then, enjoying his brazenness. He is an adrenaline junkie—mountain climbing, cave diving, pissing off Alex's mother. Flirting with death, basically. It's the flip side of the way he approaches work, which is methodical and precise, or the way he approaches parenting, which is laid-back and indulgent.

It's nice, now, to see him more than he ever did in high school, since Oscar spends most of his year in DC. During the busiest congressional sessions, they'll convene Los Bastardos— weekly beers in Oscar's office after hours, just him, Alex, and Rafael Luna, talking shit. And it's nice that proximity has forced his parents through the era of mutually assured destruction to now, where they have one Christmas instead of two.

As the days go by, Alex catches himself remembering sometimes, just for a second, how much he misses having everyone under one roof.

His dad was always the cook of the family. Alex's childhood was perfumed with simmering peppers and onions and stew meat in a cast iron pot for caldillo, fresh masa waiting on the butcher block. He remembers his mom swearing and laughing when she opened the oven for her guilty-pleasure pizza bagels only to find all the pots and pans stored there, or when she'd go for the tub of butter in the fridge and find it filled with homemade salsa verde. There used to be a lot of laughter in that kitchen, a lot of good food and loud music and parades of cousins and homework done at the table.

Except eventually there was a lot of yelling, followed by a lot of quiet, and soon Alex and June were teenagers and both their parents were in Congress, and Alex was student body president and lacrosse cocaptain and prom king and valedictorian, and, very intentionally, it stopped being a thing he had time to think about.

Still, his dad's been in the Residence for three days without incident, and one day Alex catches him in the kitchens with two of the cooks, laughing and dumping peppers into a pot. It's just, you know, sometimes he thinks it might be nice if it could be like this more often.

Zahra's heading to New Orleans to see her family for Christmas, only at the president's insistence, and only because her sister had a baby and Amy threatened to stab her if she didn't deliver the onesie she knitted. Which means Christmas dinner is happening on Christmas Eve so Zahra won't miss it. For all her late nights cursing their names, Zahra is family.

"Merry Christmas, Z!" Alex tells her cheerfully in the hall outside the family dining room. For holiday flare, she's wearing a sensible red turtleneck; Alex is wearing a sweater covered in bright green tinsel. He smiles and presses a button on the inside of the sleeve, and "O Christmas Tree" plays from a speaker near his armpit.

"I can't wait to not see you for two days," she says, but there's real affection in her voice.

This year's dinner is small, since his dad's parents are on vacation, so the table is set for six in glittering white and gold. The conversation is pleasant enough that Alex almost forgets it's not always like this.

Until it shifts to the election.

"I was thinking," Oscar says, carefully cutting his filet, "this time, I can campaign with you."

At the other end of the table, Ellen puts her fork down. "You can what?"

"You know." He shrugs, chewing. "Hit the trail, do some speeches. Be a surrogate."

"You can't be serious."

Oscar puts down his own fork and knife now on the cloth-covered table, a soft thump of *oh, shit*. Alex glances across the table at June.

"You really think it's such a bad idea?" Oscar says.

"Oscar, we went through all of this last time," Ellen tells him. Her tone is instantly clipped. "People don't like women, but they like mothers and wives. They like *families*. The last thing we need to do is remind them that I'm divorced by parading my ex-husband around."

He laughs a little grimly. "So, you'll pretend he's their dad then, eh?"

"Oscar," Leo speaks up, "you know I'd never—"

"You're missing the *point*," Ellen interrupts.

"It could help your approval ratings," he says. "Mine are quite high, El. Higher than yours ever were in the House."

"Here we go," Alex says to Leo next to him, whose face remains pleasantly neutral.

"We've done *studies*, Oscar! Okay?" Ellen's voice has risen in volume and pitch, her palms planted flat on the table. "The data shows, I track worse with undecided voters when they're reminded of the divorce!"

"People know you're divorced!"

"Alex's numbers are high!" she shouts, and Alex and June both wince. "June's numbers are high!"

"They're not *numbers!*"

"Fuck off, I know that," she spits, "I never said they were!"

"You think sometimes you use them like they are?"

"How *dare* you, when you don't seem to have any problem trotting them out every time you're up for reelection!" she says, slicing one hand through the air beside her. "Maybe if they were just Claremonts, you wouldn't have so much luck. It'd sure as hell be less confusing—it's the name everybody knows them by anyway!"

"Nobody's taking any of our names!" June jumps in, her voice high.

"June," Ellen says.

Their dad pushes on. "I'm trying to help you, Ellen!"

"I don't need your help to win an election, Oscar!" she says, hitting the table so hard with her open palm that the dishes rattle. "I didn't need it when I was in Congress, and I didn't need it to become president the first time, and I don't need it now!"

"You need to get serious about what you're up against! You think the other side is going to play fair this time? Eight years of Obama, and now you? They're angry, Ellen, and Richards is out for blood! You need to be ready!"

"I will be! You think I don't have a team on all this shit already? I'm the President of the United fucking States! I don't need you to come here and—and—"

"Mansplain?" Zahra offers.

"Mansplain!" Ellen shouts, jabbing a finger across the table at Oscar, eyes wide. "This presidential race to me!"

Oscar throws his napkin down. "You're still so *fucking* stubborn!"

"Fuck you!"

"Mom!" June says sharply.

"Jesus Christ, are you kidding me?" Alex hears himself shout before he even consciously decides to say it. "Can we not be civil for one fucking meal? It's *Christmas,* for fuck's sake. Aren't y'all supposed to be running the country? Get your shit together."

He pushes his chair back and stalks out of the dining room, knowing he's being a dramatic asshole and not really caring. He slams his bedroom door behind him, and his stupid sweater plays a few depressingly off-key notes when he yanks it off and throws it at the wall.

It's not that he doesn't lose his temper often, it's just . . . he doesn't usually lose it with his family. Mostly because he doesn't usually *deal* with his family.

He digs an old lacrosse T-shirt out of his dresser, and when he turns and catches his reflection in the mirror by the closet, he's right back in his teens, caring too much about his parents and helpless to change his situation. Except now he doesn't have any AP classes to enroll in as a distraction.

His hand twitches for his phone. His brain is a two-passenger minimum ride as far as he's concerned—alone and busy or thinking with company.

But Nora's doing Hanukkah in Vermont, and he doesn't want to annoy her, and his best friend from high school, Liam, has barely spoken to him since he moved to DC.

Which leaves . . .

"What could I possibly have done to have brought this upon myself now?" says Henry's voice, low and sleepy. It sounds like "Good King Wenceslas" is playing in the background

"Hey, um, sorry. I know it's late, and it's Christmas Eve and everything. You probably have, like, family stuff, I'm just realizing. I don't know why I didn't think of it before. Wow, this is why I don't have friends. I'm a dick. Sorry, man. I'll, uh, I'll just—"

"Alex, Christ," Henry interrupts. "It's fine. It's half two here, everyone's gone to bed. Except Bea. Say hi, Bea."

"Hi, Alex!" says a clear, giggly voice on the other end of the line. "Henry's got his candy-cane jim-jams on—"

"That's quite enough," Henry's voice comes back through, and there's a muffled sound like maybe a pillow has been shoved in Bea's direction. "What's happening, then?"

"Sorry," Alex blurts out, "I know this is weird, and you're with your sister and everything, and, like, argh. I kind of didn't have anyone else to call who would be awake? And I know we're, uh, not really friends, and we don't really talk about this stuff, but my dad came in for Christmas, and he and my mom are like fucking tiger sharks fighting over a baby seal when you put them in the same room together for more than an hour, and they got in this huge fight, and it shouldn't *matter,* because they're already divorced and everything, and I don't know why I lost my shit, but I wish they could give it a rest for *once* so we could have one single normal holiday, you know?"

There's a long pause before Henry says, "Hang on. *Bea, can I have a minute? Hush. Yes, you can take the biscuits.* All right, I'm listening."

Alex exhales, wondering faintly what the hell he's doing, but plows onward.

Telling Henry about the divorce—those weird, tumultuous years, the day he came home from a Boy Scout camp-out to discover his dad's things moved out, the nights of Helados ice cream—doesn't feel as uncomfortable as it probably should. He's never bothered to filter himself with Henry, at first because he honestly didn't care what Henry thought, and now because it's how they are. Maybe it should be different, bitching about his course load versus spilling his guts about this. It isn't.

He doesn't realize he's been talking for an hour until he finishes retelling what happened at dinner and Henry says, "It sounds like you did your best."

Alex forgets what he was going to say next.

He just . . . Well, he gets told he's great a lot. He just doesn't often get told he's good enough.

Before he can think of a response, there's a soft triple knock on the door—June.

"Ah—okay, thanks, man, I gotta go," Alex says, his voice low as June eases the door open.

"Alex—"

"Seriously, um. Thank you," Alex says. He really does not want to explain this to June. "Merry Christmas. Night."

He hangs up and tosses the phone aside as June settles down on the bed. She's wearing her pink bathrobe, and her hair is wet from the shower.

"Hey," she says. "You okay?"

"Yeah, I'm fine," he says. "Sorry, I don't know what's up with me. I didn't mean to lose it. I've been . . . I don't know. I've been kind of . . . off . . . lately."

"It's okay," she says. She tosses her hair over her shoulder, flicking droplets of water onto him. "I was a total basket case for the last six months of college. I would lose it at anybody. You know, you don't have to do everything all the time."

"It's fine. I'm fine," he tells her automatically. June tilts an unconvinced look at him, and he kicks at one of her knees with his bare foot. "So, how did things go after I left? Did they finish cleaning up the blood yet?"

June sighs, kicking him back. "Somehow it shifted to the topic of how they were a political power couple before the divorce and how good those times were, Mom apologized, and it was whiskey and nostalgia hour until everybody went to bed." She sniffs. "Anyway, you were right."

"You don't think I was out of line?"

"Nah. Though . . . I kind of agree with what Dad was saying. Mom can be . . . you know . . . Mom."

"Well, that's what got her where she is now."

"You don't think it's ever a problem?"

Alex shrugs. "I think she's a good mom."

"Yeah, to you," June says. There's no accusation behind it, just observation. "The effectiveness of her nurturing kind of depends on what you need from her. Or what you can do for her."

"I mean, I get what she's saying, though," Alex hedges. "Sometimes it still sucks that Dad decided to pack up and move just to run for the seat in California."

"Yeah, but, I mean, how is that different from the stuff Mom's done? It's all politics. I'm just saying, he has a point about how Mom pushes us without always giving us the other Mom stuff."

Alex is opening his mouth to answer when June's phone buzzes from her robe pocket. "Oh. Hmm," she says when she slides it out to eye the screen.

"What?"

"Nothing, uh." She thumbs open the message. "Merry Christmas text. From Evan."

"Evan . . . as in ex-boyfriend Evan, in California? Y'all still text?"

June's biting her lip now, her expression a little distant as she types out a response. "Yeah, sometimes."

"Cool," Alex says. "I always liked him."

"Yeah. Me too," June says softly. She locks her phone and drops it on the bed, blinking a couple times as if to reset. "Anyway, what'd Nora say when you told her?"

"Hmm?"

"On the phone?" she asks him. "I figured it was her, you never talk to anyone else about this crap."

"Oh," Alex says. He feels inexplicable, traitorous warmth flash up the back of his neck. "Oh, um, no. Actually, this is gonna sound weird, but I was talking to Henry?"

June's eyebrows shoot up, and Alex instinctively scans the room for cover. "Really."

"Listen, I know, but we kind of weirdly have stuff in common and, I guess, similar weird emotional baggage and neuroses, and for some reason I felt like he would get it."

"Oh my God, Alex," she says, lunging at him to yank him into a rough hug, "you made a friend!"

"I have friends! Get off me!"

"You made a friend!" She is literally giving him a noogie. "I'm so proud of you!"

"I'm gonna murder you, *stop it*," he says, alligator-rolling out of her clutches. He lands on the floor. "He's not my friend. He's someone I like to antagonize all the time, and *one* time I talked to him about something real."

"That's a friend, Alex."

Alex's mouth starts and stops several silent sentences before he points to the door. "You can leave, June! Go to bed!"

"Nope. Tell me everything about your new best friend, who is a *royal*. That is so bougie of you. Who would have guessed it?" she says, peering over the edge of the bed at him. "Oh my God, this is like all those romantic comedies where the girl hires a male escort to pretend to be her wedding date and then falls in love with him for real."

"That is *not at all* what this is like."

The staff has barely finished packing up the Christmas trees when it starts.

There's the dance floor to set up, menu to finalize, Snapchat filter to approve. Alex spends the entire 26th holed up in the Social Secretary's office with June, going over the waivers they've gotten for everyone to sign after a daughter of a Real Housewife fell down the rotunda stairs last year; Alex remains impressed that she didn't spill her margarita.

It's time once more for the Legendary Balls-Out Bananas White House Trio New Year's Eve Party.

Technically, the title is the Young America New Year's Eve Gala, or as at least one late-night host calls it, the Millennial Correspondents' Dinner. Every year, Alex, June, and Nora fill up the East Room on the first floor with three hundred or so of their friends, vague celebrity acquaintances, former hookups, potential political connections, and otherwise notable twenty-somethings. The party is, officially, a fund-raiser, and it generates so much money for charity and so much good PR for the First Family that even his mom approves of it.

"Um, excuse me," Alex is saying from a first-floor conference table, one hand full of confetti samples—do they want a metallic color palette or a more subdued navy and gold?—while staring at a copy of the finalized guest list. June and Nora are stuffing their faces with cake samples. "Who put Henry on here?"

Nora says through a mouthful of chocolate cake, "Wasn't me."

"June?"

"Look, you should have invited him yourself!" June says, by way of admission. "It's really nice you're making friends who aren't us. Sometimes when you get too isolated, you start to go a little crazy. Remember last year when Nora and I were both out of the country for a week, and you almost got a tattoo?"

"I still think we should have let him get a tramp stamp."

"It wasn't going to be a *tramp stamp*," Alex says hotly. "You were in on this, weren't you?"

"You know I love chaos," Nora tells him serenely.

"I have friends who aren't y'all," Alex says.

"Who, Alex?" June says. "Literally who?"

"People!" he says defensively. "People from class! Liam!"

"Please. We all know you haven't talked to Liam in a year," June says. "You need friends. And I know you like Henry."

"Shut up," Alex says. He brushes a finger under his collar and finds his skin damp. Do they always have to crank the heat up this high when it's snowing outside?

"This is interesting," Nora observes.

"No, it's not," Alex snaps. "Fine, he can come. But if he doesn't know anybody else, I'm not babysitting him all night."

"I gave him a plus-one," June says.

"Who is he bringing?" Alex asks immediately, reflexively. Involuntarily. "Just wondering."

"Pez," she says. She's giving him a weird look he can't parse, and he decides to chalk it up to June being confusing and strange. She often works in mysterious ways, organizes and orchestrates things he never sees coming until all the threads come together.

So, Henry is coming, he guesses, confirmed when he checks Instagram the day of the party and sees a post from Pez of him and Henry on a private jet. Pez's hair has been dyed pastel pink for the occasion, and beside him, Henry is smiling in a soft-looking gray sweatshirt, his socked feet up on the windowsill. He actually looks well-rested for once.

USA bound! #YoungAmericaGala2019 Pez's caption reads.

Alex smiles despite himself and texts Henry.

ATTN: will be wearing a burgundy velvet suit tonight. please do not attempt to steal my shine. you will fail and i will be embarrassed for you.

Henry texts back seconds later.

Wouldn't dream of it.

From there everything speeds up, and a hairstylist is wrangling him into the Cosmetology Room, and he gets to watch the girls transform into their camera-ready selves. Nora's short curls are swept to one side with a silver pin shaped to match the sharp geometric lines on the bodice of her black dress; June's gown is a plunging Zac Posen number in a shade of midnight blue that perfectly complements the navy-and-gold color palette they chose.

The guests start arriving around eight, and the liquor starts flowing, and Alex orders a middle-shelf whiskey to get things going. There's live music, a pop act that owed June a personal favor, and they're covering "American Girl" right now, so Alex grabs June's hand and spins her onto the dance floor.

First arrivals are always the first-time political types: a small gaggle of White House interns, an event planner for Center for American Progress, the daughter of a first-term senator with a punk rock–looking girlfriend who Alex makes a mental note to introduce himself to later. Then, the wave of politically strategic invites chosen by the press team, and lastly, the fashionably late—minor to mid-range pop stars, teen soap actors, children of major celebrities.

He's just wondering when Henry's going to make his appearance, when June appears at his side and yells, "Incoming!"

Alex's gaze is met by a bright burst of color that turns out to be Pez's bomber jacket, which is a shiny silk thing in such an elaborate, colorful floral print that Alex almost has to squint. The colors fade slightly, though, when his eyes slide to the right.

It's the first time Alex has seen Henry in person since the weekend in London and the hundreds of texts and weird in-jokes and late-night phone calls that came after, and it almost feels like meeting a new person. He knows more about Henry, understands him better, and he can appreciate the rarity of a genuine smile on the same famously beautiful face.

It's a weird cognitive dissonance, Henry present and Henry past. That must be why something feels so restless and hot somewhere beneath his sternum. That and the whiskey.

Henry's wearing a simple dark blue suit, but he's opted for a bright coppery-mustard tie in a narrow cut. He spots Alex, and his smile broadens, giving Pez's arm a tug.

"Nice tie," Alex says as soon as Henry is close enough to hear over the crowd.

"Thought I might be escorted off the premises for anything less exciting," Henry says, and his voice is somehow different than Alex remembers. Like very expensive velvet, something moneyed and lush and fluid all at once.

"And *who* is this?" June asks from Alex's side, interrupting his train of thought.

"Ah yes, you've not officially met, have you?" Henry says. "June, Alex, this is my best mate, Percy Okonjo."

"Pez, like the sweets," Pez says cheerfully, extending his hand to Alex. Several of his fingernails are painted blue. When he redirects his attention to June, his eyes grow brighter, his grin spreading. "Please do smack me if this is out of line, but you are the most exquisite woman I have ever seen in my life, and I would like to procure for you the most lavish drink in this establishment if you will let me."

"Uh," Alex says.

"You're a charmer," June says, smiling indulgently.

"And you are a goddess."

He watches them disappear into the crowd, Pez a blazing streak of color, already spinning June in a pirouette as they go. Henry's smile has gone sheepish and reserved, and Alex understands their friendship at last. Henry doesn't want the spotlight, and Pez naturally absorbs what Henry deflects.

"That man has been begging me to introduce him to your sister since the wedding," Henry says.

"Seriously?"

"We've probably just saved him a tremendous amount of money. He was going to start pricing skywriters soon."

Alex tosses his head back and laughs, and Henry watches, still grinning. June and Nora had a point. He does, against all odds, really like this person.

"Well, come on," Alex says. "I'm already two whiskeys in. You've got some catching up to do."

More than one conversation drops out as Alex and Henry pass, mouths hanging open over entremets. Alex tries to imagine what they must look like: the prince and the First Son, the two leading heartthrobs of their respective countries, shoulder to shoulder on their way to the bar. It's intimidating and thrilling, living up to that kind of rich, untouchable fantasy. That's what people *see,* but none of them know about the Great Turkey Calamity. Only Alex and Henry do.

He scores the first round and the crowd swallows them up. Alex is surprised how pleased he is by the physical presence of Henry next to him. He doesn't even mind having to look up at him anymore. He introduces Henry to some White House interns and laughs as they blush and stutter, and Henry's face goes pleasantly neutral, an expression Alex used to mistake as unimpressed but can now read for what it is: carefully concealed bemusement.

There's dancing, and mingling, and a speech by June about the immigration fund they're supporting with their donations tonight, and Alex ducks out of an aggressive come-on by a girl from the new Spider-Man movies and into a haphazard conga line, and Henry actually seems to have fun. June finds them at some point and steals Henry away to gab at the bar. Alex watches them from afar, wondering what they could possibly be talking about that has June nearly falling off her barstool laughing, until the crowd overtakes him again.

After a while, the band breaks and a DJ takes over with a mix of early 2000s hip-hop, all the greatest hits that came out when Alex was a child and were somehow still in rotation at dances in his teens. That's when Henry finds him, like a man lost at sea.

"You don't dance?" he says, watching Henry, who is very visibly trying to figure out what to do with to do with his hands. It's endearing. Wow, Alex is drunk.

"No, I do," Henry says. "It's just, the family-mandated ball-room dancing lessons didn't exactly cover this?"

"C'mon, it's, like, in the hips. You have to loosen up." He reaches down and puts both hands on Henry's hips, and Henry instantly tenses under the touch. "That's the opposite of what I said."

"Alex, I don't—"

"Here," Alex says, moving his own hips, "watch me."

With a grave gulp of champagne, Henry says, "I am."

The song crossfades into another *buh-duh dum-dum-dum, dum-duh-dum duh-duh-dum*—

"*Shut up,*" Alex yells, cutting off whatever else Henry was saying, "shut your dumb face, this is my *shit!*" He throws his hands up in the air as Henry stares at him blankly, and around them, people start cheering too, hundreds of shoulders shimmying to the shouty, Lil Jon–flavored nostalgia of "Get Low."

"Did you seriously never go to an awkward middle school dance and watch a bunch of teenagers dry hump to this song?"

Henry is holding on to his champagne for dear life. "You absolutely must know I did not."

Alex flails one arm out and snatches Nora from a nearby huddle, where she's been flirting with Spider-Man girl. "Nora! *Nora!* Henry has never watched a bunch of teenagers dry hump to this song!"

"*What?*"

"Please tell me nobody is going to *dry hump* me," Henry says.

"Oh my God, Henry," Alex yells, seizing Henry by one lapel as the music pounds on, "you have to dance. You *have to* dance. You need to understand this formative American coming-of-age experience."

Nora grabs Alex, pulling him away from Henry and spinning him around, her hands on his waist, and starts grinding with abandon. Alex whoops and Nora cackles and the crowd jumps around and Henry just gawks at them.

"Did that man just say '*sweat drop down my balls*'?"

It's *fun*—Nora against his back, sweat on his brow, bodies pushing in around him. To one side, a podcast producer and that guy from *Stranger Things* are hitting the Kid 'n Play, and to the other, Pez is literally bending over to the front and touching his toes as instructed. Henry's face is shocked and confused, and it's hilarious. Alex accepts a shot off a passing tray and drinks to the strange spark in his gut at the way Henry watches them. Alex pouts his lips and shakes his ass, and with extreme trepidation, Henry starts bopping his head a little.

"Fuck it up, vato!" Alex yells, and Henry laughs despite himself. He even gives his hips a little shake.

"I thought you weren't going to babysit him all night," June stage-whispers in his ear as she twirls by.

"I thought *you* were too busy for guys," Alex replies, nodding significantly at Pez in the periphery. She winks at him and disappears.

From there, it's a series of crowd-pleasers until midnight, the lights and music blasting at full capacity. Confetti, somehow blasting into the air. Did they arrange for confetti cannons? More drinks—Henry starts drinking directly from a bottle of Moët & Chandon. Alex likes the look on Henry's face, the sure curl of his hand around the neck of the bottle, the way his lips wrap around the mouth of it. Henry's willingness to dance is directly proportionate to his proximity to Alex's hands, and the amount of giddy warmth bubbling under Alex's skin is directly proportionate to the cut of Henry's mouth when he watches him with Nora. It's an equation he is not nearly sober enough to parse.

They all huddle up at 11:59 for the countdown, eyes blurry and arms around one another. Nora screams "three, two, one" right in his ear and slings her arm around his neck as he yells his approval and kisses her sloppily, laughing through it. They've done this every year, both of them perpetually single and affectionately drunk and happy to make everyone else intrigued and jealous. Nora's mouth is warm and tastes horrifying, like peach schnapps, and she bites his lip and messes up his hair for good measure.

When he opens his eyes, Henry's looking back at him, expression unreadable.

He feels his own smile grow wider, and Henry turns away and toward the bottle of champagne clutched in his fist, from which he takes a hearty swig before disappearing into the crowd.

Alex loses track of things after that, because he's very, very drunk and the music is very, very loud and there are very, very many hands on him, carrying him through the tangle of dancing bodies and passing him more drinks. Nora bobs by on the back of some hot rookie NFL running back.

It's loud and messy and wonderful. Alex has always loved these parties, the sparkling joy of it all, the way champagne bubbles on his tongue and confetti sticks to his shoes. It's a reminder that even though he stresses and stews in private rooms, there will always be a sea of people he can disappear into, that the world can be warm and welcoming and fill up the walls of this big old house he lives in with something bright and infectiously alive.

But somewhere, beneath the liquor and the music, he can't stop noticing that Henry has disappeared.

He checks the bathrooms, the buffet, the quiet corners of the ballroom, but he's nowhere. He tries asking Pez, shouting Henry's name at him over the noise, but Pez just smiles and shrugs and steals a snapback off a passing yacht kid.

He's . . . worried isn't exactly the word. Bothered. Curious. He was having fun watching everything he did play out on Henry's face. He keeps looking, until he trips over his own feet by one of the big windows in the hallway. He's pulling himself up when he glances outside, down into the garden.

There, under a tree in the snow, exhaling little puffs of steam, is a tall, lean, broad-shouldered figure that can only be Henry.

He slips out onto the portico without really thinking about it, and the instant the door closes behind him, the music snuffs out into silence, and it's just him and Henry and the garden. He's got the hazy tunnel vision of a drunk person when they lock eyes on a goal. He follows it down the stairs and onto the snowy lawn.

Henry stands quietly, hands in his pockets, contemplating the sky, and he'd almost look sober if not for the wobbly lean to the left he's doing. Stupid English dignity, even in the face of champagne. Alex wants to push his royal face into a shrub.

Alex trips over a bench, and the sound catches Henry's attention. When he turns, the moonlight catches on him, and his face looks softened in half shadows, inviting in a way Alex can't quite work out.

"What're you doing out here?" Alex says, trudging up to stand next to him under the tree.

Henry squints. Up close, his eyes go a little crossed, focused somewhere between himself and Alex's nose. Not so dignified after all.

"Looking for Orion," Henry says.

Alex huffs a laugh, looking up to the sky. Nothing but fat winter clouds. "You must be really bored with the commoners to come out here and stare at the clouds."

"'m not bored," Henry mumbles. "What are *you* doing out here? Doesn't America's golden boy have some swooning crowds to beguile?"

"Says Prince fucking Charming," Alex answers, smirking.

Henry pulls a very unprincely face up at the clouds. "Hardly."

His knuckle brushes the back of Alex's hand at their sides, a little zip of warmth in the cold night. Alex considers his face in profile, blinking through the booze, following the smooth line of his nose and the gentle dip at the center of his lower lip, each touched by moonlight. It's freezing and Alex is only wearing his suit jacket, but his chest feels warmed from the inside with liquor and something heady his brain keeps stumbling over, trying to name. The garden is quiet except for the blood rushing in his ears.

"You didn't really answer my question, though," Alex notes.

Henry groans, rubbing a hand across his face. "You can't ever leave well enough alone, can you?" He leans his head back. It thumps gently against the trunk of the tree. "Sometimes it gets a bit . . . much."

Alex keeps looking at him. Usually, there's something about the set of Henry's mouth that betrays a bit of friendliness, but sometimes, like right now, his mouth pinches in the corner instead, pins his guard resolutely in place.

Alex shifts, almost involuntarily, leaning back against the tree too. He nudges their shoulders together and catches that corner of Henry's mouth twitching, sees something move featherlight across his face. These things—big events, letting other people feed on his own energy—are rarely too much for Alex. He's not sure how Henry feels, but some part of his brain that is likely soaked in tequila thinks maybe it would be helpful if Henry could take what he can handle, and Alex could handle the rest. Maybe he can absorb some of the "much" from the place where their shoulders are pressed together.

A muscle in Henry's jaw moves, and something soft, almost like a smile, tugs at his lips. "D'you ever wonder," he says slowly, "what it's like to be some anonymous person out in the world?"

Alex frowns. "What do you mean?"

"Just, you know," Henry says. "If your mum weren't the president and you were just a normal bloke living a normal life, what things might be like? What you'd be doing instead?"

"Ah," Alex says, considering. He stretches one arm out in front of him, makes a dismissive gesture with a flick of his wrist. "Well, I mean, obviously I'd be a model. I've been on the cover of *Teen Vogue* twice. These genetics transcend all circumstance." Henry rolls his eyes again. "What about you?"

Henry shakes his head ruefully. "I'd be a writer."

Alex gives a little laugh. He thinks he already knew this about Henry, somehow, but it's still kind of disarming. "Can't you do that?"

"Not exactly seen as a worthwhile pursuit for a man in line

for the throne, scribbling verses about quarter-life angst," Henry says dryly. "Besides, the traditional family career track is military, so that's about it, isn't it?"

Henry bites his lip, waits a beat, and opens his mouth again. "I'd date more, probably, as well."

Alex can't help laughing again. "Right, because it's so hard to get a date when you're a prince."

Henry cuts his eyes back down to Alex. "You'd be surprised."

"How? You're not exactly lacking for options."

Henry keeps looking at him, holding his gaze for two seconds too long. "The options I'd like . . ." he says, dragging the words out. "They don't quite seem to be *options* at all."

Alex blinks. "What?"

"I'm saying that I have . . . people . . . who interest me," Henry says, turning his body toward Alex now, speaking with a fumbling pointedness, as if it means something. "But I shouldn't pursue them. At least not in my position."

Are they too drunk to communicate in English? He wonders distantly if Henry knows any Spanish.

"I don't know what the hell you're talking about," Alex says.

"You don't?"

"No."

"You really don't?"

"I really, really don't."

Henry's whole face grimaces in frustration, his eyes casting skyward like they're searching for help from an uncaring universe. "Christ, you are as thick as it gets," he says, and he grabs Alex's face in both hands and kisses him.

Alex is frozen, registering the press of Henry's lips and the wool cuffs of his coat grazing his jaw. The world fuzzes out into static, and his brain is swimming hard to keep up, adding up the equation of teenage grudges and wedding cakes and two a.m. texts and not understanding the variable that got him here, except it's . . . well, surprisingly, he really doesn't mind. Like, at all.

In his head, he tries to cobble a list together in a panic, gets as far as, *One, Henry's lips are soft,* and short-circuits.

He tests leaning into the kiss and is rewarded by Henry's mouth sliding and opening against his, Henry's tongue brushing against his, which is, *wow.* It's nothing like kissing Nora earlier—nothing like kissing anyone he's ever kissed in his life. It feels as steady and huge as the ground under their feet, as encompassing of every part of him, as likely to knock the wind out of his lungs. One of Henry's hands pushes into his hair and grabs it at the roots at the back of his head, and he hears himself make a sound that breaks the breathless silence, and—

Just as suddenly, Henry releases him roughly enough that he staggers backward, and Henry's mumbling a curse and an apology, eyes wide, and he's spinning on his heel, crunching off through the snow at double time. Before Alex can say or do anything, he's disappeared around the corner.

"Oh," Alex says finally, faintly, touching one hand to his lips. Then: "Shit."

FIVE

So, the thing about the kiss is, Alex absolutely cannot stop thinking about it.

He's tried. Henry and Pez and their bodyguards were long gone by the time Alex made it back inside. Not even a drunken stupor or the next morning's pounding hangover can scrub the image from his brain.

He tries listening in on his mom's meetings, but they can't hold his attention, and Zahra bans him from the West Wing. He studies every bill trickling through Congress and considers making rounds to sweet-talk senators, but can't muster the enthusiasm. Not even starting a rumor with Nora sounds enticing.

He starts his last semester, goes to class, sits with the social secretary to plan his graduation dinner, buries himself in highlighted annotations and supplemental readings.

But beneath it all, there's the Prince of England kissing him under a linden tree in the garden, moonlight in his hair, and Alex's insides feel positively *molten,* and he wants to throw himself down the presidential stairs.

He hasn't told anyone, not even Nora or June. He has no idea what he'd even say if he *did.* Is he even technically allowed to tell anyone, since he signed an NDA? Was this *why* he had to sign it? Is this something Henry always had in mind? Does that mean Henry has *feelings* for him? Why would Henry have acted like a tedious prick for so long if he liked him?

Henry's not offering any insights, or anything at all. He hasn't answered a single one of Alex's texts or calls.

"Okay, that's it," June says on a Wednesday afternoon, stomping out of her room and into the sitting room by their shared hallway. She's in her workout clothes with her hair tied up. Alex hastily shoves his phone back into his pocket. "I don't know what your problem is, but I have been trying to write for two hours and I can't do it when I can hear you pacing." She throws a baseball cap at him. "I'm going for a run, and you're coming with me."

Cash accompanies them to the Reflecting Pool, where June kicks the back of Alex's knee to get him going, and Alex grunts and swears and picks up the pace. He feels like a dog that has to be taken on walks to get his energy out. Especially when June says, "You're like a dog that has to be taken on walks to get his energy out."

"I hate you sometimes," he tells her, and he shoves his earbuds in and cranks up Kid Cudi.

He thinks, as he runs and runs and runs, the stupidest thing of all is that he's straight.

Like, he's pretty sure he's straight.

He can pinpoint moments throughout his life when he thought to himself, *See, this means I can't possibly be into guys.* Like when he was in middle school and he kissed a girl for the first time, and he didn't think about a guy when it was happening, just that her hair was soft and it felt nice. Or when he was a sophomore in high school and one of his friends came out as gay, and he couldn't imagine ever doing anything like that.

Or his senior year, when he got drunk and made out with Liam in his twin bed for an hour, and he didn't have a sexual crisis about it—that had to mean he was straight, right? Because if he were into guys, it would have felt scary to be with one, but it wasn't. That was just how horny teenage best friends were sometimes, like when they would get off at the same time watching porn in Liam's bedroom . . . or that one time Liam reached over, and Alex didn't stop him.

He glances over at June, at the suspicious quirk of her lips. Can she hear what he's thinking? Does she know, somehow? June always knows things. He doubles his pace, if only to get the expression on her mouth out of his periphery.

On their fifth lap, he thinks back over his hormonal teens and remembers thinking about girls in the shower, but he also remembers fantasizing about a boy's hands on him, about hard jawlines and broad shoulders. He remembers pulling his eyes off a teammate in the locker room a couple times, but that was, like, an objective thing. How was he supposed to know back then if he wanted to look like other guys, or if he *wanted* other guys? Or if his horny teenage urges actually even meant anything?

He's a son of Democrats. It's something he's always been around. So, he always assumed if he weren't straight, he would just *know,* like how he knows that he loves cajeta on his ice cream or that he needs a tediously organized calendar to get anything done. He thought he was smart enough about his own identity that there weren't any questions left.

They're rounding the corner for their eighth lap now, and he's starting to see some flaws in his logic. Straight people, he thinks, probably don't spend this much time convincing themselves they're straight.

There's another reason he never cared to examine things beyond the basic benchmark of being attracted to women. He's been in the public eye since his mom became the favored 2016 nominee, the White House Trio the administration's door to the teen and twenty-something demographic almost as long. All three of them—himself, June, and Nora—have their roles.

Nora is the cool brainy one, the one who makes inappropriate jokes on Twitter about whatever sci-fi show everyone's watching, a bar trivia team ringer. She's not straight—she's never been straight—but to her, it's an incidental part of who she is. She doesn't worry about going public with it; feelings don't consume her the way his do.

He looks at June—ahead of him now, caramel highlights in her swinging ponytail catching the midday sun—and he knows her place too. The intrepid *Washington Post* columnist, the fashion trendsetter everyone wants to have at their wine-and-cheese night.

But Alex is the golden boy. The heartthrob, the handsome rogue with a heart of gold. The guy who moves through life effortlessly, who makes everyone laugh. Highest approval ratings of the entire First Family. The whole point of him is that his appeal is as universal as possible.

Being . . . whatever he's starting to suspect he might be, is definitely not universally appealing to voters. He has a hard enough time being half-Mexican.

He wants his mom to keep her approval ratings up without having to manage a complication from her own family. He wants to be the youngest congressman in US history. He's absolutely sure that guys who kissed a Prince of England and liked it don't get elected to represent Texas.

But he thinks about Henry, and, *oh.*

He thinks about Henry, and something twists in his chest, like a stretch he's been avoiding for too long.

He thinks about Henry's voice low in his ear over the phone at three in the morning, and suddenly he has a name for what ignites in the pit of his stomach. Henry's hands on him, his thumbs braced against his temples back in the garden, Henry's hands other places, Henry's mouth, what he might do with it if Alex let him. Henry's broad shoulders and long legs and narrow waist, the place his jaw meets his neck and the place his neck meets his shoulder and the tendon that stretches the length between them, and the way it looks when Henry turns his head to shoot him a challenging glare, and his impossibly blue eyes—

He trips on a crack in the pavement and goes tumbling down, skinning his knee and ripping his earbuds out.

"Dude, what the hell?" June's voice cuts through the ringing in his ears. She's standing over him, hands on her knees, brow furrowed, panting. "Your brain could not be more clearly in another solar system. Are you gonna tell me or what?"

He takes her hand and lets her pull him and his bloody knee up. "It's fine. I'm fine."

June sighs, shooting him another look before finally dropping it. Once he's limped back home behind her, she disappears to shower and he stems the bleeding with a Captain America Band-Aid from his bathroom cabinet.

He needs a list. So: Things he knows right now.

One. He's attracted to Henry.

Two. He wants to kiss Henry again.

Three. He has maybe wanted to kiss Henry for a while. As in, probably this whole time.

He ticks off another list in his head. Henry. Shaan. Liam. Han Solo. Rafael Luna and his loose collars.

Sidling up to his desk, he pulls out the binder his mother gave him: DEMOGRAPHIC ENGAGEMENT: WHO THEY ARE AND HOW TO REACH THEM. He drags his finger down to the LGBTQ+ tab and turns to the page he's looking for, titled with mother's typical flair: THE B ISN'T SILENT: A CRASH COURSE ON BISEXUAL AMERICANS.

"I wanna start now," Alex says as he slams into the Treaty Room.

His mother lowers her glasses to the tip of her nose, eyeing him over a pile of papers. "Start what? Getting your ass beat for barging in here while I'm working?"

"The job," he says. "The campaign job. I don't wanna wait until I graduate. I already read all the materials you gave me. Twice. I have time. I can start now."

She narrows her eyes at him. "You got a bug up your butt?"

"No, I just . . ." One of his knees is bouncing impatiently. He forces it to stop. "I'm ready. I've got less than one semester left. How much more could I possibly need to know to do this? Put me in, Coach."

Which is how he finds himself out of breath on a Monday afternoon after class, following a staffer who's managed to surpass even him in the caffeination department, on a breakneck tour of the campaign offices. He gets a badge with his name and photo on it, a desk in a shared cubicle, and a WASPy cubicle mate from Boston named Hunter with an extremely punchable face.

Alex is handed a folder of data from the latest focus groups and told to start drafting policy ideas for the end of the following week, and WASPy Hunter asks him five hundred questions about his mom. Alex very professionally does not punch him. He just gets to work.

He's definitely not thinking about Henry.

He's not thinking about Henry when he puts in twenty-three hours in his first week of work, or when he's filling the rest of his hours with class and papers and going for long runs and drinking triple-shot coffees and poking around the Senate offices. He's not thinking about Henry in the shower or at night, alone and wide awake in his bed.

Except for when he is. Which is always.

This usually works. He doesn't understand why it's not working.

When he's in the campaign offices, he keeps gravitating over to the big, busy whiteboards of the polling section, where Nora sits every day enshrined in graphs and spreadsheets. She's made easy friends with her coworkers, since competence translates directly to popularity in the campaign social culture, and nobody's better at numbers than her.

He's not jealous, exactly. He's popular in his own department, constantly cornered at the Keurig for second opinions on people's drafts and invited to after-work drinks he never has time for. At least four staffers of various genders have hit on him, and WASPy Hunter won't stop trying to convince him to come to his improv shows. He smiles handsomely over his coffee and makes sarcastic jokes and the Alex Claremont-Diaz Charm Initiative is as effective as ever.

But Nora makes *friends,* and Alex ends up with acquaintances who think they know him because they've read his profile in *New York* magazine, and perfectly fine people with perfectly fine bodies who want to take him home from the bar. None of it is satisfying—it never has been, not really, but it never mattered as much as it does now that there's the sharp counterpoint of Henry, who *knows* him. Henry who's seen him in glasses and tolerates him at his most annoying and still kissed him like he wanted him, singularly, not the idea of him.

So it goes, and Henry is there, in his head and his lecture notes and his cubicle, every single stupid day, no matter how many shots of espresso he puts in his coffee.

Nora would be the obvious choice for help, if not for the fact that she's neck deep in polling numbers. When she gets into her work like this, it's like trying to have a meaningful conversation with a high-speed computer that loves Chipotle and makes fun of what you're wearing.

But she's his best friend, and she's sort of vaguely bisexual. She never dates—no time or desire—but if she did, she says it'd be an even distribution of the intern pool. She's as knowledgeable about the topic as she is about everything else.

"Hello," she says from the floor as he drops a bag of burritos and a second bag of chips with guacamole on the coffee table. "You might have to put guacamole directly into my mouth with a spoon because I need both hands for the next forty-eight hours."

Nora's grandparents, the Veep and Second Lady, live at the Naval Observatory, and her parents live just outside of Montpelier, but she's had the same airy one-bedroom in Columbia Heights since she transferred from MIT to GW. It's full of books and plants she tends to with complex spreadsheets of watering schedules. Tonight, she's sitting on her living room floor in a glowing circle of screens like some kind of Capitol Hill séance.

To her left, her campaign laptop is open to an indecipherable page of data and bar graphs. To her right, her personal computer is running three news aggregators at the same time. In front of her, the TV is broadcasting CNN's Republican primary coverage, while the tablet in her lap is playing an old episode of *Drag Race*. She's holding her iPhone in her hand, and Alex hears the little whoosh of an email sending before she looks up at him.

"Barbacoa?" she says hopefully as Alex drops onto the couch.

"I've met you before today, so, obviously."

"There's my future husband." She leans over to pull a burrito out of the bag, rips off the foil, and shoves it into her mouth.

"I'm not going to have a marriage of convenience with you if you're always embarrassing me with the way you eat burritos," Alex says, watching her chew. A black bean falls out of her mouth and lands on one of her keyboards.

"Aren't you from Texas?" she says through her mouthful. "I've seen you shotgun a bottle of barbecue sauce. Watch yourself or I'm gonna marry June instead."

This might be his opening into "the conversation." *Hey, you know how you're always joking about dating June? Well, like, what if I dated a guy?* Not that he wants to date Henry. At all. Ever. But just, like, hypothetically.

Nora goes off on a data nerd tangent for the next twenty minutes about her updated take on whatever the fuck the Boyer–Moore majority vote algorithm is and variables and how it can be used in whatever work she's doing for the campaign, or something. Honestly, Alex's concentration is drifting in and out. He's just working on summoning up courage until she talks herself into submission.

"Hey, so, uh," Alex attempts as she takes a burrito break. "Remember when we dated?"

Nora swallows a massive bite and grins. "Why yes, I do, Alejandro."

Alex forces a laugh. "So, knowing me as well as you do—"

"In the biblical sense."

"Numbers on me being into dudes?"

That pulls Nora up short, before she cocks her head to the side and says, "Seventy-eight percent probability of latent bisexual tendencies. One hundred percent probability this is not a hypothetical question."

"Yeah. So." He coughs. "Weird thing happened. You know how Henry came to New Year's? He kinda . . . kissed me?"

"Oh, no shit?" Nora says, nodding appreciatively. "Nice."

Alex stares at her. "You're not surprised?"

"I mean." She shrugs. "He's gay, and you're hot, so."

He sits up so quickly he almost drops his burrito on the floor. "Wait, wait—what makes you think he's gay? Did he tell you he was?"

"No, I just . . . like, you know." She gesticulates as if to describe her usual thought process. It's as incomprehensible as her brain. "I observe patterns and data, and they form logical conclusions, and he's just gay. He's always been gay."

"I . . . what?"

"Dude. Have you met him? Isn't he supposed to be your best friend or whatever? He's gay. Like, Fire-Island-on-the-Fourth-of-July gay. Did you really not know?"

Alex lifts his hands helplessly. "No?"

"Alex, I thought you were supposed to be smart."

"Me too! How can he—how can he spring a kiss on me without even telling me he's gay first?"

"I mean, like," she attempts, "is it possible he assumed you knew?"

"But he goes on dates with girls all the time."

"Yeah, because princes aren't allowed to be gay," Nora says as if it's the most obvious thing in the world. "Why do you think they're always photographed?"

Alex lets that sink in for half a second and remembers this is supposed to be about *his* gay panic, not Henry's. "Okay, so. Wait. Jesus. Can we go back to the part where he kissed me?"

"Ooh, yes," Nora says. She licks a glob of guacamole off the screen of her phone. "Happily. Was he a good kisser? Was there tongue? Did you like it?"

"Never mind," Alex says instantly. "Forget I asked."

"Since when are you a prude?" Nora demands. "Last year you made me listen to every nasty detail about going down on Amber Forrester from June's internship."

"Do *not*," he says, hiding his face behind the crook of his elbow.

"Then spill."

"I seriously hope you die," he says. "Yes, he was a good kisser, and there was tongue."

"I fucking knew it," she says. "Still waters, deep dicking."

"*Stop,*" he groans.

"Prince Henry is a biscuit," Nora says, "let him sop you up."

"I'm *leaving.*"

She throws her head back and cackles, and seriously, Alex has *got* to get more friends. "Did you like it, though?"

A pause.

"What, um," he starts. "What do you think it would mean . . . if I did?"

"Well. Babe. You've been wanting him to dick you down forever, right?"

Alex almost chokes on his tongue. "*What?*"

Nora looks at him. "Oh, shit. Did you not know that either? Shit. I didn't mean to, like, tell you. Is it time for this conversation?"

"I . . . maybe?" he says. "Um. What?"

She puts her burrito down on the coffee table and shakes her fingers out like she does when she's about to write a complicated code. Alex suddenly feels intimidated at having her undivided attention.

"Let me lay out some observations for you," she says. "You extrapolate. First, you've been, like, Draco Malfoy–level obsessed with Henry for years—*do not interrupt me*—and since the royal wedding, you've gotten his phone number and used it not to set up any appearances but instead to long-distance flirt with him all day every day. You're constantly making big cow eyes at your phone, and if somebody asks you who you're texting, you act like you got caught watching porn. You know his sleep schedule, he knows your sleep schedule, and you're in a noticeably worse mood if you go a day without talking to him. You spent the entire New Year's party straight-up ignoring the who's who of hot people who want to fuck America's most eligible bachelor to literally watch Henry stand next to the croquembouche. And he kissed you—with tongue!—and you liked it. So, objectively. What do you think it means?"

Alex stares. "I mean," he says slowly. "I don't . . . know."

Nora frowns, visibly giving up, resumes eating her burrito, and returns her attention to the newsfeed on her laptop. "Okay."

"No, okay, look," Alex says. "I know, like, objectively, on a fucking graphing calculator, it sounds like a huge embarrassing crush. But, ugh. I don't know! He was my sworn enemy until a couple months ago, and then we were friends, I guess, and now he's kissed me, and I don't know what we . . . *are*."

"Uh-huh," Nora says, very much not listening. "Yep."

"And, still," he barrels on. "In terms of, like, sexuality, what does that make me?"

Nora's eyes snap back up to him. "Oh, like, I thought we were already there with you being bi and everything," she says. "Sorry, are we not? Did I skip ahead again? My bad. Hello, would you like to come out to me? I'm listening. Hi."

"I don't know!" he half yells, miserably. "Am I? Do you think I'm bi?"

"I can't tell you that, Alex!" she says. "That's the whole point!"

"Shit," he says, dropping his head back on the cushions. "I need someone to just tell me. How did you know you were?"

"I don't know, man. I was in my junior year of high school, and I touched a boob. It wasn't very profound. Nobody's gonna write an Off-Broadway play about it."

"Really helpful."

"Yup," she says, chewing thoughtfully on a chip. "So, what are you gonna do?"

"I have no idea," Alex says. "He's totally ghosted me, so I guess it was awful or a stupid drunk mistake he regrets or—"

"Alex," she says. "He *likes* you. He's freaking out. You're gonna have to decide how you feel about him and do something about it. He's not in a position to do anything else."

Alex has no idea what else to say about any of it. Nora's eyes drift back to one of her screens, where Anderson Cooper is unpacking the latest coverage of the Republican presidential hopefuls.

"Any chance someone other than Richards gets the nomination?"

Alex sighs. "Nope. Not according to anybody I've talked to."

"It's almost cute how hard the others are still trying," she says, and they lapse into silence.

Alex is late, again.

His class is reviewing for the first exam today, and he's late because he lost track of time going over his speech for the campaign event he's doing in fucking *Nebraska* this weekend, of all godforsaken places. It's Thursday, and he's hauling ass straight from work to the lecture hall, and his exam is next Tuesday, and he's going to *fail* because he's missing the *review*.

The class is Ethical Issues in International Relations. He really has got to stop taking classes so painfully relevant to his life.

He gets through the review in a haze of half-distracted shorthand and books it back toward the Residence. He's pissed, honestly. Pissed at everything; a crawling, directionless bad mood that's carrying him up the stairs toward the East and West Bedrooms.

He throws his bag down at the door of his room and kicks his shoes into the hallway, watching them bounce crookedly across the ugly antique rug.

"Well, good afternoon to you too, honey biscuit," June's voice says. When Alex glances up, she's in her room across the hall, perched on a pastel-pink wingback chair. "You look like shit."

"Thanks, asshole."

He recognizes the stack of magazines in her lap as her weekly tabloid roundup, and he's just decided he doesn't want to know when she chucks one at him.

"New *People* for you," she says. "You're on page fifteen. Oh, and your BFF's on page thirty-one."

He casually extends her the finger over his shoulder and retreats into his room, slumping down onto the couch by the door with the magazine. Since he has it, he might as well.

Page fifteen is a picture of him the press team took two weeks ago, a nice, neat little package on him helping the Smithsonian with an exhibit about his mom's historic presidential campaign. He's explaining the story behind a CLAREMONT FOR CONGRESS '04 yard sign, and there's a brief write-up alongside it about how dedicated he is to the family legacy, blah blah blah.

He turns to page thirty-one and almost swears out loud.

The headline: WHO IS PRINCE HENRY'S MYSTERY BLONDE?

Three photos: the first, Henry out at a cafe in London, smiling over coffees at some anonymously pretty blond woman; the second, Henry, slightly out of focus, holding her hand as they duck behind the cafe; the third, Henry, halfway obscured by a shrub, kissing the corner of her mouth.

"What the *fuck*?"

There's a short article accompanying the photos that gives the girl's name, Emily something, an actress, and Alex was generally pissed before, but now he's very singularly pissed, his entire shitty mood funneled down to the point on the page where Henry's lips touch somebody's skin that's not *his*.

Who the fuck does Henry think he is? How fucking—how entitled, how aloof, how *selfish* do you have to be, to spend months becoming someone's friend, let them show you all their weird gross weak parts, kiss them, make them question *everything*, ignore them for *weeks*, and go out with someone else and *put it in the press*? Everyone who's ever had a publicist knows the only way anything gets into *People* is if you want the world to know.

He throws the magazine down and lunges to his feet, pacing. *Fuck* Henry. He should never have trusted the silver-spoon little shit. He should have listened to his gut.

He inhales, exhales.

The thing is. The thing. Is. He doesn't know if, beyond the initial rush of anger, he actually believes Henry would do this. If he takes the Henry he saw in a teen magazine when he was twelve, the Henry who was so cold to him at the Olympics, the Henry who slowly came unraveled to him over months, and the Henry who kissed him in the shadow of the White House, and he adds them up, he doesn't get this.

Alex has a tactical brain. A politician's brain. It works fast, and it works in many, many directions at once. And right now, he's thinking through a puzzle. He's not always good at thinking: *What if you were him? How would your life be? What would you have to do?* Instead, he's thinking: *How do these pieces slot together?*

He thinks about what Nora said: "Why do you think they're always photographed?"

And he thinks about Henry's guardedness, the way he carries himself with a careful separation from the world around him, the tension at the corner of his mouth. Then he thinks: *If there was a prince, and he was gay, and he kissed someone, and maybe it mattered, that prince might have to run a little bit of interference.*

And in one great mercurial swing, Alex is not just angry anymore. He's sad too.

He paces back over to the door and slides his phone out of his messenger bag, thumbs open his messages. He doesn't know which impulse to follow and wrestle into words that he can say to someone and make something, *anything*, happen.

Faintly, under it all, it occurs to him: This is all a very not-straight way to react to seeing your male frenemy kissing someone else in a magazine.

A little laugh startles out of him, and he walks over to his bed and sits on the edge of it, considering. He considers texting Nora, asking her if he can come over to finally have some big epiphany. He considers calling Rafael Luna and meeting him for beers and asking to hear all about his first gay sexual exploits as an REI-wearing teenage antifascist. And he considers going downstairs and asking Amy about her transition and her wife and how she knew she was different.

But in the moment, it feels right to go back to the source, to ask someone who's seen whatever is in his eyes when a boy touches him.

Henry's out of the question. Which leaves one person.

"Hello?" says the voice over the phone. It's been at least a year since they last talked, but Liam's Texas drawl is unmistakable and warm in Alex's eardrum.

He clears his throat. "Uh, hey, Liam. It's Alex."

"I know," Liam says, desert-dry.

"How, um, how have you been?"

A pause. The sound of quiet talking in the background, dishes. "You wanna tell me why you're really calling, Alex?"

"Oh," he starts and stops, tries again. "This might sound weird. But, um. Back in high school, did we have, like, a thing? Did I miss that?"

There's a clattering sound on the other side of the phone, like a fork being dropped on a plate. "Are you seriously calling me right now to talk about this? I'm at lunch with my boyfriend."

"Oh." He didn't know Liam had a boyfriend. "Sorry."

The sound goes muffled, and when Liam speaks again, it's to someone else. "It's Alex. Yeah, him. I don't know, babe." His voice comes back clear again. "What exactly are you asking me?"

"I mean, like, we messed around, but did it, like, mean something?"

"I don't think I can answer that question for you," Liam tells him. If he's still anything like Alex remembers, he's rubbing one hand on the underside of his jaw, raking through the stubble. He wonders faintly if, perhaps, his clear-as-day memory of Liam's stubble has just answered his own question for him.

"Right," he says. "You're right."

"Look, man," Liam says. "I don't know what kind of sexual crisis you're having right now, like, four years after it would have been useful, but, well. I'm not saying what we did in high school makes you gay or bi or whatever, but I can tell you *I'm* gay, and that even though I acted like what we were doing wasn't gay back then, it super was." He sighs. "Does that help, Alex? My Bloody Mary is here and I need to talk to it about this phone call."

"Um, yeah," Alex says. "I think so. Thanks."

"You're welcome."

Liam sounds so long-suffering and tired that Alex thinks about all those times back in high school, the way Liam used to look at him, the silence between them since, and feels obligated to add, "And, um. I'm sorry?"

"Jesus *Christ*," Liam groans, and hangs up.

SIX

Henry can't avoid him forever.

There's one part of the post-royal wedding arrangement left to fulfill: Henry's presence at a state dinner at the end of January. England has a relatively new prime minister, and Ellen wants to meet him. Henry's coming too, staying in the Residence as a courtesy.

Alex smooths out the lapels on his tux and hovers close to June and Nora as the guests roll in, waiting at the north entrance near the photo line. He's aware that he's rocking anxiously on his heels but can't seem to stop. Nora smirks but says nothing. She's keeping it quiet. He's still not ready to tell June. Telling his sister is irreversible, and he can't do that until he's figured out what exactly this is.

Henry enters stage right.

His suit is black, smooth, elegant. Perfect. Alex wants to rip it off.

His face is reserved, then downright ashen when he sees Alex in the entrance hall. His footsteps stutter, as if he's thinking of making a run for it. Alex is not above a flying tackle.

Instead, he keeps walking up the steps, and—

"All right, photos," Zahra hisses over Alex's shoulder.

"Oh," Henry says, like an idiot. Alex hates how much he likes the way that one stupid vowel curls in his accent. He's not even into British accents. He's into *Henry's* British accent.

"Hey," Alex says under his breath. Fake smile, handshake, cameras flashing. "Cool to see you're not dead or anything."

"Er," Henry says, adding to the list of vowel sounds he has to show for himself. It is, unfortunately, also sexy. After all these weeks, the bar is low.

"We need to talk," Alex says, but Zahra is physically shoving them into a friendly formation, and there are more photos until Alex is being shepherded off with the girls to the State Dining Room while Henry is hauled into photo ops with the prime minister.

The entertainment for the night is a British indie rocker who looks like a root vegetable and is popular with people in Alex's demographic for reasons he can't even begin to understand. Henry is seated with the prime minister, and Alex sits and chews his food like it's personally wronged him and watches Henry from across the room, seething. Every so often, Henry will look up, catch Alex's eye, go pink around the ears, and return to his rice pilaf as if it's the most fascinating dish on the planet.

How *dare* Henry come into Alex's house looking like the goddamn James Bond offspring that he is, drink red wine with the prime minister, and act like he didn't slip Alex the tongue and ghost him for a month.

"Nora," he says, leaning over to her while June is off

chatting with an actress from *Doctor Who*. The night is starting to wind down, and Alex is over it. "Can you get Henry
away from his table?"

She slants a look at him. "Is this a diabolical scheme of se-
duction?" she asks. "If so, yes."

"Sure, yes, that," he says, and he gets up and heads for the
back wall of the room, where the Secret Service is stationed.

"Amy," he hisses, grabbing her by the wrist. She makes a
quick, aborted movement, clearly fighting a hardwired take-
down reflex. "I need your help."

"Where's the threat?" she says immediately.

"No, no, Jesus." Alex swallows. "Not like that. I need to get
Prince Henry alone."

She blinks. "I don't follow."

"I need to talk to him in private."

"I can accompany you outside if you need to speak with
him, but I'll have to get it approved with his security first."

"No," Alex says. He scrubs a hand across his face, glancing
back over his shoulder to confirm Henry's where he left him,
being aggressively talked at by Nora. "I need him *alone*."

The slightest of expressions crosses over Amy's face. "The
best I can do is the Red Room. You take him any farther and
it's a no-go."

He looks over his shoulder again at the tall doors across the
State Dining Room. The Red Room is empty on the other
side, awaiting the after-dinner cocktails.

"How long can I have?" he says.

"Five min—"

"I can make that work."

He turns on his heel and stalks over to the ornamental dis-
play of chocolates, where Nora has apparently lured Henry

with the promise of profiteroles. He plants himself between them.

"Hi," he says. Nora smiles. Henry's mouth drops open. "Sorry to interrupt. Important, um. International. Relations. Stuff." And he seizes Henry by the elbow and yanks him bodily away.

"Do you mind?" Henry has the nerve to say.

"Shut your face," Alex says, briskly leading him away from the tables, where people are too busy mingling and listening to the music to notice Alex frog-marching an heir to the throne out of the dining room.

They reach the doors, and Amy is there. She hesitates, hand on the knob.

"You're not going to kill him, are you?" she says.

"Probably not," Alex tells her.

She opens the door just enough to let them through, and Alex hauls Henry into the Red Room with him.

"What on God's earth are you doing?" Henry demands.

"Shut *up*, shut all the way up, oh my God," Alex hisses, and if he weren't already hell-bent on destroying Henry's infuriating idiot face with his mouth right now, he would consider doing it with his fist. He's focused on the burst of adrenaline carrying his feet over the antique rug, Henry's tie wrapped around his fist, the flash in Henry's eyes. He reaches the nearest wall, shoves Henry against it, and crushes their mouths together.

Henry's too shocked to respond, mouth falling open slackly in a way that's more surprise than invitation, and for a horrified moment Alex thinks he calculated all wrong, but then Henry's kissing him back, and it's *everything*. It feels as good as—better than—he remembered, and he can't recall why they haven't been doing this the whole time, why they've been running belligerent circles around each other for so long without doing anything about it.

"Wait," Henry says, breaking off. He pulls back to look at Alex, wild-eyed, mouth a vivid red, and Alex could fucking scream if he weren't worried dignitaries in the next room might hear him. "Should we—"

"What?"

"I mean, er, should we, I dunno, slow down?" Henry says, cringing so hard at himself that one eye closes. "Go for dinner first, or—"

Alex is actually going to kill him.

"We just had dinner."

"Right. I meant—I just thought—"

"Stop thinking."

"Yes. Gladly."

In one frantic motion, Alex knocks the candelabra off the table next to them and pushes Henry onto it so he's sitting with his back against—Alex looks up and almost breaks into deranged laughter—a portrait of Alexander Hamilton. Henry's legs fall open readily and Alex crowds up between them, wrenching Henry's head back into another searing kiss.

They're really moving now, wrecking each other's suits, Henry's lip caught between Alex's teeth, the portrait's frame rattling against the wall when Henry's head drops back and bangs into it. Alex is at his throat, and he's somewhere between angry and giddy, caught up in the space between years of sworn hate and something else he's begun to suspect has always been there. It's white-hot, and he feels crazy with it, lit up from the inside.

Henry gives as good as he gets, hooking one knee around

the back of Alex's thigh for leverage, delicate royal sensibilities nowhere in the cut of his teeth. Alex has been learning for a while Henry isn't what he thought, but it's something else to feel it this close up, the quiet burn in him, the pent-up person under the perfect veneer who tries and pushes and wants.

He drops a hand onto Henry's thigh, feeling the electrical pulse there, the smooth fabric over hard muscle. He pushes up, up, and Henry's hand slams down over his, digging his nails in.

"Time's up!" comes Amy's voice through a crack in the doors.

They freeze, Alex falling back onto his heels. They can both hear it now, the sounds of bodies moving too close for comfort, wrapping up the night. Henry's hips give one tiny push up into him, involuntary, surprised, and Alex swears.

"I'm going to die," Henry says helplessly.

"I'm going to kill you," Alex tells him.

"Yes, you are," Henry agrees.

Alex takes an unsteady step backward.

"People are gonna be coming in here soon," Alex says, reaching down and trying not to fall on his face as he scoops up the candelabra and shoves it back onto the table. Henry is standing now, looking wobbly, his shirt untucked and his hair a mess. Alex reaches up in a panic and starts patting it back into place. "Fuck, you look—*fuck*."

Henry fumbles with his shirt tail, eyes wide, and starts humming "God Save the Queen" under his breath.

"What are you doing?"

"Christ, I'm trying to make it"—he gestures inelegantly at the front of his pants—"*go away*."

Alex very pointedly does not look down.

"Okay, so," Alex says. "Yeah. So here's what we're gonna do. You are gonna go be, like, five hundred feet away from me for the rest of the night, or else I am going to do something that I will deeply regret in front of a lot of very important people."

"All right . . ."

"And then," Alex says, and he grabs Henry's tie again, close to the knot, and draws his mouth up to a breath away from Henry's. He hears Henry swallow. He wants to follow the sound down his throat. "And then you are going to come to the East Bedroom on the second floor at eleven o'clock tonight, and I am going to do very bad things to you, and if you fucking ghost me again, I'm going to get you put on a fucking no-fly list. Got it?"

Henry bites down on a sound that tries to escape his mouth, and rasps, "Perfectly."

Alex is. Well, Alex is probably losing his mind.

It's 10:48. He's pacing.

He threw his jacket and tie over the back of the chair as soon as he returned to his room, and he's got the first two buttons of his dress shirt undone. His hands are twisted up in his hair.

This is fine. It's fine.

It's definitely a terrible idea. But it's fine.

He's not sure if he should take anything else off. He's unsure of the dress code for inviting your sworn-enemy-turned-fake-best-friend to your room to have sex with you, especially when that room is in the White House, and especially when that person is a guy, and especially when that guy is a prince of England.

The room is dimly lit—a single lamp, in the corner by the

couch, washing the deep blues of the walls neutral. He's moved all his campaign files from the bed to the desk and straightened out the bedspread. He looks at the ancient fireplace, the carved details of the mantel almost as old as the country itself, and it may not be Kensington Palace, but it looks all right.

God, if any ghosts of Founding Fathers are hanging around the White House tonight, they must really be suffering.

He's trying not to think too hard about what comes next. He may not have experience in practical application, but he's done research. He has diagrams. He can do this.

He really, really wants to do this. That much he's sure about.

He closes his eyes, grounds himself with his fingertips on the cool surface of his desk, the feathery little edges of papers there. His mind flashes to Henry, the smooth lines of his suit, the way his breath brushed Alex's cheek when he kissed him. His stomach does some embarrassing acrobatics he plans to never tell anyone about, ever.

Henry, the prince. Henry, the boy in the garden. Henry, the boy in his bed.

He doesn't, he reminds himself, even have feelings for the guy. Really.

There's a knock on the door. Alex checks his phone: 10:54. He opens the door.

Alex stands there and exhales slowly, eyes on Henry. He's not sure he's ever let himself just *look*.

Henry is tall and gorgeous, half royalty, half movie star, red wine lingering on his lips. He's left his jacket and tie behind, and the sleeves of his shirt are pushed up to his elbows. He looks nervous around the corners of his eyes, but he smiles at Alex with one side of his pink mouth and says, "Sorry I'm early."

Alex bites his lip. "Find your way here okay?"

"There was a very helpful Secret Service agent," Henry says. "I think her name was Amy?"

Alex smiles fully now. "Get in here."

Henry's grin takes over his entire face, not his photograph grin, but one that is crinkly and unguarded and infectious. He hooks his fingertips behind Alex's elbow, and Alex follows his lead, bare feet nudging between Henry's dress shoes. Henry's breath ghosts over Alex's lips, their noses brushing, and when he finally connects, he's smiling into it.

Henry shuts and locks the door behind them, sliding one hand up the nape of Alex's neck, cradling it. There's something different about the way he's kissing now—it's measured, deliberate. *Soft.* Alex isn't sure why, or what to do with it.

He settles for pulling Henry in by the sway of his waist, pressing their bodies flush. He kisses back, but lets himself be kissed however Henry wants to kiss him, which right now is exactly how he would have expected Prince Charming to kiss in the first place: sweet and deep and like they're standing at sunrise in the fucking moors. He can practically feel the wind in his hair. It's ridiculous.

Henry breaks off and says, "How do you want to do this?"

And Alex remembers, suddenly, this is not a sunrise-in-the-moors type of situation. He grabs Henry by his loosened collar, pushes a little, and says, "Get on the couch."

Henry's breath hitches and he complies. Alex moves to stand over him, looking down at that soft pink mouth. He feels himself standing at a very tall, very dangerous precipice, with no intention of backing away. Henry looks up at him, expectant, hungry.

"You've been dodging me for *weeks,*" Alex says, widening his stance so his knees bracket Henry's. He leans down and braces one hand against the back of the couch, the other grazing over the vulnerable dip of Henry's throat. "You went out with a *girl*."

"I'm gay," Henry tells him flatly. One of his broad palms flattens over Alex's hip, and Alex inhales sharply, either at the touch or at hearing Henry finally say it out loud. "Not something wise to pursue as a member of the royal family. And I wasn't sure you weren't going to murder me for kissing you."

"Then why'd you do it?" Alex asks him. He leans into Henry's neck, dragging his lips over the sensitive skin just behind his ear. He thinks Henry might be holding his breath.

"Because I—I hoped you wouldn't. Murder me. I had . . . suspicions you might want me too," Henry says. He hisses a little when Alex bites down lightly on the side of his neck. "Or I thought, until I saw you with Nora, and then I was . . . jealous . . . and I was drunk and an idiot who got sick of waiting for the answer to present itself."

"You were *jealous*," Alex says. "You *want* me."

Henry moves abruptly, heaving Alex off balance with both hands and down into his lap, eyes blazing, and he says in a low and deadly voice Alex has never heard from him before, "Yes, you preening arse, I've wanted you long enough that I won't have you tease me for another *fucking* second."

Turns out being on the receiving end of Henry's royal authority is an extreme fucking turn-on. He thinks, as he's hauled into a bruising kiss, that he'll never forgive himself for it. So, like, fuck the moors.

Henry gets a grip on Alex's hips and pulls him close, so Alex is properly straddling his lap, and he kisses hard now, more like he had in the Red Room, with teeth. It shouldn't work so perfectly—it makes absolutely no *sense*—but it does. There's something about the two of them, the way they ignite at different temperatures, Alex's frenetic energy and Henry's aching sureness.

He grinds down into Henry's lap, grunting as he's met with Henry already half-hard under him, and Henry's curse in response is buried in Alex's mouth. The kisses turn messy, then, urgent and graceless, and Alex gets lost in the drag and slide and press of Henry's lips, the sweet liquor of it. He pushes his hands into Henry's hair, and it's as soft as he always imagined when he would trace the photo of Henry in June's magazine, lush and thick under his fingers. Henry melts at the touch, wraps his arms around Alex's waist and holds him there. Alex isn't going anywhere.

He kisses Henry until it feels like he can't breathe, until it feels like he's going to forget both of their names and titles, until they're only two people tangled up in a dark room making a brilliant, epic, unstoppable mistake.

He manages to get the next two buttons on his shirt undone before Henry grabs it by the tails and pulls it off over his head and makes quick work of his own. Alex tries not to be in awe of the simple agility of his hands, tries not to think about classical piano or how swift and smooth years of polo have trained Henry to be.

"Hang on," Henry says, and Alex is already groaning in protest, but Henry pulls back and rests his fingertips on Alex's lips to shush him. "I want—" His voice starts and stops, and he's looking like he's resolving not to cringe at himself again. He gathers himself, stroking a finger up to Alex's cheek before jutting his chin out defiantly. "I want you on the bed."

Alex goes fully silent and still, looking into Henry's eyes and the question there: *Are you going to stop this now that it's real?*

"Well, come on, Your Highness," Alex says, shifting his weight to give Henry a last tease before he stands.

"You're a dick," Henry says, but he follows, smiling.

Alex climbs onto the bed, sliding back to prop himself up on his elbows by the pillows, watching as Henry kicks off his shoes and regains his bearings. He looks transformed in the lamplight, like a god of debauchery, painted gold with his hair all mussed up and his eyes heavy-lidded. Alex lets himself stare; the whipcord muscle under his skin, lean and long and lithe. The spot right at the dip of his waist below his ribs looks impossibly soft, and Alex might die if he can't fit his hand into that little curve in the next five seconds.

In an instant of sudden, vivid clarity, he can't believe he ever thought he was straight.

"Quit stalling," Alex says, pointedly interrupting the moment.

"Bossy," Henry says, and he complies.

Henry's body settles over him with a warm, steady weight, one of his thighs sliding between Alex's legs and his hands bracing on the pillows, and Alex feels the points of contact like a static shock at his shoulders, his hips, the center of his chest.

One of Henry's hands slides up his stomach and stops, having encountered the old silver key on the chain resting over his sternum.

"What's this?"

Alex huffs impatiently. "The key to my mom's house in Texas," he says, winding a hand back into Henry's hair. "I started wearing it when I moved here. I guess I thought it would remind me of where I came from or something—did I or did I not tell you to quit stalling?"

Henry looks up into his eyes, speechless, and Alex tugs him

down into another all-consuming kiss, and Henry bears down on him fully, pressing him into the bed. Alex's other hand finds that dip of Henry's waist, and he swallows a sound at how devastating it feels under his palm. He's never been kissed like this, as if the feeling could swallow him up whole, Henry's body grinding down and covering every inch of his. He moves his mouth from Henry's to the side of his neck, the spot below his ear, kisses and kisses it, and bares his teeth. Alex knows it'll probably leave a mark, which is against rule number one of clandestine hookups for political offspring—and probably royals too. He doesn't care.

He feels Henry find the waistband of his pants, the button, the zipper, the elastic of his underwear, and then everything goes very hazy, very quickly.

He opens his eyes to see Henry bringing his hand demurely up to his elegant royal mouth to *spit* on it.

"Oh my fucking God," Alex says, and Henry grins crookedly as he gets back to work. "Fuck." His body is moving, his mouth spilling words. "I can't believe—God, you are the most insufferable goddamn bastard on the face of the planet, do you know that—fuck—you're infuriating, you're the worst—you're—"

"Do you *ever* stop talking?" Henry says. "Such a *mouth* on you." And when Alex looks again, he finds Henry watching him raptly, eyes bright and smiling. He keeps eye contact and his rhythm at the same time, and Alex was wrong before, Henry's going to be the one to kill him, not the other way around.

"Wait," Alex says, clenching his fist in the bedspread, and Henry immediately stills. "I mean, *yes,* obviously, *oh my God,* but, like, if you keep doing that I'm gonna"—Alex's breath catches—"it's, that's just—that's not *allowed* before I get to see you naked."

Henry tilts his head and smirks. "All right."

Alex flips them over, kicking off his pants until only his underwear is left slung low on his hips, and he climbs up the length of Henry's body, watching his face grow anxious, eager.

"Hi," he says, when he reaches Henry's eye level.

"Hello," Henry says back.

"I'm gonna take your pants off now," Alex tells him.

"Yes, good, carry on."

Alex does, and one of Henry's hands slides down, leveraging one of Alex's thighs up so their bodies meet again right at the hard crux between them, and they both groan. Alex thinks, dizzily, that it's been nearly five years of foreplay, and enough is enough.

He moves his lips down to Henry's chest, and he feels under his mouth the beat Henry's heart skips at the realization of what Alex intends. His own heartbeat is probably falling out of rhythm too. He's in so far over his head, but that's good—that's pretty much his comfort zone. He kisses Henry's solar plexus, his stomach, the stretch of skin above his waistband.

"I've, uh," Alex begins. "I've never actually done this before."

"Alex," Henry says, reaching down to stroke at Alex's hair, "you don't have to, I'm—"

"No, I want to," Alex says, tugging at Henry's waistband. "I just need you to tell me if it's awful."

Henry is speechless again, looking as if he can't believe his fucking luck. "Okay. Of course."

Alex pictures Henry barefoot in a Kensington Palace kitchen and the little sliver of vulnerability he got to see so early on, and he thrills at Henry now, in his bed, spread out and naked and wanting. This can't be really happening after everything, but miraculously, it is.

If he's going by the way Henry's body responds, by the way Henry's hand sweeps up into his hair and clutches a fistful of curls, he guesses he does okay for a first try. He looks up the length of Henry's body and is met with burning eye contact, a red lip caught between white teeth. Henry drops his head back on the pillow and groans something that sounds like "fucking *eyelashes*." He's maybe a little bit in awe of how Henry arches up off the mattress, at hearing his sweet, posh voice reciting a litany of profanities to the ceiling. Alex is living for it, watching Henry come undone, letting him be whatever he needs to be while alone with Alex behind a locked door.

He's surprised to find himself hauled up to Henry's mouth and kissed hungrily. He's been with girls who didn't like to be kissed afterward and girls who didn't mind it, but Henry revels in it, based on the deep and comprehensive way he's kissing him. It occurs to him to make a comment about narcissism, but instead—

"Not awful?" Alex says between kisses, resting his head on the pillow next to Henry's to catch his breath.

"Definitely adequate," Henry answers, grinning, and he scoops Alex up against his chest greedily as if he's trying to touch all of him at once. Henry's hands are huge on his back, his jaw sharp and rough with a long day's stubble, his shoulders broad enough to eclipse Alex when he rolls them over and pins Alex to the mattress. None of it feels anything like anything he's felt before, but it's just as good, maybe better.

Henry's kissing him aggressively once more, confident in a way that's rare from Henry. Messy earnestness and rough focus, not a dutiful prince but any other twenty-something boy enjoying himself doing something he likes, something he's good at. And he is *good* at it. Alex makes a mental note to figure out which shadowy gay noble taught Henry all this and send the man a fruit basket.

Henry returns the favor happily, hungrily, and Alex doesn't know or care what sounds or words come out of his mouth. He thinks one of them is "sweetheart" and another is "motherfucker." Henry is one talented bastard, a man of many hidden gifts, Alex muses half-hysterically. A true prodigy. God Save the Queen.

When he's done, he presses a sticky kiss in the crease of Alex's leg where he'd slung it over his shoulder, managing to come off polite, and Alex wants to drag Henry up by the hair, but his body is boneless and wrecked. He's blissed out, dead. Ascended to the next plane, merely a pair of eyes floating through a dopamine haze.

The mattress shifts, and Henry moves up to the pillows, nuzzling his face into the hollow of Alex's throat. Alex makes a vague noise of approval, and his arms fumble around Henry's waist, but he's helpless to do much else. He's sure he used to know quite a lot of words, in more than one language, in fact, but he can't seem to recall any of them.

"Hmm," Henry hums, the tip of his nose catching on Alex's. "If I had known this was all it took to shut you up, I'd have done it ages ago."

With a feat of Herculean strength, he summons up two whole words: "Fuck you."

Distantly, through a slowly clearing fog, through a messy kiss, Alex can't help marveling at the knowledge that he's crossed some kind of Rubicon, here in this room that's almost as old as the country it's in, like Washington crossing the Delaware. He laughs into Henry's mouth, instantly caught up in his own dramatic mental portrait of the two them painted in oils, young icons of their nations, naked and shining wet in the lamplight. He wishes Henry could see it, wonders if he'd find the image as funny.

Henry rolls over onto his back. Alex's body wants to follow and tuck into his side, but he stays where he is, watching from a few safe inches away. He can see a muscle in Henry's jaw flexing.

"Hey," he says. He pokes Henry in the arm. "Don't freak out."

"I'm not *freaking out*," he says, enunciating the words.

Alex wriggles an inch closer in the sheets. "It was fun," Alex says. "I had fun. You had fun, right?"

"Definitely," he says, in a tone that sends a lazy spark up Alex's spine.

"Okay, cool. So, we can do this again, anytime you want," Alex says, dragging the back of his knuckles down Henry's shoulder. "And you know this doesn't, like, change anything between us, right? We're still . . . whatever we were before, just, you know. With blowjobs."

Henry covers his eyes with one hand. "Right."

"So," Alex says, changing tracks by stretching languidly, "I guess I should tell you, I'm bisexual."

"Good to know," Henry says. His eyes flicker down to Alex's hip, where it's bared above the sheet, and he says as much to himself as to Alex, "I am very, very gay."

Alex watches his small smile, the way it wrinkles the corners of his eyes, and very deliberately does not kiss it.

Part of his brain keeps getting stuck on how strange, and strangely wonderful, it is to see Henry like this, open and bare in every way. Henry leans across the pillow to Alex and presses a soft kiss to his mouth, and Alex feels fingertips brush over his jaw. The touch is so gentle he has to once again remind himself not to care too much.

"Hey," Alex tells him, sliding his mouth closer to Henry's ear, "you're welcome to stay as long as you want, but I should warn you it's probably in both of our best interests if you go back to your room before morning. Unless you want the PPOs to lock the Residence down and come requisition you from my boudoir."

"Ah," Henry says. He pulls away from Alex and rolls back over, looking up to the ceiling again like a man seeking penance from a wrathful god. "You're right."

"You can stay for another round, if you want to," Alex offers.

Henry coughs, scrubs a hand through his hair. "I rather think I'd—I'd better get back to my room."

Alex watches him fish his boxers from the foot of the bed and start pulling them back on, sitting up and shaking out his shoulders.

It's for the best this way, he tells himself; nobody will get any wrong ideas about what exactly this arrangement is. They're not going to spoon all night or wake up in each other's arms or eat breakfast together. Mutually satisfying sexual experiences do not a relationship make.

Even if he did want that, there are a million reasons why this will never, ever be possible.

Alex follows him to the door, watching him turn to hover there awkwardly.

"Well, er . . ." Henry attempts, looking down at his feet.

Alex rolls his eyes. "For fuck's sake, man, you just had my dick in your mouth, you can kiss me good-night."

Henry looks back up at him, his mouth open and incredulous, and he throws his head back and *laughs,* and it's only him, the nerdy, neurotic, sweet, insomniac rich guy who constantly sends Alex photos of his dog, and something slots into place. He leans down and kisses him fiercely, and then he's grinning and gone.

"You're doing *what*?"

It's sooner than either of them expected—only two weeks since the state dinner, two weeks of wanting Henry back under him as soon as possible and saying everything short of that in their texts. June keeps looking at him like she's going to throw his phone in the Potomac.

"An invitation-only charity polo match this weekend," Henry says over the phone. "It's in . . ." He pauses, probably referring back to whatever itinerary Shaan has given him. "Greenwich, Connecticut? It's $10,000 a seat, but I can have you added to the list."

Alex almost fumbles his coffee all over the south entryway. Amy glares at him. "Jesus *fuck*. That is *obscene*, what are you raising money for, monocles for babies?" He covers the mouthpiece of the phone with his hand. "Where's Zahra? I need to clear my schedule for this weekend." He uncovers the phone. "Look, I guess I'll *try* to make it, but I'm really busy right now."

"I'm sorry, Zahra said you're bailing on the fund-raiser this weekend because you're going to a *polo match* in *Connecticut*?" June asks from his bedroom doorway that night, almost startling another cup of coffee out of his hands.

"Listen," Alex tells her, "I'm trying to keep up a geopolitical public relations ruse here."

"Dude, people are writing *fan fiction* about y'all—"

"Yeah, Nora sent me that."

"—I think you can give it a *rest*."

"The crown wants me to be there!" he lies quickly. She seems unconvinced and leaves him with a parting look he'd probably be concerned about if he cared more about things that aren't Henry's mouth right now.

Which is how he ends up in his J. Crew best on a Saturday at the Greenwich Polo Club, wondering what the hell he's gotten himself into. The woman in front of him is wearing a hat with an entire taxidermied pigeon on it. High school lacrosse did not prepare him for this kind of sporting event.

Henry on horseback is nothing new. Henry in full polo gear—the helmet, the polo sleeves capped right at the bulge of his biceps, the snug white pants tucked into tall leather boots, the intricately buckled leather knee padding, the leather gloves—is familiar. He has seen it before. Categorically, it should be boring. It should not provoke anything visceral, carnal, or bodice-ripping in nature in him at all.

But Henry urging his horse across the field with the power of his thighs, his ass bouncing hard in the saddle, the way the muscles in his arms stretch and flex when he swings, looking the way he does and wearing the things he's wearing—it's a lot.

He's sweating. It's February in Connecticut, and Alex is sweating under his coat.

Worst of all, Henry is *good*. Alex doesn't pretend to care about the rules of the game, but his primary turn-on has always been competence. It's too easy to look at Henry's boots digging into the stirrups for leverage and conjure up a memory of bare calves underneath, bare feet planted just as firmly on the mattress. Henry's thighs open the same way, but with Alex between them. Sweat dripping down Henry's brow onto his throat. Just, uh . . . well, just like that.

He wants—God, after all this time ignoring it, he wants it again, now, *right now.*

The match ends after a circle-of-hell amount of time, and Alex feels like he'll pass out or scream if he doesn't get his hands on Henry soon, like the only thought possible in the universe is Henry's body and Henry's flushed face and every other molecule in existence is just an inconvenience.

"I don't like that look," Amy says when they reach the bottom of the stands, peering into his eyes. "You look . . . sweaty."

"I'm gonna go, uh," Alex says. "Say hi to Henry."

Amy's mouth settles into a grim line. "Please don't elaborate."

"Yeah, I know," Alex says. "Plausible deniability."

"I don't know what you could possibly mean."

"Sure." He rakes a hand through his hair. "Yep."

"Enjoy your summit with the English delegation," she tells him flatly, and Alex sends up a vague prayer of thanks for staff NDAs.

He legs it toward the stables, limbs already buzzing with the steady knowledge of Henry's body getting incrementally closer to his. Long, lean legs, grass stains on pristine, tight pants, why does this sport have to be so completely *repulsive* while Henry looks so damn *good* doing it—

"Oh shit—"

He barely stops himself from running headfirst into Henry in the flesh, who has rounded the corner of the stables.

"Oh, hello."

They stand there staring at each other, fifteen days removed from Henry swearing at the ceiling of Alex's bedroom and unsure how to proceed. Henry is still in his full polo regalia, gloves and all, and Alex can't decide if he is pleased or wants to brain him with a polo stick. Polo bat? Polo club? Polo . . . mallet? This sport is a travesty.

Henry breaks the silence by adding, "I was coming to find you, actually."

"Yeah, hi, here I am."

"Here you are."

Alex glances over his shoulder. "There's, uh. Cameras. Three o'clock."

"Right," Henry says, straightening his shoulders. His hair is messy and slightly damp, color still high in his cheeks from exertion. He's going to look like goddamn Apollo in the photos when they go to press. Alex smiles, knowing they'll sell.

"Hey, isn't there, uh, a thing?" Alex says. "You needed to. Uh. Show me?"

Henry looks at him, glances at the dozens of millionaires and socialites milling around, and back at him. "Now?"

"It was a four-and-a-half-hour car ride up here, and I have to go back to DC in an hour, so I don't know when else you're expecting to show it to me."

Henry takes a beat, his eyes flickering to the cameras again before he switches on a stage smile and a laugh, cuffing Alex on the shoulder. "Ah, yes. Right. This way."

He turns on his boot heel and leads the way around the back of the stables, veering right into a doorway, and Alex follows. It's a small, windowless room attached to the stables, fragrant with leather polish and stained wood from floor to ceiling, the walls lined with heavy saddles, riding crops, bridles, and reins.

"What in the rich-white-people-sex-dungeon hell?" Alex wonders aloud as Henry crosses behind him. He whips a thick leather strap off a hook on the wall, and Alex almost blacks out.

"What?" Henry says offhandedly, bypassing him to bind the doors shut. He turns around, sweet-faced and unbelievable. "It's called a tack room."

Alex drops his coat and takes three swift steps toward him. "I don't actually care," he says, and grabs Henry by the stupid collar of his stupid polo and kisses his stupid mouth.

It's a good kiss, solid and hot, and Alex can't decide where to put his hands because he wants to put them everywhere at once.

"Ugh," he groans in exasperation, shoving Henry backward by the shoulders and making a disgusted show of looking him up and down. "You look *ridiculous.*"

"Should I—" He steps back and puts a foot up on a nearby bench, moving to undo his kneepads.

"What? No, of course not, keep them on," Alex says. Henry freezes, standing there all artistically posed with his thighs apart and one knee up, the fabric straining. "Oh my God, what are you doing? I can't even look at you." Henry frowns. "No, Jesus, I just meant—I'm so *mad* at you." Henry gingerly puts his boot back on the floor. Alex wants to die. "Just, come here. *Fuck.*"

"I'm quite confused."

"Me fucking too," Alex says, profoundly suffering for something he must have done in a previous life. "Listen, I don't know why, but this whole *thing*"—he gestures at Henry's entire physical presence—"is . . . really doing it for me, so, I just need to." Without any further ceremony, he drops to his knees and starts undoing Henry's belt, tugging at the fastenings of his pants.

"Oh, God," Henry says.

"Yeah," Alex agrees, and he gets Henry's boxers down.

"Oh, *God,*" Henry repeats, this time with feeling.

It's all still so new to Alex, but it's not difficult to follow through on what's been playing out in elaborate detail in his head for the past hour. When he looks up, Henry's face is flushed and transfixed, his lips parted. It almost hurts to look at him—the athlete's focus, all the dressings of aristocracy laid wide open for him. He's watching Alex, eyes blown dark and hazy, and Alex is watching him right back, every nerve in both bodies narrowed down to a single point.

It's fast and dirty and Henry is swearing up a storm, which is still disarmingly sexy, but this time it's punctuated by the occasional word of praise, and somehow that's even hotter. Alex isn't prepared for the way "that's good" sounds in Henry's rounded Buckingham vowels, or for how luxury leather feels when it strokes approvingly down his cheek, a gloved thumb brushing the corner of his mouth.

As soon as Henry's finished, he's got Alex on the bench and is putting his kneepads to use.

"I'm still fucking mad at you," Alex says, destroyed, slumped forward with his forehead resting on Henry's shoulder.

"Of course you are," Henry says vaguely.

Alex completely undermines his point by pulling Henry into a deep and lingering kiss, and another, and they kiss for an amount of time he decides not to count or think about.

They sneak out quietly, and Henry touches Alex's shoulder at the gate near where his SUV waits, presses his palm into the wool of his coat and the knot of muscle.

"I don't suppose you'll be anywhere near Kensington anytime soon?"

"That shithole?" he says with a wink. "Not if I can help it."

"Oi," Henry says. He's grinning now. "That's disrespect of

the crown, that is. Insubordination. I've thrown men in the dungeons for less."

Alex turns, walking backward toward the car, hands in the air. "Hey, don't threaten me with a good time."

Paris?

A <agcd@eclare45.com>   3/3/20 7:32 PM
to Henry

His Royal Highness Prince Henry of Whatever,

Don't make me learn your actual title.

Are you going to be at the Paris fund-raiser for rainforest conservation this weekend?

Alex
First Son of Your Former Colony

Re: Paris?

Henry <hwales@kensingtonemail.com>   3/4/20 2:14 AM
to A

Alex, First Son of Off-Brand England:

First, you should know how terribly inappropriate it is for you to intentionally botch my title. I could have you made into a

royal settee cushion for that kind of lèse-majesté.
Fortunately for you, I do not think you would complement my
sitting room decor.

Secondly, no, I will not be attending the Paris fund-raiser;
I have a previous engagement. You shall have to find
someone else to accost in a cloakroom.

Regards,
His Royal Highness Prince Henry of Wales

Re: Paris?

 A <agcd@eclare45.com>   3/4/20 2:27 AM
to Henry

Huge Raging Headache Prince Henry of Who Cares,

It is amazing you can sit down to write emails with that
gigantic royal stick up your ass. I seem to remember you
really enjoying being "accosted."

Everyone there is going to be boring anyway. What are you
doing?

Alex
First Son of Hating Fund-raisers

Re: Paris?

 Henry <hwales@kensingtonemail.com>   3/4/20 2:32 AM
to A

Alex, First Son of Shirking Responsibilities:

A royal stick is formally known as a "scepter."

I've been sent to a summit in Germany to act as if I know anything about wind power. Primarily, I'll be getting lectured by old men in lederhosen and posing for photos with windmills. The monarchy has decided we care about sustainable energy, apparently—or at least that we want to appear to. An utter romp.

Re: fund-raiser guests, I thought you said *I* was boring?

Regards,
Harangued Royal Highness

Re: Paris?

 A \<agcd@eclare45.com\>   3/4/20 2:34 AM
to Henry

Horrible Revolting Heir,

It's recently come to my attention you're not quite as boring
as I thought. Sometimes. Namely when you're doing the
thing with your tongue.

Alex
First Son of Questionable Late Night Emails

Re: Paris?

 Henry \<hwales@kensingtonemail.com\>   3/4/20 2:37 AM
to A

Alex, First Son of Inappropriately Timed Emails When I'm in
Early Morning Meetings:

Are you trying to get fresh with me?

Regards,
Handsome Royal Heretic

Re: Paris?

 A <agcd@eclare45.com>   3/4/20 2:41 AM
to Henry

His Royal Horniness,

If I were trying to get fresh with you, you would know it.

For example: I've been thinking about your mouth on me all
week, and I was hoping I'd see you in Paris so I could put it
to use.

I was also thinking you might know how to pick French
cheeses. Not my area of expertise.

Alex
First Son of Cheese Shopping and Blowjobs

Re: Paris?

 Henry <hwales@kensingtonemail.com>   3/4/20 2:43 AM
to A

Alex, First Son of Making Me Spill My Tea in Said Early
Morning Meeting:

Hate you. Will try to get out of Germany.

x

SEVEN

Henry does get out of Germany, and he meets Alex near a herd of crêpe-eating tourists by Place du Tertre, wearing a sharp blue blazer and a wicked smile. They stumble back to his hotel after two bottles of wine, and Henry sinks to his knees on the white marble and looks up at Alex with big, blue, bottomless eyes, and Alex doesn't know a word in any language to describe it.

He's so drunk, and Henry's mouth is so soft, and it's all so fucking French that he forgets to send Henry back to his own hotel. He forgets they don't spend the night. So, they do.

He discovers Henry sleeps curled up on his side, his spine poking out in little sharp points that are actually soft if you reach out and touch them, very carefully so as not to wake him because he's actually sleeping for once. In the morning, room service brings up crusty baguettes and sticky tarts filled with fat apricots and a copy of *Le Monde* that Alex makes Henry translate out loud.

He vaguely remembers telling himself they weren't going to do things like this. It's all a little hazy right now.

When Henry's gone, Alex finds the stationery by the bed: *Fromagerie Nicole Barthélémy*. Leaving your clandestine hookup directions to a Parisian cheese shop. Alex has to admit: Henry really has a solid handle on his personal brand.

Later, Zahra texts him a screencap of a *BuzzFeed* article about his "best bromance ever" with Henry. It's a mix of photos: the state dinner, a couple of shots of them grinning outside the stables in Greenwich, one picked up from a French girl's Twitter of Alex leaning back in his chair at a tiny cafe table while Henry finishes off the bottle of red between them.

Beneath it, Zahra has begrudgingly written: **Good work, you little shit.**

He guesses this is how they're going to do this—the world is going to keep thinking they're best friends, and they're going to keep playing the part.

He knows, objectively, he should pace himself. It's only physical. But Perfect Stoic Prince Charming laughs when he comes, and texts Alex at weird hours of the night: **You're a mad, spiteful, unmitigated demon, and I'm going to kiss you until you forget how to talk.** And Alex is kind of obsessed with it.

Alex decides not to think too hard. Normally they'd only cross paths a few times a year; it takes creative schedule wrangling and a little sweet-talking of their respective teams to see each other as often as their bodies demand. At least they've got a ruse of international public relations.

Their birthdays, it turns out, are less than three weeks

apart, which means, for most of March, Henry is twenty-three and Alex is twenty-one. ("I knew he was a goddamn Pisces," June says). Alex happens to have a voter registration drive at NYU at the end of March, and when he texts Henry about it, he gets a brisk response fifteen minutes later: Have rescheduled visit to New York for nonprofit business to this weekend. Will be in the city ready to carry out birthday floggings &c.

The photographers are readily visible when they meet in front of the Met, so they clasp each other's hands and Alex says through his big on-camera smile, "I want you alone, now."

They're more careful in the States, and they go up to the hotel room one at a time—Henry through the back flanked by two tall PPOs, and later, Alex with Cash, who grins and knows and says nothing.

There's a lot of champagne and kissing and buttercream from a birthday cupcake Henry's inexplicably procured smeared around Alex's mouth, Henry's chest, Alex's throat, between Henry's hips. Henry pins his wrists to the mattress and swallows him down, and Alex is drunk and fucking transported, feeling every moment of twenty-two years and not a single day older, some kind of hedonistic youth of history. Birthday head from another country's prince will do that.

It's the last time they see each other for weeks, and after a lot of teasing and maybe some begging, he convinces Henry to download Snapchat. Henry mostly sends tame, fully clothed thirst traps that make Alex sweat in his lectures: a mirror shot, mud-stained white polo pants, a sharp suit. On a Saturday, the C-SPAN stream on his phone gets interrupted by Henry on a sailboat, smiling into the camera with the sun bright on his bare shoulders, and Alex's heart goes so fucking weird that he has to put his head in his hands for a full minute.

(But, like. It's fine. It's not a whole thing.)

Between it all, they talk about Alex's campaign job, Henry's nonprofit projects, both of their appearances. They talk about how Pez is now proclaiming himself fully in love with June and spends half his time with Henry rhapsodizing about her or begging him to ask Alex if she likes flowers (yes) or exotic birds (to look at, not to own) or jewelry in the shape of her own face (no).

There are a lot of days when Henry is happy to hear from him and quick to respond, a fast, cutting sense of humor, hungry for Alex's company and the tangle of thoughts in Alex's head. But sometimes, he's taken over by a dark mood, an unusually acerbic wit, strange and vitrified. He'll withdraw for hours or days, and Alex comes to understand this as grief time, little bouts of depression, or times of "too much." Henry hates those days completely. Alex wishes he could help, but he doesn't particularly mind. He's just as attracted to Henry's cloudy tempers, the way he comes back from them, and the millions of shades in between.

He's also learned that Henry's placid demeanor is shattered with the right poking. He likes to bring up things he knows will get Henry going, including:

"Listen," Henry is saying, heated, over the phone on a Thursday night. "I don't give a damn what *Joanne* has to say, Remus John Lupin is gay as the day is long, and I won't hear a word against it."

"Okay," Alex says. "For the record, I agree with you, but also, tell me more."

He launches into a long-winded tirade, and Alex listens,

amused and a little awed, as Henry works his way to his point: "I just think, as the prince of this bloody country, that when it comes to Britain's *positive* cultural landmarks, it would be nice if we could not throw our own marginalized people under the proverbial bus. People sanitize Freddie Mercury or Elton John or Bowie, who was shagging Jagger up and down Oakley Street in the seventies, I might add. It's just not the *truth*."

It's another thing Henry does—whipping out these analyses of what he reads or watches or listens to that confronts Alex with the fact that he has both a degree in English literature and a vested interest in the gay history of his family's country. Alex has always *known* his gay American history—after all, his parents' politics have been part of it—but it wasn't until he figured himself out that he started to *engage* with it like Henry.

He's starting to understand what swelled in his chest the first time he read about Stonewall, why he ached over the SCOTUS decision in 2015. He starts catching up voraciously in his spare time: Walt Whitman, the Laws of Illinois 1961, The White Night Riot, *Paris Is Burning*. He's pinned a photo over his desk at work, a man at a rally in the '80s in a jacket that says across the back: IF I DIE OF AIDS—FORGET BURIAL— JUST DROP MY BODY ON THE STEPS OF THE F.D.A.

June's eyes stick on it one day when she drops by the office to have lunch with him, giving him the same strange look she gave him over coffee the morning after Henry snuck into his room. But she doesn't say anything, carries on through sushi about her latest project, pulling all her journals together into a memoir. Alex wonders if any of this stuff would make it into there. Maybe, if he tells her soon. He should tell her soon.

It's weird that the thing with Henry could make him understand this huge part of himself, but it does. When he sinks into thoughts of Henry's hands, square knuckles and elegant fingers, he wonders how he never realized it before. When he sees Henry next at a gala in Berlin, and he feels that gravitational pull, chases it down in the back of a limo, and binds Henry's wrists to a hotel bedpost with his own necktie, he knows himself better.

When he shows up for a weekly briefing two days later, Zahra grabs his jaw with one hand and turns his head, peering closer at the side of his neck. "Is that a *hickey*?"

Alex freezes. "I . . . um, no?"

"Do I look stupid to you, Alex?" Zahra says. "Who is giving you hickeys, and why have you not gotten them to sign an NDA?"

"Oh my God," he says, because really, the last person Zahra needs to be concerned about leaking sordid details is Henry. "If I needed an NDA, you would know. Chill."

Zahra does not appreciate being told to chill.

"Look at me," she says. "I have known you since you were still leaving skid marks in your drawers. You think I don't know when you're lying to me?" She jabs a pointy, polished nail into his chest. "However you got that, it better be somebody off the approved list of girls you are allowed to be seen with during the election cycle, which I will email to you again as soon as you get out of my sight in case you have misplaced it."

"Jesus, okay."

"And to remind you," she goes on, "I will chop my own tit off before I let you pull some idiotic stunt to cause your mother, our first female president, to be the first president to lose re-election since H fucking W. Do you understand me? I will lock you in your room for the next year if I have to, and you can take your finals by fucking smoke signal. I will staple your dick to the inside of your leg if that keeps it in your fucking pants."

She returns to her notes with smooth professionalism, as if she has not just threatened his life. Behind her, he can see June at her place at the table, very clearly aware that he's lying too.

"Do you have a last name?"

Alex has never actually offered a greeting when calling Henry.

"What?" The usual bemused, elongated, one-syllable response.

"A last name," Alex repeats. It's late afternoon and stormy outside the Residence, and he's on his back in the middle of the Solarium, catching up on drafts for work. "That thing I have two of. Do you use your dad's? Henry Fox? That sounds fucking dope. Or does royalty outrank? Do you use your mom's name, then?"

He hears some shuffling over the phone and wonders if Henry's in bed. They haven't been able to see each other in a couple weeks, so his mind is quick to supply the image.

"The official family name is Mountchristen-Windsor," Henry says. "Hyphenate, like yours. So my full name is . . . Henry George Edward James Fox-Mountchristen-Windsor."

Alex gapes up at the ceiling. "Oh . . . my God."

"Truly."

"I thought Alexander Gabriel Claremont-Diaz was bad."

"Is that after someone?"

"Alexander after the founding father, Gabriel after the patron saint of diplomats."

"That's a bit on the nose."

"Yeah, I didn't have a chance. My sister got Catalina June after the place and the Carter Cash, but I got all the self-fulfilling prophecies."

"I did get both of the gay kings," Henry points out. "There's a prophecy for you."

Alex laughs and kicks his files for the campaign away. He's not coming back to them tonight. "Three last names is just mean."

Henry sighs. "In school, we all went by Wales. Philip is Lieutenant Windsor in the RAF now, though."

"Henry Wales, then? That's not too bad."

"No, it's not. Is this the reason you phoned?"

"Maybe," Alex says. "Call it historical curiosity." Except the truth is closer to the slight drag in Henry's voice and the half step of hesitation before he speaks that's been there all week. "Speaking of historical curiosity, here's a fun fact: I'm sitting in the room Nancy Reagan was in when she found out Ronald Reagan got shot."

"Good Lord."

"And it's also where ol' Tricky Dick told his family he was gonna resign."

"I'm sorry—who or what is a *Tricky Dick*?"

"*Nixon!* Listen, you're undoing everything this country's crusty forefathers fought for and deflowering the darling of the republic. You at least need to know *basic* American history."

"I hardly think deflowering is the word," Henry deadpans. "These arrangements are supposed to be with virgin brides, you know. That certainly didn't seem to be the case."

"Uh-huh, and I'm sure you picked up all those skills from books."

"Well, I did go to uni. It just wasn't necessarily the reading that did it."

Alex hums in suggestive agreement and lets the rhythm of banter fall out. He looks across the room—the windows that were once only gauzy curtains on a sleeping room for Taft's family on hot nights, the corner now stacked with Leo's old comic book collectibles where Eisenhower used to play cards. The stuff underneath the surface. Alex has always sought those things out.

"Hey," he says. "You sound weird. You good?"

Henry's breath catches and he clears his throat. "I'm fine."

Alex doesn't say anything, letting the silence stretch in a thin thread between them before he cuts it. "You know, this whole arrangement we have . . . you can tell me stuff. I tell you stuff all the time. Politics stuff and school stuff and nutso family stuff. I know I'm, like, not the paragon of normal human communication, but. You know."

Another pause.

"I'm not . . . historically great at talking about things," Henry says.

"Well, I wasn't historically great at blowjobs, but we all gotta learn and grow, sweetheart."

"Wasn't?"

"Hey," Alex huffs. "Are you trying to say I'm still not good at them?"

"No, no, I wouldn't dream of it," Henry says, and Alex can hear the small smile in his voice. "It was just the first one that was . . . Well. It was enthusiastic, at least."

"I don't remember you complaining."

"Yes, well, I'd only been fantasizing about it for *ages.*"

"See, there's a thing," Alex points out. "You just told me that. You can tell me other stuff."

"It's hardly the same."

He rolls over onto his stomach, considers, and very deliberately says, "Baby."

It's become a thing: *baby*. He knows it's become a thing. He's
slipped up and accidentally said it a few times, and each time,
Henry positively melts and Alex pretends not to notice, but
he's not above playing dirty here.

There's a slow hiss of an exhale across the line, like air es-
caping through a crack in a window.

"It's, ah. It's not the best time," he says. "How did you put
it? Nutso family stuff."

Alex purses his lips, bites down on his cheek. There it is.

He's wondered when Henry would finally start talking
about the royal family. He makes oblique references to Philip
being wound so tight as to double as an atomic clock, or to his
grandmother's disapproval, and he mentions Bea as often as
Alex mentions June, but Alex knows there's more to it than
that. He couldn't tell you when he started noticing, though,
just like he doesn't know when he started ticking off the days
of Henry's moods.

"Ah," he says. "I see."

"I don't suppose you keep up with any British tabloids, do
you?"

"Not if I can help it."

Henry offers the bitterest of laughs. "Well, the *Daily Mail*
has always had a bit of an affinity for airing our dirty laundry.
They, er, they gave my sister this nickname years ago. 'The
Powder Princess.'"

A ding of recognition. "Because of the . . ."

"Yes, the cocaine, Alex."

"Okay, that does sound familiar."

Henry sighs. "Well, someone's managed to bypass security
to spray paint 'Powder Princess' on the side of her car."

"Shit," Alex says. "And she's not taking it well?"

"Bea?" Henry laughs, a little more genuinely this time. "No, she doesn't usually care about those things. She's fine. More shaken up that someone got past security than anything. Gran had an entire PPO team sacked. But . . . I dunno."

He trails off, and Alex can guess.

"But you care. Because you want to protect her even though you're the little brother."

"I . . . yes."

"I know the feeling. Last summer I almost punched a guy at Lollapalooza because he tried to grab June's ass."

"But you didn't?"

"June had already dumped her milkshake on him," Alex explains. He shrugs a little, knowing Henry can't see it. "And then Amy Tased him. The smell of burnt strawberry milkshake on a sweaty frat guy is really something."

Henry laughs fully at that. "They never do need us, do they?"

"Nope," Alex agrees. "So you're upset because the rumors aren't true."

"Well . . . they are true, actually," Henry says.

Oh, Alex thinks.

"Oh," Alex says. He's not sure how else to respond, reaching into his mental store of political platitudes and finding them all clinical and intolerable.

Henry, with a little trepidation, presses on. "You know, Bea has only ever wanted to play music," he starts. "Mum and Dad played too much Joni Mitchell for her growing up, I think. She wanted guitar lessons; Gran wanted violin since it was more proper. Bea was allowed to learn both, but she went to uni for classical violin. Anyway, her last year of uni, Dad died. It happened so . . . quickly. He just *went.*"

Alex shuts his eyes. "Fuck."

"Yeah," Henry says, voice rough. "We all went round the bend a bit. Philip just *had* to be the man of the family, and I was an arsehole, and Mum didn't leave her rooms. Bea just stopped seeing the point in anything. I was starting uni when she finished, and Philip was deployed halfway round the globe, and she was out every single night with all the posh London hipsters, sneaking out to play guitar at secret shows and doing mountains of cocaine. The papers *loved* it."

"Jesus," Alex hisses. "I'm sorry."

"It's fine," Henry says, steadiness rising in his voice as if he's stuck out his chin in that stubborn way he does sometimes. Alex wishes he could see it. "In any event, the speculation and paparazzi photos and the goddamn nickname got to be too much, and Philip came home for a week, and he and Gran literally put her in a car and had her driven to rehab and called it a *wellness retreat* to the press."

"Wait—sorry," Alex says before he can stop himself. "Just. Where was your mom?"

"Mum hasn't been involved in much since Dad died," Henry says on an exhale, then stops short. "Sorry. That's not fair. It's . . . the grief has been total for her. It was paralyzing. It *is* paralyzing. She was such a spitfire. I dunno. She still listens, and she tries, and she wants us to be happy. But I don't know if she has it in her anymore to be a part of anyone's happiness."

"That's . . . horrible."

A pause, heavy.

"Anyway, Bea went," Henry goes on, "against her will, and didn't think she had a problem at all, even though you could see her bloody ribs and she'd barely spoken to me in months, when we grew up inseparable. Checked herself out after six hours. I remember her calling me that night from a club, and I lost it. I was, what, eighteen? I drove there and she was sitting on the back steps, high as a kite, and I sat down next to her and cried and told her she wasn't allowed to kill herself because Dad was gone and I was gay and I didn't know what the hell to do, and that was how I came out to her.

"The next day, she went back, and she's been clean ever since, and neither of us has ever told anyone about that night. Until now, I suppose. And I'm not sure why I've said all this, I just, I've never really said any of it. I mean, Pez was there for most of it, so, and I—I don't know." He clears his throat. "Anyway, I don't think I've ever said this many words out loud in a row in my entire life, so please feel free to put me out of my misery any time now."

"No, no," Alex says, stumbling over his own tongue in a rush. "I'm glad you told me. Does it feel better at all to have said it?"

Henry goes silent, and Alex wants so badly to see the shadows of expressions moving across his face, to be able to touch them with his fingertips. Alex hears a swallow across the line, and Henry says, "I suppose so. Thank you. For listening."

"Yeah, of course," Alex tells him. "I mean, it's good to have times when it's not all about me, as tedious and exhausting as it may be."

That earns him a groan, and he bites back a smile when Henry says, "You are a *wanker*."

"Yeah, yeah," Alex says, and he takes the opportunity to ask a question he's been wanting to ask for months. "So, um. Does anybody else know? About you?"

"Bea's the only one in the family I've told, though I'm sure the rest have suspected. I was always a bit different, never quite had the stiff upper lip. I think Dad knew and never cared. But Gran sat me down the day I finished my A levels and made it abundantly clear I was not to let anyone know about any deviant desires I might be beginning to harbor that might reflect poorly upon the crown, and there were appropriate channels to maintain appearances if necessary. So."

Alex's stomach turns over. He pictures Henry, a teenager, back-broken with grief and told to keep it and the rest of him shut up tight.

"What the fuck. Seriously?"

"The wonders of the monarchy," Henry says loftily.

"God." Alex scrubs a hand across his face. "I've had to fake some shit for my mom, but nobody's ever outright told me to *lie* about who I am."

"I don't think she sees it as lying. She sees it as doing what must be done."

"Sounds like bullshit."

Henry sighs. "Hardly any other options, are there?"

There's a long pause, and Alex is thinking about Henry in his palace, Henry and the years behind him, how he got here. He bites his lip.

"Hey," Alex says. "Tell me about your dad."

Another pause.

"Sorry?"

"I mean, if you don't—if you want to. I was just thinking I don't know much about him except that he was James Bond. What was he like?"

Alex paces the Solarium and listens to Henry talk, stories about a man with Henry's same sandy hair and strong, straight nose, someone Alex has met in shadows that pass through the way Henry speaks and moves and laughs. He hears about sneaking out of the palace and joyriding around the country-side, learning to sail, being propped up in director's chairs. The man Henry remembers is both superhuman and heartbreak-ingly flesh and blood, a man who encompassed Henry's en-tire childhood and charmed the world but was also simply a man.

The way Henry talks about him is a physical feat, drifting up in the corners with fondness but sagging in the middle under the weight. He tells Alex in a low voice how his parents met—Princess Catherine, dead set on being the first princess with a doctorate, mid-twenties and wading through Shake-speare. How she went to see *Henry* V at the RSC and Arthur was starring, how she pushed her way backstage and shook off her security to disappear into London with him and dance all night. How the Queen forbid it, but she married him anyway.

He tells Alex about growing up in Kensington, how Bea sang and Philip clung to his grandmother, but they were happy, buttoned up in cashmere and knee socks and whisked through foreign countries in helicopters and shiny cars. A brass tele-scope from his father for his seventh birthday. How he real-ized by the time he was four that every person in the country knew his name, and how he told his mother he didn't know if he wanted them to, and how she knelt down and told him she'd let nothing touch him, not ever.

Alex starts talking too. Henry already hears nearly every-thing about Alex's current life, but talking about how they grew up has always been some invisible line of demarcation. He talks about Travis County, making campaign posters with construction paper for fifth-grade student council, family trips to Surfside, running headlong into the waves. He talks about the big bay window in the house where he grew up, and Henry doesn't tell him he's crazy for all the things he used to write and hide under there.

It starts to grow dark outside, a dull and soggy evening around the Residence, and Alex makes his way down to his room and his bed. He hears about the assortment of guys from Henry's university days, all of them enamored with the idea of sleeping with a prince, almost all of them immediately alienated by the paperwork and secrecy and, occasionally, Henry's dark moods about the paperwork and secrecy.

"But of course, er," Henry says, "nobody since . . . well, since you and I—"

"No," Alex says, faster than he expects, "me neither. Nobody else."

He hears words coming out of his mouth, ones he can't believe he's saying out loud. About Liam, about those nights, but also how he'd sneak pills out of Liam's Adderall bottle when his grades were slipping and stay awake for two, three days at a time. About June, the unspoken knowledge that she only lives here to watch out for him, the quiet sense of guilt he carries when he can't tear himself away. About how much some of the lies people tell about his mother hurt, the fear she'll lose.

They talk for so long Alex has to plug his phone in to keep the battery from dying. He rolls onto his side and listens, trails the back of his hand across the pillow next to him and imagines Henry lying opposite in his own bed, two parentheses enclosing 3,700 miles. He looks at his chewed-up cuticles and imagines Henry there under his fingers, speaking into only inches of distance. He imagines the way Henry's face would look in the bluish-gray dark. Maybe he would have a faint shadow of stubble on his jaw, waiting for a morning shave, or maybe the circles under his eyes would wash out in the low light.

Somehow, this is the same person who had Alex so convinced he didn't care about anything, who still has the rest of the world convinced he's a mild, unfettered Prince Charming. It's taken months to get here: the full realization of just how wrong he was.

"I miss you," Alex says before he can stop himself.

He instantly regrets it, but Henry says, "I miss you too."

"Hey, wait."

Alex rolls his chair back out of his cubicle. The woman from the after-hours cleaning crew stops, her hand on the handle of the coffeepot. "I know it looks disgusting, but would you mind leaving that? I was gonna finish it."

She gives him a dubious look but leaves the last burnt, sludgy vestiges of coffee where they are and rolls off with her cart.

He peers down into his CLAREMONT FOR AMERICA mug and frowns at the almond milk that's pooled in the middle. Why doesn't this office keep normal milk around? This is why people from Texas hate Washington elites. Ruining the goddamn dairy industry.

On his desk, there are three stacks of papers. He keeps staring at them, hoping if he recites them enough times in his head, he'll figure out how to feel like he's doing enough.

One. The Gun File. A detailed index of every kind of insane gun Americans can own and state-by-state regulations, which he has to comb through for research on a new set of federal assault rifle policies. It's got a giant smudge of pizza sauce on it because it makes him stress-eat.

Two. The Trans-Pacific Partnership File, which he knows
he needs to work on but has barely touched because it's mind-
numbingly boring.

Three. The Texas File.

He's not supposed to have this file. It wasn't given to him
by the policy chief of staff or anyone on the campaign. It's not
even about policy. It's also more of a binder than a file. He
guesses he should call it: The Texas Binder.

The Texas Binder is his baby. He guards it jealously, stuffing it into his messenger bag to take home with him when he
leaves the office and hiding it from WASPy Hunter. It contains a county map of Texas with complex voter demographic
breakdowns, matched up with the populations of children of
undocumented immigrants, unregistered voters who are legal
residents, voting patterns over the last twenty years. He's
stuffed it with spreadsheets of data, voting records, projections
he had Nora calculate for him.

Back in 2016, when his mother squeezed out a victory in
the general election, the bitterest sting was losing Texas. She
was the first president since Nixon to win the presidency but
lose her own state of residence. It wasn't exactly a surprise,
considering Texas had been polling red, but they were all
secretly holding out for the Lometa Longshot to take it in the
end. She didn't.

Alex keeps coming back to the numbers from 2016 and
2018 precinct by precinct, and he can't shake this nagging feeling of hope. There's something there, something shifting, he
swears it.

He doesn't mean to be ungrateful for the policy job, it's
just . . . not what he thought it was going to be. It's frustrating
and slow-moving. He should stay focused, give it more time,
but instead, he keeps coming back to the binder.

He plucks a pencil out of WASPy Hunter's Harvard pencil cup and starts sketching lines on the map of Texas for the millionth time, redrawing the districts old white men drew years ago to force votes their way.

Alex has this spark at the base of his spine to do the most good he can, and when he sits here in his cubicle for hours a day and fidgets under all the minutiae, he doesn't know if he is. But if he could only figure out a way to make Texas' vote reflect its soul . . . he's nowhere near qualified to single-handedly dismantle Texas' iron curtains of gerrymandering, but what if he—

An incessant buzzing snaps him present, and he digs out his phone from the bottom of his bag.

"Where are you?" June's voice demands over the line.

Fuck. He checks the time: 9:44. He was supposed to meet June for dinner over an hour ago.

"Shit, June, I'm so sorry," he says, jumping up from his desk and shoving his things into his bag. "I got caught up at work— I, I completely forgot."

"I sent you like a million texts," she says. She sounds like she's vision-boarding his funeral.

"My phone was on silent," he says helplessly, booking it for the elevator. "I'm seriously so sorry. I'm a complete jackass. I'm leaving now."

"Don't worry about it," she says. "I got mine to go. I'll see you at home."

"Bug."

"I'm gonna need you to *not* call me that right now."

"June—"

The call drops.

When he gets back to the Residence, she's sitting on her bed, eating pasta out of a plastic container, with *Parks &*

Recreation playing on her tablet. She pointedly ignores him when he comes to her doorway.

He's reminded of when they were kids—around eight and eleven years old. He recalls standing next to her at the bathroom mirror, looking at the similarities between their faces: the same round tips of their noses, the same thick, unruly brows, the same square jaw inherited from their mother. He remembers studying her expression in the reflection as they brushed their teeth, the morning of the first day of school, their dad having braided June's hair for her because their mom was in DC and couldn't be there.

He recognizes the same expression on her face now: carefully tucked-away disappointment.

"I'm sorry," he tries again. "I honestly feel like complete and total shit. Please don't be mad at me."

June keeps chewing, looking steadfastly at Leslie Knope chirping away.

"We can do lunch tomorrow," Alex says desperately. "I'll pay."

"I don't care about a stupid meal, Alex."

Alex sighs. "Then what do you want me to do?"

"I want you not to be Mom," June says, finally looking up at him. She closes her food container and gets up off her bed, pacing across the room.

"Okay," Alex says, raising both hands, "is that what's happening right now?"

"I—" She takes a deep breath. "No. I shouldn't have said that."

"No, you obviously meant it," Alex says. He drops his messenger bag and steps into the room. "Why don't you say whatever it is you need to say?"

She turns to face him, arms folded, her spine braced against her dresser. "You really don't see it? You never sleep, you're always throwing yourself into something, you're willing to let Mom use you for whatever she wants, the tabloids are always after you—"

"June, I've always been this way," he interrupts gently. "I'm gonna be a politician. You always knew that. I'm starting as soon as I graduate . . . in a month. This is how my life is gonna be, okay? I'm choosing it."

"Well, maybe it's the wrong choice," June says, biting her lip.

He rocks back on his heels. "Where the hell is this coming from?"

"Alex," she says, "come on."

He doesn't know what the hell she's getting at. "You've always backed me up until now."

She flings one arm out emphatically enough to upset an entire potted cactus on her dresser and says, "Because until now you weren't *fucking the Prince of England*!"

That effectively snaps Alex's mouth shut. He crosses to the sitting area in front of the fireplace, sinking down into an armchair. June watches him, cheeks bright scarlet.

"Nora told you."

"What?" she says. "No. She wouldn't do that. Although it kinda sucks you told her and not me." She folds her arms again. "I'm sorry, I was trying to wait for you to tell me yourself, but, Jesus, Alex. How many times was I supposed to believe you were volunteering to take those international appearances we always found excuses to get out of? And, like, did you forget I've lived across the hall from you for almost my entire life?"

Alex looks down at his shoes, June's perfectly curated mid-century rug. "So you're mad at me because of Henry?"

June makes a strangled noise, and when he looks back up, she's digging through the top drawer of her dresser. "Oh my God, how are you so smart and so dumb at the same time?" she says, pulling a magazine out from underneath her underwear. He's about to tell her he's not in the mood to look at her tabloids when she throws it at him.

An ancient issue of *J14*, opened to a center page. The photograph of Henry, age thirteen.

He glances up. "You knew?"

"Of course I knew!" she says, flopping dramatically into the chair opposite him. "You were always leaving your greasy little fingerprints all over it! Why do you always assume you can get away with things?" She releases a long-suffering sigh. "I never really . . . got what he was to you, until I *got* it. I thought you had a crush or something, or that I could help you make a friend, but, Alex. We meet so many people. I mean, thousands and thousands of people, and a lot of them are morons, and a lot of them are incredible, unique people, but I almost never meet somebody who's a match for you. Do you know that?" She leans forward and touches his knee, pink fingernails on his navy chinos. "You have so much in you, it's almost impossible to match it. But he's your match, dumbass."

Alex stares at her, trying to process what she's said.

"I feel like this is your starry-eyed romantic thing projecting onto me," is what he decides to say, and she immediately withdraws her hand from his leg and returns to glaring at him.

"You know Evan didn't break up with me?" she says. "I broke up with him. I was gonna go to California with him, live in the same time zone as Dad, get a job at the fucking *Sacramento Bee* or something. But I gave all that up to come *here*, because it was the right thing to do. I did what Dad did—I went where I was most needed, because it was my responsibility."

"And you regret it?"

"No," she says. "I don't know. I don't think so. But I—I wonder. Dad wonders, sometimes. Alex, you don't have to wonder. You don't have to be our parents. You can keep Henry, and figure the rest out." Now she's looking at him evenly, steadily. "Sometimes you have a fire under your ass for no good goddamn reason. You're gonna burn out like this."

Alex leans back, thumbing the stitching on the armrest of the chair.

"So, what?" he asks. "You want me to quit politics and go become a princess? That's not very feminist of you."

"That's not how feminism works," she says, rolling her eyes. "And that's not what I mean. I mean . . . I don't know. Have you ever considered there might be more than one path to use what you have? Or to get where you want to be to make the most difference in the world?"

"I'm not sure I'm following."

"Well." She looks down at her cuticles. "It's like the whole *Sac Bee* thing—it never actually would have worked out. It was a dream I had before Mom was president. The kind of journalism I wanted to do is the kind of journalism that being a First Daughter pretty much disqualifies you from. But the world is better with her where she is, and right now I'm looking for a new dream that's better too." Her big brown Diaz eyes blink up at him. "So, I don't know. Maybe there's more than one dream for you, or more than one way to get there."

She gives a crooked shrug, tilting her head to look at him openly. June is often a mystery, a big ball of complex emotions and motivations, but her heart is honest and true. She's very much what Alex holds in his memory as the sanctified idea of Southerness at its best: always generous and warm and sincere, work-strong and reliable, a light left on. She wants the best for him, plainly, in an unselfish and uncalculating way. She's been trying to talk to him for a while, he realizes.

He looks down at the magazine and feels the corner of his mouth tug upward. He can't believe June kept it all these years.

"He looks so different," he says after a long minute, gazing down at the baby Henry on the page and his easy, unfledged sureness. "I mean, like, obviously. But the way he carries himself." His fingertips brush the page in the same place they did when he was young, over the sun-gold hair, except now he knows its exact texture. It's the first time he's seen it since he learned where this version of Henry went. "It pisses me off sometimes, thinking about everything he's been through. He's a good person. He really cares, and he *tries*. He never deserved any of it."

June leans forward, looking at the picture too. "Have you ever told him that?"

"We don't really . . ." Alex coughs. "I don't know. Talk like that?"

June inhales deeply and makes an enormous fart noise with her mouth, shattering the serious mood, and Alex is so grateful for it that he melts onto the floor in a fit of hysterical laughter.

"Ugh! Men!" she groans. "No emotional vocabulary. I can't believe our ancestors survived centuries of wars and plagues and genocide just to wind up with your sorry ass." She throws a pillow at him, and Alex scream-laughs as it hits him in the face. "You should try saying some of that stuff to *him*."

"Stop trying to Jane Austen my life!" he yells back.

"Listen, it's not my fault he's a mysterious and retiring young royal and you're the tempestuous ingénue that caught his eye, okay?"

He laughs and tries to crawl away, even as she claws at his ankle and wallops another pillow at his head. He still feels guilty for blowing her off, but he thinks they're okay now. He'll do better. They fight for a spot on her big canopy bed, and she makes him spill what it's like to be secretly hooking up with a real-life prince. And so June knows; she knows about him and she hugs him and doesn't care. He didn't realize how terrified he was of her knowing until the fear is gone.

She puts *Parks* back on and has the kitchen send up ice cream, and Alex thinks about how she said, "You don't have to be our parents"—she's never mentioned their dad in the same context as their mom like that before. He's always known part of her resents their mom for the position they occupy in the world, for not having a normal life, for taking herself away from them. But he never really realized she felt the same sense of loss he does deep down about their dad, that it's something she dealt with and moved past. That the stuff with their mom is something she's still going through.

He thinks she's wrong about him, mostly—he doesn't necessarily believe he has to choose between politics and this thing with Henry yet, or that he's moving too fast in his career. But . . . there's the Texas Binder, and the knowledge of other states like Texas and millions of other people who need someone to fight for them, and the feeling at the base of his spine, like there's a lot of fight in him that could be honed down to a more productive point.

There's law school.

Every time he looks at the Texas Binder, he knows it's a big fat case for him to go take the damn LSAT like he knows both his parents wish he would instead of diving headfirst into politics. He's always, always said no. He doesn't wait for things. Doesn't put in the time like that, do what he's told.

He's never given much thought to options other than a crow's path ahead of him. Maybe he should.

"Is now a good time to point out Henry's very hot, very rich best friend is basically in love with you?" Alex says to June. "He's like some kind of billionaire, genius, manic-pixie-dream philanthropist. I feel like you would be into that."

"Please shut up," she says, and she steals the ice cream back.

Once June knows, their circle of "knowing" is up to a tight seven.

Before Henry, most of his romantic entanglements as FSOTUS were one-off incidents that involved Cash or Amy confiscating phones before the act and pointing at the dotted line on the NDA on the way out—Amy with mechanical professionalism, Cash with the air of a cruise ship director. It was inevitable they be looped in.

And there's Shaan, the only member of the royal staff who knows Henry is gay, excluding his therapist. Shaan ultimately doesn't care about Henry's sexual preferences as long as they're not getting him into trouble. He's a consummate professional parceled in immaculately tailored Tom Ford, ruffled by absolutely nothing, whose affection for his charge shows in the way he tends to him like a favorite houseplant. Shaan knows for the same reason Amy and Cash know: absolute necessity.

Then Nora, who still looks smug every time the subject arises. And Bea, who found out when she walked in on one of their after-dark FaceTime sessions, leaving Henry capable of nothing but flustered British stammering and thousand-yard stares for the next day and a half.

Pez seems to have been in on the secret all along. Alex imagines he demanded an explanation when Henry literally made them flee the country under the cover of night after putting his tongue in Alex's mouth in the Kennedy Garden.

It's Pez who answers when Alex FaceTimes Henry at four a.m. DC time, expecting to catch Henry over his morning tea. Henry is holidaying in one of the family's country homes while Alex suffocates under his last week of college. He doesn't reflect on why his migraine demands soothing images of Henry looking cozy and picturesque, sipping tea by a lush green hillside. He just hits the buttons on the phone.

"Alexander, babes," Pez says when he picks up. "How lovely for you to give your auntie Pezza a ring on this magnificent Sunday morning." He's smiling from what looks like the passenger seat of a luxury car, wearing a cartoonishly large sunhat and a striped pashmina.

"Hi, Pez," Alex says, grinning back. "Where are y'all?"

"We are out for a drive, taking in the scenery of Carmarthenshire," Pez tells him. He tilts the phone over toward the driver's seat. "Say good morning to your strumpet, Henry."

"Good morning, strumpet," Henry says, glancing away from the road to wink at the camera. He's looking fresh-faced and relaxed, all rolled-up sleeves and soft gray linen, and Alex feels calmer knowing somewhere in Wales, Henry got a decent night's sleep. "What's got you up at four in the morning this time?"

"My fucking economics final," Alex says, rolling over onto his side to squint at the screen. "My brain isn't working anymore."

"Can't you get one of those Secret Service earpieces with Nora on the other end?"

"I can take it for you," Pez interjects, turning the camera back to himself. "I'm aces with money."

"Yes, yes, Pez, we know there's nothing you can't do," says Henry's voice off-camera. "No need to rub it in."

Alex laughs under his breath. From the angle Pez is holding the phone, he can see Wales rolling by though the car window, dramatic and plunging. "Hey, Henry, say the name of the house you're staying at again."

Pez turns the camera to catch Henry in a half smile. "Llwynywermod."

"One more time."

"Llwynywermod."

Alex groans. "Jesus."

"I was *hoping* you two would start talking dirty," Pez says. "Please, do go on."

"I don't think you could keep up, Pez," Alex tells him.

"Oh *really*?" The picture returns to Pez. "What if I put my co—"

"Pez," comes the sound of Henry's voice, and a hand with a signet ring on the smallest finger covers Pez's mouth. "I beg of you. Alex, what part of 'nothing he cannot do' did you think was worth testing? Honestly, you are going to get us all killed."

"That's the goal," Alex says happily. "So what are y'all gonna do today?"

Pez frees himself by licking Henry's palm and continues talking. "Frolic naked in the hills, frighten the sheep, return to the house for the usual: tea, biscuits, casting ourselves upon the Thighmaster of love to moan about Claremont-Diaz siblings, which has become tragically one-sided since Henry took up with you. It used to be all bottles of cognac and shared malaise and 'When will they notice us'—"

"Don't tell him that!"

"—and now I just ask Henry, 'What is your secret?' And he says, 'I insult Alex all the time and that seems to work.'"

"I will *turn this car around.*"

"That won't work on June," Alex says.

"Let me get a pen—"

It turns out they're spending their holiday workshopping philanthropy projects. Henry's been telling Alex for months about their plans to go international, and now they're talking three refugee programs around Western Europe, HIV clinics in Nairobi and Los Angeles, LGBT youth shelters in four different countries. It's ambitious, but since Henry still staunchly covers all his own expenses with his inheritance from his father, his royal accounts are untouched. He's determined to use them for nothing but this.

Alex curls around his phone and his pillow as the sun comes up over DC. He's always wanted to be a person with a legacy in this world. Henry is undoubtedly, determinedly that. It's a little intoxicating. But it's fine. He's just a little sleep-deprived.

All in all, finals come and go with much less fanfare than Alex imagined. It's a week of cramming and presentations and the usual amount of all-nighters, and it's over.

The whole college thing in general went by like that. He didn't really have the experiences everyone else has, always isolated by fame or harangued by security. He never got a stamp on his forehead on his twenty-first birthday at The Tombs, never jumped in Dalhgren Fountain. Sometimes it's like he barely went to Georgetown, merely powered through a series of lectures that happened to be in the same geographical area.

Anyway, he graduates, and the whole auditorium gives him a standing ovation, which is weird but kind of cool. A dozen of his classmates want to take a photo with him afterward. They all know him by name. He's never spoken to any of them before. He smiles for their parents' iPhones and wonders if he should have tried.

Alex Claremont-Diaz graduates summa cum laude from Georgetown University with a bachelor's degree in Government, his Google alerts read when he checks them from the back seat of the limo, before he's even taken his cap and gown off.

There's a huge garden party at the White House, and Nora is there in a dress and blazer and a sly smile, pressing a kiss to the side of Alex's jaw.

"The last of the White House Trio finally graduates," she says, grinning. "And he didn't even have to bribe any professors with political or sexual favors to do it."

"I think some of them might finally manage to purge me from their nightmares soon," Alex says.

"Y'all do school weird," June says, crying a little.

There's a mixed bag of political power players and family friends in attendance—including Rafael Luna, who falls under the heading of both. Alex spots him looking tired but handsome by the ceviche, involved in animated conversation with Nora's grandfather, the Veep. His dad is in from California, freshly tanned from a recent trek through Yosemite, grinning and proud. Zahra hands him a card that says, *Good job doing what was expected of you,* and nearly shoves him into the punch bowl when he tries to hug her.

An hour in, his phone buzzes in his pocket, and June gives him a mild glare when he diverts his attention mid-sentence to check it. He's ready to brush it off, but all around him iPhones and Blackberries are coming out in a flurry of movement.

It's WASPy Hunter: Jacinto just called a presser, word is he's dropping out of the primary a.k.a. officially Claremont vs. Richards 2020.

"Shit," Alex says, turning his phone around to show June the message.

"So much for the party."

She's right—in a matter of seconds, half the tables are empty as campaign staffers and congresspeople leave their seats to huddle together over their phones.

"This is a bit dramatic," Nora observes, sucking an olive off the end of a toothpick. "We all knew he was gonna give Richards the nomination eventually. They probably got Jacinto in a windowless room and bench-clamped his dick to the table until he said he'd concede."

Alex doesn't hear whatever Nora says next because a rush of movement at the doors of the Palm Room near the edge of the garden catches his eye. It's his dad, pulling Luna by the arm. They disappear into a side door, toward the housekeeper's office.

He leaves his champagne with the girls and weaves a circuitous path toward the Palm Room, pretending to check his phone. Then, after considering whether the scolding he'll get from the dry-cleaning crew will be worth it, he ducks into the shrubbery.

There's a loose windowpane in the bottom of the third fixture of the south-facing wall of the housekeeper's office. It's popped out of its frame slightly, enough that its bulletproof, soundproof seal isn't totally intact. It's one of three windowpanes like this in the Residence. He found them during his first six months at the White House, before June graduated and Nora transferred, when he was alone, with nothing better to do than these little investigative projects around the grounds.

He's never told anyone about the loose panes; he always suspected they might come in handy one day.

He crouches down and creeps up toward the window, soil rolling into his loafers, hoping he guessed their destination right, until he finds the pane he's looking for. He leans in, tries to get his ear as close to it as he can. Over the sound of the wind rustling the bushes around him, he can hear two low, tense voices.

". . . hell, Oscar," says one voice, in Spanish. Luna. "Did you tell her? Does she know you're asking me to do this?"

"She's too careful," his father's voice says. He's speaking Spanish too—a precaution the two of them occasionally take when they're concerned about being overheard. "Sometimes it's best that she doesn't know."

There's the sound of a hissing exhale, weight shifting. "I'm not going behind her back to do something I don't even want to do."

"You mean to tell me, after what Richards did to you, there's not a part of you that wants to burn all his shit to the ground?"

"Of course there is, Oscar, Jesus," Luna says. "But you and I both know it's not that fucking simple. It never is."

"Listen, Raf. I know you kept the files on everything. You don't even have to make a statement. You could leak it to the press. How many other kids do you think since—"

"Don't."

"—and how many more—"

"You don't think she can win on her own, do you?" Luna cuts across him. "You still don't have faith in her, after everything."

"It's not about that. This time is different."

"Why don't you leave me and something that happened *twenty fucking years ago* out of your unresolved feelings for your ex-wife and focus on winning this goddamn election, Oscar? I don't—"

Luna cuts himself off because there's the sound of the door-knob turning, someone entering the offices.

Oscar switches to clipped English, making an excuse about discussing a bill, then says to Luna, in Spanish, "Just think about it."

There are muffled sounds of Oscar and Luna clearing out of the office, and Alex sinks down onto his ass in the mulch, wondering what the hell he's missing.

It starts with a fund-raiser, a silk suit and a big check, a nice white-tablecloth event. It starts, as it always does, with a text: Fund-raiser in LA next weekend. Pez says he's going to get us all matching embroidered kimonos. Put you down for a plus-two?

He grabs lunch with his dad, who flat-out changes the subject every time Alex brings up Luna, and afterward heads to the gala, where Alex gets to properly meet Bea for the first time. She's much shorter than Henry, shorter even than June, with Henry's clever mouth but their mom's brown hair and heart-shaped face. She's wearing a motorcycle jacket over her cocktail dress and has a slight posture he recognizes from his own mother as a reformed chainsmoker. She smiles at Alex, wide and mischievous, and he gets her immediately: another rebel kid.

It's a lot of champagne and too many handshakes and a speech by Pez, charming as always, and as soon as it's over, their collective security convenes at the exit and they're off.

Pez has, as promised, six matching silk kimonos waiting in the limo, each one embroidered across the back with a different riff on a name from a movie. Alex's is a lurid teal and says HOE DAMERON. Henry's lime-green one reads PRINCE BUTTERCUP.

They end up somewhere in West Hollywood at a shitty, sparkling karaoke bar Pez somehow knows about, neon bright enough that it feels spontaneous even though Cash and the rest of their security have been checking it and warning people against taking photos for half an hour before they arrive. The bartender has immaculate pink lipstick and stubble poking through thick foundation, and they rapidly line up five shots and a soda with lime.

"Oh, dear," Henry says, peering down into his empty shot glass. "What's in these? Vodka?"

"Yep," Nora confirms, to which both Pez and Bea break out into fits of giggles.

"What?" Alex says.

"Oh, I haven't had vodka since uni," Henry says. "It tends to make me, erm. Well—"

"Flamboyant?" Pez offers. "Uninhibited? *Randy?*"

"Fun?" Bea suggests.

"*Excuse* you, I am *loads* of fun all the time! I am a *delight*!"

"Hello, excuse me, can we get another round of these please?" Alex calls down the bar.

Bea screams, Henry laughs and throws up a V, and it all goes hazy and warm in the way Alex loves. They all tumble into a round booth, and the lights are low, and he and Henry are keeping a safe distance, but Alex can't stop staring at how the special-effect beams keep hitting Henry's cheekbones, hollowing his face out in blues and greens. He's something else—half-drunk and grinning in a $2,000 suit and a kimono, and Alex can't tear his eyes away. He waves over a beer.

Once things get going, it's impossible to tell how Bea is the one persuaded up to the stage first, but she unearths a plastic crown from the prop chest onstage and rips through a cover of "Call Me" by Blondie. They all wolf whistle and cheer, and the bar crowd finally realizes they've got two members of the royal family, a millionaire philanthropist, and the White House Trio crammed into one of the sticky booths in a rainbow of vivid silk. Three rounds of shots appear—one from a drunk bachelorette party, one from a herd of surly butch chicks at the bar, and one from a table of drag queens. They raise a toast, and Alex feels more welcomed than he ever has before, even at his family's victory rallies.

Pez gets up and launches into "So Emotional" by Whitney Houston in a shockingly flawless falsetto that has the whole club on their feet in a matter of moments, shouting their approval as he belts out the glory notes. Alex looks over in giddy awe at Henry, who laughs and shrugs.

"I told you, there's nothing he can't do," he shouts over the noise.

June is watching the whole performance with her hands clapped to her face, her mouth hanging open, and she leans over to Nora and drunkenly yells, "Oh, *no* . . . he's . . . so . . . hot . . ."

"I know, babe," Nora yells back.

"I want to . . . put my fingers in his mouth . . ." she moans, sounding horrified.

Nora cackles and nods appreciatively and says, "Can I help?"

Bea, who has gone through five different lime and sodas so far, politely passes over a shot that's been handed to her as Pez pulls June up on stage, and Alex throws it back. The burn makes his smile and his legs spread a little wider, and his phone is in his hand before he registers sliding it out of his pocket. He texts Henry under the table: wanna do something stupid?

He watches Henry pull his own phone out, grin, and arch a brow over at him.

What could be stupider than this?

Henry's mouth falls open into a very unflattering expression of drunken, bewildered arousal, like a hot halibut, at his reply several beats later. Alex smiles and leans back into the booth, making a show of wrapping wet lips around the bottle of his beer. Henry looks like his entire life might be flashing before his eyes, and he says, an octave too high, "Right, well, I'll just—nip to the loo!"

And he's off while the rest of the group is still caught up Pez and June's performance. Alex gives it to the count of ten before slipping past Nora and following. He swaps a glance with Cash, who's standing against one wall, gamely wearing a bright pink feather boa. He rolls his eyes but peels off to watch the door.

Alex finds Henry leaning against the sink, arms folded.

"Have I mentioned lately that you're a *demon*?"

"Yeah, yeah," Alex says, double-checking the coast is clear before grabbing Henry by the belt and backing into a stall. "Tell me again later."

"You—you know this is still not convincing me to sing, don't you?" Henry chokes out as Alex mouths along his throat.

"You really think it's a good idea to present me with a challenge, sweetheart?"

Which is how, thirty minutes and two more rounds later, Henry is in front of a screaming crowd, absolutely butchering "Don't Stop Me Now" by Queen while Nora sings backup and Bea throws glittery gold roses at his feet. His kimono is dangling off one shoulder so the embroidery across the back reads PRINCE BUTT. Alex does not know where the roses came from, and he can't imagine asking would get him anywhere. He also wouldn't be able to hear the answer because he's been screaming at the top of his lungs for two minutes straight.

"*I wanna make a supersonic woman of youuu!*" Henry shouts, lunging violently sideways, catching Nora by both arms. "*Don't stop me! Don't stop me! Don't stop me!*"

"Hey, hey, hey!" the entire bar yells back. Pez is practically on top of the table now, pounding the back of the booth with one hand and helping June up onto a chair with the other.

"*Don't stop me! Don't stop me!*"

Alex cups his hands around his mouth. "*Ooh, ooh, ooh!*"

In a cacophony of shouting and kicking and pelvic-thrusting and flashing lights, the song blasts into the guitar solo, and there's not a single person in the bar in their seat, not when a Prince of England is knee-sliding across the stage, playing passionate and somewhat erotic air guitar.

Nora has produced a bottle of champagne and starts spraying Henry with it, and Alex loses his *mind* laughing, climbs on top of his seat and wolf whistles. Bea is absolutely beside herself, tears streaming down her face, and Pez actually is on top of the table now, June dancing beside him, with a bright fuschia smear of lipstick in his platinum hair.

Alex feels a tug on his arm—Bea, dragging him down to the

stage. She grabs his hand and spins him in a ballerina twirl, and he puts one of her roses between his teeth, and they watch Henry and grin at each other through the noise. Alex feels somewhere, under the fifty layers of booze, something crystal clear radiating off her, a shared knowledge of how rare and wonderful this version of Henry is.

Henry is yelling into the microphone again, stumbling to his feet, his suit and kimono stuck to him with champagne and sweat in a confusingly sexy mess. His eyes flick upward, hazy and hot, and unmistakably lock with Alex's at the edge of the stage, smiling broad and messy. *"I wanna make a supersonic man outta youuuuu!"*

By the end, there's a standing ovation awaiting him, and Bea, with a steady hand and a devilish smile, ruffling his champagne-sticky hair. She steers him into the booth and Alex's side, and he pulls her in after him, and the six of them fall together in a tangle of hoarse laughter and expensive shoes.

He looks at all of them. Pez, his broad smile and glowing joy, the way his white-blond hair flashes against smooth, dark skin. The curve of Bea's waist and hip and her punk-rock grin as she sucks on the rind of a lime. Nora's long legs, one of which is propped up on the table and the other crossed over one of Bea's, her thigh bare where her dress has ridden up. And Henry, flushed and callow and lean, elegant and thrown wide open, his face always turned toward Alex, his mouth unguarded around a laugh, willing.

He turns to June and slurs, "Bisexuality is truly a rich and complex tapestry," and she screams with laughter and shoves a napkin in his mouth.

Alex doesn't catch much of the next hour—the back of the limo, Nora and Henry jostling for a spot in his lap, an In-N-

Out drive-thru and June screaming next to his ear, "Animal Style, did you hear me say Animal Style? Stop fucking laughing, Pez." There's the hotel, three suites booked for them on the very top floor, riding through the lobby on Cash's impossibly broad back.

June keeps shushing them as they stumble to their rooms with hands full of grease-soaked burger bags, but she's louder than any of them, so it's a zero-sum game. Bea, perpetually the lone sober voice of the group, picks one of the suites at random and deposits June and Nora in the king-size bed and Pez in the empty bathtub.

"I trust you two can handle yourselves?" she says to Alex and Henry in the hallway, a glimmer of mischief in her eyes as she hands them the third key. "I fully intend to put on a robe and investigate this french-fries-dipped-in-milkshake thing Nora told me about."

"Yes, Beatrice, we shall behave in a manner befitting the crown," Henry says. His eyes are slightly crossed.

"Don't be a tosser," she says, and quickly kisses them both on the cheek before vanishing around the corner.

Henry's laughing into the curls at the nape of Alex's neck by the time Alex is fumbling the door open, and they stumble together into the wall, and then toward the bed, clothes dropping in their wake. Henry smells like expensive cologne and champagne and a distinctly Henry smell that never goes away, clean and grassy, and his chest encompasses Alex's back when he crowds up behind him at the edge of the bed, splaying his hands over his hips.

"Supersonic man out of youuuu," Alex mumbles low, craning his head back into Henry's ear, and Henry laughs and kicks his knees out from under him.

It's a clumsy, sideways tumble into bed, both of them grabbing greedy handfuls of the other, Henry's pants still dangling from one ankle, but it doesn't matter because Henry's eyes are fluttered shut and Alex is finally kissing him again.

His hands start traveling south on instinct, sweet muscle memory of Henry's body against his, until Henry reaches down to stop him.

"Hold on, hold on," Henry says. "I'm just realizing. All that earlier, and you haven't gotten off yet tonight, have you?" He drops his head back on the pillow, regards him with narrowed eyes. "Well. That just shall not do."

"Hmm, yeah?" Alex says. He takes advantage of the moment to kiss the column of Henry's throat, the hollow at his collarbone, the knot of his Adam's apple. "What are you gonna do about it?"

Henry pushes a hand into his hair and gives it a little pull. "I shall just have to make it the best orgasm of your life. What can I do to make it good for you? Talk about American tax reform during the act? Have you got talking points?"

Alex looks up, and Henry is grinning at him. "I hate you."

"Maybe some light lacrosse role-play?" He's laughing now, arms coming up around Alex's shoulders to squeeze him to his chest. *"O captain, my captain."*

"You're literally the worst," Alex says, and undercuts it by leaning up to kiss him once more, gently, then deeply, long and slow and heated. He feels Henry's body shifting beneath his, opening up.

"Hang on," Henry says, breaking off breathlessly. "Wait." Alex opens his eyes, and when he looks down, the expression on Henry's face is a more familiar one: nervous, unsure. "I do actually. Er. Have an idea."

He slides a hand up Henry's chest to the side of his jaw, ghosting over his cheek with one finger. "Hey," he says, serious now. "I'm listening. For real."

Henry bites his lip, visibly searching for the right words, and apparently comes to a decision.

"C'mere," he says, surging up to kiss Alex, and he's putting his whole body into it now, sliding his hands down to palm at Alex's ass as he kisses him. Alex feels a sound tear itself from his throat, and he's following Henry's lead blindly now, kissing him deep into the mattress, riding a continuous wave of Henry's body.

He feels Henry's thighs—those goddamn horseback-riding, polo-playing thighs—moving around him, soft, warm skin wrapping around his waist, heels pressing into his back. When Alex breaks off to look at him, the intention on Henry's face is as plain as anything he's ever read there.

"You sure?"

"I know we haven't," Henry says quietly. "But, er. I have, before, so, I can show you."

"I mean, I'm familiar with the mechanics," Alex says, smirking a little, and he sees a corner of Henry's mouth quirk up to mirror him. "But you want me to?"

"Yeah," he says. He pushes his hips up, and they both make some unflattering, involuntary noises. "Yes. Absolutely."

Henry's shaving kit is on the nightstand, and he reaches over and fumbles blindly through it before finding what he's looking for—a condom and a tiny bottle of lube.

Alex almost laughs at the sight. Travel-size lube. He's had some experimental sex in his lifetime, but it never occurred to him to consider if such a thing existed, much less if Henry was jetting around with it alongside his dental floss.

"This is new."

"Yes, well," Henry says, and he takes one of Alex's hands in his and brings it to his own mouth, kissing his fingertips. "We all must learn and grow, mustn't we?"

Alex rolls his eyes, ready to snark, except Henry sucks two fingers into his mouth, very effectively shutting him the hell up. It's incredible and baffling, the way Henry's confidence comes in waves like this, how he struggles so much to get through the asking for what he wants and then readily takes it the moment he's given permission, like at the bar, how the right push had him dancing and shouting as if he'd been waiting for someone to tell him he was allowed to do it.

They're not as drunk as they were, but there's enough alcohol in their systems, and it doesn't feel as daunting as it would otherwise, the first time, even as his fingers start to find their way. Henry's head falls back onto the pillows, and he closes his eyes and lets Alex take over.

The thing about sex with Henry is, it's never the same twice. Sometimes he moves easily, caught up in the rush, and other times he's tense and taut and wants Alex to work him loose and take him apart. Sometimes nothing gets him off faster than being talked back to, but other times they both want him to use every inch of authority in his blood, not to let Alex get there until he's told, until he begs.

It's unpredictable and it's intoxicating and it's *fun,* because Alex has never met a challenge he didn't love, and he—well, Henry is a challenge, head to toe, beginning to end.

Tonight, Henry's silly and warm and ready, his body quick and smooth to give Alex what he's looking for, laughing and incredulous at his own responsiveness to touch. Alex leans down to kiss him, and Henry murmurs into the corner of his mouth, "Ready when you are, love."

Alex takes a breath, holds it. He's ready. He thinks he's ready.

Henry's hand comes up to stroke along his jaw, his sweaty hairline, and Alex settles himself between his legs, lets Henry lace the fingers of his right hand with Alex's left.

He's watching Henry's face—he can't imagine looking at anything other than Henry's face right now—and his expression goes so soft and his mouth so happy and astonished that Alex's voice speaks without his permission, a hoarse "baby." Henry nods, so small that someone who didn't know all his tics might miss it, but Alex knows exactly what it means, so he leans down and sucks Henry's earlobe between his lips and calls him *baby* again, and Henry says, "Yes," and, "Please," and tugs his hair at the root.

Alex nips at Henry's throat and palms at his hips and sinks into the white-out bliss of being that impossibly close to him, of getting to share his body. Somehow it still amazes him that all this seems to be as unbelievably, singularly *good* for Henry as it is for him. Henry's face should be illegal, the way it's turned up toward him, flushed and undone. Alex feels his own lips spreading into a pleased smile, awed and proud.

Afterward, he comes back into his own body in increments— his knees, still dug into the mattress and shaking; his stomach, slick and sticky; his hands, twisted up in Henry's hair, stroking it gently.

He feels like he's stepped outside of himself and returned to find everything slightly rearranged. When he pulls his face back to look at Henry, the feeling comes back into his chest: an ache in answer to the curve of Henry's top lip over white teeth.

"Jesus Christ," Alex says at last, and when he looks over at Henry again, he's squinting at him impishly out of one eye, smirking.

"Would you describe it as *supersonic?*" he says, and Alex groans and slaps him across the chest, and they both dissolve into messy laughter.

They slide apart and make out and argue over who has to sleep in the wet spot until they pass out around four in the morning. Henry rolls Alex onto his side and burrows behind him until he's covering him completely, his shoulders a brace for Alex's shoulders, one of his thighs pressed on top of Alex's thighs, his arms over Alex's arms and his hands over Alex's hands, nowhere left untouched. It's the best Alex has slept in years.

Their alarms go off three hours later for their flights home.

They shower together. Henry's mood turns dark and sour over morning coffee at the harsh reality of returning to London so soon, and Alex kisses him dumbly and promises to call and wishes there was more he could do.

He watches Henry lather up and shave, put pomade in his hair, put on his Burberry for the day, and he catches himself wishing he could watch it every day. He likes taking Henry apart, but there's something incredibly intimate about sitting on the bed they wrecked the night before, the only one who watches him create Prince Henry of Wales for the day.

Through his throbbing hangover, he's got a suspicion all these feelings are why he held off on fucking Henry for so long.

Also, he might puke. It's probably unrelated.

They meet the others in the hallway, Henry passing for hungover but handsome, and Alex just doing his best. Bea is looking well-rested, fresh, and very smug about it. June, Nora, and Pez all emerge disheveled from their suite looking like the cats that caught the canaries, but it's impossible to tell who is a cat and who is a canary. Nora has a smudge of lipstick on the back of her neck. Alex doesn't ask.

Cash chuckles under his breath when he meets them at the elevators, a tray of six coffees balanced on one hand. Hang-over tending isn't part of his job description, but he's a mother hen.

"So this is the gang now, huh?"

And through it all, Alex realizes with a start: He has friends now.

EIGHT

You are a dark sorcerer

 Henry <hwales@kensingtonemail.com>   6/8/20 3:23 PM
to A

Alex,

I can't think of a single other way to start this email except to say, and I do hope you will forgive both my language and my utter lack of restraint: You are so fucking beautiful.

I've been useless for a week, driven around for appearances and meetings, lucky if I've made a single meaningful contribution to any of them. How is a man to get anything done knowing Alex Claremont-Diaz is out there on the loose? I am driven to distraction.

It's all bloody useless because when I'm not thinking about your face, I'm thinking about your arse or your hands or your smart mouth. I suspect the latter is what got me into this predicament in the first place. Nobody's ever got the nerve to be cheeky to a prince, except you. The moment you first called me a prick, my fate was sealed. O, fathers of my bloodline! O, ye kings of olde! Take this crown from me, bury me in my ancestral soil. If only you had known the mighty work of thine loins would be undone by a gay heir who likes it when American boys with chin dimples are mean to him.

Actually, remember those gay kings I mentioned? I feel that James I, who fell madly in love with a very fit and exceptionally dim knight at a tilting match and immediately made him a gentleman of the bedchamber (a real title), would take mercy upon my particular plight.

I'll be damned but I miss you.

x
Henry

Re: You are a dark sorcerer

A <agcd@eclare45.com>   6/8/20 5:02 PM
to Henry

H,

Are you implying that you're James I and I'm some hot,
dumb jock? I'm more than fantastic bone structure and an
ass you can bounce a quarter on, Henry!!!!

Don't apologize for calling me pretty. Because then you're
putting me in a position where I have to apologize for saying
you blew my fucking mind in LA and I'm gonna die if it
doesn't happen again soon. How's that for lack of restraint,
huh? You really wanna play that game with me?

Listen: I'll fly to London right now and pull you out of
whatever pointless meeting you're in and make you admit
how much you love it when I call you "baby." I'll take you
apart with my teeth, sweetheart.

xoxo
A

Re: You are a dark sorcerer

 Henry <hwales@kensingtonemail.com>   6/8/20 7:21 PM
to A

Alex,

You know, when you go to Oxford to get a degree in English literature, as I have, people always want to know who your favorite English author is.

The press team compiled a list of acceptable answers. They wanted a realist, so I suggested George Eliot— no, Eliot was actually Mary Anne Evans under a pen name, not a strong male author. They wanted one of the inventors of the English novel, so I suggested Daniel Defoe—no, he was a dissenter from the Church of England. At one point, I threw out Jonathan Swift just to watch the collective coronary they had at the thought of an Irish political satirist.

In the end they picked Dickens, which is hilarious. They wanted something less fruity than the truth, but truly, what is gayer than a woman who languishes away in a crumbling mansion wearing her wedding gown every day of her life, for the drama?

The fruity truth: My favorite English author is Jane Austen.

So, to borrow a passage from *Sense and Sensibility*: "You want nothing but patience—or give it a more fascinating

name, call it hope." To paraphrase: I hope to see you
put your green American money where your filthy mouth is
soon.

Yours in sexual frustration,
Henry

Alex feels like somebody has probably warned him about private email servers before, but he's a little fuzzy on the details.
It doesn't feel important.

At first, like most things that require time when instant
gratification is possible, he doesn't see the point of Henry's
emails.

But when Richards tells Sean Hannity that his mother
hasn't accomplished anything as president, Alex screams into
his elbow and goes back to: The way you speak sometimes
is like sugar spilling out of a bag with a hole in the bottom.
When WASPy Hunter brings up the Harvard rowing team
for the fifth time in one workday: Your arse in those trousers
is a crime. When he's tired of being touched by strangers:
Come back to me when you're done being flung through
the firmament, you lost Pleiad.

Now he gets it.

His dad wasn't wrong about how ugly things would get
with Richards leading the ticket. Utah ugly, Christian ugly,
ugliness couched in dog whistles and toothy white smiles.
Right-wing think pieces about entitlement thrown in his
and June's direction, reeking of: *Mexicans stole the First Family
jobs too.*

He can't allow the fear of losing in. He drinks coffee and

brings his policy work on the campaign trail and drinks more coffee, reads emails from Henry, and drinks even more coffee.

The first DC Pride since his "bisexual awakening" happens while Alex is in Nevada, and he spends the day jealously checking Twitter—confetti raining down on the Mall, grand marshal Rafael Luna with a rainbow bandana around his head. He goes back to his hotel and talks to his minibar about it.

The biggest bright spot in all the chaos is that his lobbying with one of the campaign chairs (and his own mother) has finally paid off: They're doing a massive rally at Minute Maid Park in Houston. Polls are shifting in directions they've never seen before. Politico's top story of the week: IS 2020 THE YEAR TEXAS BECOMES A TRUE BATTLEGROUND STATE?

"Yes, I will make sure everyone knows the Houston rally was your idea," his mother says, barely paying attention, as she goes over her speech on the plane to Texas.

"You should say 'grit,' not 'fortitude' there," June says, reading the speech over her shoulder. "Texans like grit."

"Can y'all both go sit somewhere else?" she says, but she adds a note.

Alex knows a lot of the campaign is skeptical, even when they've seen the numbers. So when they pull up to Minute Maid and the line wraps around the block twice, he feels beyond gratified. He feels *smug*. His mom gets up to make her speech to thousands, and Alex thinks, *Hell yeah, Texas. Prove the bastards wrong.*

He's still riding the high when he swipes his badge at the door of the campaign office the following Monday. He's been getting tired of sitting at a desk and going through focus groups again and again and again, but he's ready to pick the fight back up.

The fact that he rounds the corner into his cubicle to find WASPy Hunter holding the Texas Binder brings him right the fuck back down.

"Oh, you left this on your desk," WASPy Hunter says casually. "I thought maybe it was a new project they were putting us on."

"Do I go on *your* side of the cubicle and turn off your Dropkick Murphys Spotify station, no matter how much I want to?" Alex demands. "No, *Hunter,* I don't."

"Well, you do kind of steal my pencils a lot—"

Alex snatches the binder away before he can finish. "It's private."

"What is it?" WASPy Hunter asks as Alex shoves it back into his bag. He can't believe he left it out. "All that data, and the district lines—what are you doing with all that?"

"Nothing."

"Is it about the Houston rally you pushed for?"

"Houston was a good idea," he says, instantly defensive.

"Dude . . . you don't honestly think Texas can go blue, do you? It's one of the most backward states in the country."

"You're from *Boston,* Hunter. You really want to talk about all the places bigotry comes from?"

"Look, man, I'm just saying."

"You know what?" Alex says. "You think y'all are off the hook for institutional bigotry because you come from a blue state. Not every white supremacist is a meth-head in Bumfuck, Mississippi—there are *plenty* of them at Duke or UPenn on Daddy's money."

WASPy Hunter looks startled but not convinced. "None

of that changes that red states have been red forever," he says, laughing, like it's something to joke about, "and none of those populations seem to care enough about what's good for them to vote."

"Maybe *those populations* might be more motivated to vote if we made an actual effort to campaign to them and showed them that we care, and how our platform is designed to help them, not leave them behind," Alex says hotly. "Imagine if nobody who claims to have your interests at heart ever came to your state and tried to talk to you, man. Or if you were a felon, or—fucking voter ID laws, people who can't access polls, who can't leave work to get to one?"

"Yeah, I mean, it'd be great if we could magically mobilize every eligible marginalized voter in red states, but political campaigns have a finite amount of time and resources, and we have to prioritize based on projections," WASPy Hunter says, as if Alex, the First Son of the United States, is unfamiliar with how campaigns work. "There just aren't the same number of bigots in blue states. If they don't want to be left behind, maybe people in red states should do something about it."

And Alex has, quite frankly, had it.

"Did you forget that you're working on the campaign of someone Texas fucking created?" he says, and his voice has officially risen to the point where staffers in the neighboring cubicles are staring, but he doesn't care. "Why don't we talk about how there's a chapter of the Klan in every state? You think there aren't racists and homophobes growing up in Vermont? Man, I appreciate that you're doing the work here, but you're not special. You don't get to sit up here and pretend like it's someone else's problem. None of us do."

He takes his bag and his binder and storms out.

The minute he's outside the building, he pulls out his phone on impulse, opens up Google. There are test dates this month. He knows there are.

LSAT washington dc area test center, he types.

3 Geniuses and Alex

June 23, 2020, 12:34 PM

juniper

BUG
Not my name, not anyone's name,
stop

leading member of korean pop
band bts kim nam-june

BUG
I'm blocking your number

HRH Prince Dickhead 💩
Alex, please don't tell me Pez has
indoctrinated you with K-pop.

well you let nora get you into
drag race so

irl chaos demon
[latrice royale eat it.gif]

BUG

What did you want Alex????

> where's my speech for
> milwaukee? i know you took it

HRH Prince Dickhead 💩

Must you have this conversation in
the group chat?

BUG

Part of it needed to be rewritten!!! I
put it back with edits in the outside
pocket of your messenger bag

> davis is gonna kill you if you
> keep doing this

BUG

Davis saw how well my tweaks to
the talking points went over on Seth
Meyers last week so he knows
better

> why is there a rock in here too

BUG

That is a clear quartz crystal for
clarity and good vibes do not @ me.
We need all the help we can get
right now

> stop putting SPELLS on my
> STUFF

irl chaos demon
BURN THE WITCH

irl chaos demon
hey what do we think of this #look
for the college voter thing tomorrow

irl chaos demon
[Attached Image]

irl chaos demon
i'm going for, like, depressed
lesbian poet who met a hot yoga
instructor at a speakeasy who got
her super into meditation and
pottery, and now she's starting a
new life as a high-powered
businesswoman selling her own line
of hand-thrown fruit bowls

> . . .

HRH Prince Dickhead 💩
Bitch, you took me there.

> alskdjfadslfjad

> NORA YOU BROKE HIM

irl chaos demon

lmaoooooo

The invitation comes certified airmail straight from Buckingham Palace. Gilded edges, spindly calligraphy: THE CHAIRMAN AND COMMITTEE OF MANAGEMENT OF THE CHAMPIONSHIPS REQUEST THE PLEASURE OF THE COMPANY OF ALEXANDER CLAREMONT-DIAZ IN THE ROYAL BOX ON THE 6TH OF JULY, 2020.

Alex takes a picture and texts it to Henry.

1. tf is this? aren't there poor people in your country?

2. i've already been in the royal box

Henry sends back, You are a delinquent and a plague, and then, Please come?

And here Alex is, spending his one day off from the campaign at Wimbledon, only to get his body next to Henry's again.

"So, as I've warned you," Henry says as they approach the doors to the Royal Box, "Philip will be here. And assorted other nobility with whom you may have to make conversation. People named Basil."

"I think I've proven that I can handle royals."

Henry looks doubtful. "You're brave. I could use some of that."

The sun is, for once, bright over London when they step outside, flooding the stands around them, which have already mostly filled with spectators. He notices David Beckham in a well-tailored suit—once again, how had he convinced himself he was straight?—before David Beckham turns away and Alex sees it was Bea he was talking to, her face bright when she spots them.

"Oi, Alex! Henry!" she chirps over the murmur of the Box. She's a vision in a lime-green, drop-waist silk dress, a pair of huge, round Gucci sunglasses embellished with gold honeybees perched on her nose.

"You look gorgeous," Alex says, accepting a kiss on his cheek.

"Why *thank* you, darling," Bea says. She takes one of their arms in each of hers and whisks them off down the steps. "Your sister helped me pick the dress, actually. It's McQueen. She's a genius, did you know?"

"I've been made aware."

"Here we are," Bea says when they've reached the front row. "These are ours."

Henry looks at the lush green cushions of the seats topped with thick and shiny *WIMBLEDON 2020* programs, right at the front edge of the box.

"Front and center?" he says with a note of nervousness. "Really?"

"Yes, Henry, in case you have forgotten, you are a royal and this is the Royal Box." She waves down to the photographers below, who are already snapping photos of them, before leaning into them and whispering, "Don't worry, I don't think they can detect the thick air of horn-town betwixt you two from the lawn."

"Ha-ha, Bea," Henry monotones, ears pink, and despite his apprehension, he takes his seat between Alex and Bea. He keeps his elbows carefully tucked into his sides and out of Alex's space.

It's halfway through the day when Philip and Martha arrive, Philip looking as generically handsome as ever. Alex wonders how such rich genetics conspired to make Bea and Henry both so interesting to look at, all mischievous smiles and swooping cheekbones, but punted so hard on Philip. He looks like a stock photo.

"Morning," Philip says as he takes his reserved seat to the side of Bea. His eyes track over Alex twice, and Alex can sense skepticism as to why Alex was even allowed. Maybe it's weird Alex is here. He doesn't care. Martha's looking at him weird too, but maybe she's simply holding a grudge about her wedding cake.

"Afternoon, Pip," Bea says politely. "Martha."

Beside him, Henry's spine stiffens.

"Henry," Philip says. Henry's hand is tense on the program in his lap. "Good to see you, mate. Been a bit busy, have you? Gap year and all that?"

There's an implication under his tone. *Where exactly have you been? What exactly have you been doing?* A muscle flexes in Henry's jaw.

"Yes," Henry says. "Loads of work with Percy. It's been mad."

"Right, the Okonjo Foundation, isn't it?" he says. "Shame he couldn't make it today. Suppose we'll have to make do with our American friend, then?"

At that, he tips a dry smile at Alex.

"Yep," Alex says, too loud. He grins broadly.

"Though, I do suppose Percy would look a bit out of place in the Box, wouldn't he?"

"*Philip,*" Bea says.

"Oh, don't be so dramatic, Bea," Philip says dismissively. "I only mean he's a peculiar sort, isn't he? Those frocks he wears? A bit much for Wimbledon."

Henry's face is calm and genial, but one of his knees has shifted over to dig into Alex's. "They're called dashikis, Philip, and he wore one *once.*"

"Right," Philip says. "You know I don't judge. I just think, you know, remember when we were younger and you'd spend time with my mates from uni? Or Lady Agatha's son, the one that's always quail hunting? You could consider more mates of . . . similar standing."

Henry's mouth is a thin line, but he says nothing.

"We can't all be best mates with the Count of Monpezat like you, Philip," Bea mutters.

"In any event," Philip presses on, ignoring her, "you're unlikely to find a wife unless you're running in the right circles, aren't you?" He chuckles a little and returns to watching the match.

"If you'll excuse me," Henry says. He drops his program in his seat and vanishes.

Ten minutes later, Alex finds him in the clubhouse by a gigantic vase of lurid fuschia flowers. His eyes are intent on Alex the moment he sees him, his lip chewed the same furious red as the embroidered Union Jack on his pocket square.

"Hello, Alex," he says placidly.

Alex takes his tone. "Hi."

"Has anyone shown you round the clubhouse yet?"

"Nope."

"Well, then."

Henry touches two fingers to the back of his elbow, and Alex obeys immediately.

Down a flight of stairs, through a concealed side door and a second hidden corridor, there is a small room full of chairs and tablecloths and one old, abandoned tennis racquet. As soon as the door is closed behind them, Henry slams him up against it.

He gets right up in Alex's space, but he doesn't kiss him. He hovers there, a breath away, his hands at Alex's hips and his mouth split open in a crooked smirk.

"D'you know what I want?" he says, his voice so low and hot that it burns right through Alex's solar plexus, right into the core of him.

"What?"

"I want," he says, "to do the absolute last thing I'm supposed to be doing right now."

Alex juts out his chin, grinningly defiant. "Then tell me to do it, sweetheart."

And Henry, tonguing the corner of his own mouth, tugs hard to undo Alex's belt and says, "Fuck me."

"Well," Alex grunts, "when at Wimbledon."

Henry laughs hoarsely and leans down to kiss him, open-mouthed and eager. He's moving fast, knowing they're on borrowed time, quick to follow the lead when Alex groans and pulls at his shoulders to change their positions. He gets Henry's back to his chest, Henry's palms braced against the door.

"Just so we're clear," Alex says, "I'm about to have sex with you in this storage closet to spite your family. Like, that's what's happening?"

Henry, who has apparently been carrying his travel-size lube with him this entire time in his jacket, says, "Right," and tosses it over his shoulder.

"Awesome, fuckin' love doing things out of spite," he says without a hint of sarcasm, and he kicks Henry's feet apart.

And it should be—it should be funny. It should be hot, stupid, ridiculous, obscene, another wild sexual adventure to add to the list. And it is, but . . . it shouldn't also feel like last time, like Alex might die if it ever stops. There's a laugh in his mouth, but it won't get past his tongue, because he knows this is him helping Henry get through something. Rebellion.

You're brave. I could use some of that.

After, he kisses Henry's mouth fiercely, pushes his fingers deep into Henry's hair, sucks the air out of him. Henry smiles breathlessly against his neck, looking extremely pleased with himself, and says, "I'm rather finished with tennis, aren't you?"

So, they steal away behind a crowd, blocked by PPOs and umbrellas, and back at Kensington, Henry brings Alex up to his rooms.

His "apartment" is a sprawling warren of twenty-two rooms on the northwest side of the palace closest to the Orangery. He splits it with Bea, but there's not much of either of them in any of the high ceilings and heavy, jacquard furniture. What is there is more Bea than Henry: a leather jacket flung over the back of a chaise, Mr. Wobbles preening in a corner, a seventeenth-century Dutch oil painting on one landing literally called *Woman at her Toilet* that only Bea would have selected from the royal collection.

Henry's bedroom is as cavernous and opulent and insufferably beige as Alex could have imagined, with a gilded baroque bed and windows overlooking the gardens. He watches Henry shrug out of his suit and imagines having to live in it, wondering if Henry simply isn't allowed to choose what his rooms look like or if he never wanted to ask for something different. All those nights Henry can't sleep, just knocking around these endless, impersonal rooms, like a bird trapped in a museum.

The only room that really feels like both Henry and Bea is a small parlor on the second floor converted into a music studio. The colors are richest here: hand-woven Turkish rugs in deep reds and violets, a tobacco-colored settee. Little poufs and tables of knickknacks spring up like mushrooms, and the walls are lined with Stratocasters and Flying Vs, violins, an assortment of harps, one stout cello propped up in the corner.

In the center of the room is the grand piano, and Henry sits down at it and plucks away idly, toying with the melody of something that sounds like an old song by The Killers. David the beagle naps quietly near the pedals.

"Play something I don't know," Alex says.

Back in high school in Texas, Alex was the most cultured of the jock crowd because he was a book nerd, a politics junkie, the only varsity letterman debating the finer points of Dred Scott in AP US History. He listens to Nina Simone and Otis Redding, likes expensive whiskey. But Henry's got an entirely different compendium of knowledge.

So he just listens and nods and smiles a little while Henry explains that *this* is what Brahms sounds like, and *this* is Wagner, and how they were on the two opposing sides of the Romantic movement. "Do you hear the difference there?" His hands are fast, almost effortless, even as he goes off into a tangent about the War of the Romantics and how Liszt's daughter left her husband for Wagner, *quel scandale*.

He switches to an Alexander Scriabin sonata, winking over at Alex at the composer's first name. The andante—the third movement—is his favorite, he explains, because he read once that it was written to evoke the image of a castle in ruins, which he found darkly funny at the time. He goes quiet, focused, lost in the piece for long minutes. Then, without warning, it changes again, turbulent chords circling back into something familiar—the Elton John songbook. Henry closes his eyes, playing from memory. It's "Your Song." *Oh.*

And Alex's heart doesn't spread itself out in his chest, and he doesn't have to grip the edge of the settee to steady himself. Because that's what he would do if he were here in this palace to fall in love with Henry, and not just continuing this thing where they fly across the world to touch each other and don't talk about it. That's not why he's here. It's not.

They make out lazily for what could be hours on the settee— Alex wants to do it on the piano, but it's a priceless antique or whatever—and then they stagger up to Henry's room, the palatial bed. Henry lets Alex take him apart with painstaking patience and precision, moans the name of God so many times that the room feels consecrated.

It pushes Henry over some kind of edge, melted and overwhelmed on the lush bedclothes. Alex spends nearly an hour afterward coaxing little tremors out of him, in awe of his elaborate expressions of wonder and blissful agony, ghosting featherlight fingertips over his collarbone, his ankles, the insides of his knees, the small bones of the backs of his hands, the dip of his lower lip. He touches and touches until he brings Henry to another brink with only his fingertips, only his breath on the inside of his thighs, the promise of Alex's mouth where he'd pressed his fingers before.

Henry says the same two words from the secret room at Wimbledon, this time dressed up in, "Please, I need you to." He still can't believe Henry can talk like this, that he gets to be the only one who hears it.

So he does.

When they come back down, Henry practically passes out on his chest without another word, fucked-out and boneless, and Alex laughs to himself and pets his sweaty hair and listens to the soft snores that come almost immediately.

It takes him hours to fall asleep, though.

Henry drools on him. David finds his way onto the bed and

curls up at their feet. Alex has to be back on a plane for DNC prep in a matter of hours, but he can't sleep. It's jet lag. It's just jet lag.

He remembers, as if from a million miles away, telling Henry once not to overthink this.

"As your president," Jeffrey Richards is saying on one of the flat screens in the campaign office, "one of my many priorities will be encouraging young people to get involved with their government. If we're going to hold our control of the Senate and take back the House, we need the next generation to stand up and join the fight."

The College Republicans of Vanderbilt University cheer on the live feed, and Alex pretends to barf onto his latest policy draft.

"Why don't you come up here, Brittany?" A pretty blond student joins Richards at the podium, and he puts an arm around her. "Brittany here was the main organizer we worked with for this event, and she couldn't have done a better job getting us this amazing turnout!"

More cheers. A mid-level staffer lobs a ball of paper at the screen.

"It's young people like Brittany who give us hope for the future of our party. Which is why I'm pleased to announce that, as president, I'll be launching the Richards Youth Congress program. Other politicians don't want people—especially discerning young people like you—to get up close in our offices and see just how the sausage gets made—"

i want to see a cage match between your grandmother and this fucking ghoul running against my mom, Alex texts Henry as he turns back to his cubicle.

It's the last days before the DNC, and he hasn't been able to catch the coffeepot before it's empty in a week. The policy inboxes are overflowing since they released the official platform two days ago, and WASPy Hunter has been firing off emails like his life depends on it. He hasn't said anything else to Alex about his rant from last month, but he has started wearing headphones to spare Alex his musical choices.

He types out another text, this one to Luna: can you please go on anderson cooper or something and explain that paragraph you ghostwrote on tax law for the platform so people will stop asking? ain't got the time, vato.

He's been texting Luna all week, ever since the Richards campaign leaked that they've tapped an Independent senator for his prospective cabinet. That old bastard Stanley Connor flat-out denied every last request for an endorsement—by the end, Luna privately told Alex they were lucky Connor didn't try to primary them. Nothing's official, but everyone knows Connor is the one joining Richards's ticket. But if Luna knows when the announcement's coming, he's not sharing.

It's a *week*. The polls aren't great, Paul Ryan is getting sanctimonious about the Second Amendment, and there's some *Salon* hot take going around, WOULD ELLEN CLAREMONT HAVE GOTTEN ELECTED IF SHE WEREN'T CONVENTIONALLY BEAUTIFUL? If it weren't for her morning meditation sessions, Alex is sure his mom would have throttled an aide by now.

For his part, he misses Henry's bed, Henry's body, Henry and a place a few thousand miles removed from the factory line of the campaign. That night after Wimbledon from a week ago feels like something out of a dream now, all the more tantalizing because Henry is in New York for a few days with Pez to do paperwork for an LGBT youth shelter in Brooklyn. There aren't enough hours in the day for Alex to find a pretense to get there, and no matter how much the world enjoys their public friendship, they're running out of plausible excuses to be seen together.

This time is nothing like their first breathless trip to the DNC in 2016. His dad had been the delegate to cast the votes from California that put her over, and they all cried. Alex and June introduced their mother before her acceptance speech, and June's hands were shaking but his were steady. The crowd roared, and Alex's heart roared back.

This year, they're all frizzy-haired and exhausted from trying to run the country and a campaign simultaneously, and even one day of the DNC is a stretch. On the second night of the convention, they pile onto Air Force One to New York—it'd be Marine One, but they won't all fit in one helicopter.

"Have you run a cost-benefit analysis on this?" Zahra is saying into her phone as they take off. "Because you know I'm right, and these assets can be transferred at any time if you disagree. Yes. Yeah, I know. Okay. That's what I thought." A long pause, then, under her breath, "Love you too."

"Um," Alex says when she's hung up. "Something you'd like to share with the class?"

Zahra doesn't even look up from her phone. "Yes, that was my boyfriend, and no, you may not ask me any further questions about him."

June has shut her journal in sudden interest. "How could you possibly have a boyfriend we don't know about?"

"I see you more than I see clean underwear," Alex says.

"You're not changing your underwear often enough, sugar," his mother interjects from across the cabin.

"I go commando a lot," Alex says dismissively. "Is this like a 'my Canadian girlfriend' thing? Does he"—he does very animated air quotes—"'go to a different school'?"

"You really are determined to get shoved out of an emergency hatch one day, huh?" she says. "It's long distance. But not like that. No more questions."

Cash jumps in too, insisting he deserves to know as the resident love guru of the staff, and there's a debate about appropriate information to share with your coworkers, which is laughable considering how much Cash already knows about Alex's personal life. They're circling New York when June suddenly stops talking, focused again on Zahra, who has gone silent.

"Zahra?"

Alex turns and sees Zahra sitting perfectly still, such a departure from her usual constant motion that everyone else freezes too. She's staring at her phone, mouth open.

"Zahra," his mother echoes now, deadly serious. "What?"

She looks up finally, her grip on her phone tight. "The *Post* just broke the name of the Independent senator joining Richards's cabinet," she says. "It's not Stanley Connor. It's Rafael Luna."

"No," June is saying. Her heels are dangling from her hand, her eyes bright in the warm light near the hotel elevator where they've agreed to meet. Her hair is coming out of its braid in angry spikes. "You're damn lucky I agreed to talk to you in the first place, so you get this or you get nothing."

The *Post* reporter blinks, fingers faltering on his recorder. He's been hounding June on her personal phone since the minute they landed in New York for a quote about the convention, and now he's demanding something about Luna. June is not typically an angry person, but it's been a long day, and she looks about three seconds from using one of those heels to stab the guy through the eye socket.

"What about you?" the guy asks Alex.

"If she's not giving it to you, I'm not giving it to you," Alex says. "She's much nicer than me."

June snaps her fingers in front of the guy's hipster glasses, eyes blazing. "You don't get to speak to him," June says. "Here is my quote: My mother, the president, still fully intends to win this race. We're here to support her and to encourage the party to stay united behind her."

"But about Senator Luna—"

"Thank you. Vote Claremont," June says tightly, slapping her hand over Alex's mouth. She sweeps him off and into the waiting elevator, elbowing him when he licks her palm.

"That goddamn fucking *traitor*," Alex says when they reach their floor. "Duplicitous fucking *bastard*! I—I fucking helped him get elected. I canvassed for him for twenty-seven hours straight. I went to his sister's wedding. I memorized his goddamn *Five Guys order*!"

"I fucking know, Alex," June says, shoving her keycard into the slot.

"How did that Vampire Weekend–looking little shit even have your personal number?"

June throws her shoes at the bed, and they bounce off onto the floor in different directions. "Because I slept with him last year, Alex, how do you think? You're not the only one who makes stupid sexual decisions when you're stressed out." She drops onto the bed and starts taking off her earrings. "I just don't understand what the point is. Like, what is Luna's endgame here? Is he some kind of fucking sleeper agent sent from the future to give me an ulcer?"

It's late—they got into New York after nine, hurtling into crisis management meetings for hours. Alex still feels wired, but when June looks up at him, he can see some of the brightness in her eyes has started to look like frustrated tears, and he softens a little.

"If I had to guess, Luna thinks we're going to lose," he tells her quietly, "and he thinks he can help push Richards farther left by joining the ticket. Like, putting the fire out from inside the house."

June looks at him, eyes tired, searching his face. She may be the oldest, but politics is Alex's game, not hers. He knows he would have chosen this life for himself given the option; he knows she wouldn't have.

"I think . . . I need to sleep. For, like, the next year. At least. Wake me up after the general."

"Okay, Bug," Alex says. He leans down to kiss the top of her head. "I can do that."

"Thanks, baby bro."

"Don't call me that."

"Tiny, miniature, itty-bitty, baby brother."

"Fuck off."

"Go to bed."

Cash is waiting for him out in the hallway, his suit abandoned for plainclothes.

"Hanging in there?" he asks Alex.

"I mean, I kind of have to."

Cash pats him on the shoulder with one gigantic hand. "There's a bar downstairs."

Alex considers. "Yeah, okay."

The Beekman is thankfully quiet this late, and the bar is low-lit with warm, rich shades of gold on the walls and deep-green leather on the high-backed barstools. Alex orders a whiskey neat.

He looks at his phone, swallowing down his frustration with the whiskey. He texted Luna three hours ago, a succinct: what the fuck? An hour ago, he got back: I don't expect you to understand.

He wants to call Henry. He guesses it makes sense—they've always been fixed points in each other's worlds, little magnetic poles. Some laws of physics would be reassuring right now.

God, whiskey makes him maudlin. He orders another.

He's contemplating texting Henry, even though he's probably somewhere over the Atlantic, when a voice curls around his ear, smooth and warm. He's sure he must be imagining it.

"I'll have a gin and tonic, thanks," it says, and there's Henry in the flesh, sidled up next to him at the bar, looking a little tousled in a soft gray button-down and jeans. Alex wonders for an insane second if his brain has conjured up some kind of stress-induced sex mirage, when Henry says, voice lowered, "You looked rather tragic drinking alone."

Definitely the real Henry, then. "You're—what are you doing here?"

"You know, as a figurehead of one of the most powerful countries in the world, I do manage to keep abreast on international politics."

Alex raises an eyebrow.

Henry inclines his head, sheepish. "I sent Pez home without me because I was worried."

"There it is," Alex says with a wink. He goes for his drink to hide what he suspects is a small, sad smile; the ice clacks against his teeth. "Speak not the bastard's name."

"Cheers," Henry says as the bartender returns with his drink.

Henry takes the first sip, sucking lime juice off his thumb, and fuck, he looks *good*. There's color in his cheeks and lips, the glow of Brooklyn summertime warmth that his English blood isn't accustomed to. He looks like something soft and downy Alex wants to sink into, and he realizes the knot of anxiety in his chest has finally slackened.

It's rare anyone other than June goes out of their way to check on him. It's by his own design, mostly, a barricade of charm and fitful monologues and hard-headed independence. Henry looks at him like he's not fooled by any of it.

"Get moving on that drink, Wales," Alex says. "I've got a king-size bed upstairs that's calling my name." He shifts on his stool, letting one of his knees graze against Henry's under the bar, nudging them apart.

Henry squints at him. "Bossy."

They sit there until Henry finishes his drink, Alex listening to the placating murmur of Henry talking about different brands of gin, thankful that for once Henry seems happy to carry the conversation alone. He closes his eyes, wills the disaster of the day away, and tries to forget. He remembers Henry's words in the garden months ago: "D'you ever wonder what it's like to be some anonymous person out in the world?"

If he's some anonymous, normal person, removed from history, he's twenty-two and he's tipsy and he's pulling a guy into his hotel room by the belt loop. He's pulling a lip between his teeth, and he's fumbling behind his back to switch on a lamp, and he's thinking, *I like this person.*

They break apart, and when Alex opens his eyes, Henry is watching him.

"Are you sure you don't want to talk about it?"

Alex groans.

The thing is, he *does,* and Henry knows this too.

"It's . . ." Alex starts. He paces backward, hands on his hips. "He was supposed to be me in twenty years, you know? I was fifteen the first time I met him, and I was . . . in awe. He was everything I wanted to be. And he cared about people, and about doing the work because it was the right thing to do, because we were making people's lives better."

In the low light of the single lamp, Alex turns and sits down on the edge of the bed.

"I've never been more sure that I wanted to go into politics than when I went to Denver. I saw this young, queer guy who looked like me, sleeping at his desk because he wants kids at public schools in his state to have free lunches, and I was like, I could do this. I honestly don't know if I'm good enough or smart enough to ever be either of my parents. But I could be *that.*" He drops his head down. He's never said the last part out loud to anyone before. "And now I'm sitting here thinking, that son of a bitch sold out, so maybe it's all bullshit, and maybe I really am just a naive kid who believes in magical shit that doesn't happen in real life."

Henry comes to stand in front of Alex, his thigh brushing against the inside of Alex's knee, and he reaches one hand down to still Alex's nervous fidgeting.

"Someone else's choice doesn't change who you are."

"I feel like it does," Alex tells him. "I wanted to believe in some people being good and doing this job because they want to do good. Doing the right things most of the time and most things for the right reasons. I wanted to be the kind of person who believes in that."

Henry's hands move, brushing up to Alex's shoulders, the dip of his throat, the underside of his jaw, and when Alex finally looks up, Henry's eyes are soft and steady. "You still are. Because you still bloody care so much." He leans down and presses a kiss into Alex's hair. "And you are good. Most things are awful most of the time, but you're good."

Alex takes a breath. There's this way Henry has of listening to the erratic stream of consciousness that pours out of Alex's mouth and answering with the clearest, crystallized truth that Alex has been trying to arrive at all along. If Alex's head is a storm, Henry is the place lightning hits ground. He wants it to be true.

He lets Henry push him backward on the bed and kiss him until his mind is blissfully blank, lets Henry undress him carefully. He pushes into Henry and feels the tight cords of his shoulders start to release, like how Henry describes unfurling a sail.

Henry kisses his mouth over and over again and says quietly, "You are good."

The pounding on his door comes much too early for Alex to handle loud noises. There's a sharpness to it he recognizes instantly as Zahra before she even speaks, and he wonders why the hell she didn't just call before he reaches for his phone and finds it dead. Shit. That would explain the missed alarm.

"Alex Claremont-Diaz, it is almost seven," Zahra shouts through the door. "You have a strategy meeting in fifteen minutes and I have a key, so I don't care how naked you are, if you don't answer this door in the next thirty seconds, I'm coming in."

He is, he realizes as he rubs his eyes, extremely naked. A cursory examination of the body pressed up against his back: Henry, very comprehensively naked as well.

"Oh fuck me," Alex swears, sitting up so fast he gets tangled in the sheet and flails sideways out of bed.

"Blurgh," Henry groans.

"Fucking shit," says Alex, whose vocabulary is apparently now only expletives. He yanks himself free and scrambles for his chinos. "Goddammit ass fucker."

"What," Henry says flatly to the ceiling.

"I can hear you in there, Alex, I swear to God—"

There's another sound from the door, like Zahra has kicked it, and Henry flies out of bed too. He is truly a picture, wearing an expression of bewildered panic and absolutely nothing else. He eyes the curtains furtively, as if considering hiding in them.

"Jesus tits," Alex continues as he fumbles to pull his pants up. He snatches a shirt and boxers at random from the floor, shoves them at Henry's chest, and points him toward the closet. "Get in there."

"Quite," he observes.

"Yes, we can unpack the ironic symbolism later. *Go,*" Alex says, and Henry does, and when the door swings open, Zahra is standing there with her thermos and a look on her face that says she did not get a master's degree to babysit a fully grown adult who happens to be related to the president.

"Uh, morning," he says.

Zahra's eyes do a quick sweep of the room—the sheets on the floor, the two pillows that have been slept on, the two phones on the nightstand.

"Who is she?" she demands, marching over to the bathroom

and yanking open the door like she's going to find some Hollywood starlet in the bathtub. "You let her bring a *phone* in here?"

"Nobody, Jesus," Alex says, but his voice cracks in the middle. Zahra arches an eyebrow. "What? I got kinda drunk last night, that's all. It's chill."

"Yes, it is so very, very chill that you're going to be hungover for today," Zahra says, rounding on him.

"I'm fine," he says. "It's fine."

As if on cue, there's a series of bumps from the other side of the closet door, and Henry, halfway into Alex's boxers, comes literally tumbling out of the closet.

It is, Alex thinks half-hysterically, a very solid visual pun.

"Er," Henry says from the floor. He finishes pulling Alex's boxers up his hips. Blinks. "Hello."

The silence stretches.

"I—" Zahra begins. "Do I even want you to explain to me what the fuck is happening here? Literally how is he even *here,* like, physically or geographically, and *why*—no, nope. Don't answer that. Don't tell me anything." She unscrews the top of her thermos and takes a pull of coffee. "Oh my God, did *I* do this? I never thought . . . when I set it up . . . oh my *God.*"

Henry has pulled himself off the floor and put on a shirt, and his ears are bright red. "I think, perhaps, if it helps. It was. Er. Rather inevitable. At least for me. So you shouldn't blame yourself."

Alex looks at him, trying to think of something to add, when Zahra jabs a manicured finger into his shoulder.

"Well, I hope it was *fun,* because if anyone ever finds out about this, we're all fucked," Zahra says. She points at Henry.

"You too. Can I assume I don't have to make you sign an NDA?"

"I've already signed one for him," Alex offers up, while Henry's ears turn from red to an alarming shade of purple. Six hours ago, he was sinking drowsily into Henry's chest, and now he's standing here half-naked, talking about the paperwork. He fucking hates paperwork. "I think that covers it."

"Oh, wonderful," Zahra says. "I'm so glad you thought this through. Great. How long has this been happening?"

"Since, um. New Year's," Alex says.

"New Year's?" Zahra repeats, eyes wide. "This has been going on for *seven months?* That's why you—Oh my God, I thought you were getting into international relations or something."

"I mean, technically—"

"If you finish that sentence, I'm gonna spend tonight in jail." Alex winces. "Please don't tell Mom."

"Seriously?" she hisses. "You're literally putting your dick in *the leader of a foreign state,* who is a *man,* at *the biggest political event before the election,* in a hotel full of *reporters,* in a city full of *cameras,* in a race close enough to fucking *hinge* on some bullshit like this, like a manifestation of my fucking *stress dreams,* and you're asking me *not* to tell the president about it?"

"Um. Yeah? I haven't, um, come out to her. Yet."

Zahra blinks, presses her lips together, and makes a noise like she's being strangled. "Listen," she says. "We don't have time to deal with this, and your mother has enough to manage without having to process her son's fucking quarter-life NATO sexual crisis, so—I won't tell her. But once the convention is over, you have to."

"Okay," Alex says on an exhale.

"Would it make any difference at all if I told you not to see him again?"

Alex looks over at Henry, looking rumpled and nauseated and terrified at the corner of the bed. "No."

"God fucking dammit," she says, rubbing the heel of her hand against her forehead. "Every time I see you, it takes another year off my life. I'm going downstairs, and you better be dressed and there in five minutes so we can try to save this goddamn campaign. And *you*"—she rounds on Henry—"you need to get back to fucking England now, and if anyone sees you leave, I will personally end you. Ask me if I'm afraid of the crown."

"Duly noted," he says in a faint voice.

Zahra fixes him with a final glare, turns on her heel, and stalks out of the room, slamming the door behind her.

NINE

"Okay," he says.

His mother sits across the table, hands folded, looking at him expectantly. His palms are starting to sweat. The room is small, one of the lesser conference rooms in the West Wing. He knows he could have asked her to lunch or something, but, well, he kind of panicked.

He guesses he should just do it.

"I've been, um," he starts. "I've been figuring some stuff out about myself, lately. And . . . I wanted to let you know, because you're my mom, and I want you to be a part of my life, and I don't want to hide things from you. And also it's, um, relevant to the campaign, from an image perspective."

"Okay," Ellen says, her voice neutral.

"Okay," he repeats. "All right. Um. So, I've realized I'm not straight. I'm actually bisexual."

Her expression clears, and she laughs, unclasping her hands. "Oh, that's it, sugar? God, I was worried it was gonna be something worse!" She reaches across the table, covering his hand with hers. "That's great, baby. I'm so glad you told me."

Alex smiles back, the anxious bubble in his chest shrinking slightly, but there's one more bomb to drop. "Um. There's something else. I kind of . . . met somebody."

She tilts her head. "You did? Well, I'm happy for you, I hope you had them do all the paperwork—"

"It's, uh," he interrupts her. "It's Henry."

A beat. She frowns, her brow knitting together. "Henry . . . ?"

"Yeah, Henry."

"Henry, as in . . . the prince?"

"Yes."

"Of England?"

"Yes."

"So, not another Henry?"

"No, Mom. Prince Henry. Of Wales."

"I thought you hated him?" she says. "Or . . . now you're friends with him?"

"Both true at different points. But uh, now we're, like, a thing. Have been. A thing. For, like, seven-ish months? I guess?"

"I . . . see."

She stares at him for a very long minute. He shifts uncomfortably in his chair.

Suddenly, her phone is in her hand, and she's standing, kicking her chair under the table. "Okay, I'm clearing my schedule for the afternoon," she says. "I need, uh, time to prepare some materials. Are you free in an hour? We can reconvene here. I'll order food. Bring, uh, your passport and any receipts and relevant documents you have, sugar."

She doesn't wait to hear if he's free, just walks backward out of the room and disappears into the corridor. The door isn't even finished closing when a notification pops up on his phone. CALENDAR REQUEST FROM MOM: 2 P.M. WEST WING FIRST FLOOR, INTERNATIONAL ETHICS & SEXUAL IDENTITY DEBRIEF.

An hour later, there are several cartons of Chinese food and a PowerPoint cued up. The first slide says: SEXUAL EXPERIMENTATION WITH FOREIGN MONARCHS: A GRAY AREA. Alex wonders if it's too late to swan dive off the roof.

"Okay," she says when he sits down, in almost exactly the same tone he used on her earlier. "Before we start, I—I want to be clear, I love you and support you always. But this is, quite frankly, a logistical and ethical clusterfuck, so we need to make sure we have our ducks in a row. Okay?"

The next slide is titled: EXPLORING YOUR SEXUALITY: HEALTHY, BUT DOES IT HAVE TO BE WITH THE PRINCE OF ENGLAND? She apologizes for not having time to come up with better titles. Alex actively wishes for the sweet release of death.

The one after is: FEDERAL FUNDING, TRAVEL EXPENSES, BOOTY CALLS, AND YOU.

She's mostly concerned with making sure he hasn't used any federally funded private jets to see Henry for exclusively personal visits—he hasn't—and with making him fill out a bunch of paperwork to cover both their asses. It feels clinical and wrong, checking little boxes about his relationship, especially when half are asking things he hasn't even discussed with Henry yet.

It's agonizing, but eventually it's over, and he doesn't die, which is something. His mother takes the last form and seals it up in an envelope with the rest. She sets it aside and takes off her reading glasses, setting those aside too.

"So," she says. "Here's the thing. I know I put a lot on you. But I do it because I trust you. You're a dumbass, but I trust you, and I trust your judgment. I promised you years ago I would never tell you to be anything you're not. So I'm not gonna be the president or the mother who forbids you from seeing him."

She takes another breath, waiting for Alex to nod that he understands.

"But," she goes on, "this is a really, really big fucking deal. This is not just some person from class or some intern. You need to think really long and hard because you are putting yourself and your career and, above all, this campaign and this entire administration, in danger here. I know you're young, but this is a forever decision. Even if you don't stay with him forever, if people find out, that sticks with you forever. So you need to figure out if you feel forever about him. And if you don't, you need to cut it the fuck out."

She rests her hands on the table in front of her, and the silence hangs in the air between them. Alex feels like his heart is caught somewhere between his tonsils.

Forever. It seems like an impossibly huge word, something he's supposed to grow into ten years from now.

"Also," she says. "I am so sorry to do this, sugar. But you're off the campaign."

Alex snaps back into razor sharp reality, stomach plummeting.

"Wait, no—"

"This is not up for debate, Alex," she tells him, and she does look sorry, but he knows the set of her jaw too well. "I can't risk this. You're way too close to the sun. We're telling the press you're focusing on other career options. I'll have your desk cleaned out for you over the weekend."

She holds out one hand, and Alex looks down into her palm, the worried lines there, until the realization clicks.

He reaches into his pocket, pulls out his campaign badge. The first artifact of his entire career, a career he's managed to derail in a matter of months. And he hands it over.

"Oh, one last thing," she says, her tone suddenly business-like again, shuffling something from the bottom of her files. "I know Texas public schools don't have sex ed for shit, and we didn't go over this when we had the talk—which is on me for assuming—so I just wanted to make sure you know you still need to be using condoms even if you're having anal interc—"

"Okay, thanks, Mom!" Alex half yells, nearly knocking over his chair in his rush for the door.

"Wait, honey," she calls after him, "I had Planned Parenthood send over all these pamphlets, take one! They sent a bike messenger and everything!"

A mass of fools and knaves

 A <agcd@eclare45.com>   8/10/20 1:04 AM
to Henry

H,

Have you ever read any of Alexander Hamilton's letters to John Laurens?

What am I saying? Of course you haven't. You'd probably be disinherited for revolutionary sympathies.

Well, since I got the boot from the campaign, there is literally nothing for me to do but watch cable news (diligently chipping away at my brain cells by the day), reread Harry Potter, and sort through all my old shit from college. Just looking at papers, thinking: Excellent, yes, I'm so glad I stayed up all night writing this for a 98 in the class, only to get summarily fired from the first job I ever had and exiled to my bedroom! Great job, Alex!

Is this how you feel in the palace all the time? It fucking *sucks,* man.

So anyway, I'm going through my college stuff, and I find this analysis I did of Hamilton's wartime correspondence, and hear me out: I think Hamilton could have been bi. His letters to Laurens are almost as romantic as his letters to his wife. Half of them are signed "Yours" or "Affectionately yrs," and the last one before Laurens died is signed "Yrs for ever." I can't figure out why nobody talks about the possibility of a Founding Father being not straight (outside of Chernow's biography, which is great btw, see attached bibliography). I mean, I *know* why, but.

Anyway, I found this part of a letter he wrote to Laurens, and it made me think of you. And me, I guess:

The truth is I am an unlucky honest man, that speak my sentiments to all and with emphasis. I say this to you

because you know it and will not charge me with vanity.
I hate Congress—I hate the army—I hate the world—I hate
myself. The whole is a mass of fools and knaves; I could
almost except you . . .

Thinking about history makes me wonder how I'll fit into it
one day, I guess. And you too. I kinda wish people still wrote
like that.

History, huh? Bet we could make some.

Affectionately yrs, slowly going insane,
Alex, First Son of Founding Father Sacrilege

Re: A mass of fools and knaves

 Henry <hwales@kensingtonemail.com>   8/10/20 4:18 AM
to A

Alex, First Son of Masturbatory Historical Readings:

The phrase "see attached bibliography" is the single sexiest
thing you have ever written to me.

Every time you mention your slow decay inside the
White House, I can't help but feel it's my fault, and I
feel absolutely shit about it. I'm sorry. I should have
known better than to turn up at a thing like that. I got
carried away; I didn't think. I know how much that job meant
to you.

I just want to . . . you know. Extend the option. If you wanted less of me, and more of that—the work, the uncomplicated things—I would understand. Truly.

In any event . . . Believe it or not, I have actually done a bit of reading on Hamilton, for a number of reasons. First, he was a brilliant writer. Second, I knew you were named after him (the pair of you share an alarming number of traits, by the by: passionate determination, never knowing when to shut up, &c &c). And third, some saucy tart once tried to impugn my virtue against an oil painting of him, and in the halls of memory, some things demand context.

Are you angling for a revolutionary soldier role-play scenario? I must inform you, any trace of King George III blood I have would curdle in my very veins and render me useless to you.

Or are you suggesting you'd rather exchange passionate letters by candlelight?

Should I tell you that when we're apart, your body comes back to me in dreams? That when I sleep, I see you, the dip of your waist, the freckle above your hip, and when I wake up in the morning, it feels like I've just been with you, the phantom touch of your hand on the back of my neck fresh and not imagined? That I can feel your skin against mine, and it makes every bone in my body ache? That, for a few moments, I can hold my breath and be back there with you, in a dream, in a thousand rooms, nowhere at all?

I think perhaps Hamilton said it better in a letter to Eliza:

You engross my thoughts too intirely to allow me to think of any thing else—you not only employ my mind all day; but you intrude upon my sleep. I meet you in every dream—and when I wake I cannot close my eyes again for ruminating on your sweetness.

If you did decide to take the option mentioned at the start of this email, I do hope you haven't read the rest of this rubbish.

Regards,
Haplessly Romantic Heretic Prince Henry the Utterly Daft

Re: A mass of fools and knaves

 A <agcd@eclare45.com>   8/10/20 5:36 AM
to Henry

H,

Please don't be stupid. No part of any of this will ever be uncomplicated.

Anyway, you should be a writer. You are a writer.

Even after all this, I still always feel like I want to know more of you. Does that sound crazy? I just sit here and wonder, who is this person who knows stuff about Hamilton and writes like this? Where does someone like that even come from? How was I so wrong?

It's weird because I always know things about people, gut feelings that usually lead me in more or less the right direction. I do think I got a gut feeling with you, I just didn't have what I needed in my head to understand it. But I kind of kept chasing it anyway, like I was just going blindly in a certain direction and hoping for the best. I guess that makes you the North Star?

I wanna see you again and soon. I keep reading that one paragraph over and over again. You know which one. I want you back here with me. I want your body and I want the rest of you too. And I want to get the fuck out of this house. Watching June and Nora on TV doing appearances without me is torture.

We have this annual thing at my dad's lake house in Texas. Whole long weekend off the grid. There's a lake with a pier, and my dad always cooks something fucking amazing. You wanna come? I kind of can't stop thinking about you all sunburned and pretty sitting out there in the country. It's the weekend after next. If Shaan can talk to Zahra or somebody about flying you into Austin, we can pick you up from there. Say yes?

Yrs,
Alex

P.S. Allen Ginsberg to Peter Orlovsky—1958:

Tho I long for the actual sunlight contact between us I miss you like a home. Shine back honey & think of me.

Re: A mass of fools and knaves

Henry <hwales@kensingtonemail.com>   8/10/20 8:22 PM
to A

Alex,

If I'm north, I shudder to think where in God's name we're going.

I'm ruminating on identity and your question about where a person like me comes from, and as best as I can explain it, here's a story:

Once, there was a young prince who was born in a castle. His mother was a princess scholar, and his father was the most handsome, feared knight in all the land. As a boy, people would bring him everything he could ever dream of wanting. The most beautiful silk clothes, ripe fruit from the orangery. At times, he was so happy, he felt he would never grow tired of being a prince.

He came from a long, long line of princes, but never before had there been a prince quite like him: born with his heart on the outside of his body.

When he was small, his family would smile and laugh and say he would grow out of it one day. But as he grew, it stayed where it was, red and visible and alive. He didn't mind it very much, but every day, the family's fear grew that the people of the kingdom would soon notice and turn their backs on the prince.

His grandmother, the queen, lived in a high tower, where she spoke only of the other princes, past and present, who were born whole.

Then, the prince's father, the knight, was struck down in battle. The lance tore open his armor and his body and left him bleeding in the dust. And so, when the queen sent new clothes, armor for the prince to parcel his heart away safe, the prince's mother did not stop her. For she was afraid, now: afraid of her son's heart torn open too.

So the prince wore it, and for many years, he believed it was right.

Until he met the most devastatingly gorgeous peasant boy from a nearby village who said absolutely ghastly things to him that made him feel alive for the first time in years and who turned out to be the most mad sort of sorcerer, one who could conjure up things like gold and vodka shots and apricot tarts out of absolutely nothing, and the prince's whole life went up in a puff of dazzling purple smoke, and the kingdom said, "I can't believe we're all so surprised."

I'm in for the lake house. I must admit, I'm glad you're getting out of the house. I worry you may burn the thing down. Does this mean I'll be meeting your father?

I miss you.

x

Henry

P.S. This is mortifying and maudlin and, honestly, I hope you forget it as soon as you've read it.

P.P.S. From Henry James to Hendrik C. Andersen, 1899:

May the terrific U.S.A. be meanwhile not a brute to you. I feel in you a confidence, dear Boy—which to show is a joy to me. My hopes and desires and sympathies right heartily and most firmly, go with you. So keep up your heart, and tell me, as it shapes itself, your (inevitably, I imagine, more or less weird) American story. May, at any rate, tutta quella gente be good to you.

"Do *not*," Nora says, leaning over the passenger seat. "There is a system and you must respect the system."

"I don't believe in systems when I'm on vacation," June says, her body folded halfway over Alex's, trying to slap Nora's hand out of the way.

"It's math," Nora says.

"Math has no authority here," June tells her.

"Math is *everywhere*, June."

"Get off me," Alex says, shoving June off his shoulder.

"You're supposed to back me up on this!" June yelps, pulling his hair and receiving a very ugly face in response.

"I'll let you look at one boob," Nora tells him. "The good one."

"They're both good," June says, suddenly distracted.

"I've seen both of them. I can practically see both of them now," Alex says, gesturing at what Nora is wearing for the day, which is a ratty pair of short overalls and the most perfunctory of bra-like things.

"Hashtag vacation nips," she says. "Pleeeeeease."

Alex sighs. "Sorry, Bug, but Nora did put more hours into her playlist, so she should get the aux cord."

There's a combination of girl sounds from the back seat, disgust and triumph, and Nora plugs her phone in, swearing she's developed some kind of foolproof algorithm for the perfect road trip playlist. The first trumpets of "Loco in Acapulco" by the Four Tops blast, and Alex finally pulls out of the gas station.

The jeep is a refurb, a project his dad took on when Alex was around ten. It lives in California now, but he drives it into Texas once a year for this weekend, leaves it in Austin so Alex and June can drive it in. Alex learned to drive one summer in the valley in this jeep, and the accelerator feels just as good under his foot now as he falls into formation with two black Secret Service SUVs and heads for the interstate. He hardly ever gets to drive himself anywhere anymore.

The sky is wide open and bluebonnet blue for miles, the sun low and heavy with an early morning start, and Alex has his sunglasses on and his arms bare and the doors and roof off. He cranks up the stereo and feels like he could throw anything away on the wind whipping through his hair and it would just float away like it never was, as if nothing matters but the rush and skip in his chest.

But it's all right behind the haze of dopamine: losing the campaign job, the restless days pacing his room, *Do you feel forever about him?*

He tips his chin up to the warm, sticky hometown air, catches his own eye in the rearview mirror. He looks bronzed and soft-mouthed and young, a Texas boy, the same kid he was when he left for DC. So, no more big thoughts for today.

Outside the hangar are a handful of PPOs and Henry in a short-sleeved chambray, shorts, and a pair of fashionable sunglasses, Burberry weekender over one shoulder—a goddamn summer dream. Nora's playlist has segued into "Here You Come Again" by Dolly Parton by the time Alex swings out of the side of the jeep by one arm.

"Yes, hello, hello, it's good to see you too!" Henry is saying from somewhere inside a smothering hug from June and Nora. Alex bites his lip and watches Henry squeeze their waists in return, and then Alex has him, inhaling the clean smell of him, laughing into the crook of his neck.

"Hi, love," he hears Henry say quietly, privately, right into the hair above his ear, and Alex's breath forgets how to do anything but laugh helplessly.

"Drums, please!" erupts from the jeep's stereo and the beat on "Summertime" kicks in, and Alex whoops his approval. Once Henry's security team has fallen in with the Secret Service cars, they're off.

Henry is grinning wide beside him as they cruise down 45, happily bopping his head along to the music, and Alex can't help glancing over at him, feeling giddy that Henry—Henry the prince—is *here,* in Texas, coming home with him. June pulls four bottles of Mexican Coke out of the cooler under her seat and passes them around, and Henry takes the first sip and practically melts. Alex reaches over and takes Henry's free hand into his own, lacing their fingers together on the console between them.

It takes an hour and a half to get out to Lake LBJ from Austin, and when they start weaving their way toward the water, Henry asks, "Why is it called Lake LBJ?"

"Nora?" Alex says.

"Lake LBJ," Nora says, "or Lake Lyndon B. Johnson, is one of six reservoirs formed by dams on the Colorado River known as the Texas Highland Lakes. Made possible by LBJ enacting the Rural Electrification Act when he was president. And LBJ had a place out here."

"That's true," Alex says.

"Also, fun fact: LBJ was obsessed with his own dick," Nora adds. "He called it Jumbo and would whip it out all the time. Like, in front of colleagues, reporters, anybody."

"Also true."

"American politics," Henry says. "Truly fascinating."

"You wanna talk, Henry VIII?" Alex says.

"*Anyway,*" Henry says airily, "how long have you lot come out here?"

"Dad bought it when he and Mom split up, so when I was twelve," Alex tells him. "He wanted to have a place close to us after he moved. We used to spend so much time here in the summers."

"Aw, Alex, remember when you got drunk for the first time out here?" June says.

"Strawberry daiquiris all *day.*"

"You threw up *so much,*" she says fondly.

They pull into a driveway flanked by thick trees and drive up to the house at the top of the hill, the same old vibrant orange exterior and smooth arches, tall cactuses and aloe plants. His mom was never into the whole hacienda school of home decor, so his dad went all in when he bought the lake house, tall teal doors and heavy wooden beams and Spanish tile accents in pinks and reds. There's a big wrap-around porch and stairs leading down the hill to the dock, and all the windows facing the water have been flung open, the curtains drifting out on a warm breeze.

Their teams fall back to check the perimeter—they're renting out the place next door for added privacy and the obligatory security presence. Henry effortlessly lifts June's cooler up onto one shoulder and Alex pointedly does not swoon about it.

There's the loud yell of Oscar Diaz coming around the corner, dripping and apparently fresh from a swim. He's wearing his old brown huaraches and a pair of swim trunks with parrots on them, both arms extended to the sun, and June is summarily scooped up into them.

"CJ!" he says as he spins her around and deposits her on the stucco railing. Nora is next, and then a bone-crushing hug for Alex.

Henry steps forward, and Oscar looks him up and down—the Burberry bag, the cooler on his shoulder, the elegant smile, the extended hand. His dad had been confused but ultimately willing to roll with it when Alex asked if he could bring a friend and casually mentioned the friend would be the Prince of Wales. He's not sure how this will go.

"Hello," Henry says. "Good to meet you. I'm Henry."

Oscar slaps his hand into Henry's. "Hope you're ready to fucking party."

———

Oscar may be the cook of the family, but Alex's mom was the one who grilled. It didn't always track in Pemberton Heights— his Mexican dad in the house diligently soaking a tres leches while his blond mom stood out in the yard flipping burgers— but it worked. Alex determinedly picked up the best from both of them, and now he's the only one here who can handle racks of ribs while Oscar does the rest.

The kitchen of the lake house faces the water, always smelling like citrus and salt and herbs, and his dad keeps it stocked with plump tomatoes and clay-soft avocados when they're visiting. He's standing in front of the big open windows now, three racks of ribs spread out on pans on the counter in front of him. His dad is at the sink, shucking ears of corn and humming along to an old Chente record.

Brown sugar. Smoked paprika. Onion powder. Chili powder. Garlic powder. Cayenne pepper. Salt. Pepper. More brown sugar. Alex measures each one out with his hands and dumps them into the bowl.

Down by the dock, June and Nora are embroiled in what looks like an improvised jousting match, charging at each other on the backs of inflatable animals with pool noodles. Henry is tipsy and shirtless and attempting to referee, standing on the dock with one foot on a piling and waving a bottle of Shiner around like a madman.

Alex smiles a little to himself, watching them. Henry and his girls.

"So, you wanna talk about it?" says his father's voice, in Spanish, from somewhere to his left.

Alex jumps a little, startled. His dad has relocated to the

bar a few feet down from him, mixing up a big batch of cotija and crema and seasonings for elotes.

"Uh." Has he been that obvious already?

"About Raf."

Alex exhales, his shoulders dropping, and returns his attention to the dry rub.

"Ah. That motherfucker," he says. They've only broached the topic in passing obscenities over text since the news broke. There's a mutual sting of betrayal. "Do you have any idea what he's thinking?"

"I don't have anything kinder to say about him than you do. And I don't have an explanation either. But . . ." He pauses thoughtfully, still stirring. Alex can sense him weighing out several thoughts at once, as he often does. "I don't know. After all this time, I want to believe there's a reason for him to put himself in the same room as Jeffrey Richards. But I can't figure out what."

Alex thinks about the conversation he overheard in the housekeeper's office, wondering if his dad is ever going to let him in on the full picture. He doesn't know how to ask without revealing that he literally climbed into a bush to eavesdrop on them. His dad's relationship with Luna has always been like that—grown-up talk.

Alex was at the fund-raiser for Oscar's Senate run where they first met Luna, Alex only fifteen and already taking notes. Luna showed up with a pride flag unapologetically stuck in his lapel; Alex wrote that down.

"Why'd you pick him?" Alex asks. "I remember that campaign. We met a lot of people who would've made great politicians. Why wouldn't you pick someone easier to elect?"

"You mean, why'd I roll the dice on the gay one?"

Alex concentrates on keeping his face neutral.

"I wasn't gonna put it like that," he says, "but yeah."

"Raf ever tell you his parents kicked him out when he was sixteen?"

Alex winces. "I knew he had a hard time before college, but he didn't specify."

"Yeah, they didn't take the news so well. He had a rough couple of years, but it made him tough. The night we met him, it was the first time he'd been back in California since he got kicked out, but he was damn sure gonna come in to support a brother out of Mexico City. It was like when Zahra showed up at your mom's office in Austin and said she wanted to prove the bastards wrong. You know a fighter when you see one."

"Yeah," Alex says.

There's another pause of Chente crooning in the background while his dad stirs, before he speaks again.

"You know . . ." he says. "That summer, I sent you to work on his campaign because you're the best point man I got. I knew you could do it. But I really thought there was a lot you could learn from him too. You got a lot in common."

Alex says nothing for a long moment.

"I gotta be honest," his dad says, and when Alex looks up again, he's watching the window. "I thought a prince would be more of a candy-ass."

Alex laughs, glancing back out at Henry, the sway of his back under the afternoon sun. "He's tougher than he looks."

"Not bad for a European," his dad says. "Better than half the idiots June's brought home." Alex's hands freeze, and his head jerks back to his dad, who's still stirring with his heavy wooden spoon, face impartial. "Half the girls you've brought around too. Not better than Nora, though. She'll always be my favorite." Alex stares at him, until his dad finally looks up. "What? You're not as subtle as you think."

"I—I don't know," Alex sputters. "I thought you might need to, like, have a Catholic moment about this or something?"

His dad slaps him on the bicep with the spoon, leaving a splatter of crema and cheese behind. "Have a little more faith in your old man than that, eh? A little appreciation for the patron saint of gender-neutral bathrooms in California? Little shit."

"Okay, okay, sorry!" Alex says, laughing. "I just know it's different when it's your own kid."

His dad laughs too, rubbing a hand over his goatee. "It's really not. Not to me, anyway. I see you."

Alex smiles again. "I know."

"Does your ma know?"

"Yeah, I told her a couple weeks ago."

"How'd she take it?"

"I mean, she doesn't care that I'm bi. She kind of freaked out it was him. There was a PowerPoint."

"That sounds about right."

"She fired me. And, uh. She told me I need to figure out if the way I feel about him is worth the risk."

"Well, is it?"

Alex groans. "Please, for the love of God, do not ask me. I'm on *vacation*. I want to get drunk and eat barbecue in peace."

His dad laughs ruefully. "You know, in a lot of ways, your mom and me were a stupid idea. I think we both knew it wouldn't be forever. We're both too fucking proud. But God, that woman. Your mother is, without question, the love of my life. I'll never love anyone else like that. It was wildfire. And I got you and June out of it, best things that ever happened to an old asshole like me. That kind of love is rare, even if it was a complete disaster." He sucks his teeth, considering. "Sometimes you just jump and hope it's not a cliff."

Alex closes his eyes. "Are you done with dad monologues for the day?"

"You're such a shit," he says, throwing a kitchen towel at his head. "Go put the ribs on. I wanna eat today." He calls after Alex's back, "You two better take the bunk beds tonight! Santa Maria is watching!"

They eat later that evening, big piles of elotes, pork tamales with salsa verde, a clay pot of frijoles charros, ribs. Henry gamely piles his plate with some of each and eyeballs it as if waiting for it to reveal its secrets to him, and Alex realizes Henry has never eaten barbecue with his hands before.

Alex demonstrates and watches with poorly concealed glee as Henry gingerly picks up a rib with his fingertips and considers his approach, cheering as Henry dives in face-first and rips a hunk of meat off with his teeth. He chews proudly, a huge smear of barbecue sauce across his upper lip and the tip of his nose.

His dad keeps an old guitar in the living room, and June brings it out on the porch so the two of them can pass it back and forth. Nora, one of Alex's chambrays thrown on over her bikini, floats barefoot in and out, keeping all their glasses filled from a pitcher of sangria brimming with white peaches and blackberries.

They sit around the fire pit and play old Johnny Cash songs, Selena, Fleetwood Mac. Alex sits and listens to the cicadas and the water and his dad's rough ranger voice, and when his dad slumps off to bed, June's songbird one. He feels wrapped up and warm, turning slowly under the moon.

He and Henry drift to a swing at the edge of the porch, and he curls into Henry's side, buries his face in the collar of his shirt. Henry puts an arm around him, touches the hinge of Alex's jaw with fingers that smell like smoke.

June plucks away at "Annie's Song," *you fill up my senses like a night in a forest,* and the breeze keeps moving to meet the highest branches of the trees, and the water keeps rising to meet the bulkheads, and Henry leans down to meet Alex's mouth, and Alex is. Well, Alex is so in love he could die.

Alex falls out of bed the following morning with a low-grade hangover and one of Henry's swimsuits tangled around his elbow. They did, technically, sleep in separate bunks. They just didn't *start* there.

Over the kitchen sink, he chugs a glass of water and stares out the window, the sun blinding and bright on the lake, and there's an incandescent little stone of certainty at the bottom of his chest.

It's this place—the absolute separation from DC, the familiar old smells of cedar trees and dried chile de árbol, the sanity of it. The roots. He could go outside and dig his fingers into the springy ground and understand anything about himself.

And he does understand, really. He loves Henry, and it's nothing new. He's been falling in love with Henry for years, probably since he first saw him in glossy print on the pages of *J14,* almost definitely since Henry pinned Alex to the floor of a medical supply closet and told him to shut the hell up. That long. That much.

He smiles as he reaches for a frying pan, because he knows it's exactly the kind of insane risk he can't resist.

By the time Henry comes wandering into the kitchen in his pajamas, there's an entire breakfast spread on the long green table, and Alex is at the stove, flipping his dozenth pancake.

"Is that an *apron*?"

Alex flourishes toward the polka-dotted thing he's got on over his boxers with his free hand, as if showing off one of his tailored suits. "Morning, sweetheart."

"Sorry," Henry says. "I was looking for someone else. Handsome, petulant, short, not pleasant until after ten a.m.? Have you seen him?"

"Fuck off, five-nine is average."

Henry crosses the room with a laugh and nudges up behind him at the stove to peck him on the cheek. "Love, you and I both know you're rounding up."

It's only a step on the way to the coffeemaker, but Alex reaches back and gets a hand in Henry's hair before he can move, pulling him into a kiss on the mouth this time. Henry huffs a little in surprise but returns it fully.

Alex forgets, momentarily, about the pancakes and everything else, not because he wants to do absolutely filthy things to Henry—maybe even with the apron still on—but because he *loves* him, and isn't that wild, to know that *that's* what makes the filthy things so good.

"I didn't realize this was a jazz brunch," says Nora's voice suddenly, and Henry springs backward so fast he almost puts his ass in the bowl of batter. She sidles up to the forgotten coffeemaker, grinning slyly at them.

"That doesn't seem sanitary," June is saying with a yawn as she folds herself into a chair at the table.

"Sorry," Henry says sheepishly.

"Don't be," Nora tells him.

"I'm not," Alex says.

"I'm hungover," June says as she reaches for the pitcher of mimosas. "Alex, you did all this?"

Alex shrugs, and June squints at him, bleary but knowing.

That afternoon, over the sounds of the boat's engine, Henry talks to Alex's dad about the sailboats that jut up from the horizon, getting into a complex discussion on outboard motors that Alex can't hope to follow. He leans back against the bow and watches, and it's so easy to imagine it: a future Henry who comes to the lake house with him every summer, who learns how to make elotes and ties neat cleat hitches and fits right into place in his weird family.

They go swimming, yell over one another about politics, pass the guitar around again. Henry takes a photo of himself with June and Nora, one under each arm and both in their bikinis. Nora is holding his chin in one hand and licking the side of his face, and June has her fingers tangled up in his hair and her head in the crook of his neck, smiling angelically at the camera. He sends it to Pez and receives anguished keysmashes and crying emojis in response, and they all almost piss themselves laughing.

It's good. It's really, really good.

Alex lies awake that night, drunk on Shiner and way too many campfire marshmallows, and he stares at whorls in the wood panels of the top bunk and thinks about coming of age out here. He remembers when he was a kid, freckly and unafraid, when the world seemed like it was blissfully endless but everything still made perfect sense. He used to leave his clothes in a pile on the pier and dive headfirst into the lake. Everything was in its right place.

He wears a key to his childhood home around his neck, but he doesn't know the last time he actually thought about the boy who used to push it into the lock.

Maybe losing the job isn't the worst thing that could have happened.

He thinks about roots, about first and second languages.

What he wanted when he was a kid and what he wants now and where those things overlap. Maybe that place, the meeting of the two, is here somewhere, in the gentle insistence of the water around his legs, crude letters carved with an old pocket knife. The steady thrum of another person's pulse against his.

"H?" he whispers. "You awake?"

Henry sighs. "Always."

They sneak through the grass in hushed voices past one of Henry's PPOs dozing on the porch, racing down the pier, shoving at each other's shoulders. Henry's laugh is high and clear, his sunburned shoulders bright pink in the dark, and Alex looks at him and something so buoyant fills up his chest that he feels like he could swim the length of the lake without stopping for air. He throws his T-shirt down at the end of the pier and starts to shuck his boxers, and when Henry arches an eyebrow at him, Alex laughs and jumps.

"You're a menace," Henry says when Alex breaks back to the surface. But he only hesitates briefly before he's stripping out of his clothes.

He stands naked at the edge of the pier, looking at Alex's head and shoulders bobbing in the water. The lines of him are long and languid in the moonlight, just skin and skin and skin lit soft and blue, and he's so beautiful that Alex thinks this moment, the soft shadows and pale thighs and crooked smile, should be the portrait of Henry that goes down in history. There are fireflies winking around his head, landing in his hair. A crown.

His dive is infuriatingly graceful.

"Can't you ever just do one thing without having to be so goddamn extra about it?" Alex says, splashing him as soon as he surfaces.

"That is bloody rich coming from you," Henry says, and he's grinning like he does when he's drinking in a challenge, like nothing in the world pleases him more than Alex's antagonizing elbow in his side.

"I don't know what you're talking about," Alex says, kicking over to him.

They chase each other around the pier, race down to the lake's shallow bottom and shoot back up in the moonlight, all elbows and knees. Alex finally manages to catch Henry around the waist, and he pins him, slides his wet mouth over the thudding pulse of Henry's throat. He wants to stay tangled up in Henry's legs forever. He wants to match the new freckles across Henry's nose to the stars above them and make him name the constellations.

"Hey," he says, his mouth right up in a breath's space from Henry's. He watches a drop of water roll down Henry's perfect nose and disappear into his mouth.

"Hi," Henry says back, and Alex thinks, *Goddamn, I love him.* It keeps coming back to him, and it's getting harder to look into Henry's soft smiles and not say it.

He kicks out a little to turn them in a slow circle. "You look good out here."

Henry's grin goes crooked and a little shy, dipping down to brush against Alex's jaw. "Yeah?"

"Yeah," Alex says. He twists Henry's wet hair around his fingers. "I'm glad you came this weekend," Alex hears himself say. "It's been so intense lately. I . . . I really needed this."

Henry's fingers give a little jab to his ribs, gently scolding. "You carry too much."

His instinct has always been to shoot back, *No, I don't,* or, *I want to*, but he bites it back and says, "I know," and he realizes it's the truth. "You know what I'm thinking right now?"

"What?"

"I'm thinking about, after inauguration, like next year, taking you back out here, just the two of us. And we can sit under the moon and not stress about anything."

"Oh," Henry says. "That sounds nice, if unlikely."

"Come on, think about it, babe. Next year. My mom'll be in office again, and we won't have to worry about winning any more elections. I'll finally be able to breathe. Ugh, it'll be amazing. I'll cook migas in the mornings, and we'll swim all day and never put clothes on and make out on the pier, and it won't even matter if the neighbors see."

"Well. It will matter, you know. It will always matter."

He pulls back to find Henry's face indecipherable.

"You know what I mean."

Henry's looking at him and looking at him, and Alex can't shake the feeling Henry's really seeing him for the first time. He realizes it's probably the only time he's ever invited love into a conversation with Henry on purpose, and it must be lying wide open on his face.

Something moves behind Henry's eyes. "Where are you going with all this?"

Alex tries to figure out how the hell to funnel everything he needs to tell Henry into words.

"June says I have a fire under my ass for no good reason," he says. "I don't know. You know how they always say to take it one day at a time? I think I take it ten years in the future. Like when I was in high school, it was all: Well, my parents hate each other, and my sister is leaving for college, and sometimes I look at other guys in the shower, but if I keep looking directly ahead, that stuff can't catch up to me. Or if I take this class, or this internship, or this job. I used to think, if I pictured the person I wanted to be and took all the crazy anxiety in my brain and narrowed it down to that point, I could rewire it. Use it to power something else. It's like I never learned how to just be where I am." Alex takes a breath. "And where I am is here. With you. And I'm thinking maybe I should start trying to take it day by day. And just . . . feel what I feel."

Henry doesn't say anything.

"Sweetheart." The water ripples quietly around him as he slides his hands up to hold Henry's face in both palms, tracing his cheekbones with the wet pads of his thumbs.

The cicadas and the wind and the lake are probably still making sounds, somewhere, but it's all faded into silence. Alex can't hear anything but his heartbeat in his ears.

"Henry, I—"

Abruptly Henry shifts, ducking beneath the surface and out of his arms before he can say anything else.

He pops back up near the pier, hair sticking to his forehead, and Alex turns around and stares at him, breathless at the loss. Henry spits out lake water and sends a splash in his direction, and Alex forces a laugh.

"Christ," Henry says, slapping at a bug that's landed on him, "what are these infernal creatures?"

"Mosquitos," Alex supplies.

"They're awful," Henry says loftily. "I'm going to catch an exotic plague."

"I'm . . . sorry?"

"I just mean to say, you know, Philip is the heir and I'm the spare, and if that nervy bastard has a heart attack at thirty-five and I've got malaria, whither the spare?"

Alex laughs weakly again, but he's got a distinct feeling of something being pulled out of his hands right before he could grasp it. Henry's tone has gone light, clipped, superficial. His press voice.

"At any rate, I'm knackered," Henry is saying now. And Alex watches helplessly as he turns and starts hauling himself out of the water and onto the dock, pulling his shorts back up shivering legs. "If it's all the same to you, I think I'll go to bed."

Alex doesn't know what to say, so he watches Henry walk the long line of the dock, disappearing into the darkness.

A ringing, scooped-out sensation starts behind his molars and rolls down his throat, into his chest, down to the pit of his stomach. Something's wrong, and he knows it, but he's too afraid to push back or ask. That, he realizes suddenly, is the danger of allowing love into this—the acknowledgment that if something goes wrong, he doesn't know how he will stand it.

For the first time since Henry grabbed him and kissed him with so much certainty in the garden, the thought enters Alex's mind: What if it was never his decision to make? What if he got so wrapped up in everything Henry is—the words he writes, the earnest heartsickness of him—he forgot to take into account that it's just *how* he is, all the time, with everyone?

What if he's done the thing he swore he would never do, the thing he hates, and fallen in love with a prince because it was a fantasy?

When he gets back to their room, Henry's already in his bunk and silent, his back turned.

In the morning, Henry is gone.

Alex wakes up to find his bunk empty and made up, the pillow tucked neatly beneath the blanket. He practically throws the door off its hinges running out onto the patio, only to find it empty as well. The yard is empty, the pier is empty. It's like he was never even there.

He finds the note in the kitchen:

> *Alex,*
> *Had to go early for a family matter. Left with the PPOs.*
> *Didn't want to wake you.*
> *Thank you for everything.*
> *X*

It's the last message Henry sends him.

TEN

He sends Henry five texts the first day. Two the second. By day three, none. He's spent too much of his life talking, talking, talking not to know the signs when someone doesn't want to hear him anymore.

He starts forcing himself to only check his phone once every two hours instead of once an hour, makes himself hang on by his fingernails until the minutes tick down. A few times, he gets wrapped up in obsessively reading press coverage of the campaign and realizes he hasn't checked in hours, and every time he's hit with a hiccupping, desperate hope that there will be something. There never is.

He thought he was reckless before, but he understands now—holding love off was the only thing keeping him from losing himself in this completely, and he's gone, stupid, lovesick, a fucking disaster. No work to distract him. The tripwire of "Things Only People in Love Say and Do" set off.

So, instead:

A Tuesday night, hiding on the roof of the Residence, pacing so many furious laps that the skin on the backs of his heels splits open and blood soaks into his loafers.

His CLAREMONT FOR AMERICA mug, returned in a carefully marked box from his desk at the campaign office, a concrete reminder of what this already cost him smashed in his bathroom sink.

The smell of Earl Grey curling up from the kitchens, and his throat going painfully tight.

Two and a half different dreams about sandy hair wrapped around his fingers.

A three-line email, an excerpt dug up from an archived letter, Hamilton to Laurens, *You should not have taken advantage of my sensibility to steal into my affections without my consent,* drafted and deleted.

On day five, Rafael Luna makes his fifth campaign stop as a surrogate, the Richards campaign's token twofer minority. Alex hits a momentary emotional impasse: either destroy something or destroy himself. He ends up smashing his phone on the pavement outside the Capitol. The screen is replaced by the end of the day. It doesn't make any messages from Henry magically appear.

On the morning of day seven, he's digging in the back of his closet when he stumbles upon a bundle of teal silk—the stupid kimono Pez had made for him. He hasn't taken it out since LA.

He's about to shove it back into the corner when he feels something in the pocket. He finds a small folded square of paper. It's stationery from their hotel that night, the night everything inside Alex rearranged. Henry's cursive.

Dear Thisbe,
I wish there weren't a wall.
Love, Pyramus

He fumbles his phone out so fast he almost drops it on the floor and smashes it again. The search tells him Pyramus and Thisbe were lovers in a Greek myth, children of rival families, forbidden to be together. Their only way to speak to each other was through a thin crack in the wall built between them.

And that is, officially, too fucking much.

What he does next, he's sure he'll have no memory of doing, simply a white-noise gap of time that got him from point A to point B. He texts Cash, what are you doing for the next 24 hours? Then he unearths the emergency credit card from his wallet and buys two plane tickets, first class, nonstop. Boarding in two hours. Dulles International to Heathrow.

Zahra nearly refuses to secure a car after Alex "had the goddamn nerve" to call her from the runway at Dulles. It's dark and pissing down rain when they land in London around nine in the evening, and he and Cash are both soaked the second they climb out of the car inside the back gates of Kensington.

Clearly, someone has radioed for Shaan, because he's standing there at the door to Henry's apartments in an impeccable gray peacoat, dry and unmoved under a black umbrella.

"Mr. Claremont-Diaz," he says. "What a treat."

Alex has not got the damn time. "Move, Shaan."

"Ms. Bankston called ahead to warn me that you were on the

way," he says. "As you might have guessed by the ease with which you were able to get through our gates. We thought it best to let you kick up a fuss somewhere more private."

"Move."

Shaan smiles, looking as if he might be genuinely enjoying watching two hapless Americans become slowly waterlogged. "You're aware it's quite late, and it's well within my power to have security remove you. No member of the royal family has invited you into the palace."

"Bullshit," Alex bites out. "I need to see Henry."

"I'm afraid I can't do that. The prince does not wish to be disturbed."

"Goddammit—Henry!" He sidesteps Shaan and starts shouting up at Henry's bedroom windows, where there's a light on. Fat raindrops are pelting his eyeballs. "Henry, you motherfucker!"

"Alex—" says Cash's nervous voice behind him.

"Henry, you piece of shit, get your ass down here!"

"You are making a scene," Shaan says placidly.

"Yeah?" Alex says, still yelling. "How 'bout I just keep yelling and we see which of the papers show up first!" He turns back to the window and starts flailing his arms too. "Henry! Your Royal fucking Highness!"

Shaan touches a finger to his earpiece. "Team Bravo, we've got a situa—"

"For Christ's sake, Alex, what are you doing?"

Alex freezes, his mouth open around another shout, and there's Henry standing behind Shaan in the doorway, barefoot in worn-in sweats. Alex's heart is going to fall out of his ass. Henry looks unimpressed.

He drops his arms. "Tell him to let me in."

Henry sighs, pinching the bridge of his nose. "It's fine. He can come in."

"*Thank* you," he says, pointedly looking at Shaan, who does not seem to care at all if he dies of hypothermia. He sloshes into the palace, ditching his soaked shoes as Cash and Shaan disappear behind the door.

Henry, who led the way in, hasn't even stopped to speak to him, and all Alex can do is follow him up the grand staircase toward his rooms.

"Really nice," Alex yells after him, dripping as aggressively as he can manage along the way. He hopes he ruins a rug. "Fuckin' ghost me for a week, make me stand in the rain like a brown John Cusack, and now you won't even talk to me. I'm really just having a great time here. I can see why all y'all had to marry your fucking cousins."

"I'd rather not do this where we might be overheard," Henry says, taking a left on the landing.

Alex stomps up after him, following him into his bedroom. "Do what?" he says as Henry shuts the door behind them. "What are you gonna do, Henry?"

Henry turns to face him at last, and now that Alex's eyes aren't full of rainwater, he can see the skin under his eyes is papery and purple, rimmed pink at his eyelashes. There's a tense set to his shoulders Alex hasn't seen in months, not directed at him at least.

"I'm going to let you say what you need to say," Henry says flatly, "so you can leave."

Alex stares. "What, and then we're over?"

Henry doesn't answer him.

Something rises in Alex's throat—anger, confusion, hurt, bile. Unforgivably, he feels like he might cry.

"Seriously?" he says, helpless and indignant. He's still dripping. "What the *fuck* is going on? A week ago it was emails about how much you missed me and meeting my fucking *dad*, and that's it? You thought you could fucking *ghost me*? I can't shut this off like you do, Henry."

Henry paces over to the elaborately carved fireplace across the room and leans on the mantelpiece. "You think I don't *care* as much as you?"

"You're sure as hell acting like it."

"I honestly haven't got the time to explain to you all the ways you're wrong—"

"Jesus, could you stop being an obtuse fucking asshole for, like, twenty seconds?"

"So glad you flew here to *insult me*—"

"*I fucking love you, okay?*" Alex half yells, finally, irreversibly. Henry goes very still against the mantelpiece. Alex watches him swallow, watches the muscle that keeps twitching in his jaw, and feels like he might shake out of his skin. "Fuck, I swear. You don't make it fucking easy. But I'm in love with you."

A small *click* cuts the silence: Henry has taken his signet ring off and set it down on the mantel. He holds his naked hand to his chest, kneading the palm, the flickering light from the fire painting his face in dramatic shadows. "Do you have any idea what that means?"

"Of course I do—"

"Alex, *please*," Henry says, and when he finally turns to look at him, he looks wretched, miserable. "Don't. This is the entire goddamned reason. I can't do this, and you *know* why I can't do this, so *please* don't make me say it."

Alex swallows hard. "You're not even gonna try to be happy?"

"For Christ's sake," Henry says, "I've been trying to be happy my entire idiot life. My birthright is a *country,* not happiness."

Alex yanks the soggy note out of his pocket, *I wish there wasn't a wall,* and throws it at Henry viciously, watches him pick it up. "Then what is *that* supposed to mean, if you don't want this?"

Henry stares down at his words from months ago. "Alex, Thisbe and Pyramus both *die* at the end."

"Oh my *God,*" Alex groans. "So, what, was this all never going to be anything real to you?"

And Henry snaps.

"You really are a *complete* idiot if you believe that," Henry hisses, the note balled in his fist. "When have I *ever,* since the first instant I touched you, pretended to be anything less than in love with you? Are you so fucking self-absorbed as to think this is about you and whether or not I love you, rather than the fact I'm an heir to the fucking throne? You at least have the *option* to not choose a public life eventually, but I will live and die in these palaces and in this family, so don't you dare come to me and question if I love you when it's the thing that could bloody well ruin everything."

Alex doesn't speak, doesn't move, doesn't breathe, his feet rooted to the spot. Henry isn't looking at him, but staring at a point on the mantel somewhere, tugging at his own hair in exasperation.

"It was never supposed to be an issue," he goes on, his voice hoarse. "I thought I could have some part of you, and just never say it, and you'd never have to know, and one day you'd get tired of me and leave, because I'm—" He stops short, and one shaking hand moves through the air in front of him in a helpless sort of gesture at everything about himself. "I never thought I'd be stood here faced with a choice I can't make, because I never . . . I never imagined you would love me back."

"Well," Alex says. "I do. And you *can* choose."

"You know bloody well I can't."

"You can *try,*" Alex tells him, feeling as if it should be the simplest fucking truth in the world. "What do you *want?*"

"I want you—"

"Then fucking *have me.*"

"—but I don't want *this.*"

Alex wants to grab Henry and shake him, wants to scream in his face, wants to smash every priceless antique in the room. "What does that even *mean?*"

"I don't *want* it!" Henry practically shouts. His eyes are flashing, wet and angry and afraid. "Don't you bloody see? I'm not *like* you. I can't afford to be *reckless.* I don't have a family who will support me. I don't go about shoving who I am in everyone's faces and dreaming about a career in fucking *politics,* so I can be *more* scrutinized and picked apart by the entire godforsaken world. I can love you and want you and still not want that life. I'm allowed, all right, and it doesn't make me a liar; it makes me a man with some infinitesimal shred of self-preservation, unlike *you,* and you don't get to come here and call me a coward for it."

Alex takes a breath. "I never said you were a coward."

"I." Henry blinks. "Well. The point stands."

"You think *I* want *your* life? You think I want *Martha's?* Gilded fucking cage? Barely allowed to *speak* in public, or have a goddamn opinion—"

"Then what are we even doing here? Why are we fighting, then, if the lives we have to lead are so incompatible?"

"Because you don't want that either!" Alex insists. "You don't want any of this bullshit. You *hate* it."

"Don't tell me what I want," Henry says. "You haven't a clue how it feels."

"Look, I might not be a fucking royal," Alex says, crosses the horrible rug, moves into Henry's space, "but I know what it's like for your whole life to be determined by the family you were born into, okay? The lives we want—they're *not that different*. Not in the ways that matter. You want to take what you were given and leave the world better than you found it. So do I. We can—we can figure out a way to do that together."

Henry stares at him silently, and Alex can see the scales balancing in his head.

"I don't think I can."

Alex turns away from him, falling back on his heels like he's been slapped. "Fine," he finally says. "You know what? Fucking fine. I'll leave."

"Good."

"I'll leave," he says, and he turns back and leans in, "as soon as you tell me to leave."

"*Alex.*"

He's in Henry's face now. If he's getting his heart broken tonight, he's sure as hell going to make Henry have the guts to do it right. "Tell me you're done with me. I'll get back on the plane. That's it. And you can live here in your tower and be miserable forever, write a whole book of sad fucking poems about it. Whatever. Just say it."

"Fuck you," Henry says, his voice breaking, and he gets a handful of Alex's shirt collar, and Alex knows he's going to love this stubborn shithead forever.

"Tell me," he says, a ghost of a smile around his lips, "to leave."

He feels before he registers being shoved backward into a wall, and Henry's mouth is on his, desperate and wild. The faint taste of blood blooms on his tongue, and he smiles as he opens up to it, pushes it into Henry's mouth, tugs at his hair with both hands. Henry groans, and Alex feels it in his spine.

They grapple along the wall until Henry physically picks him up off the floor and staggers backward, toward the bed. Alex bounces when his back hits the mattress, and Henry stands over him for several breaths, staring. Alex would give anything to know what's going through that fucking head of his.

He realizes, suddenly, Henry's crying.

He swallows.

That's the thing: he doesn't know. He doesn't know if this is supposed to be some kind of consummation, or if it's one last time. He doesn't think he could go through with it if he knew it was the latter. But he doesn't want to go home without having this.

"C'mere."

He fucks Henry slow and deep, and if it's the last time, they go down shivering and gasping and epic, all wet mouths and wet eyelashes, and Alex is a cliché on an ivory bedspread, and he hates himself but he's so in love. He's in stupid, unbearable love, and Henry loves him too, and at least for one night it matters, even if they both have to pretend to forget in the morning.

Henry comes with his face turned into Alex's open palm, his bottom lip catching on the knob of his wrist, and Alex tries to memorize every detail down to how his lashes fan across his cheeks and the pink flush that spreads all the way up to his ears. He tells his too-fast brain: *Don't miss it this time. He's too important.*

It's pitch-black outside when Henry's body finally subsides, and the room is impossibly quiet, the fire gone out. Alex rolls over onto his side and touches two fingers to his chest, right next to where the key on the chain rests. His heart is beating the same as ever under his skin. He doesn't know how that can be true.

It's a long stretch of silence before Henry shifts in the bed beside him and rolls onto his back, pulling a sheet over them. Alex reaches for something to say, but there's nothing.

Alex wakes up alone.

It takes a moment for everything to reorient around the fixed point in his chest where last night settled. The elaborate gilded headboard, the heavy embroidered duvet, the soft twill blanket beneath that's the only thing in the room Henry actually chose. He slides his hand across the sheet, over to Henry's side of the bed. It's cool to the touch.

Kensington Palace is gray and dull in the early morning. The clock on the mantelpiece says it's not even seven, and there's a violent rain lashing against the big picture window, half-revealed by parted curtains.

Henry's room has never felt much like Henry, but in the quiet of morning, he shows up in pieces. A pile of journals on the desk, the topmost splotched with ink from a pen exploding in his bag on a plane. An oversized cardigan, worn through and patched at the elbows, slung over an antique wingback chair near the window. David's leash hanging from the doorknob.

And beside him, there's a copy of *Le Monde* on the nightstand, tucked under a gigantic leather-bound volume of Wilde's complete works. He recognizes the date: Paris. The first time they woke up next to each other.

He squeezes his eyes shut, feeling for once in his life that he should stop being so damn nosy. It's time, he realizes, to start accepting only what Henry can give him.

The sheets smell like Henry. He knows:

One. Henry isn't here.

Two. Henry never said yes to any kind of future last night.

Three. This could very well be the last time he gets to inhale Henry's scent on anything.

But, four. Next to the clock on the mantel, Henry's ring still sits.

The doorknob turns, and Alex opens his eyes to find Henry, holding two mugs and smiling a wan, unreadable smile. He's in soft sweats again, brushed with morning mist.

"Your hair in the mornings is truly a wonder to behold," is how he breaks the silence. He crosses and kneels on the edge of the mattress, offering Alex a mug. It's coffee, one sugar, cinnamon. He doesn't want to feel anything about Henry knowing how he likes his coffee, not when he's about to be dumped, but he does.

Except, when Henry looks at him again, watches him take the first blessed sip of coffee, the smile comes back in earnest. He reaches down and palms one of Alex's feet through the duvet.

"Hi," Alex says carefully, squinting over his coffee. "You seem . . . less pissy."

Henry huffs a laugh. "You're one to talk. I wasn't the one who stormed the palace in a fit of pique to call me an 'obtuse fucking asshole.'"

"In my defense," Alex says, "you *were* an obtuse fucking asshole."

Henry pauses, takes a sip of his tea, and places it on the nightstand. "I was," he agrees, and he leans forward and presses his mouth to Alex's, one hand steadying his mug so it doesn't spill. He tastes like toothpaste and Earl Grey, and maybe Alex isn't getting dumped after all.

"Hey," he says when Henry pulls back. "Where were you?"

Henry doesn't answer, and Alex watches him kick his wet sneakers onto the floor before climbing up to sit between Alex's open legs. He places his hands on Alex's thighs, bracketing him with his full attention, and when he looks up into Alex's eyes, his are clear blue and focused.

"I needed a run," he says. "To clear my head a bit, figure out . . . what's next. Very Mr. Darcy brooding at Pemberley. And I ran into Philip. I hadn't mentioned it, but he and Martha are here for the week while they're doing renovations on Anmer Hall. He was up early for some appearance or other, eating toast. Plain toast. Have you ever seen someone eat toast without anything on it? Harrowing, truly."

Alex chews his lip. "Where's this going, babe?"

"We chatted for a bit. He didn't seem to know about your . . . visitation . . . last night, thankfully. But he was on about Martha, and land holdings, and the hypothetical heirs they have to start working on, even though Philip hates children, and suddenly it was as if . . . as if everything you said last night came back to me. I thought, God, that's it, isn't it? Just following the plan. And it's not that he's unhappy. He's fine. It's all very deeply fine. A whole lifetime of fine." He's been pulling at a thread on the duvet, but he looks back up, squarely into Alex's eyes, and says, "That's not good enough for me."

There's a desperate stutter in Alex's heartbeat. "It's not?"

He reaches up and touches a thumb to Alex's cheekbone. "I'm not . . . good at saying these things like you are, but. I've always thought . . . ever since I knew about me, and even before, when I could sense I was *different*—and, after everything the past few years, all the mad things my head does—I've always thought of myself as a problem that deserved to stay hidden. Never quite trusted myself, or what I wanted. Before you, I was all right letting everything happen to me. I honestly have never thought I deserved to choose." His hand moves, fingertips brushing a curl behind Alex's ear. "But you treat me like I do."

There's something painfully hard in Alex's throat, but he pushes past it. He reaches over and sets his mug down next to Henry's on the nightstand.

"You do," he says.

"I think I'm actually beginning to believe that," Henry says. "And I don't know how long it would have taken if I didn't have you to believe for me."

"And there's nothing wrong with you," Alex tells him. "I mean, aside from the fact that you're occasionally an obtuse fucking asshole."

Henry laughs again, wetly, his eyes crinkling up in the corners, and Alex feels his heart lift into his throat, up to the embellished ceilings, pushing out to fill the whole room all the way to the glinting gold ring still sitting above the fireplace.

"I am sorry about that," Henry says. "I—I wasn't ready to hear it. That night, at the lake . . . it was the first time I let myself think you might actually say it. I panicked, and it was daft and unfair, and I won't do it again."

"You better not," Alex tells him. "So, you're saying . . . you're in?"

"I'm saying," Henry begins, and the knit of his brow is nervous but his mouth keeps speaking, "I'm terrified, and my whole life is completely mad, but trying to give you up this week nearly killed me. And when I woke up this morning and looked at you . . . there's no trying to get by for me anymore. I don't know if I'll ever be allowed to tell the world, but I . . . I want to. One day. If there's any legacy for me on this bloody earth, I want it to be true. So I can offer you all of me, in whatever way you'll have me, and I can offer you the chance of a life. If you can wait, I want you to help me try."

Alex looks at him, taking in the whole parcel of him, the centuries of royal blood sitting under an antique Kensington chandelier, and he reaches out to touch his face and looks at his fingers and thinks about holding the Bible at his mother's inauguration with the same hand.

It hits him, fully: the weight of this. How completely neither of them will ever be able to undo it.

"Okay," he says. "I'm into making history."

Henry rolls his eyes and seals it with a smiling kiss, and they fall back into the pillows together, Henry's wet hair and sweatpants and Alex's naked limbs all tangled up in the lavish bedclothes.

When Alex was a kid, before anyone knew his name, he dreamed of love like it was a fairy tale, as if it would come sweeping into his life on the back of a dragon one day. When he got older, he learned about love as a strange thing that could fall apart no matter how badly you wanted it, a choice you make anyway. He never imagined it'd turn out he was right both times.

Henry's hands on him are unhurried and soft, and they make out lazily for hours or days, basking in the rare luxury of it. They take breaks to finish their lukewarm coffee and tea, and Henry has scones and blackcurrant jam sent up. They waste away the morning in bed, watching Mel and Sue squawk over tea cakes on Henry's laptop, listening to the rain slow to a drizzle.

At some point, Alex disentangles his jeans from the foot of the bed and fishes out his phone. He's got three missed calls from Zahra, one ominous voicemail from his mother, and forty-seven unread messages in his group text with June and Nora.

ALEX, Z JUST TOLD ME YOU'RE IN
LONDON???????

Alex oh my god

I swear to god if you do something
stupid and get yourself caught, I'm
gonna kill you myself

But you went after him!!! That's SO
Jane Austen

I'm gonna punch you in the face
when you get back. I can't believe
you didn't tell me

How did it go??? Are you with
Henry now?????

GONNA PUNCH YOU

It turns out forty-six out of forty-seven texts are June and the forty-seventh is Nora asking if either of them know where she left her white Chuck Taylors. Alex texts back: your chucks are under my bed and henry says hi.

The message has barely delivered before his phone erupts with a call from June, who demands to be put on speaker and told everything. After, rather than facing Zahra's wrath himself, he convinces Henry to call Shaan.

"D'you think you could, er, phone Ms. Bankston and let her know Alex is safe and with me?"

"Yes, sir," Shaan says. "And shall I arrange a car for his departure?"

"Er," Henry says, and he looks at Alex and mouths, *Stay?* Alex nods. "Tomorrow?"

There's a very long pause over the line before Shaan says, "I'll let her know," in a voice like he'd rather do literally anything else.

Alex laughs as Henry hangs up, but he returns to his phone again, to the voicemail waiting from his mother. Henry sees his thumb hovering over the play button and nudges his ribs.

"I suppose we do have to face the consequences at some point," he says.

Alex sighs. "I don't think I told you, but she, uh. Well, when she fired me, she told me that if I wasn't a thousand percent serious about you, I needed to break things off."

Henry nuzzles his nose behind Alex's ear. "A thousand percent?"

"Yeah, don't let it go to your head."

Henry elbows him again, and Alex laughs and grabs his head and aggressively kisses his cheek, smashing his face into the pillow. When Alex finally relents, Henry is pink-faced and mussed and definitely pleased.

"I was thinking about that, though," Henry says, "the chance being with me is going to keep ruining your career. Congress by thirty, wasn't it?"

"Come on. Look at this face. People love this face. I'll figure out the rest." Henry looks deeply skeptical, and Alex sighs again. "Look, I don't know. I don't even exactly know, like, how being a legislator would work if I'm with a prince of another country. So, you know. There's stuff to figure out. But way worse people with way bigger problems than me get elected all the time."

Henry's looking at him in the piercing way he has sometimes that makes Alex feel like a bug stuck under a shadowbox with a pushpin. "You're really not frightened of what might happen?"

"No, I mean, of course I am," he says. "It definitely stays secret until after the election. And I know it'll be messy. But if we can get ahead of the narrative, wait for the right time and do it on our own terms, I think it could be okay."

"How long have you been thinking about this?"

"Consciously? Since, like, the DNC. Subconsciously, in total denial? A long-ass time. At least since you kissed me."

Henry stares at him from the pillow. "That's . . . kind of incredible."

"What about you?"

"What about *me*?" Henry says. "Christ, Alex. The whole bloody time."

"The whole time?"

"Since the Olympics."

"The *Olympics*?" Alex yanks Henry's pillow out from under him. "But that's, that's like—"

"Yes, Alex, the day we met, nothing gets past you, does it?" Henry says, reaching to steal the pillow back. "'What about you,' he says, as if he doesn't *know*—"

"Shut your *mouth*," Alex says, grinning like an idiot, and he stops fighting Henry for the pillow and instead straddles him and kisses him into the mattress. He pulls the blankets up and they disappear into the pile, a laughing mess of mouths and hands, until Henry rolls onto his phone and his ass presses the button on the voicemail.

"Diaz, you insane, hopeless romantic little shit," says the voice of the President of the United States, muffled in the bed. "It had better be forever. Be safe."

Sneaking out of the palace without security at two in the morning was, surprisingly, Henry's idea. He pulled hoodies and hats out for both of them—the incognito uniform of the internationally recognizable—and Bea staged a noisy exit from the opposite end of the palace while they sprinted through the gardens. Now they're on the deserted, wet pavement of South Kensington, flanked by tall, red brick buildings and a sign for—

"Stop, are you kidding me?" Alex says. "*Prince Consort Road?* Oh my God, take a picture of me with the sign."

"Not there yet!" Henry says over his shoulder. He gives Alex's arm another pull to keep him running. "Keep moving, you wastrel."

They cross to another street and duck into an alcove between two pillars while Henry fishes a keyring with dozens of keys out of his hoodie. "Funny thing about being a prince—people will give you keys to just about anything if you ask nicely."

Alex gawks, watching Henry feel around the edge of a seemingly plain wall. "All this time, I thought *I* was the Ferris Bueller of this relationship."

"What, did you think I was Sloane?" Henry says, pushing the panel open a crack and yanking Alex into a wide, dark plaza.

The grounds are sloping, white tiles carrying the sounds of their feet as they run. Sturdy Victorian bricks tower into the night, framing the courtyard, and Alex thinks, *Oh*. The Victoria and Albert Museum. Henry has a key to the V&A.

There's a stout old security guard waiting at the doors.

"Can't thank you enough, Gavin," Henry says, and Alex notices the thick wad of cash Henry slips into their handshake.

"Renaissance City tonight, yeah?" Gavin says.

"If you would be so kind," Henry tells him.

And they're off again, hustling through rooms of Chinese art and French sculptures. Henry moves fluidly from room to room, past a black stone sculpture of a seated Buddha and John the Baptist nude and in bronze, without a single false step.

"You do this a lot?"

Henry laughs. "It's, ah, sort of my little secret. When I was young, my mum and dad would take us early in the morning, before opening. They wanted us to have a sense of the arts, I suppose, but mostly history." He slows and points to a massive piece, a wooden tiger mauling a man dressed as a European soldier, the sign declaring: *TIPU'S TIGER*. "Mum would take us to look at this one and whisper to me, 'See how the tiger is eating him up? That's because my great-great-great-great grandad *stole* this from India. I think we should give it back, but your gran says no.'"

Alex watches Henry's face in quarter profile, the slight pain that moves under his skin, but he shakes it off quickly and takes Alex's hand back up. They're running again.

"Now, I like to come at night," he says. "A few of the

higher-up security guards know me. Sometimes I think I keep coming because, no matter how many places I've been or people I've met or books I read, this place is proof I'll never learn it all. It's like Westminster: You can look at every individual carving or pane of stained glass and know there's this wealth of stories there, that everything was put in a specific place for a reason. Everything has a meaning, an intention. There are pieces in here—*The Great Bed of Ware,* it's mentioned in *Twelfth Night, Epicoene, Don Juan,* and it's here. Everything is a story, never finished. Isn't it incredible? And the archives, God, I could spend hours in the archives, they—*mmph.*"

He's cut off mid-sentence because Alex has stopped in the middle of the corridor and yanked him backward into a kiss.

"Hello," Henry says when they break apart. "What was that for?"

"I just, like." Alex shrugs. "Really love you."

The corridor dumps them out into a cavernous atrium, rooms sprawling out in each direction. Only some of the overhead lighting has been left on, and Alex can see an enormous chandelier looming high in the rotunda, tendrils and bubbles of glass in blues and greens and yellows. Behind it, there's an elaborate iron choir screen standing broad and gorgeous on the landing above.

"This is it," Henry says, pulling Alex by the hand to the left, where light spills out of an immense archway. "I called ahead to Gavin to make sure they left a light on. It's my favorite room."

Alex has personally helped with exhibitions at the Smithsonian and sleeps in a room once occupied by Ulysses S. Grant's father-in-law, but he still loses his breath when Henry pulls him through the marble pillars.

In the half light, the room is alive. The vaulted roof seems to stretch up forever into the inky London sky, and beneath it the room is arranged like a city square somewhere in Florence, climbing columns and towering altars and archways. Deep basins of fountains are planted in the floor between statues on heavy pedestals, and effigies lie behind black doorways with the Resurrection carved into their slate. Dominating the entire back wall is a colossal, Gothic choir screen carved from marble and adorned with ornate statues of saints, black and gold and imposing, holy.

When Henry speaks again, it's soft, as if he's trying not to break the spell.

"In here, at night, it's almost like walking through a real piazza," Henry says. "But there's nobody else around to touch you or gawk at you or try to steal a photo of you. You can just *be*."

Alex looks over to find Henry's expression careful, waiting, and he realizes this is the same as when Alex took Henry to the lake house—the most sacred place he has.

He squeezes Henry's hand and says, "Tell me everything."

Henry does, leading him around to each piece in turn. There's a life-size sculpture of Zephyr, the Greek god of the west wind brought to life by Francavilla, a crown on his head and one foot on a cloud. Narcissus on his knees, mesmerized by his own reflection in the pool, once thought to be Michelangelo's lost Cupid but actually carved by Cioli—"Do you see here, where they had to repair his knuckles with stucco?"— Pluto stealing Proserpina away to the underworld, and Jason with his golden fleece.

They wind up back at the first statue, *Samson Slaying a Philistine*, the one that knocked the wind out of Alex when they walked in. He's never seen anything like it—the smooth muscles, the indentations of flesh, the breathing, bleeding life of it, all carved by Giambologna out of marble. If he could touch it, he swears the skin would be warm.

"It's a bit ironic, you know," Henry says, gazing up at it. "Me, the cursed gay heir, standing here in Victoria's museum, considering how much she *loved* those sodomy laws." He smirks. "Actually . . . you remember how I told you about the gay king, James I?"

"The one with the dumb jock boyfriend?"

"Yes, that one. Well, his most beloved favorite was a man named George Villiers. 'The handsomest-bodied man in all of England,' they called him. James was completely besotted. Everyone knew. This French poet, de Viau, wrote a poem about it." He clears his throat and starts to recite: "'One man fucks Monsieur le Grand, another fucks the Comte de Tonnerre, and it is well known that the King of England, fucks the Duke of Buckingham.'" Alex must be staring, because he adds, "Well, it rhymes in French. Anyway. Did you know the reason the King James translation of the Bible exists is because the Church of England was so displeased with James for flaunting his relationship with Villiers that he had the translation commissioned to appease them?"

"You're kidding."

"He stood in front of the Privy Council and said, 'Christ had John, and I have George.'"

"Jesus."

"Precisely." Henry's still looking up at the statue, but Alex can't stop looking at him and the sly smile on his face, lost in his own thoughts. "And James's son, Charles I, is the reason we have dear Samson. It's the only Giambologna that ever left Florence. He was a gift to Charles from the King of Spain, and

Charles gave it, this massive, absolutely priceless masterpiece of a sculpture, to Villiers. And a few centuries later, here he is. One of the most beautiful pieces we own, and we didn't even steal it. We only needed Villiers and his trolloping ways with the queer monarchs. To me, if there were a registry of national gay landmarks in Britain, Samson would be on it."

Henry's beaming like a proud parent, like Samson is his, and Alex is hit with a wave of pride in kind.

He takes his phone out and lines up a shot, Henry standing there all soft and rumpled and smiling next to one of the most exquisite works of art in the world.

"What are you doing?"

"I'm taking a picture of a national gay landmark," Alex tells him. "And also a statue."

Henry laughs indulgently, and Alex closes the space between them, takes Henry's baseball cap off and stands on his toes to kiss the ridge of his brow.

"It's funny," Henry says. "I always thought of the whole thing as the most unforgivable thing about me, but you act like it's one of the best."

"Oh, yeah," Alex says. "The top list of reasons to love you goes brain, then dick, then imminent status as a revolutionary gay icon."

"You are quite literally Queen Victoria's worst nightmare."

"And that's why *you* love *me*."

"My God, you're right. All this time, I was just after the bloke who'd most infuriate my homophobic forebears."

"Ah, and we can't forget they were also racist."

"Certainly not." Henry nods seriously. "Next time we shall visit some of the George III pieces and see if they burst into flame."

Through the marble choir screen at the back of the room is a second, deeper chamber, this one filled with church relics. Past stained glass and statues of saints, at the very end of the room, is an entire high altar chapel removed from its church. The sign explains its original setting was the apse of the convent church of Santa Chiara in Florence in the fifteenth century, and it's stunning, set deep into an alcove to create a real chapel, with statues of Santa Chiara and Saint Francis of Assisi.

"When I was younger," Henry says, "I had this very elaborate idea of taking somebody I loved here and standing inside the chapel, that he'd love it as much as I did, and we'd slow dance right in front of the Blessed Mother. Just a . . . daft pubescent fantasy."

Henry hesitates, before finally sliding his phone out of his pocket. He presses a few buttons and extends a hand to Alex, and, quietly, "Your Song" starts to play from the tiny speaker.

Alex exhales a laugh. "Aren't you gonna ask if I know how to waltz?"

"No waltzing," Henry says. "Never cared for it."

Alex takes his hand, and Henry turns to face the chapel like a nervous postulant, his cheeks hollowed out in the low light, before pulling Alex into it.

When they kiss, Alex can hear a half-remembered old proverb from catechism, mixed up between translations of the book: "Come, hijo mío, de la miel, porque es buena, and the honeycomb, sweet to thy taste." He wonders what Santa Chiara would think of them, a lost David and Jonathan, turning slowly on the spot.

He brings Henry's hand to his mouth and kisses the little knob of his knuckle, the skin over the blue vein there, bloodlines, pulses, the old blood kept in perpetuity within these walls, and he thinks, *Father, Son, and Holy Spirit, amen.*

Henry charters a private plane to get him back home, and Alex is dreading the dressing-down he's going to get the minute he's stateside, but he's trying not to think about it. At the airstrip, the wind whipping his hair across his forehead, Henry fishes inside his jacket for something.

"Listen," he says, pulling a curled fist out of his pocket. He takes one of Alex's hands and turns it to press something small and heavy into his palm. "I want you to know, I'm sure. A thousand percent."

He removes his hand and there, sitting in the center of Alex's callused palm, is the signet ring.

"What?" Alex's eyes flash up to search Henry's face and find him smiling softly. "I can't—"

"Keep it," Henry tells him. "I'm sick of wearing it."

It's a private airstrip, but it's still risky, so he folds Henry in a hug and whispers fiercely, "I completely fucking love you."

At cruising altitude, he takes the chain off his neck and slides the ring on next to the old house key. They clink together gently as he tucks them both under his shirt, two homes side by side.

ELEVEN

Hometown stuff

A <agcd@eclare45.com>   9/2/20 5:12 PM
to Henry

H,

Have been home for three hours. Already miss you. This is
some bullshit.

Hey, have I told you lately that you're brave? I still
remember what you said to that little girl in the hospital about
Luke Skywalker: "He's proof that it doesn't matter where you
come from or who your family is." Sweetheart, you're proof
too.

(By the way, in this relationship, I am absolutely the Han and you are absolutely the Leia. Don't try to argue because you'll be wrong.)

I was also thinking about Texas again, which I guess I do a lot when I'm stressed about election stuff. There's so much stuff I haven't shown you yet. We haven't even done Austin! I wanna take you to Franklin Barbecue. You have to wait in line for hours, but that's part of the experience. I really wanna see a member of the royal family wait in line for hours to eat cow parts.

Have you thought any more about what you said before I left? About coming out to your family? Obviously, you're not obligated. You just seemed kind of hopeful when you talked about it.

I'll be over here, still quarantined in the White House (at least Mom didn't kill me for London), rooting for you.

Love you.

xoxoxoxoxo
A

P.S. Vita Sackville-West to Virginia Woolf—1927:

With me it is quite stark: I miss you even more than I could have believed; and I was prepared to miss you a good deal.

Re: Hometown stuff

 Henry <hwales@kensingtonemail.com>   9/3/20 2:49 AM
to A

Alex,

It is, indeed, bullshit. It's all I can do not to pack a bag and be
gone forever. Perhaps I could live in your room like a recluse.
You could have food sent up for me, and I'll be lurking in
disguise in a shadowy corner when you answer the door. It'll
all be very dreadfully *Jane Eyre.*

The Mail will write mad speculations about where I've gone,
if I've offed myself or vanished to St. Kilda, but only you and
I will know that I'm just sprawled in your bed, reading books
and feeding myself profiteroles and making love to you
endlessly until we both expire in a haze of chocolate sauce.
It's how I'd want to go.

I'm afraid, though, I'm stuck here. Gran keeps asking
Mum when I'm going to enlist, and did I know Philip had
already served a year by the time he was my age. I do
need to figure out what I'm going to do, because I'm
certainly closing in on the end of what's an acceptable
amount of time for a gap year. Please do keep me in your—
what is it American politicians say?—thoughts and
prayers.

Austin sounds brilliant. Maybe in a few months, after things
settle down a bit? I could take a long weekend. Can we visit

your mum's house? Your room? Do you still have your lacrosse trophies? Tell me you still have posters up. Let me guess: Han Solo, Barack Obama, and . . . Ruth Bader Ginsburg.

(I'll agree with your assessment that you're the Han to my Leia in that you are, without doubt, a scruffy-looking nerf herder who would pilot us into an asteroid field. I happen to like nice men.)

I have thought more about coming out to my family, which is part of why I'm staying here for now. Bea has offered to be there when I tell Philip if I want, so I think I will. Again, thoughts and prayers.

I love you terribly, and I want you back here soon. I need your help picking a new bed for my room; I've decided to get rid of that gold monstrosity.

Yours,
Henry

P.S. From Radclyffe Hall to Evguenia Souline, 1934:

Darling—I wonder if you realize how much I am counting on your coming to England, how much it means to me—it means all the world, and indeed my body shall be all, all yours, as yours will be all, all mine, beloved. . . . And nothing will matter but just we two, we two longing loves at last come together.

Re: Hometown stuff

 A <agcd@eclare45.com>   9/3/20 6:20 AM
to Henry

H,

Shit. Do you think you're going to enlist? I haven't done
any research on it yet. I'm gonna ask Zahra to have one
of our people put together a binder on it. What would
that mean? Would you have to be gone a lot? Would it
be dangerous??? Or is it just like, wear the uniform and sit
at a desk? How did we not talk about this when I was
there?????

Sorry. I'm panicking. I somehow forgot this was a thing
looming on the horizon. I'm there for whatever you decide
you want to do, just, like, let me know if I need to start
practicing gazing wistfully out the window, waiting for my
love to return from the war.

It drives me nuts sometimes that you don't get to have
more say in your life. When I picture you happy, I see
you with your own apartment somewhere outside of the
palace and a desk where you can write anthologies of
queer history. And I'm there, using up your shampoo
and making you come to the grocery store with me and
waking up in the same damn time zone with you every
morning.

When the election is over, we can figure out what we'll do next. I would love to be in the same place for a bit, but I know you have to do what you have to do. Just know, I believe in you.

Re: telling Philip, sounds like a great plan. If all else fails, just do what I did and act like a huge jackass until most of your family figures it out on their own.

Love you. Tell Bea hi.
A

P.S. Eleanor Roosevelt to Lorena Hickock—1933:

I miss you greatly dear. The nicest time of the day is when I write to you. You have a stormier time than I do but I miss you as much, I think. . . . Please keep most of your heart in Washington as long as I'm here for most of mine is with you!

Re: Hometown stuff

 Henry <hwales@kensingtonemail.com>   9/4/20 7:58 PM
to A

Alex,

Have you ever had something go so horribly, horribly, unbelievably badly that you'd like to be loaded into a cannon and jettisoned into the merciless black maw of outer space?

I wonder sometimes what is the point of me, or anything. I should have just packed a bag like I said. I could be in your bed, languishing away until I perish, fat and sexually conquered, snuffed out in the spring of my youth. *Here lies Prince Henry of Wales. He died as he lived: avoiding plans and sucking cock.*

I told Philip. Not about you, precisely—about me.

Specifically, we were discussing enlistment, Philip and Shaan and I, and I told Philip I'd rather not follow the traditional path and that I hardly think I'd be useful to anyone in the military. He asked why I was so intent on disrespecting the traditions of the men of this family, and I truly think I dissociated straight (ha) out of the conversation, because I opened my blasted mouth and said, "Because I'm not like the rest of the men of this family, beginning with the fact that I am very deeply gay, Philip."

Once Shaan managed to dislodge him from the chandelier, Philip had quite a few words for me, some of which were "confused or misguided" and "ensuring the perpetuity of the bloodline" and "respecting the legacy." Honestly, I don't recall much of it. Essentially, I gathered that he was not surprised to discover I am not the heterosexual heir I'm supposed to be, but rather surprised that I do not intend to keep pretending to be the heterosexual heir I'm supposed to be.

So, yes, I know we discussed and hoped that coming out to my family would be a good first step. I cannot say this was

an encouraging sign re: our odds of going public. I don't
know. I've eaten a tremendous amount of Jaffa Cakes about
it, to be frank.

Sometimes I imagine moving to New York to take over
launching Pez's youth shelter there. Just leaving. Not coming
back. Maybe burning something down on the way out. It
would be nice.

Here's an idea: Do you know, I've realised I've never actually
told you what I thought the first time we met?

You see, for me, memories are difficult. Very often, they
hurt. A curious thing about grief is the way it takes your
entire life, all those foundational years that made you
who you are, and makes them so painful to look
back upon because of the absence there, that
suddenly they're inaccessible. You must invent an entirely
new system.

I started to think of myself and my life and my whole
lifetime worth of memories as all the dark, dusty rooms of
Buckingham Palace. I took the night Bea left rehab and I
begged her to take it seriously, and I put it in a room with
pink peonies on the wallpaper and a golden harp in
the center of the floor. I took my first time, with one of
my brother's mates from uni when I was seventeen, and
I found the smallest, most cramped little broom cupboard
I could muster, and I shoved it in. I took my father's last night,
the way his face went slack, the smell of his hands, the fever,
the waiting and waiting and terrible waiting and the even

worse not-waiting anymore, and I found the biggest room, a ballroom, wide open and dark, windows drawn and covered. Locked the doors.

But the first time I saw you. Rio. I took that down to the gardens. I pressed it into the leaves of a silver maple and recited it to the Waterloo Vase. It didn't fit in any rooms.

You were talking with Nora and June, happy and animated and fully alive, a person living in dimensions I couldn't access, and so beautiful. Your hair was longer then. You weren't even a president's son yet, but you weren't afraid. You had a yellow ipê-amarelo in your pocket.

I thought, this is the most incredible thing I have ever seen, and I had better keep it a safe distance away from me. I thought, if someone like that ever loved me, it would set me on fire.

And then I was a careless fool, and I fell in love with you anyway. When you rang me at truly shocking hours of the night, I loved you. When you kissed me in disgusting public toilets and pouted in hotel bars and made me happy in ways in which it had never even occurred to me that a mangled-up, locked-up person like me could be happy, I loved you.

And then, inexplicably, you had the absolute audacity to love me back. Can you believe it?

Sometimes, even now, I still can't.

I'm sorry things didn't go better with Philip. I wish I could send hope.

Yours,
Henry

P.S. From Michelangelo to Tommaso Cavalieri, 1533:

I know well that, at this hour, I could as easily forget your name as the food by which I live; nay, it were easier to forget the food, which only nourishes my body miserably, than your name, which nourishes both body and soul, filling the one and the other with such sweetness that neither weariness nor fear of death is felt by me while memory preserves you to my mind. Think, if the eyes could also enjoy their portion, in what condition I should find myself.

Re: Hometown stuff

 A <agcd@eclare45.com>   9/4/20 8:31 PM
to Henry

H,

Fuck.

I'm so sorry. I don't know what else to say. I'm so sorry. June and Nora send their love. Not as much love as me. Obviously.

Please don't worry about me. We'll figure it out. It just might take time. I've been working on patience. I've picked up all kinds of things from you.

God, what can I possibly write to make this better?

Here: I can't decide if your emails make me miss you more or less. Sometimes I feel like a funny-looking rock in the middle of the most beautiful clear ocean when I read the kinds of things you write to me. You love so much bigger than yourself, bigger than everything. I can't believe how lucky I am to even witness it—to be the one who gets to have it, and so much of it, is beyond luck and feels like fate. Catholic God made me to be the person you write those things about. I'll say five Hail Marys. Muchas gracias, Santa Maria.

I can't match you for prose, but what I *can* do is write you a list.

AN INCOMPLETE LIST: THINGS I LOVE ABOUT HRH PRINCE HENRY OF WALES

1. The sound of your laugh when I piss you off.
2. The way you smell underneath your fancy cologne, like clean linens but somehow also fresh grass (what kind of magic is this?).
3. That thing you do where you stick out your chin to try to look tough.
4. How your hands look when you play piano.
5. All the things I understand about myself now because of you.

6. How you think *Return of the Jedi* is the best Star Wars (wrong) because deep down you're a gigantic, sappy, embarrassing romantic who just wants the happily ever after.

7. Your ability to recite Keats.

8. Your ability to recite Bernadette's "Don't let it drag you down" monologue from *Priscilla, Queen of the Desert*.

9. How hard you try.

10. How hard you've always tried.

11. How determined you are to keep trying.

12. That when your shoulders cover mine, nothing else in the entire stupid world matters.

13. The goddamn issue of *Le Monde* you brought back to London with you and kept and have on your nightstand (yes, I saw it).

14. The way you look when you first wake up.

15. Your shoulder-to-waist ratio.

16. Your huge, generous, ridiculous, indestructible heart.

17. Your equally huge dick.

18. The face you just made when you read that last one.

19. The way you look when you first wake up (I know I already said this, but I really, really love it).

20. The fact that you loved me all along.

I keep thinking about that last one ever since you told me, and what an idiot I was. It's so hard for me to get out of my own head sometimes, but now I'm coming back to what I said to you the night in my room when it all started, and how I brushed you off when you offered to let me go after the DNC, how I used to try to act like it was nothing sometimes. I didn't even know what you were offering to do to yourself. God, I want to fight everyone who's ever hurt you, but it was me too, wasn't it? All that time. I'm so sorry.

Please stay gorgeous and strong and unbelievable. I miss you I miss you I miss you I love you. I'm calling you as soon as I send this, but I know you like to have these things written down.

A

P.S. Richard Wagner to Eliza Wille, re: Ludwig II–1864 (Remember when you played Wagner for me? He's an asshole, but this is something.)

It is true that I have my young king who genuinely adores me. You cannot form an idea of our relations. I recall one of the dreams of my youth. I once dreamed that Shakespeare was alive: that I really saw and spoke to him: I can never forget the impression that dream made on me. Then I would have wished to see Beethoven, though he was already dead. Something of the same kind must pass in the mind of this lovable man when with me. He says he can hardly believe that he really possesses me. None can read without astonishment, without enchantment, the letters he writes to me.

TWELVE

There's a diamond ring on Zahra's finger when she shows up with her coffee thermos and a thick stack of files. They're in June's room, scarfing down breakfast before Zahra and June leave for a rally in Pittsburgh, and June drops her waffle on the bedspread.

"Oh my God, Z, what is *that*? Did you get *engaged*?"

Zahra looks down at the ring and shrugs. "I had the weekend off."

June gapes at her.

"When are you going to tell us who you're dating?" Alex asks. "Also, *how*?"

"Uh-uh, nope," she says. "*You* don't get to say shit to me about secret relationships in and around this campaign, princess."

"Point," Alex concedes.

She brushes past the topic as June starts wiping syrup off the bed with her pajama pants. "We've got a lot of ground to cover this morning, so focus up, little Claremonts."

She's got detailed agendas for each of them, bullet-pointed and double-sided, and she dives right in. They're already on Thursday's voter registration drive in Cedar Rapids (Alex is pointedly not invited) when her phone pings with a notification. She picks it up, scrolling through the screen offhandedly.

"So I need both of you to be dressed and ready . . . by . . ." She's looking more closely at the screen, distracted. "By, uh . . ." Her face is taken over with a horrified gasp. "Oh, *fuck my ass.*"

"What—?" Alex starts, but his own phone buzzes in his lap, and he looks down to find a push notification from CNN: LEAKED SURVEILLANCE FOOTAGE SHOWS PRINCE HENRY AT DNC HOTEL.

"Oh, shit," Alex says.

June reads over his shoulder; somehow, some "anonymous source" got the security camera footage from the lobby of the Beekman that night of the DNC.

It's not . . . explicitly damning, but it very clearly does show the two of them walking out of the bar together, shoulder to shoulder, flanked by Cash, and it cuts to footage from the elevator, Henry's arm around Alex's waist while they talk with Cash. It ends with the three of them getting off together at the top floor.

Zahra looks up at him, practically murderous. "Can you explain to me why this one day of our lives will not stop haunting me?"

"I don't know," Alex says miserably. "I can't believe this is the one that's—I mean, we've done riskier things than this—"

"That's supposed to make me feel better *how*?"

"I just mean, like, who is leaking fucking elevator tapes? Who's checking for that? It's not like Solange was in there—"

A chirp from June's phone interrupts him, and she swears when she looks at it. "Jesus, that *Post* reporter just texted to ask for a comment on the speculation surrounding your relationship with Henry and whether it—whether it has to do with you leaving the campaign after the DNC." She looks between Alex and Zahra, eyes wide. "This is really bad, isn't it?"

"It ain't great," Zahra says. She's got her nose buried in her phone, furiously typing out what are probably very strongly worded emails to the press team. "What we need is a fucking diversion. We have to—to send you on a date or something."

"What if we—" June attempts.

"Or, fuck, send *him* on a date," Zahra says. "Send you *both* on dates."

"I could—" June tries again.

"Who the fuck do I call? What girl is gonna want to wade into this shitstorm to fake date either of you at this point?" Zahra grinds the heels of both hands against her eyes. "Jesus, be a gay beard."

"I have an idea!" June finally half shouts. When they both look at her, she's biting her lip, looking at Alex. "But I don't know if you're gonna like it."

She turns her phone around to show them the screen. It's a photo he recognizes as one of the ones they took for Pez in Texas, June and Henry lounging on the dock together. She's cropped Nora out so it's just the two of them, Henry sporting a wide, teasing grin under his sunglasses and June planting a kiss on his cheek.

"I was on that floor too," she says. "We don't have to, like, confirm or deny anything. But we can imply something. Just to take the heat off."

Alex swallows.

He's always known June was one inch from taking a bullet for him, but this? He would never ask her to do this.

But the thing is . . . it would work. Their social media friendship is well documented, even if half of it is GIFs of Colin Firth. Out of context, the photo looks as couple-y as anything, like a nice, gorgeous, heterosexual couple on vacation together. He looks over to Zahra.

"It's not a bad idea," Zahra says. "We'd have to get Henry on board. Can you do that?"

Alex releases a breath. He absolutely doesn't want this, but he's also not sure what other choice he has. "Um. Yeah, I. Yeah, I think so."

"This is kind of exactly what we said we didn't want to do," Alex says into his phone.

"I know," Henry tells him across the line. His voice is shaky. Philip is waiting on Henry's other line. "But."

"Yeah," Alex says. "But."

June posts the picture from Texas, and it immediately burns through her stats to become her new most-liked post.

Within hours, it's everywhere. *BuzzFeed* puts up a comprehensive guide to Henry and June's relationship, leading off with that goddamn photo of them dancing at the royal wedding. They dig up photos from the night in LA, analyze Twitter interactions. "Just when you thought June Claremont-Diaz couldn't get any more #goals," one article writes, "has she secretly had her own Prince Charming all along?" Another one speculates, "Did HRH's best friend Alex introduce them?"

June's relieved, only because she managed to find a way to protect him, even though it means the world is digging through *her* life for answers and evidence, which makes Alex want to murder everyone. He also wants to grab people by the shoulders and shake them and tell them Henry is *his,* you idiots, even though the whole point of this was for it to be believable. He shouldn't feel wronged deep in his gut. But that everyone seems enamored, when the only difference between the lie and the truth that would burn up Fox News is the gender involved . . . well, it fucking stings.

Henry is quiet. He says enough for Alex to glean that Philip is apoplectic and Her Majesty is annoyed but pleased Henry has finally found himself a girlfriend. Alex feels horrible about it. The stifling orders, pretending to be someone he's not—Alex has always tried to be a refuge for Henry from it all. It was never supposed to come from his side too.

It's bad. It's stomach-cramps, walls-closing-in, no-plan-B-if-this-fails bad. He was in London barely two weeks ago, kissing Henry in front of a Giambologna. Now, this.

There's another piece in their back pocket that'll sell it. The only relationship in his life that can get more mileage than any of this. Nora comes to him at the Residence wearing bright red lipstick and presses cool, patient fingers against his temples and says, "Take me on a date."

They choose a college neighborhood full of people who'll sneak shots on their phones and post them everywhere. Nora slides her hand into his back pocket, and he tries to focus on the comfort of her physical presence against his side, the familiar frizz of her curls against his cheek.

For half a second, he allows a small part of him to think about how much easier things would be if this were the truth: sliding back into comfortable, easy harmony with his best friend, leaving greasy fingerprints along her waistline outside Jumbo Slice, laughing at her crass jokes. If he could love her like people wanted him to, and she loved him, and there wasn't any more to it than that.

But she doesn't, and he can't, and his heart is on a plane over the Atlantic right now, coming to DC to seal the deal over a well-photographed lunch with June the next day. Zahra sends him an email full of Twitter threads about him and Nora that night when he's in bed, and he feels sick.

Henry lands in the middle of the night and isn't even allowed to come near the Residence, instead sequestered in a hotel across town. He sounds exhausted when he calls in the morning, and Alex holds the phone close and promises he'll try to find a way to see him before he flies back out.

"Please," Henry says, paper-thin.

His mother, the rest of the administration, and half of the press at this point are caught up for the day dealing with news of a North Korean missile test; nobody notices when June lets him climb into her SUV with her that morning. June holds onto his elbow and makes half-hearted jokes, and when they pull up a block from the cafe, she offers him an apologetic smile.

"I'll tell him you're here," she says. "If nothing else, maybe that'll make it a little easier for him."

"Thanks," he says. Before she opens the door to leave, he catches her by the wrist and says, "Seriously. Thank you."

She gives his hand a squeeze, and she and Amy are gone, and he's alone in a tiny, secluded alleyway with the second car of backup security and a twisted-up feeling in his stomach.

It takes all of an hour before June texts him, All done, followed by, Bringing him to you.

They worked it out before they left: Amy brings June and Henry back to the alley, they have him swap cars like a political prisoner. Alex leans forward to the two agents sitting silently in the front seats. He doesn't know if they've figured out what this really is yet, and he honestly doesn't care.

"Hey, can I have a minute?"

They exchange a look but get out, and a minute later, there's another car alongside him and the door is opening, and he's there. Henry, looking tense and unhappy, but within arm's reach.

Alex pulls him in by the shoulder on instinct, the door shutting behind him. He holds him there, and this close he can see the faint gray tinge to Henry's complexion, the way his eyes aren't connecting. It's the worst he's ever seen him, worse than a violent fit or the verge of tears. He looks hollowed-out, vacant.

"Hey," Alex says. Henry's gaze is still unfocused, and Alex shifts toward the middle of the seat and into his line of vision. "Hey. Look at me. Hey. I'm right here."

Henry's hands are shaking, his breaths coming shallow, and Alex knows the signs, the low hum of an impending panic attack. He reaches down and wraps his hands around one of Henry's wrists, feeling the racing pulse under his thumbs.

Henry finally meets his eyes. "I hate it," he says. "I *hate* this."

"I know," Alex says.

"It was . . . *tolerable* before, somehow," Henry says. "When there was never—never the possibility of anything else. But, Christ, this is—it's *vile*. It's a bloody farce. And June and Nora, what, they just get to be *used*? Gran wanted me to bring my own photographers for this. Did you know that?" He inhales, and it gets caught in his throat and shudders violently on the way back out. "Alex. I don't want to *do* this."

"I know," Alex tells him again, reaching up to smooth out Henry's brow with the pad of his thumb. "I know. I hate it too."

"It's not fucking *fair!*" he goes on, his voice nearly breaking. "My shit ancestors walked around doing a thousand times worse than any of this, and nobody *cared!*"

"*Baby,*" Alex says, moving his hand to Henry's chin to bring him back down. "I know. I'm so sorry, babe. But it won't be like this forever, okay? I promise."

Henry closes his eyes and exhales through his nose. "I want to believe you. I do. But I'm so afraid I'll never be allowed."

Alex wants to go to war for this man, wants to get his hands on everything and everyone that ever hurt him, but for once, he's trying to be the steady one. So he rubs the side of Henry's neck gently until his eyes drift back open, and he smiles softly, tipping their foreheads together.

"Hey," he says. "I'm not gonna let that happen. Listen, I'm telling you right now, I will physically fight your grandmother myself if I have to, okay? And, like, she's old. I know I can take her."

"I wouldn't be so cocky," Henry says with a small laugh. "She's full of dark surprises."

Alex laughs, cuffing him on the shoulder.

"Seriously," he says. Henry's looking back at him, beautiful and vital and heartsick and still, always, the person Alex is willing to risk ruining his life for. "I hate this so much. I know. But we're gonna do it together. And we're gonna make it work. You and me and history, remember? We're just gonna fucking fight. Because you're it, okay? I'm never gonna love anybody in the world like I love you. So, I promise you, one day we'll be able to just *be,* and fuck everyone else."

He pulls Henry in by the nape of his neck and kisses him hard, Henry's knee knocking against the center console as his hands move up to Alex's face. Even though the windows are tinted black, it's the closest they've ever come to kissing in public, and Alex knows it's reckless, but all he can think is a supercut of other people's letters they've quietly sent to each other. Words that went down in history. "Meet you in every dream . . . Keep most of your heart in Washington . . . Miss you like a home . . . We two longing loves . . . My young king."

One day, he tells himself. *One day, us too.*

The anxiety feels like buzzing little wings in his ear in the silence, like a petulant wasp. It catches him when he tries to sleep and startles him awake, follows him on laps paced up and down the floors of the Residence. It's getting harder to brush off the feeling he's being watched.

The worst part is that there's no end in sight. They'll definitely have to keep it up at least until the election is over, and even then, there's the always looming possibility of the queen outright forbidding it. His idealistic streak won't let him fully accept it, but that doesn't mean it isn't there.

He keeps waking up in DC, and Henry keeps waking up in London, and the whole world keeps waking up to talk about the two of them in love with other people. Pictures of Nora's hand in his. Speculation about whether June will get an official announcement of royal courtship. And the two of them, Henry and Alex, like the world's worst illustration of the *Symposium*: split down the middle and sent bleeding into separate lives.

Even that thought depresses him because Henry's the only

reason he's become a person who cites Plato. Henry and his classics. Henry in his palace, in love, in misery, not talking much anymore.

Even with both of them trying as hard as they are, it's impossible to feel like it's not pulling them apart. The whole charade takes and takes from them, takes days that were sacred—the night in LA, the weekend at the lake, the missed chance in Rio—and records over the tape with something more palatable. The narrative: two fresh-faced young men who love two beautiful young women and definitely not ever each other.

He doesn't want Henry to know. Henry has a hard enough time as it is, looked at sideways by his whole family, Philip who knows and has not been kind. He tries to sound calm and whole over the phone when they talk, but he doesn't think it's convincing.

When he was younger and the anxiety got this bad, when the stakes in his life were much, much lower, this would be the point of self-destruction. If he were in California, he'd sneak the jeep out and drive way too fast down the 101, doors off, blasting N.W.A., inches from being painted on the pavement. In Texas, he'd steal a bottle of Maker's from the liquor cabinet and get wasted with half the lacrosse team and maybe, afterward, climb through Liam's window and hope to forget by morning.

The first debate is in a matter of weeks. He doesn't even have work to keep him busy, so he stews and stresses and goes for long, punishing runs until he has the satisfaction of blisters. He wants to set himself on fire, but he can't afford for anyone to see him burn.

He's returning a box of borrowed files to his dad's office in the Dirksen Building after hours when he hears the faint sound of Muddy Waters from the floor above, and it hits him. There's one person he can burn down instead.

He finds Rafael Luna hunched at his office's open window, sucking down a cigarette. There are two empty, crumpled packs of Marlboros next to a lighter and an overflowing ashtray on the sill. When he turns around at the slam of the door, he coughs out a startled cloud of smoke.

"Those things are gonna fucking kill you," Alex says. He said the same thing about five hundred times that summer in Denver, but now he means, *I kinda wish they would.*

"Kid—"

"*Don't* call me that."

Luna turns, stubbing out his cigarette in the ashtray, and Alex can see a muscle clenching in his jaw. As handsome as he always is, he looks like shit. "You shouldn't be here."

"No shit," Alex says. "I just wanted to see if you would have the balls to actually talk to me."

"You do realize you're talking to a United States senator," he says placidly.

"Yeah, big fucking man," Alex says. He's advancing on Luna now, kicking a chair out of the way. "Important fucking job. Hey, how 'bout you tell me how you're serving the people who voted for you by being Jeffrey Richards's chickenshit little sellout?"

"What the hell did you come here for, Alex, eh?" Luna asks him, unmoved. "You gonna fight me?"

"I want you to tell me *why.*"

His jaw clenches again. "You wouldn't understand. You're—"

"I swear to God, if you say I'm too young, I'm gonna lose my shit."

"This isn't you losing your shit?" Luna asks mildly, and the look that crosses Alex's face must be murderous because he immediately puts a hand up. "Okay, bad timing. Look, I know. I know it seems shitty, but there's—there are moving parts at work here that you can't even imagine. You know I'll always be indebted to your family for what you all have done for me, but—"

"I don't give a shit about what you *owe* us. I *trusted* you," he says. "Don't condescend to me. You know as much as anyone what I'm capable of, what I've seen. If you told me, I would get it."

He's so close he's practically breathing Luna's reeking cigarette smoke, and when he looks into his face, there's a flicker of recognition at the bloodshot, blackened eyes and the gaunt cheekbones. It reminds him of how Henry looked in the back of the Secret Service car.

"Does Richards have something on you?" he asks. "Is he making you do this?"

Luna hesitates. "I'm doing this because it's what needs to be done, Alex. It was my choice. Nobody else's."

"Then tell me why."

Luna takes a deep breath and says, "*No.*"

Alex imagines his fist in Luna's face and removes himself by two steps, out of range.

"You remember that night in Denver," he says, measured, his voice quavering, "when we ordered pizza and you showed me pictures of all the kids you fought for in court? And we drank that nice bottle of scotch from the mayor of Boulder? I remember lying on the floor of your office, on the ugly-ass carpet, drunk off my ass, thinking, 'God, I hope I can be like him.' Because you were brave. Because you stood up for things. And I couldn't stop wondering how you had the nerve to get up and do what you do every day with everyone knowing what they know about you."

Briefly, Alex thinks he's gotten through to Luna, from the way he closes his eyes and braces himself against the sill. But when he faces Alex again, his stare is hard.

"People don't know a damn thing about me. They don't know the half of it. And neither do you," he says. "Jesus, Alex, please, don't be like me. Find another fucking role model."

Alex, finally at his limit, lifts his chin and spits out, "I already *am* like you."

It hangs in the air between them, as physical as the kicked-over chair. Luna blinks. "What are you saying?"

"You know what I'm saying. I think you always knew, before I even did."

"You don't—" he says, stammering, trying to put it off. "You're not like me."

Alex levels his stare. "Close enough. And you know what I mean."

"Okay, fine, kid," Luna finally snaps, "you want me to be your fucking sherpa? Here's my advice: Don't tell anyone. Go find a nice girl and marry her. You're luckier than me—you can do that, and it wouldn't even be a lie."

And what comes out of Alex's mouth, comes so fast he has no chance to stop it, only divert it out of English at the last second in case it's overheard: "Sería una mentira, porque no sería él." It would be a lie, because it wouldn't be *him.*

He knows immediately Raf has caught his meaning, because he takes a sharp step backward, his back hitting the sill again.

"You can't tell me this shit, Alex!" he says, clawing inside his jacket until he finds and removes another pack of cigarettes. He shakes one out and fumbles with the lighter. "What are you even *thinking*? I'm on the opponent's fucking campaign! I can't hear this! How can you possibly think you can be a politician like this?"

"Who fucking decided that politics had to be about lying and hiding and being something you're not?"

"It's *always* been that, Alex!"

"Since when did *you* buy into it?" Alex spits. "You, me, my family, the people we run with—we were gonna be the honest ones! I have absolutely zero interest in being a politician with some perfect veneer and two-point-five kids. Didn't we decide it was supposed to be about helping people? About the fight? What part of that is so fucking irreconcilable with letting people see who I really am? Who *you* are, Raf?"

"Alex, please. Please. Jesus Christ. You have to leave. I can't know this. You can't tell me this. You have to be more careful than this."

"God," Alex says, voice bitter, his hands on his hips. "You know, it's worse than trust. I *believed* in you."

"I know you did," Luna says. He's not even looking at Alex anymore. "I wish you hadn't. Now, I need you to get out."

"Raf—"

"Alex. Get. Out."

He goes, slamming the door behind him.

Back at the Residence, he tries to call Henry. He doesn't pick up, but he texts: Sorry. Meeting with Philip. Love you.

He reaches under the bed and gropes in the dark until he finds it: a bottle of Maker's. The emergency stash.

"Salud," he mutters under his breath, and he unscrews the top.

bad metaphors about maps

A <agcd@eclare45.com>   9/25/20 3:21 AM
to Henry

h,

i have had whiskey. bear with me.

there's this thing you do. this thing. it drives me crazy. i think
about it all the time.

there's a corner of your mouth, and a place that it goes.
pinched and worried like you're afraid you're forgetting
something. i used to hate it. used to think it was your little tic
of disapproval.

but i've kissed your mouth, that corner, that place it goes,
so many times now. i've memorized it. topography on the
map of you, a world i'm still charting. i know it. i added it
to the key. here: inches to miles. i can multiply it out, read
your latitude and longitude. recite your coordinates like la
rosaria.

this thing, your mouth, its place. it's what you do when you're
trying not to give yourself away. not in the way that you do all
the time, those empty, greedy grabs for you. i mean the truth
of you. the weird, perfect shape of your heart. the one on the
outside of your chest.

on the map of you, my fingers can always find the green
hills, wales. cool waters and a shore of white chalk. the
ancient part of you carved out of stone in a prayerful circle,
sacrosanct. your spine's a ridge i'd die climbing.

if i could spread it out on my desk, i'd find the corner of your
mouth where it pinches with my fingers, and i'd smooth it
away and you'd be marked with the names of saints like all
the old maps. i get the nomenclature now—saints' names
belong to miracles.

give yourself away sometimes, sweetheart. there's so much
of you.

fucking yrs,
a

p.s. wilfred owen to siegfried sassoon—1917:

*And you have fixed my Life—however short. You did not light
me: I was always a mad comet; but you have fixed me. I
spun round you a satellite for a month, but shall swing out
soon, a dark star in the orbit where you will blaze.*

Re: Bad metaphors about maps

 Henry <hwales@kensingtonemail.com>   9/25/20 6:07 AM
to A

From Jean Cocteau to Jean Marais, 1939:

*Thank you from the bottom of my heart for having saved me.
I was drowning and you threw yourself into the water without
hesitation, without a backward look.*

The sound of Alex's phone buzzing on his nightstand startles
him out of a dead sleep. He falls halfway out of bed, fumbling
to answer it.

"Hello?"

"*What did you do?*" Zahra's voice nearly shouts. By the clicking of heels in the background and muttered swearing, she's
running somewhere.

"Um," Alex says. He rubs his eyes, trying to get his brain
back online. What *did* he do? "Be more specific?"

"Check the fucking news, you horny little miscreant—how
could you possibly be *stupid enough to get photographed*? I swear to
God—"

Alex doesn't even hear the last part of what she says, because
his stomach has just dropped all the way down through the
floor and into the fucking basements two floors below.

"Fuck."

Hands shaking, he switches Zahra to speaker, opens up
Google, and types his own name.

BREAKING: Photos Reveal Romantic Relationship Between Prince Henry and Alex Claremont-Diaz

OMFG: FSOTUS and Prince Henry—Totally Doing It

THE ORAL OFFICE: READ FSOTUS'S STEAMY EMAILS TO PRINCE HENRY

Royal Family Declines to Comment on Reports of Prince Henry's Relationship with First Son

25 GIFs That Perfectly Describe Our Reaction When We Heard About Prince Henry & FSOTUS

DON'T LET FIRST SON GO DOWN ON ME

A bubble of hysterical laughter emerges from his throat.

His bedroom door flies open, and Zahra slams on the light, a steely expression of rage barely concealing the sheer terror on her face. Alex's brain flashes to the panic button behind his headboard and wonders if the Secret Service will be able to find him before he bleeds out.

"You're on communications lockdown," she says, and instead of punching him, she snatches his phone out of his hand and shoves it down the front of her blouse, which has been buttoned wrong in her rush. She doesn't even blink at his state of half-nakedness, just dumps an armload of newspapers onto his bedspread.

QUEEN HENRY! twenty copies of the *Daily Mail* proclaim

in gigantic letters. INSIDE THE PRINCE'S GAY AFFAIR WITH THE FIRST SON OF THE UNITED STATES!

The cover is splashed with a blown-up photo of what is undeniably himself and Henry kissing in the back seat of the car behind the cafe, apparently shot with a long-range lens through the windshield. Tinted windows, but he forgot about the fucking *windshield*.

Two smaller photos are inset on the bottom of the page: one of the shots of them on the Beekman's elevator and a photo of them side by side at Wimbledon, him whispering something in Henry's ear while Henry smiles a soft, private smile.

Fucking shitting hell. He is so fucked. Henry is so fucked. And, Jesus Christ, his mother's campaign is fucked, and his political career is fucked, and his ears are ringing, and he's going to throw up.

"*Fuck,*" Alex says again. "I need my phone. I have to call Henry—"

"No, you do fucking not," Zahra says. "We don't know yet how the emails got out, so it's radio silence until we find the leak."

"The—what? Is Henry okay?" God, Henry. All he can think about is Henry's big blue eyes looking terrified, Henry's breathing coming shallow and quick, locked in his bedroom in Kensington Palace and desperately alone, and his jaw locks up, something burning in the back of his throat.

"The president is sitting down right now with as many members of the Office of Communications as we could drag out of bed at three in the morning," Zahra tells him, ignoring his question. Her phone is buzzing nonstop in her hand. "It's about to be gay DEFCON five in this administration. For God's sake, put some clothes on."

Zahra disappears into Alex's closet, and he flips the

newspaper open to the story, his heart pounding. There are even more photos inside. He glances over the copy, but there's too much to even begin to process.

On the second page, he sees them: printed and annotated excerpts of their emails. One is labeled: PRINCE HENRY: SECRET POET? It begins with a line he's read about a thousand times by now.

Should I tell you that when we're apart, your body comes back to me in dreams . . .

"*Fuck!*" he says a third time, spiking the newspaper at the floor. That one was *his.* It feels obscene to see it there. "How the fuck did they *get these?*"

"Yep," Zahra agrees. "You dirty did it." She throws a white button-down and a pair of jeans at him, and he pitches himself out of bed. Zahra gamely holds out an arm for him to steady himself while he pulls his pants up, and despite it all, he's struck with overwhelming gratitude for her.

"Listen, I need to talk to Henry as soon as possible. I can't even imagine— God, I need to talk to him."

"Get some shoes, we're running," Zahra tells him. "Priority one is damage control, not feelings."

He grabs a pair of sneakers, and they take off while he's still pulling them on, running west. His brain is struggling to keep up, running through about five thousand possible ways this could go, imagining himself ten years down the road being frozen out of Congress, plummeting approval ratings, Henry's name scratched off the line of succession, his mother losing reelection on a swing state's disapproval of him. He's so screwed, and he can't even decide who to be the angriest with, himself or the *Mail* or the monarchy or the whole stupid country.

He nearly crashes into Zahra's back as she skids to a stop in front of a door.

He pushes the door open, and the whole room goes silent.

His mother stares at him from the head of the table and says flatly, "Out."

At first he thinks she's talking to him, but she cuts her eyes down to the people around the table with her.

"Was I not clear? Everyone, out, now," she says. "I need to talk to my son."

THIRTEEN

"Sit down," his mother tells him, and Alex feels dread coil deep in his stomach. He has no clue what to expect—knowing your parent as the person who raised you isn't the same as being able to guess their moves as a world leader.

He sits, and the silence hovers over them, his mother's hands folded in a considering pose against her lips. She looks exhausted.

"Are you okay?" she says finally. When he looks up in surprise, there's no anger in her eyes.

The president stands on the edge of a career-ending scandal, measures her breaths evenly, and waits for her son to answer.

Oh.

It hits him with sudden clarity that he hasn't at all stopped to consider his own feelings. There simply hasn't been the time. When he reaches for an emotion to name, he finds he can't pin one down, and something shudders inside him and shuts down completely.

He doesn't often wish away his position in life, but in this moment, he does. He wants to be having this conversation in a different life, just his mother sitting across from him at the dinner table, asking him how he feels about his nice, respectable boyfriend, if he's doing okay with figuring his identity out. Not like this, in a West Wing briefing room, his dirty emails spread out between them on the table.

"I'm . . ." he begins. To his horror, he hears something shake in his voice, which he quickly swallows down. "I don't know. This isn't how I wanted to tell people. I thought we'd get a chance to do this right."

Something softens and resolves in her face, and he suspects he's answered a question for her beyond the one she asked.

She reaches over and covers one of his hands with her own.

"You listen to me," she says. Her jaw is set, ironclad. It's the game face he's seen her use to stare down Congress, to cow autocrats. Her grip on his hand is steady and strong. He wonders, half-hysterically, if this is how it felt to charge into war under Washington. "I am your mother. I was your mother before I was ever the president, and I'll be your mother long after, to the day they put me in the ground and beyond this earth. You are my child. So, if you're serious about this, I'll back your play."

Alex is silent.

But the debates, he thinks. *But the general.*

Her gaze is hard. He knows better than to say either of those things. She'll handle it.

"So," she says. "Do you feel forever about him?"

And there's no room left to agonize over it, nothing left to do but say the thing he's known all along.

"Yeah," he says, "I do."

Ellen Claremont exhales slowly, and she grins a small, secret grin, the crooked, unflattering one she never uses in public, the one he knows best from when he was a kid around her knees in a small kitchen in Travis County.

"Then, fuck it."

The Washington Post

As details emerge about Alex Claremont-Diaz's affair with Prince Henry, White House goes silent

September 27, 2020

"Thinking about history makes me wonder how I'll fit into it one day, I guess," First Son Alex Claremont-Diaz writes in one of the many emails to Prince Henry published by the *Daily Mail* this morning. "And you too."

It seems the answer to that question may have come sooner than any anticipated with the sudden exposure of the First Son's romantic relationship with Prince Henry, an arrangement with major repercussions for two of the world's most powerful nations, less than two months before the United States casts its vote on President Claremont's second term.

As security experts within the FBI and the Claremont administration scramble to find the sources that provided the British tabloid with evidence of the affair, the usually high-profile First Family has shuttered, with no official statement from the First Son.

"The First Family has always and continues to keep their personal lives separate from the political and diplomatic dealings of the presidency," White House Press Secretary Davis Sutherland said in a brief prepared statement this morning. "They ask for patience and understanding from the American people as they handle this very private matter."

The *Daily Mail*'s report this morning revealed that First Son Alex Claremont-Diaz has been involved romantically and sexually with Prince Henry since at least February of this year, according to emails and photographs obtained by the paper.

The full email transcripts have been uploaded to WikiLeaks under the moniker "The Waterloo Letters," seemingly named for a reference to the Waterloo Vase in the Buckingham Palace Gardens in one email composed by Prince Henry. The correspondence continues regularly up to Sunday night and appears to have been lifted from a private email server used by residents of the White House.

"Setting aside the ramifications for President Claremont's ability to be impartial on issues of both international relations and traditional family values," Republican presidential candidate Senator Jeffrey Richards said at a press conference earlier today, "I'm extremely concerned about this private email server. What kind of information was being disseminated on this server?"

Richards added that he believes the American voters have a right to know everything else for which President Claremont's server may have been used.

Sources close to the Claremont administration insist the private server is similar to the one set up during President George W. Bush's administration and used only for communication within the White House about day-to-day operations and personal correspondence for the First Family and core White House personnel.

First rounds of examination of "The Waterloo Letters" by experts have yet to reveal any evidence of classified information or otherwise compromising content outside of the nature of the First Son's relationship with Prince Henry.

For five endless, unbearable hours, Alex is shuffled from room to room in the West Wing, meeting with what seems to be every strategist, press staffer, and crisis manager his mother's administration has to offer.

The only moment he recalls with any clarity is pulling his mother into an alcove to say, "I told Raf."

She stares at him. "You told Rafael Luna that you're bisexual?"

"I told Rafael Luna about Henry," he says flatly. "Two days ago."

She doesn't ask why, just sighs grimly, and they both hover over the implication before she says, "No. No, those pictures were taken before that. It couldn't have been him."

He runs through pro and con lists, models of different outcomes, fucking charts and graphs and more data than he has ever wanted to see about his own relationship and its ramifications for the world around him. *This is the damage you cause, Alex,* it all seems to say, right there in hard facts and figures. *This is who you hurt.*

He hates himself, but he doesn't regret anything, and maybe that makes him a bad person and a worse politician, but he doesn't regret Henry.

For five endless, unbearable hours, he's not allowed to even try to contact Henry. The press sec drafts a statement. It looks like any other memo.

For five hours, he doesn't shower or change his clothes or laugh or smile or cry. It's eight in the morning when he's finally released and told to stay in the Residence and stand by for further instructions.

He's handed his phone, at last, but there's no answer when he calls Henry, and no response when he texts. Nothing at all.

Amy walks him through the colonnade and up the stairs, saying nothing, and when they reach the hallway between the East and West Bedrooms, he sees them.

June, her hair in a haphazard knot on the top of her head and in a pink bathrobe, her eyes red-rimmed. His mom, in a sharp, no-nonsense black dress and pointed heels, jaw set. Leo, barefoot in his pajamas. And his dad, a leather duffel still hanging off one shoulder, looking harried and exhausted.

They all turn to look at him, and Alex feels a wave of something so much bigger than himself sweep over him, like when he was a child standing bowlegged in the Gulf of Mexico, riptide sucking at his feet. A sound escapes his throat uninvited, something that he barely even recognizes, and June has him first, then the rest of them, arms and arms and hands and hands, pulling him close and touching his face and moving him until he's on the floor, the goddamn terrible hideous antique rug that he hates, sitting on the floor and staring at the rug and the threads of the rug and hearing the Gulf rushing in his ears and thinking distantly that he's having a panic attack, and that's why he can't breathe, but he's just staring at the rug and he's having a panic attack and knowing why his lungs won't work doesn't make them work again.

He's faintly aware of being shifted into his room, to his bed, which is still covered in the godforsaken fucking *newspapers,* and someone guides him onto it, and he sits down and tries very, very hard to make a list in his head.

One.

One.

One.

He sleeps in fits and starts, wakes up sweating, wakes up shivering. He dreams in short, fractured scenes that swell and fade erratically. He dreams of himself at war, in a muddy trench, love letter soaking red in his chest pocket. He dreams of a house in Travis County, doors locked, unwilling to let him in again. He dreams of a crown.

He dreams once, briefly, of the lake house, an orange beacon under the moon. He sees himself there, standing in water up to his neck. He sees Henry, sitting naked on the pier. He sees June and Nora, hands clasped together, and Pez on the grass between them, and Bea, digging pink fingertips into the wet soil.

In the trees next to them, he hears the snap, snap, snap of branches.

"Look," Henry says, pointing up at the stars.

And Alex tries to say, *Don't you hear it?* Tries to say, *Something's coming.* He opens his mouth: a spill of fireflies, and nothing.

When he opens his eyes, June is sitting up against the pillows next to him, bitten nails pressed against her bottom lip, still in her bathrobe and keeping watch. She reaches down and squeezes his hand. He squeezes back.

Between dreams he catches the sound of muffled voices in the hallway.

"Nothing," Zahra's voice is saying. "Not a thing. Nobody is taking our calls."

"How can they not be taking our calls? I'm the goddamn president."

"Permission to do a thing, ma'am, slightly outside diplomatic protocol."

A comment: The First Family Has Been Lying To Us, The American People!!1 WHAT ELSE Are They Lying About??!?!

A tweet: I KNEW IT I KNEW ALEX WAS GAY I TOLD YOU BITCHES

A comment: My 12 y/o daughter has been crying all day. She's dreamt of marrying Prince Henry since she was a little girl. She is heartbroken.

A comment: Are we really supposed to believe that no federal funds were used to cover this up?

A tweet: lmaoooo wait look at page 22 of the emails alex is such a hoe

A tweet: OMFG DID YOU SEE somebody who went to uni with Henry posted some photos of him at a party and he is just like Profoundly Gay in them i'm screaming

A tweet: READ—My column with @WSJ on what the #WaterlooLetters say about the inner workings of the Claremont White House.

More comments. Slurs. Lies.

June takes his phone away and shoves it under a couch cushion. He doesn't bother protesting. Henry's not going to call.

At one in the afternoon, for the second time in twelve hours, Zahra bursts through his bedroom door.

"Pack a bag," she says. "We're going to London."

June helps him stuff a backpack with jeans and a pair of shoes and a broken-in copy of *Prisoner of Azkaban,* and he stumbles into a clean shirt and out of his room. Zahra is waiting in the hall with her own bag and a freshly pressed suit of Alex's, a sensible navy one that she has apparently decided is appropriate for meeting the queen.

She's told him very little, except that Buckingham Palace has shut down communication channels in and out, and they're just going to show up and demand a meeting. She seems confident Shaan will agree to it and willing to physically overpower him if not.

The feeling rolling around in his gut is bizarre. His mom has signed off on them going public with the truth, which is *incredible,* but there's no reason to expect that from the crown. He could get marching orders to deny everything. He thinks he might grab Henry and run if it comes down to that.

He's almost completely sure Henry wouldn't go along with pretending it was all fake. He trusts Henry, and he believes in him.

But they were also supposed to have more time.

There's a secluded side entrance of the Residence that Alex can sneak out of without being seen, and June and his parents meet him there.

"I know this is scary," his mom says, "but you can handle it."

"Give 'em hell," his dad adds.

June hugs him, and he shoves on his sunglasses and a hat and jogs out the door and toward whatever way this is all going to end.

Cash and Amy are waiting on the plane. Alex wonders briefly if they volunteered for the assignment, but he's trying to get his emotions back under control, and that's not going to help. He bumps his fist against Cash's as he passes, and Amy nods up from the denim jacket she's needling yellow flowers into.

It's all happened so quickly that now, knees curled up to his chin as they leave the ground, is the first time Alex is able to actually think about everything.

He's not, he thinks, upset people know. He's always been pretty unapologetic when it came to things like who he dates and what he's into, although those were never anything like this. Still, the cocky shithead part of him is slightly pleased to finally have a claim on Henry. Yep, the prince? Most eligible bachelor in the world? British accent, face like a Greek god, legs for days? *Mine.*

But that's only a tiny, tiny fraction of it. The rest is a knot of fear, anger, violation, humiliation, uncertainty, panic. There are the flaws everyone's allowed to see—his big mouth, his mercurial temper, his searing impulses—and then there's this. It's like how he only wears his glasses when nobody's around: Nobody's supposed to see how much he needs.

He doesn't care that people think about his body and write about his sex life, real or imagined. He cares that they know, in his own private words, what's pumping out of his heart.

And Henry. God, Henry. Those emails—those *letters*— were the one place Henry could say what he was really thinking. There's nothing that wasn't laid out in there: Henry being gay, Bea going to rehab, the queen tacitly keeping Henry in the closet. Alex hasn't been a good Catholic in a long time, but he knows confession is a sacrament. They were supposed to stay safe.

Fuck.

He can't sit still. He tosses *Prisoner of Azkaban* aside after four pages. He encounters a think piece on his own relationship on Twitter and has to shut down the whole app. He paces up and down the aisle of the jet, kicking at the bottoms of the seats.

"Can you *please* sit down?" Zahra says after twenty minutes of watching him twitch around the cabin. "You're giving my ulcer an ulcer."

"Are you sure they're gonna let us in when we get there?" Alex asks her. "Like, what if they don't? What if they, like, call the Royal Guard on us and have us arrested? Can they do that? Amy could probably fight them. Will she get arrested if she tries to fight them?"

"For fuck's sake," Zahra groans, and she pulls out her phone and starts dialing.

"Who are you calling?"

She sighs, holding the phone up to her ear as it rings. "Srivastava."

"What makes you think he'll answer?"

"It's his personal line."

Alex stares at her. "You have his personal line and you haven't used it until now?"

"*Shaan,*" Zahra snaps. "Listen up, you fuck. We are in the air right now. FSOTUS is with me. ETA six hours. You will have a car waiting. We will meet the queen and whoever the fuck else we have to meet to hash this shit out, or so help me God I will personally make your balls into fucking earrings. I will scorched-earth your entire motherfucking life." She pauses, presumably to listen to him agree because Alex can't imagine him doing anything else. "Now, put Henry on the phone, and do *not* try to tell me he's not there, because I know you haven't let him out of your sight."

And she shoves her phone at Alex's face.

He takes it uncertainly and lifts it to his ear. There's rustling, a confused noise.

"Hello?"

It's Henry's voice, sweet and posh and shaky and confused, and relief knocks the wind out of him.

"*Sweetheart.*"

He hears Henry's exhale over the line. "Hi, love. Are you okay?"

He laughs wetly, amazed. "Fuck, are you kidding me? I'm fine, I'm fine, are *you* okay?"

"I'm . . . managing."

Alex winces. "How bad is it?"

"Philip broke a vase that belonged to Anne Boleyn, Gran ordered a communications lockdown, and Mum hasn't spoken to anyone," Henry tells him. "But, er, other than that. All things considered. It's, er."

"I know," Alex says. "I'll be there soon."

There's another pause, Henry's breath shaky over the receiver. "I'm not sorry," he says. "That people know."

Alex feels his heart climb up into his throat.

"Henry," he attempts, "I . . ."

"Maybe—"

"I talked to my mom—"

"I know the timing isn't ideal—"

"Would you—"

"I want—"

"Hang on," Alex says. "Are we. Um. Are we both asking the same thing?"

"That depends. Were you going to ask me if I want to tell the truth?"

"Yeah," Alex says, and he thinks his knuckles must be white around the phone. "Yeah, I was."

"Then, yes."

A breath, barely. "You want that?"

Henry takes a moment to respond, but his voice is level. "I don't know if I would have chosen it yet, but it's out there now, and . . . I won't lie. Not about this. Not about you."

Alex's eyelashes are wet.

"I fucking love you."

"I love you too."

"Just hold on until I get there; we're gonna figure this out."

"I will."

"I'm coming. I'll be there soon."

Henry exhales a wet, broken laugh. "Please, do hurry."

They hang up, and he passes the phone back to Zahra, who takes it wordlessly and tucks it back into her bag.

"Thank you, Zahra, I—"

She holds up one hand, eyes closed. "Don't."

"Seriously, you didn't have to do that."

"Look, I'm only going to say this once, and if you ever repeat it, I'll have you kneecapped." She drops her hand, fixing him with a glare that manages to be both chilly and fond. "I'm rooting for you, okay?"

"Wait. Zahra. Oh my God. I just realized. You're . . . my friend."

"No, I'm not."

"Zahra, you're my *mean friend*."

"Am not." She yanks a blanket from her pile of belongings, turning her back to Alex and wrapping it around her. "Don't speak to me for the next six hours. I deserve a fucking nap."

"Wait, wait, okay, wait," Alex says. "I have one question."

She sighs heavily. "What?"

"Why'd you wait to use Shaan's personal number?"

"Because he's my fiancé, asshole, but *some* of us understand the meaning of discretion, so you wouldn't know about it," she tells him without even so much as looking at him, curled up against the window of the plane. "We agreed we'd never use our personal numbers for work contact. Now shut up and let me get some sleep before we have to deal with the rest of this. I'm running on nothing but black coffee, a Wetzel's Pretzel, and a fistful of B12. Do not even breathe in my direction."

———

It's not Henry but Bea who answers when Alex knocks on the closed door of the music room on the second floor of Kensington.

"I *told* you to stay away—" Bea is saying as soon as the door is open, brandishing a guitar over her shoulder. She drops it as soon as she sees him. "Oh, Alex, I'm so sorry, I thought you were Philip." She scoops him up with her free hand into a surprisingly bone-crushing hug. "Thank God you're here, I was about to come get you myself."

When she releases him, he's finally able to see Henry behind her, slumped on the settee with a bottle of brandy. He smiles at Alex, weakly, and says, "Bit short for a stormtrooper."

Alex's laugh comes out half sob, and it's impossible to know if he moves first or if Henry does, but they meet in the middle of the room, Henry's arms around Alex's neck, swallowing him up. If Henry's voice on the phone was a tether, his body is the gravity that makes it possible, his hand gripping the back of Alex's neck a magnetic force, a permanent compass north.

"I'm sorry," is what comes out of Alex's mouth, miserably, earnestly, muffled against Henry's throat. "It's my fault. I'm so sorry. I'm so sorry."

Henry releases him, hands on his shoulders, jaw set. "Don't you dare. I'm not sorry for a thing."

Alex laughs again, incredulous, looking into the heavy circles under Henry's eyes and the chewed-up bottom lip and, for the first time, seeing a man born to lead a nation.

"You're unbelievable," Alex says. He leans up and kisses the underside of his jaw, finding it rough from a full, fitful day without a shave. He pushes his nose, his cheek into it, feels some of the tension sap out of Henry at the touch. "You know that?"

They find their way onto the lush purples and reds of the

Persian rugs on the floor, Henry's head in Alex's lap and Bea on a pouf, plucking away at a weird little instrument she tells Alex is called an autoharp. Bea pulls over a tiny table and sets out crackers and a little chunk of soft cheese and takes away the brandy bottle.

From the sound of it, the queen is absolutely livid—not just to finally have confirmation about Henry, but because it's via something as undignified as a tabloid scandal. Philip drove in from Anmer Hall the minute the news broke and has been rebuffed by Bea every time he tries to get near Henry for what he says "will simply be a stern discussion about the consequences of his actions." Catherine has been by, once, three hours ago, stone-faced and sad, to tell Henry that she loves him and he could have told her sooner.

"And I said, 'That's great, Mum, but as long as you're letting Gran keep me trapped, it doesn't mean a fucking thing,'" Henry says. Alex stares down at him, shocked and a little impressed. Henry rests an arm over his face. "I feel awful. I was—I dunno. All the times she should have been there the past few years, it caught up to me."

Bea sighs. "Maybe it was the kick in the arse she needs. We've been trying to get her to do *anything* for years since Dad."

"Still," Henry says. "The way Gran is—Mum isn't to blame for that. And she did manage to protect us, before. It's not fair."

"H," Bea says firmly. "It's hard, but she needed to hear it." She looks down at the little buttons of the autoharp. "We deserve to have one parent, at least."

The corner of her mouth pinches, so much like Henry's.

"Are you okay?" Alex asks her. "I know I—I saw a couple articles . . ." He doesn't finish the sentence. "The Powder Princess" was the fourth-highest Twitter trend ten hours ago.

Her frown twitches into a half-smile. "Me? Honestly, it's almost a relief. I've always said that the most comfortable I could be is everyone knowing my story upfront, so I don't have hear the speculations or lie to cover the truth—or explain it. I'd rather it, you know, hadn't been this way. But here we are. At least now I can stop acting as if it's something to be ashamed of."

"I know the feeling," Henry says softly.

The quiet ebbs and flows after a while, the London night black and pressing in against the windowpanes. David the beagle curls up protectively at Henry's side, and Bea picks a Bowie song to play. She sings under her breath, "I, I will be king, and you, you will be queen," and Alex almost laughs. It feels like how Zahra has described hurricane days to him: stuck together, hoping the sandbags will hold.

Henry drifts asleep at some point, and Alex is thankful for it, but he can still feel tension in every part of Henry's body against him.

"He hasn't slept since the news," Bea tells him quietly.

Alex nods slightly, searching her face. "Can I ask you something?"

"Always."

"I feel like he's not telling me something," Alex whispers. "I believe him when he says he's in, and he wants to tell everyone the truth. But there's something else he's not saying, and it's freaking me out that I can't figure out what it is."

Bea looks up, her fingers stilling. "Oh, love," she says simply. "He misses Dad."

Oh.

He sighs, putting his head in his hands. Of course.

"Can you explain?" he attempts lamely. "What that's like? What I can do?"

She shifts on her pouf, repositioning the harp onto the floor, and reaches into her sweater. She withdraws a silver coin on a chain: her sobriety chip.

"D'you mind if I go a bit sponsor?" she asks with a smirk. He offers her a weak half smile, and she continues.

"So, imagine we're all born with a set of feelings. Some are broader or deeper than others, but for everyone, there's that ground floor, a bottom crust of the pie. That's the maximum depth of feeling you've ever experienced. And then, the worst thing happens to you. The very worst thing that could have happened. The thing you had nightmares about as a child, and you thought, it's all right because that thing will happen to me when I'm older and wiser, and I'll have felt so many feelings by then that this one worst feeling, the worst possible feeling, won't seem so terrible.

"But it happens to you when you're young. It happens when your brain isn't even fully done cooking—when you've barely experienced anything, really. The worst thing is one of the first big things that ever happens to you in your life. It happens to you, and it goes all the way down to the bottom of what you know how to feel, and it rips it open and carves out this chasm down below to make room. And because you were so young, and because it was one of the first big things to happen in your life, you'll always carry it inside you. Every time something terrible happens to you from then on, it doesn't just stop at the bottom—it goes all the way down."

She reaches across the tiny tea table and the sad little pile of water crackers and touches the back of Alex's hand.

"Do you understand?" she asks him, looking right into his eyes. "You need to understand this to be with Henry. He is the most loving, nurturing, selfless person you could hope to meet, but there is a sadness and a hurt in him that is tremendous, and you may very well never truly understand it, but you need to love it as much as you love the rest of him, because that's him. That is him, part and parcel. And he is prepared to give it all to you, which is far more than I ever, in a thousand years, thought I would see him do."

Alex sits, trying for a long moment to absorb it, and says, "I've never . . . I haven't been through anything like that," he says, voice rough. "But I've always felt it, in him. There's this side of him that's . . . unknowable." He takes a breath. "But the thing is, jumping off cliffs is kinda my thing. That's the choice. I love him, with all that, *because* of all that. On purpose. I love him on purpose."

Bea smiles gently. "Then you'll do fine."

Sometime around four in the morning, he climbs into bed behind Henry, Henry whose spine pokes out in soft points, Henry who has been through the worst thing and now the next worst thing and is still alive. He reaches out a hand and touches the ridge of Henry's shoulder blade, the skin where the sheet has slid off him, where his lungs stubbornly refuse to stop pulling air. Six feet of boy curled around kicked-in ribs and a recalcitrant heart.

Carefully, his chest to Henry's back, he slots himself into place.

"It's foolishness, Henry," Philip is saying. "You're too young to understand."

Alex's ears are ringing.

They sat down in Henry's kitchen this morning with scones and a note from Bea that she'd gone to meet with Catherine. And then suddenly, Philip was bursting through the door, suit askew, hair uncombed, shouting at Henry about the nerve to break the communications embargo, to bring Alex here while the palace is being watched, to keep embarrassing the family.

Presently, Alex is thinking about breaking his nose with the coffee percolator.

"I'm *twenty-three,* Philip," Henry says, audibly struggling to keep his voice even. "Mum was barely more than that when she met Dad."

"Yes, and you think that was a *wise* decision?" Philip says nastily. "Marrying a man who spent half our childhoods making films, who never served his country, who got sick and *left* us and Mum—"

"*Don't,* Philip," Henry says. "I swear to God. Just because your obsession with family legacy didn't impress *him*—"

"You clearly don't know the first fucking thing about what a legacy means if you can let something like this happen," Philip snaps. "The only thing to do now is bury it and hope that somehow people will believe that none of it was real. That's your duty, Henry. It's the *least* you can do."

"I'm sorry," Henry says, sounding wretched, but there's a bitter defiance rising in him too. "I'm sorry that I'm such a *disgrace* for being the way I am."

"I don't care if you're *gay,*" Philip says, dropping that big fat *if* like Henry hasn't already specifically *told* him. "I care that you've made this choice, with *him*"—he cuts his eyes sharply to Alex as if he finally exists in the same room as this conversation— "someone with a fucking target on his back, to be so stupid and naive and *selfish* as to think it wouldn't completely fuck us all."

"I knew, Philip. Christ," Henry says. "I knew it could ruin

everything. I was *terrified* of exactly this. But how could I have predicted? How?"

"As I said, *naive*," Philip tells him. "This is the life we live, Henry. You've always known it. I've tried to tell you. I wanted to be a good brother to you, but you don't bloody *listen*. It's time to remember your place in this family. Be a man. Stand up and take responsibility. *Fix this.* For once in your life, don't be a coward."

Henry flinches like he's been physically slapped. Alex can see it now—this is how he was broken down over the years. Maybe not always as explicitly, but always there, always implied. *Remember your place.*

And he does the thing Alex loves so much: He sticks his chin out, steeling himself up. "I'm not a coward," he says. "And I don't want to fix it."

Philip slants a harsh, humorless laugh at him. "You don't know what you're talking about. You can't possibly know."

"Fuck off, Philip, I love him," Henry says.

"Oh, you *love him,* do you?" It's so patronizing that Alex's hand twitches into a fist under the table. "What exactly do you intend to do, then, Henry? Hmm? *Marry him?* Make him the Duchess of Cambridge? The First Son of the United bloody States, fourth in line to be Queen of England?"

"I'll fucking abdicate!" Henry says, voice rising. "I don't care!"

"You wouldn't *dare*," Philip spits back.

"We have a great uncle who abdicated because he was a *fucking Nazi,* so it'd hardly be the worst reason anyone's done it, would it?" Henry's yelling now, and he's out of his chair, hands shaking, towering over Philip, and Alex notices that he's actually taller. "What are we even *defending* here, Philip? What kind of legacy? What kind of *family,* that says, we'll take the murder, we'll take the raping and pillaging and the colonizing, we'll scrub it up nice and neat in a museum, but oh no, you're a bloody poof? That's beyond our sense of decorum! I've bloody well *had it.* I've sat about long enough letting you and Gran and the weight of the damned world keep me pinned, and I'm finished. *I don't care.* You can take your legacy and your decorum and you can *shove it up your fucking arse,* Philip. I'm *done.*"

He huffs out an almighty breath, turns on his heel, and stalks out of the kitchen.

Alex, mouth hanging open, remains frozen in his seat for a few seconds. Across from him, Philip is looking red-faced and queasy. Alex clears his throat, stands, and buttons his jacket.

"For what it's worth," he says to Philip, "that is the bravest son of a bitch I've ever met."

And he leaves too.

Shaan looks like he hasn't slept in thirty-six hours. Well, he looks perfectly composed and groomed, but the tag is sticking out of his sweater and the strong smell of whiskey is emanating from his tea.

Next to him, in the back of the incognito van they're taking to Buckingham Palace, Zahra has her arms folded resolutely. The engagement ring on her left hand glints in the muted London morning.

"So, uh," Alex attempts. "Are you two in a fight now?"

Zahra looks at him. "No. Why would you think that?"

"Oh. I just thought because—"

"It's fine," Shaan says, still typing on his iPhone. "This is why we set rules about the personal-slash-professional lines at the outset of the relationship. It works for us."

"If you want a fight, you should have seen it when I found out he had known about you two all along," Zahra says. "Why do you think I got a rock this big?"

"It *usually* works for us," Shaan amends.

"Yep," Zahra agrees. "Plus, we banged it out last night."

Without looking up, Shaan meets her hand in a high five.

Shaan and Zahra's forces combined have managed to secure them a meeting with the queen at Buckingham Palace, but they've been told to take a winding, circumspect route to avoid the paparazzi. Alex can feel a buzzing static electricity in London this morning, millions of voices murmuring about him and Henry and what might happen next. But Henry's beside him, holding his hand, and he's holding Henry's hand back, so at least that's something.

There's a small, older woman with Bea's upturned nose and Henry's blue eyes waiting outside the conference room when they approach it. She's wearing thick glasses, a worn-in maroon sweater, and a pair of cuffed jeans, looking decidedly out of place in the halls of Buckingham Palace. She has a paperback tucked into her back pocket.

Henry's mother turns to face them, and Alex watches her expression flutter through something pained to reserved to gentle when she lays eyes on them.

"Hi, my baby," she says as Henry draws up even with her.

Henry's jaw is tight, but it's not anger, only fear. Alex can see on his face an expression he recognizes: Henry wondering if it's safe to accept the love offered to him, and wanting desperately to take it regardless. He puts his arm around her, lets her kiss his cheek.

"Mum, this is Alex," Henry says, and adds, as if it's not obvious, "my boyfriend."

She turns to Alex, and he's honestly not sure what to expect, but she pulls him toward her and kisses his cheek too.

"My Bea has told me what you've done for my son," she says, her gaze piercing. "Thank you."

Bea is behind her, looking tired but focused, and Alex can only imagine the come-to-Jesus talk she must have given her mother before they got to the palace. She locks eyes with Zahra as their little party assembles in the hall, and Alex feels like they couldn't possibly be in more capable hands. He wonders if Catherine is up to joining the ranks.

"What are you going to say to her?" Henry asks his mother.

She sighs, touching the edge of her glasses. "Well, the old bird isn't much moved by emotion, so I suppose I'll try to appeal to her with political strategy."

Henry blinks. "Sorry—what are you saying?"

"I'm saying that I've come to fight," she says, straightforward and plain. "You want to tell the truth, don't you?"

"I—yeah, Mum." A light of hope has switched on behind his eyes. "Yes, I do."

"Then we can try."

They take their seats around the long, ornately carved table in the meeting room, awaiting the queen's arrival in nervous silence. Philip is there, looking like he's about to chew through his tongue, and Henry can't stop fidgeting with his tie.

Queen Mary glides in wearing slate-gray separates and a stony expression, her gray bob arranged with razor precision around the edges of her face. Alex is struck by how tall she is, straight-backed and fine-jawed even in her early eighties. She's not exactly beautiful, but there's a definite story in her shrewd blue eyes and angular features, the heavy creases of frowns around her mouth.

The temperature in the room drops as she takes her seat at the head of the table. A royal attendant fetches the teapot from the center of the table and pours into the pristine china, and the quiet hangs as she fixes her tea at a glacial pace, making them wait. The milk, poured with one gently tremoring, ancient hand. One cube of sugar, picked up with deliberate care with the tiny silver tongs. A second cube.

Alex coughs. Shaan shoots him a look. Bea presses her lips together.

"I had a visit earlier this year," the queen says at last. She takes up her teaspoon and begins to stir slowly. "The President of China. You'll forgive me if the name escapes me. But he told me the most fascinating story about how technology has advanced in different parts of the world for these modern times. Did you know, one can manipulate a photograph to make it appear as if the most outlandish things are real? Just a simple . . . program, is it? A computer. And any manner of unbelievable falsehood could be made actual. One's eyes could hardly detect a difference."

The silence in the room is total, except for the sound of the queen's teaspoon scraping circular motions in the bottom of her teacup.

"I'm afraid I am too old to understand how things are filed away in space," she goes on, "but I have been told any number of lies can be manufactured and disseminated. One could . . . create files that never existed and plant them somewhere easy to find. None of it real. The most flagrant of evidence can be discredited and dismissed, just like that."

With the delicate tinkling of silver on porcelain, she rests her spoon on the saucer and finally looks at Henry.

"I wonder, Henry. I wonder if you think any of this had to do with these unseemly reports."

It's right on the table between them: an offer. Keep ignoring it. Pretend it was a lie. Make it all go away.

Henry grits his teeth.

"It's real," he says. "All of it."

The queen's face moves through a series of expressions, settling on a terse frown, as if she's found something unsightly on the bottom of one of her kitten heels.

"Very well. In that case." Her gaze shifts to Alex. "Alexander. Had I known you were involved with my grandson, I would have insisted upon a more formal first meeting."

"Gran—"

"Do be quiet, Henry, dear."

Catherine speaks up, then. "Mum—"

The queen holds up one wizened hand to silence her. "I thought we had been humiliated enough in the papers when Beatrice had her little *problem*. And I made myself clear, Henry, years ago, that if you were drawn in *unnatural* directions, appropriate measures could be taken. Why you have chosen to undermine the hard work I've done to maintain the crown's standing is beyond me, and why you seem set on disrupting my efforts to restore it by demanding I summit with some . . . *boy*"—here, a nasty lilt to her polite tone, under which Alex can hear epithets for everything from his race to his sexuality—"when you were told to await orders, is truly a mystery. Clearly you have taken leave of your senses. My position is unchanged, dear: Your role in this family is to perpetuate our bloodline and maintain the appearance of the monarchy as the ideal of British excellence, and I simply cannot allow anything less."

Henry is looking down, eyes distant and cast toward the grain of the table, and Alex can practically feel the energy

roiling up from Catherine across from him. An answer to the
fury tight in his own chest. The princess who ran away with
James Bond, who told her children to give back what their
country stole, making a choice.

"Mum," she says evenly. "Don't you think we ought to at
least have a conversation about other options?"

The queen's head turns slowly. "And what options might
those be, Catherine?"

"Well, I think there's something to be said for coming
clean. It could save us a great deal of face to treat it not as a
scandal, but as an intrusion upon the privacy of the family and
the victimization of a young man in love."

"Which is what it was," Bea chimes in.

"We could integrate this into our narrative," Catherine
says, choosing her words with extreme precision. "Reclaim the
dignity of it. Make Alex an official suitor."

"I see. So your plan is to allow him to choose this life?"

Here, a slight tell. "It's the only life for him that's honest,
Mum."

The queen purses her lips. "Henry," she says, returning to
him, "wouldn't you have a more pleasant go of it without all
these unnecessary complications? You know we have the resources to find a wife for you and compensate her handsomely.
You understand, I'm only trying to protect you. I know it
seems important to you in this moment, but you really must
think of the future. You do realize this would mean years of
reporters hounding you, all sorts of allegations? I can't imagine people would be as eager to welcome you into children's
hospitals—"

"Stop it!" Henry bursts out. All the eyes in the room swivel
to him, and he looks pale and shocked at the sound of his own

voice, but he goes on. "You can't—you can't intimidate me into submission forever!"

Alex's hand gropes across the space between them under the table, and the moment his fingertips catch on the back of Henry's wrist, Henry's hand is gripping his, hard.

"I know it will be difficult," Henry says. "I . . . It's terrifying. And if you'd asked me a year ago, I probably would have said it was fine, that nobody needs to know. But . . . I'm as much a person and a part of this family as you. I deserve to be happy as much as any of you do. And I don't think I ever will be if I have to spend my whole life pretending."

"Nobody's saying you don't deserve to be happy," Philip cuts in. "First love makes everyone mad—it's foolish to throw away your future because of one hormonal decision based on less than a year of your life when you were barely in your twenties."

Henry looks Philip square in the face and says, "I've been gay as a maypole since the day I came out of Mum, Philip."

In the silence that follows, Alex has to bite down very hard on his tongue to suppress the urge to laugh hysterically.

"Well," the queen eventually says. She's holding her teacup daintily in the air, eyeing Henry over it. "Even if you're willing to submit to the flogging in the papers, it doesn't erase the stipulations of your birthright: You are to produce heirs."

And Alex apparently hasn't been biting his tongue hard enough, because he blurts out, "We could still do that."

Even Henry's head whips around at that.

"I don't recall giving you permission to speak in my presence," Queen Mary says.

"*Mum—*"

"That raises the issue of surrogates, or donors," Philip jumps back in, "and rights to the throne—"

"Are those details pertinent right now, Philip?" Catherine interrupts.

"*Someone* has to bear the stewardship for the royal legacy, Mum."

"I don't care for *that* tone at all."

"We can entertain hypotheticals, but the fact of the matter is that anything but maintaining the royal image is out of the question," the queen says, setting down her teacup. "The country simply will not accept a prince of his proclivities. I am sorry, dear, but to them, it's perverse."

"Perverse to them or perverse to you?" Catherine asks her.

"That isn't fair—" Philip says.

"It's *my* life—" Henry interjects.

"We haven't even gotten a chance yet to see how people will react."

"I have been serving this country for forty-seven years, Catherine. I believe I know its heart by now. As I have told you since you were a little girl, you must remove your head from the clouds—"

"Oh, will you all shut up for a second?" Bea says. She's standing now, brandishing Shaan's tablet in one hand. "Look."

She thunks it down on the table so Queen Mary and Philip can see it, and the rest of them stand to look too.

It's a news report from the BBC, and the sound is off, but Alex reads the scroll at the bottom of the screen: WORLD-WIDE SUPPORT POURS IN FOR PRINCE HENRY AND FIRST SON OF US.

The room falls silent at the images on the screen. A rally in New York outside the Beekman, decked out in rainbows, with waving signs that say things like: FIRST SON OF OUR HEARTS. A banner on the side of a bridge in Paris that reads:

HENRY + ALEX WERE HERE. A hasty mural on a wall in Mexico City of Alex's face in blue, purple, and pink, a crown on his head. A herd of people in Hyde Park with rainbow Union Jacks and Henry's face ripped out of magazines and pasted onto poster boards reading: FREE HENRY. A young woman with a buzz cut throwing two fingers up at the windows of the *Daily Mail*. A crowd of teenagers in front of the White House, wearing homemade T-shirts that all say the same thing in crooked Sharpie letters, a phrase he recognizes from one of his own emails: HISTORY, HUH?

Alex tries to swallow, but he can't. He looks up, and Henry is looking back at him, mouth open, eyes wet.

Princess Catherine turns and crosses the room slowly, toward the tall windows on the east side of the room.

"Catherine, don't—" the queen says, but Catherine grabs the heavy curtains with both hands and throws them open.

A burst of sunlight and color pushes the air out of the room. Down on the mall in front of Buckingham Palace, there's a mass of people with banners, signs, American flags, Union Jacks, pride pennants streaming over their heads. It's not as big as the royal wedding crowd, but it's huge, filling up the pavement and pressed up to the gates. Alex and Henry were told to come in through the back of the palace—they never saw it.

Henry has carefully approached the window, and Alex watches from across the room as he reaches out and grazes his fingertips against the glass.

Catherine turns to him and says on a shaky sigh, "Oh, my love," and pulls him into her chest somehow, even though he's nearly a foot taller. Alex has to look away—even after everything, this feels too private for him to witness.

The queen clears her throat.

"This is . . . hardly representative of how the country as a whole will respond," she says.

"Jesus *Christ,* Mum," Catherine says, releasing Henry and nudging him behind her on protective reflex.

"This is precisely why I didn't want you to see. You're too softhearted to accept the truth, Catherine, given any other option. The majority of this country still wants the ways of old."

Catherine draws herself up, her posture ramrod straight as she approaches the table again. It's a product of royal breeding, but it comes off more like a bow being drawn. "Of course they do, Mum. Of course the bloody Tories in Kensington and the Brexit fools don't want it. That's not the *point.* Are you so determined to believe nothing could change? That nothing *should* change? We can have a real legacy here, of hope, and love, and *change.* Not the same tepid shite and drudgery we've been selling since World War II—"

"You will not speak to me this way," Queen Mary says icily, one tremulous, ancient hand still resting on her teaspoon.

"I'm sixty years old, Mum," Catherine says. "Can't we eschew decorum at this point?"

"No respect. Never an ounce of respect for the *sanctity*—"

"Or, perhaps I should bring some of my concerns to Parliament?" Catherine says, leaning in to lower her voice right in Queen Mary's face. Alex recognizes the glint in her eyes. He never knew—he always assumed Henry got it from his dad. "You know, I do think Labour is rather finished with the old guard. I wonder, if I were to mention those meetings you keep forgetting about, or the names of countries you can't quite keep straight, if they might decide that forty-seven is perhaps enough years for the people of Britain to expect you to serve?"

The tremor in the queen's hand has doubled, but her jaw is steely. The room is deadly silent. "You wouldn't dare."

"Wouldn't I, Mum? Would you like to find out?"

Catherine turns to face Henry, and Alex is surprised to see tears on her face.

"I'm sorry, Henry," she says. "I've failed you. I've failed all of you. You needed your mum, and I wasn't there. And I was so frightened that I started to think maybe it was for the best, to let you all be kept behind glass." She turns back to her mother. "Look at them, Mum. They're not props of a legacy. They're my *children*. And I swear on my life, and *Arthur's,* I will take you off the throne before I will let them feel the things you made me feel."

The room hangs in suspense for a few agonizing seconds, then:

"I still don't think—" Philip begins, but Bea seizes the pot of tea from the center of the table and dumps it into his lap.

"Oh, I'm *terribly* sorry, Pip!" she says, grabbing him by the shoulders and shoving him, sputtering and yelping, toward the door. "So *dreadfully* clumsy. You know, I think all that *cocaine* I did must have really done a job on my reflexes! Let's go get you cleaned up, shall we?"

She heaves him out, throwing Henry a thumbs-up over her shoulder, and shuts the door behind them.

The queen looks over at Alex and Henry, and Alex sees it in her eyes at last: She's afraid of them. She's afraid of the threat they pose to the perfect Faberge veneer she's spent her whole life maintaining. They *terrify* her.

And Catherine isn't backing down.

"Well," Queen Mary says. "I suppose. I suppose you don't leave me much choice, do you?"

"Oh, you have a choice, Mum," Catherine says. "You've always had a choice. Perhaps today you'll make the right one."

In the corridor of Buckingham Palace, as soon as the door has shut behind them, they fall sideways into a tapestry on a wall, breathless and delirious and laughing, cheeks wet. Henry pulls Alex close and kisses him, whispers, "I love you I love you I love you," and it doesn't matter, it *doesn't matter* if anyone sees.

He's on the way back to the airstrip when he sees it, emblazoned on the side of a brick building, a shock of color against a gray street.

"Wait!" Alex yells up to the driver. "Stop! Stop the car!"

Up close, it's beautiful. Two stories tall. He can't imagine how somebody was able to put together something like this so fast.

It's a mural of himself and Henry, facing each other, haloed by a bright yellow sun, depicted as Han and Leia. Henry in all white, starlight in his hair. Alex dressed as a scruffy smuggler, a blaster at his hip. A royal and a rebel, arms around each other.

He snaps a photo on his phone, and fingers shaking, types out a tweet: *Never tell me the odds.*

He calls June from the air over the Atlantic.

"I need your help," he says.

He hears the click of her pen cocking on the other end of the line. "Whatcha got?"

FOURTEEN

Jezebel ✔ @Jezebel
WATCH: DC Dykes on Bikes chase
protesters from Westboro Baptist Church
down Pennsylvania Avenue, and yes, it's as
amazing as it sounds. bit.ly/2ySPeRj
9:15 PM · 29 Sept 2020

The very first time Alex pulled up to Pennsylvania Avenue as the First Son of the United States, he almost fell into a bush.

He can remember it vividly, even though the whole day was surreal. He remembers the interior of the limo, how he was still unused to the way the leather felt under his clammy palms, still green and jittery and pressed too close to the window to look at all the crowds.

He remembers his mother, her long hair pulled back from

her face in an elegant, no-nonsense twist at the back of her head. She'd worn it down for her first day as mayor, her first day in the House, her first day as Speaker, but that day it was up. She said she didn't want any distractions. He thought it made her look tough, like she was ready for a brawl if it came down to it, as if she might have a razor in her shoe. She sat there across from him, going over the notes for her speech, a twenty-four-karat gold American flag on her lapel, and Alex was so proud he thought he'd throw up.

There was a changeover at some point—Ellen and Leo escorted to the north entrance and Alex and June shuffled off in another direction. He remembers, very specifically, a handful of things. His cuff links, custom sterling silver X-wings. A tiny scuff in the plaster on a western wall of the White House, which he was seeing up close for the first time. His own shoelace, untied. And he remembers bending over to tie his shoe, losing his balance because of nerves, and June grabbing the back of his jacket to keep him from plunging face-first into a thorny rosebush in front of seventy-five cameras.

That was the moment he decided he wasn't going to allow himself nerves ever again. Not as Alex Claremont-Diaz, First Son of the United States, and not as Alex Claremont-Diaz, rising political star.

Now, he's Alex Claremont-Diaz, center of an international political sex scandal and boyfriend of a Prince of England, and he's back in a limo on Pennsylvania Avenue, and there's another crowd, and the imminent barf feeling is back.

When the car door opens, it's June, standing there in a bright yellow T-shirt that says: HISTORY, HUH?

"You like it?" she says. "There's a guy selling them down the block. I got his card. Gonna put it in my next column for *Vogue*."

Alex launches himself at her, engulfing her in a hug that lifts her feet off the ground, and she yelps and pulls his hair, and they topple sideways into a shrub, as Alex was always destined to do.

Their mother is in a decathlon of meetings, so they sneak out onto the Truman Balcony and catch each other up over hot chocolates and a plate of donuts. Pez has been trying to play telephone between the respective camps, but it's only so effective. June cries first when she hears about the phone call on the plane, then again at Henry standing up to Philip, and a third time at the crowd outside Buckingham Palace. Alex watches her text Henry about a hundred heart emojis, and he sends her back a short video of himself and Catherine drinking champagne while Bea plays "God Save the Queen" on electric guitar.

"Okay, here's the thing," June says afterward. "Nobody has seen Nora in two days."

Alex stares at her. "What do you mean?"

"I mean, I've called her, Zahra's called her, Mike and her parents have all called her, she's not answering anyone. The guard at her apartment says she hasn't left this whole time. Apparently, she's 'fine but busy.' I tried just showing up, but she'd told the doorman not to let me in."

"That's . . . concerning. And also, uh, kind of shitty."

"Yeah, I know."

Alex turns away, pacing over to the railing. He really could have used Nora's nonplussed approach in this situation, or, really, just his best friend's company. He feels somewhat betrayed she's abandoned him when he needs her most—when he and June *both* need her most. She has a tendency to bury herself in complex calculations on purpose when especially bad things happen around her.

"Oh, hey," June says. "And here's the favor you asked for."

She reaches into the pocket of her jeans and hands him a folded-up piece of paper.

He skims the first few lines.

"Oh my God, Bug," he says. "I— Oh my God."

"Do you like it?" She looks a little nervous. "I was trying to capture, like, who you are, and your place in history, and what your role means to you, and—"

She's cut off because he's scooped her up in another bear hug, teary-eyed. "It's perfect, June."

"Hey, First Offspring," says a voice suddenly, and when Alex puts June down, Amy is waiting in the doorway connecting the balcony to the Oval Room. "Madam President wants to see you in her office." Her attention shifts, listening to her earpiece. "She says to bring the donuts."

"How does she always *know*?" June mutters, scooping up the plate.

"I have Bluebonnet and Barracuda, on the move," Amy says, touching her earpiece.

"I still can't believe you picked that for your stupid code name," June says to him. Alex trips her on the way through the door.

The donuts have been gone for two hours.

One, on the couch: June, tying and untying and retying the laces on her Keds, for lack of anything else to do with her hands. Two, against a far wall: Zahra, rapidly typing out an email on her phone, then another. Three, at the Resolute Desk: Ellen, buried in probability projections. Four, on the other couch: Alex, counting.

The doors to the Oval Office fly open and Nora comes careening in.

She's wearing a bleach-stained HOLLERAN FOR CONGRESS '72 sweatshirt and the frenzied, sun-blinded expression of someone who has emerged from a doomsday bunker for the first time in a decade. She nearly crashes into the bust of Abraham Lincoln in her rush to Ellen's desk.

Alex is already on his feet. "Where the fuck have you *been?*"

She slaps a thick folder down on the desk and turns halfway to face Alex and June, out of breath. "Okay, I know you're pissed, and you have every right to be, but"—she braces herself against the desk with both hands, gesturing toward the folder with her chin—"I have been holed up in my apartment for two days doing *this,* and you are super not gonna be mad anymore when you see what it is."

Alex's mother blinks at her, perturbed. "Nora, honey, we're trying to figure out—"

"*Ellen,*" Nora practically yells. The room goes silent, and Nora freezes, realizing. "Uh. Ma'am. Mom-in-law. Please, just. You need to read this."

Alex watches her sigh and put down her pen before pulling the folder toward her. Nora looks like she's about to pass out on top of the desk. He looks across to June on the opposite couch, who appears as clueless as he feels, and—

"Holy . . . *fucking* shit," his mother says, a dawning mix of fury and bemusement. "Is this—?"

"Yup," Nora says.

"And the—?"

"Uh-huh."

Ellen covers her mouth with one hand. "How the hell did

you *get* this? Wait, let me rephrase—how the hell did *you* get this?"

"Okay, so." Nora withdraws herself from the desk and steps backward. Alex has no idea what the fuck is happening, but it's something, something big. Nora is pacing now, both hands clutched to her forehead. "The day of the leaks, I get an anonymous email. Obvious sockpuppet account, but untraceable. I tried. They sent me a link to a fucking massive file dump and told me they were a hacker and had obtained the contents of the Richards campaign's private email server in their entirety."

Alex stares at her. "*What?*"

Nora looks back at him. "I know."

Zahra, who has been standing behind Ellen's desk with her arms folded, cuts in to ask, "And you didn't report this to any of the proper channels because?"

"Because I wasn't sure it was anything at first. And when it was, I didn't trust anybody else to handle it. They said they sent it specifically to me because they knew I was personally invested in Alex's situation and would work as fast as possible to find what they didn't have time to."

"Which is?" Alex can't believe he still has to ask.

"Proof," Nora says. And her voice is shaking now. "That Richards fucking set you up."

He hears, distantly, the sound of June swearing under her breath and getting up from the couch, walking off to a far corner of the room. His knees give out, so he sits back down.

"We . . . we suspected that maybe the RNC had somehow been involved with some of what happened," his mother says. She's coming around the desk now, kneeling on the floor in front of him in her starched gray dress, the folder held against her chest. "I had people looking into it. I never imagined . . . the whole thing, straight from Richards's campaign."

She takes the folder and spreads it open on the coffee table in the middle of the room.

"There were—I mean, just, hundreds of thousands of emails," Nora is saying as Alex climbs down onto the rug and starts staring at the pages, "and I swear a third of them were from dummy accounts, but I wrote a code that narrowed it down to about three thousand. I went through the rest manually. This is everything about Alex and Henry."

Alex notices his own face first. It's a photo: blurry, out of focus, caught on a long-range lens, only barely recognizable. It's hard to place where he is, until he sees the elegant ivory curtains at the edge of the frame. Henry's bedroom.

He looks above the photo and sees it's attached to an email between two people. *Negative. Nilsen says that's not nearly clear enough. You need to tell the P we're not paying for Bigfoot sightings.* Nilsen. Nilsen, as in Richards's campaign manager.

"Richards outed you, Alex," Nora says. "As soon as you left the campaign, it started. He hired a firm that hired the hackers who got the surveillance tapes from the Beekman."

His mother is next to him with a highlighter cap already between her teeth, slashing bright yellow lines across pages. There's movement to his right: Zahra is there too, pulling a stack of papers toward her and starting in with a red pen.

"I—I don't have any bank account numbers or anything but, if you look, there are pay stubs and invoices and requests of service," Nora says. "Everything, guys. It's all through back channels and go-between firms and fake names but it's—there's a digital paper trail for everything. Enough for a federal investigation, which could subpoena the financial stuff, I think. Basically, Richards hired a firm that hired the photographers who followed Alex and the hackers who breached your server, and then he hired another third party to buy everything and resell it to the *Daily Mail*. I mean, we're talking about having private contractors surveil a member of the First Family and infiltrate White House security to try to induce a sex scandal to win a presidential race, that is some fucked-up shi—"

"Nora, can you—?" June says suddenly, having returned to one of the couches. "Just, please."

"Sorry," Nora says. She sits down heavily. "I drank like nine Red Bulls to get through all of those and ate a weed gummy to level back out, so I'm flying at fasten-seat-belts right now."

Alex closes his eyes.

There's so fucking much in front of him, and it's impossible to process it all right now, and he's pissed, *furious,* but he can also put a name on it. He can do something about it. He can go outside. He can walk out of this office and call Henry and tell him: "We're safe. The worst is over."

He opens his eyes again, looks down at the pages on the table.

"What do we do with this now?" June asks.

"What if we just leaked it?" Alex offers. "WikiLeaks—"

"I'm not giving them shit," Ellen cuts him off immediately, not even looking up, "especially not after what they did to you. This is real shit. I'm taking this motherfucker down. It has to stick." She finally puts her highlighter down. "We're leaking it to the press."

"No major publication is going to run this without verification from someone on the Richards campaign that these emails are real," June points out, "and that kind of thing takes months."

"Nora," Ellen says, fixing her with a steely gaze, "is there anything you can do at all to trace the person who sent this to you?"

"I tried," Nora says. "They did everything to obscure their identity." She reaches down into her shirt and produces her phone. "I can show you the email they sent."

She swipes through a few screens and places her phone face-up on the table. The email is exactly as she described, with a signature at the bottom that's apparently a random combination of numbers and letters: 2021 SCB. BAC CHZ GR ON A1.

2021 SCB.

Alex's eyes stop on the last line. He picks up the phone. Stares at it.

"Goddammit."

He keeps staring at the stupid letters. 2021 SCB.

2021 South Colorado Boulevard.

The closest Five Guys to the office where he worked that summer in Denver. He still remembers the order he was sent out to pick up at least once a week. Bacon cheeseburger, grilled onions, A1 Sauce. Alex memorized the goddamn Five Guys order. He feels himself start to laugh.

It's code, for Alex and Alex only: *You're the only one I trust.*

"This isn't a hacker," Alex says. "Rafael Luna sent this to you. That's your verification." He looks at his mother. "If you can protect him, he'll confirm it for you."

[MUSICAL INTRODUCTION: 15 SECOND INSTRUMENTAL FROM DESTINY'S CHILD'S 1999 SINGLE "BILLS, BILLS, BILLS"]

VOICEOVER: This is a Range Audio podcast. You're listening to "Bills, Bills, Bills," hosted by Oliver Westbrook, Professor of Constitutional Law at NYU.

[END MUSICAL INTRODUCTION]

WESTBROOK: Hi. I'm Oliver Westbrook, and with me, as always, is my exceedingly patient, talented, merciful, and lovely producer, Sufia, without whom I would be lost, bereft, floating on a sea of bad thoughts and drinking my own piss. We love her. Say hi, Sufia.

SUFIA JARWAR, PRODUCER, RANGE AUDIO: Hello, please send help.

WESTBROOK: And this is *Bills, Bills, Bills*, the podcast where I attempt every week to break down for you, in layman's terms, what's happening in Congress, why you should care, and what you can do about it.

Well. I gotta tell you, guys, I had a very different show planned out a few days ago, but I don't really see the point in getting into any of it.

Let's just, ah. Take a minute to review the story the *Washington Post* broke this morning. We've got emails, anonymously leaked, confirmed by an anonymous source on the Richards campaign, that clearly show Jeffrey Richards—or at least high-ranking staffers at his campaign—orchestrated this fucking diabolical plan to have Alex Claremont-Diaz stalked, surveilled, hacked, and outed by the *Daily Mail* as part of an effort to take down Ellen Claremont in the general. And then, about—uh, what is it, Suf? Forty minutes?—forty minutes before we started recording this, Senator Rafael Luna tweeted he was parting ways with the Richards campaign.

So. Wow.

I don't think there's any need to discuss a leak from that campaign other than Luna. It's obviously him. From where I sit, this looks like the case of a man who—maybe he didn't really want to be there in the first place, maybe he was already having second thoughts. Maybe he even infiltrated the campaign to do something exactly like this—Sufia, am I allowed to say that?

JARWAR: Literally, when has that ever stopped you?

WESTBROOK: Point. Anyway, Casper Mattresses is paying me the big sponsorship bucks to give you a Washington analysis podcast, so I'm gonna attempt to do that here, even though what has happened to Alex Claremont-Diaz—and Prince Henry too—over the past few days has been obscene, and it feels cheap and gross to even talk about it like this. But in my opinion, here are the three big things to take away from the news we've gotten today.

First, the First Son of the United States didn't actually do anything wrong.

Second, Jeffrey Richards committed a hostile act of conspiracy against a sitting president, and I am eagerly awaiting the federal investigation that is coming to him once he loses this election.

Third, Rafael Luna is perhaps the unlikeliest hero of the 2020 presidential race.

A speech has to be made.

Not just a statement. A speech.

"You wrote this?" their mother says, holding the folded-up page June had handed Alex on the balcony. "Alex told you to scrap the statement our press secretary drafted and write this whole thing?" June bites her lip and nods. "This is—this is *good*, June. Why the hell aren't you writing all our speeches?"

The press briefing room in the West Wing is ruled too impersonal, so they've called the press pool to the Diplomatic Reception Room on the ground floor. It's the room where FDR once recorded his fireside chats, and Alex is going to walk in there and make a speech and hope the country doesn't hate him for the truth.

They've flown Henry in from London for the telecast. He'll be positioned right at Alex's shoulder, steady and sure, the emblematic politician's spouse. Alex's brain can't stop sprinting laps around it. He keeps picturing it: an hour from now, millions and millions of TVs across America simulcasting his face, his voice, June's words, Henry at his side. Everyone will

know. Everyone already knows now, but they don't *know*, not
the right way.

In an hour, every person in America will be able to look at
a screen and see their First Son and his boyfriend.

And, across the Atlantic, almost as many will look up over a
beer at a pub or dinner with their family or a quiet night in
and see their youngest prince, the most beautiful one, Prince
Charming.

This is it. October 2, 2020, and the whole world watched,
and history remembered.

Alex waits on the South Lawn, within view of the linden
trees of the Kennedy Garden, where they first kissed. Marine
One touches down in a cacophony of noise and wind and ro-
tors, and Henry emerges in head-to-toe Burberry looking dramatic and windswept, like a dashing hero here to rip bodices
and mend war-torn countries, and Alex has to laugh.

"What?" Henry shouts over the noise when he sees the look
on Alex's face.

"My life is cosmic joke and you're not a real person," Alex
says, wheezing.

"*What?*" Henry yells again.

"I said, you look great, baby!"

They sneak off to make out in a stairwell until Zahra finds
them and drags Henry off to get camera-ready, and soon
they're being shuffled to the Diplomatic Reception Room,
and it's time.

It's time.

It's been one long, long year of learning Henry inside and
out, learning himself, learning how much he still had to learn,
and just like that, it's time to walk out there and stand at a podium and confidently declare it all as fact.

He's not afraid of anything he feels. He's not afraid of saying it. He's only afraid of what happens when he does.

Henry touches his hand, gently, two fingertips against his
palm.

"Five minutes for the rest of our lives," he says, laughing a
grim little laugh.

Alex reaches for him in return, presses one thumb into the
hollow of his collarbone, slipping right under the knot of his
tie. The tie is purple silk, and Alex is counting his breaths.

"You are," he says, "the absolute worst idea I've ever had."

Henry's mouth spreads into a slow smile, and Alex kisses it.

FIRST SON ALEXANDER CLAREMONT-DIAZ'S ADDRESS
FROM THE WHITE HOUSE, OCTOBER 2, 2020

Good morning.

   I am, and have been—first, last, and
always—a child of America.

   You raised me. I grew up in the
pastures and hills of Texas, but I had
been to thirty-four states before I
learned how to drive. When I caught the
stomach flu in the fifth grade, my mother
sent a note to school written on the back
of a holiday memo from Vice President
Biden. Sorry, sir—we were in a rush, and
it was the only paper she had on hand.

   I spoke to you for the first time
when I was eighteen, on the stage of
the Democratic National Convention in

Philadelphia, when I introduced my mother
as the nominee for president. You cheered
for me. I was young and full of hope, and
you let me embody the American dream:
that a boy who grew up speaking two
languages, whose family was blended and
beautiful and enduring, could make a home
for himself in the White House.

You pinned the flag to my lapel and
said, "We're rooting for you." As I stand
before you today, my hope is that I have
not let you down.

Years ago, I met a prince. And though I
didn't realize it at the time, his country
had raised him too.

The truth is, Henry and I have been
together since the beginning of this
year. The truth is, as many of you have
read, we have both struggled every day
with what this means for our families, our
countries, and our futures. The truth is,
we have both had to make compromises that
cost us sleep at night in order to afford
us enough time to share our relationship
with the world on our own terms.

We were not afforded that liberty.

But the truth is, also, simply this:
love is indomitable. America has always
believed this. And so, I am not ashamed
to stand here today where presidents have
stood and say that I love him, the same

as Jack loved Jackie, the same as Lyndon
loved Lady Bird. Every person who bears
a legacy makes the choice of a partner
with whom they will share it, whom the
American people will hold beside them in
hearts and memories and history books.
America: He is my choice.

Like countless other Americans, I was
afraid to say this out loud because of
what the consequences might be. To you,
specifically, I say: I see you. I am one
of you. As long as I have a place in
this White House, so will you. I am the
First Son of the United States, and I'm
bisexual. History will remember us.

If I can ask only one thing of the
American people, it's this: Please, do
not let my actions influence your decision
in November. The decision you will make
this year is so much bigger than anything
I could ever say or do, and it will
determine the fate of this country for
years to come. My mother, your president,
is the warrior and the champion that each
and every American deserves for four more
years of growth, progress, and prosperity.
Please, don't let my actions send us
backward. I ask the media not to focus on
me or on Henry, but on the campaign, on
policy, on the lives and livelihoods of
millions of Americans at stake in this
election.

And finally, I hope America will
remember that I am still the son you
raised. My blood still runs from Lometa,
Texas, and San Diego, California,
and Mexico City. I still remember the
sound of your voices from that stage in
Philadelphia. I wake up every morning
thinking of your hometowns, of the
families I've met at rallies in Idaho and
Oregon and South Carolina. I have never
hoped to be anything other than what I
was to you then, and what I am to you now—
the First Son, yours in actions and words.
And I hope when Inauguration Day comes
again in January, I will continue to be.

The first twenty-four hours after the speech are a blur, but a few snapshots will stay with him for the rest of his life.

A picture: the morning after, a new crowd gathered on the Mall, the biggest yet. He stays in the Residence for safety, but he and Henry and June and Nora and all three of his parents sit in the living room on the second floor and watch the live stream on CNN. In the middle of the broadcast: Amy at the front of the cheering crowd wearing June's yellow HISTORY, HUH? T-shirt and a trans flag pin. Next to her: Cash, with Amy's wife on his shoulders in what Alex can now tell is the jean jacket Amy was embroidering on the plane in the colors of the pansexual flag. He whoops so hard he spills his coffee on George Bush's favorite rug.

A picture: Senator Jeffrey Richards's stupid Sam the Eagle face on CNN, talking about his grave concern for President

Claremont's ability to remain impartial on matters of traditional family values due to the acts her son engages in on the sacred grounds of the house our forefathers built. Followed by: Senator Oscar Diaz, responding via satellite, that President Claremont's primary value is upholding the Constitution, and that the White House was built by slaves, not our forefathers.

A picture: the expression on Rafael Luna's face when he looks up from his paperwork to see Alex standing in the doorway of his office.

"Why do you even have a staff?" Alex says. "Nobody has ever tried to stop me from walking straight in here."

Luna has his reading glasses on, and he looks like he hasn't shaved in weeks. He smiles, a little apprehensive.

After Alex decoded the message in the email, his mother called Luna directly and told him, no questions asked, she would grant him full protection from criminal charges if he helped her take Richards down. He knows his dad has been in touch too. Luna knows neither of his parents are holding a grudge. But this is the first time they've spoken.

"If you think I don't tell every hire on their first day that you have a free pass," he says, "you do not have an accurate sense of yourself."

Alex grins, and he reaches into his pocket and produces a packet of Skittles, lobbing them underhand onto Luna's desk.

Luna looks down at them.

The chair is next to his desk these days, and he pushes it out.

Alex hasn't gotten a chance to thank him yet, and he doesn't know where to start. He doesn't even feel like it's the first order of business. He watches Luna rip open the packet and dump the candy out onto his papers.

There's a question hanging in the air, and they can both see it. Alex doesn't want to ask. They just got Luna back. He's afraid of losing him again to the answer. But he has to know.

"Did you know?" he finally says. "Before it happened, did you know what he was going to do?"

Luna takes his glasses off and sets them down grimly on his blotter.

"Alex, I know I . . . completely destroyed your faith in me, so I don't blame you for asking me," he says. He leans forward on his elbows, his eye contact hard and deliberate. "But I need you to know I would never, ever intentionally let something like that happen to you. Ever. I had no idea until it came out. Same as you."

Alex releases a long breath.

"Okay," he says. He watches Luna lean back, looks at the fine lines on his face, slightly heavier than they were before. "So, what happened?"

Luna sighs, a hoarse, tired sound in the back of his throat. It's a sound that makes Alex think about what his dad told him at the lake, about how much of Luna is still hidden.

"So," he says, "you know I interned for Richards?"

Alex blinks. "What?"

Luna barks a small, humorless laugh. "Yeah, you wouldn't have heard. Richards made pretty damn sure to get rid of the evidence. But, yeah, 2000. I was nineteen. It was back when he was AG in Utah. One of my professors called in a favor."

There were rumors, Luna explains, among the low-level staffers. Usually the female interns, but occasionally an especially pretty boy—a boy like him. Promises, from Richards: mentorship, connections, if "you'd just get a drink with me after work." A strong implication that "no" was unacceptable.

"I had *nothing* back then," Luna says. "No money, no family, no connections, no experience. I thought, 'This is your only way to get your foot in the door. Maybe he means it.'"

Luna pauses, taking a breath. Alex's stomach is twisting uncomfortably.

"He sent a car, made me meet him at a hotel, got me drunk. He wanted—he tried to—" Luna grimaces away from finishing the sentence. "Anyway, I got away. I remember I got home that night, and the guy I was renting a room with took one look at me and handed me a cigarette. That's when I started smoking, by the way."

He's been looking down at the Skittles on his desk, sorting the reds from oranges, but here he looks up at Alex with a bitter, cutting smile.

"And I went back to work the next day like nothing happened. I made *small talk* with him in the *break room,* because I wanted it to be okay, and that's what I hated myself the most for. So the next time he sent me an email, I walked into his office and told him that if he didn't leave me alone, I'd take it to the paper. And that's when he pulled out the file.

"He called it an 'insurance policy.' He knew stuff I did as a teenager, how I got kicked out by my parents and a youth shelter in Seattle. That I have family who are undocumented. He told me that if I ever said a word about what happened, not only would I never have a career in politics, but he would ruin my life. He'd ruin my *family's* lives. So, I shut the fuck up."

Luna's eyes when they meet his again are ice cold, sharp. A window slammed shut.

"But I've never forgotten. I'd see him in the Senate chamber, and he'd look at me like I owed *him* something, because he hadn't destroyed me when he could have. And I knew he was going to do whatever shady shit it took to win the presidency, and I couldn't let a fucking *predator* be the most powerful man in the country if it was within my power to stop it."

He turns now, a tiny shake of his shoulders like he's dusting off a light snowfall, pivoting his chair to pluck up a few Skittles and pop them into his mouth, and he's trying for casual but his hands aren't steady.

He explains that the moment he decided was this summer, when he saw Richards on TV talking about the Youth Congress program. That he knew, with more access, he could find and leak evidence of abuse. Even if he was too old for Richards to want to fuck, he could play him. Convince him he didn't believe Ellen would win, that he'd get the Hispanic and moderate vote in exchange for power.

"I fucking hated myself every minute of working with that campaign, but I spent the whole time looking for evidence. I was close. I was so focused, so zeroed in that, that I . . . I never noticed if there were whispers about you. I had no idea. But when everything came out . . . I knew. I just couldn't prove it. But I had access to the servers. I don't know much, but I'd been around the block enough in my teenage anarchist days to know people who know how to do a file dump. Don't look at me like that. I'm not *that* old."

Alex laughs, and Luna laughs too, and it's a relief, like the air coming back in the room.

"Anyway, getting it straight to you and your mother was the fastest way to expose him, and I knew Nora could do that. And I . . . I knew you would understand."

He pauses, sucking on a Skittle, and Alex decides to ask. "Did my dad know?"

"About me going triple agent? No, nobody does. Half my

staff quit because they didn't know. My sister hasn't spoken to me in months."

"No, about what Richards did to you?"

"Alex, your father is the only other person alive I've ever told any of this to," he says. "Your father took it upon himself to help me when I wouldn't let anyone else, and I'll never stop being grateful to him. But he wanted me to come forward with what Richards did to me, and I . . . couldn't. I said it was a risk I wasn't willing to take with my own career, but truthfully, I didn't think what happened to one gay Mexican kid twenty years ago would make a difference to his base. I didn't think anyone would believe me."

"I believe you," Alex says readily. "I just wish you would have told me what you were doing. Or, like, anybody."

"You would have tried to stop me," Luna says. "You all would have."

"I mean . . . Raf, it was a fucking crazy plan."

"I know. And I don't know if I'll ever be able to fix the damage I've done, but I honestly don't care. I did what I had to do. There was no way in hell I was going to let Richards win. My whole life has been about fighting. I fought."

Alex thinks it over. He can relate—it echoes the same deliberations he's been having with himself. He thinks of something he hasn't allowed himself to think about since all this started after London: his LSAT results, unopened and tucked away inside the desk in his bedroom. How do you do all the good you can do?

"I'm sorry, by the way," Luna says. "For the things I said to you." He doesn't have to specify which things. "I was . . . fucked up."

"It's cool," Alex tells him, and he means it. He forgave Luna before he ever walked into the office, but he appreciates the apology. "I'm sorry too. But also, I hope you know that if you ever call me 'kid' again after all this, I am literally going to kick your ass."

Luna laughs in earnest. "Listen, you've had your first big sex scandal. No more sitting at the kids' table."

Alex nods appreciatively, stretching in his chair and folding his hands behind his head. "Man, it fucking sucks it has to be like this, with Richards. Even if you expose him now, straight people always want the homophobic bastards to be closet cases so they can wash their hands of it. As if ninety-nine out of a hundred aren't just regular old hateful bigots."

"Yeah, especially since I think I'm the only male intern he ever took to a hotel. It's the same as any fucking predator—it has nothing to do with sexuality and everything to do with power."

"Do you think you'll say anything?" Alex says. "At this point?"

"I've been thinking about it a lot." He leans in. "Most people have kind of already figured out that I'm the leak. And I think, sooner or later, someone is going to come to me with an allegation that is within the statute of limitations. Then we can open up a congressional investigation. *Big-time.* And *that* will make a difference."

"I heard a 'we' in there," Alex says.

"Well," Luna says. "Me and someone else with law experience."

"Is that a hint?"

"It's a suggestion," Luna says. "But I'm not gonna tell you what to do with your life. I'm busy trying to get my own shit together. Look at this." He lifts his sleeve. "Nicotine patch, bitch."

"No way," Alex says. "Are you actually quitting for real?"

"I am a changed man, unburdened by the demons of my past," Luna says solemnly, with a jerk-off hand gesture.

"You fucker, I'm proud of you."

"Hola," says a voice at the door of the office.

It's his dad, in a T-shirt and jeans, a six-pack of beer in one hand.

"Oscar," Luna says, grinning. "We were just talking about how I've decimated my reputation and killed my own political career."

"Ay," he says, dragging an extra chair over to the desk and passing out beers. "Sounds like a job for Los Bastardos."

Alex cracks open his can. "We can also discuss how I might cost Mom the election because I'm a one-man bisexual wrecking ball who exposed the vulnerability of the White House private email server."

"You think?" his dad says. "Nah. Come on. I don't think this election is gonna hinge on an email server."

Alex arches a brow. "You sure about that?"

"Listen, maybe if Richards had more time to sow those seeds of doubt, but I don't think we're there. Maybe if it were 2016. Maybe if this weren't an America that already elected a woman to the highest office once. Maybe if I weren't sitting in a room with the three assholes responsible for electing the first openly gay man to the Senate in US history." Alex whoops and Luna inclines his head and raises his beer. "But, nah. Is it gonna be a pain in your mom's ass for the second term? Shit, yeah. But she'll handle it."

"Look at you," Luna says over his beer. "Answer for everything, eh?"

"Listen," his dad says, "somebody on this damn campaign has to keep their fucking cool while everyone else catastrophizes. Everything's gonna be fine. I believe that."

"And what about me?" Alex says. "You think I got a chance in politics after going supernova in every paper in the world?"

"They got you," Oscar says, shrugging. "It happens. Give it time. Try again."

Alex laughs, but still, he reaches in and plucks up something deep down in his chest. Something shaped not like Claremont but Diaz—no better, no worse, just different.

Henry gets his own room in the White House while he's in. The crown spared him for two nights before he returns to England for his own damage control tour. Once again, they're lucky to have Catherine back in the game; Alex doubts the queen would have been so generous.

This particularly is what makes it a little funny that Henry's room—the customary quarters for royal guests—is called the Queen's Bedroom.

"It's quite . . . aggressively pink, innit?" Henry mutters sleepily.

The room is, really, aggressively pink, done up in the Federal style with pink walls and rose-covered rugs and bedding, pink upholstery on everything from the chairs and settee in the sitting area to the canopy on the four-poster bed.

Henry's agreed to sleep in the room rather than Alex's "because I respect your mother," as if every person who had a hand in raising Alex has not read in graphic detail the things they get up to when they share a bed. Alex has no such hangups and enjoys Henry's half-hearted grumblings when he sneaks in from the East Bedroom right down the hall.

They've woken up half-naked and warm, tucked in tight while the first autumn chill creeps in under the lacy curtains. Humming low in his chest, Alex presses the length of his body against Henry's under the blankets, his back to Henry's chest, the swell of his ass against—

"Argh, hello," Henry mumbles, his hips hitching at the contact. Henry can't see his face, but Alex smiles anyway.

"Morning," Alex says. He gives his ass a little wiggle.

"Time's it?"

"Seven thirty-two."

"Plane in two hours."

Alex makes a small sound in the back of his throat and turns over, finding Henry's face soft and close, eyes only half-open. "You sure you don't need me to come with you?"

Henry shakes his head without picking it up from the pillow, so his cheek squishes against it. It's cute. "You're not the one who slagged off the crown and your own family in the emails that everybody in the world has read. I've got to handle that on my own before you come back over."

"That's fair," Alex says. "But soon?"

Henry's mouth tugs into a smile. "Absolutely. You've got the royal suitor photos to take, the Christmas cards to sign . . . Oh, I wonder if they'll have you do a line of skincare products like Martha—"

"Stop," Alex groans, poking him in the ribs. "You're enjoying this too much."

"I'm enjoying it the perfect amount," Henry says. "But, in all seriousness, it's . . . frightening but a bit nice. To do this on my own. I've not gotten to do that much, well, ever."

"Yeah," Alex says. "I'm proud of you."

"Ew," Henry says in a flat American accent, and he laughs and Alex throws an elbow.

Henry's pulling him and kissing him, sandy hair on a pink bedspread, long lashes and long legs and blue eyes, elegant hands pinning his wrists to the mattress. It's like everything he's ever loved about Henry in a moment, in a laugh, in the way he shivers, in the confident roll of his spine, in happy, unfettered sex in the well-furnished eye of a storm.

Today, Henry goes back to London. Today, Alex goes back to the campaign trail. They have to figure out how to do this for real now, how to love each other in plain sight. Alex thinks they're up for it.

FIFTEEN

"Let me just get this hair, love."

"Mum."

"Soz, am I embarrassing you?" Catherine says, her glasses on the tip of her nose as she rearranges Henry's thick hair. "You'll thank me when you've not got a great cowlick in your official portrait."

Alex has to admit, the royal photographer is being exceedingly patient about the whole thing, especially considering they waffled through three different locations—Kensington Gardens, a stuffy Buckingham Palace library, the courtyard of Hampton Court Palace—before they decided to screw it all for a bench in a locked-down Hyde Park.

("Like a common vagrant?" Queen Mary asked.

"Shut up, Mum," Catherine said.)

There's a certain need for formal portraits now that Alex is officially in "courtship" with Henry. He tries not to think too hard about his face on chocolate bars and thongs in Buckingham gift shops. At least it'll be next to Henry's.

Some psychological math always goes into styling photos like these. The White House stylists have Alex in something he'd wear any day—brown leather loafers, slim-fit chinos in a soft tan, a loose-collared Ralph Lauren chambray—but in this context, it reads confident, roguish, decidedly American. Henry's in a Burberry button-down tucked into dark jeans and a navy cardigan that the royal shoppers squabbled over in Harrods for hours. They want a picture of a perfect, dignified, British intellectual, a loved-up boyfriend with a bright future as an academic and philanthropist. They even staged a little pile of books on the bench next to him.

Alex looks over at Henry, who's groaning and rolling his eyes under his mother's preening, and smiles at how much closer this packaging is to the real, messy, complicated Henry. As close as any PR campaign is ever going to get.

They take about a hundred portraits just sitting on the bench next to each other and smiling, and part of Alex keeps stumbling over the disbelief he's actually here, in the middle of Hyde Park, in front of God and everybody, holding Henry's hand atop his own knee for the camera.

"If Alex from this time last year could see this," Alex says, leaning into Henry's ear.

"He'd say, 'Oh, I'm in love with Henry? That must be why I'm such a berk to him all the time,'" Henry suggests.

"Hey!" Alex squawks, and Henry's chuckling at his own joke and Alex's indignation, one arm coming up around

Alex's shoulders. Alex gives into it and laughs too, full and deep, and that's the last hope for a serious tone for the day gone. The photographer finally calls it, and they're set loose.

Catherine's got a busy day, she says—three meetings before afternoon tea to discuss relocating into a royal residence more centrally located in London, since she's begun taking up more duties than ever. Alex can see the glint in her eye— she'll be gunning for the throne soon. He's choosing not to say anything about it to Henry yet, but he's curious to see how it all plays out. She kisses them both and leaves them with Henry's PPOs.

It's a short walk over the Long Water back to Kensington, and they meet Bea at the Orangery, where a dozen members of her event-planning team are scurrying around, setting up a stage. She's tromping up and down rows of chairs on the lawn in a ponytail and rain boots, speaking very tersely on the phone about something called "cullen skink" and why on earth would she ever request cullen skink and even if she had in fact requested cullen skink in what universe would she ever need twenty bloody liters of cullen skink for anything, ever.

"What in the hell is a 'cullen skink'?" Alex asks once she's hung up.

"Smoked haddock chowder," she says. "Enjoy your first royal dog show, Alex?"

"It wasn't too bad," Alex says, smirking.

"Mum is *beyond*," Henry says. "She offered to *edit my manuscript* this morning. It's like she's trying to make up for five years of absentee parenting all at once. Which, of course, I love her very much, and I appreciate the effort, but, Christ."

"She's trying, H," Bea says. "She's been on the bench for a while. Let her warm up a bit."

"I know," Henry says with a sigh, but his eyes are fond. "How are things over here?"

"Oh, you know," she says, waving her phone in the air. "Just the maiden voyage of my very controversial fund upon which all future endeavors will be judged, so, no pressure at all. I'm only slightly cross with you for not making it a Henry Foundation–Beatrice Fund double feature so I could unload half the stress onto you. All this fund-raising for sobriety is going to drive me to drink." She pats Alex on the arm. "That's drunk humor for you, Alex."

Bea and Henry both had an October as busy as their mother's. There were a lot of decisions to be made in that first week: Would they ignore the revelations about Bea in the emails (no), would Henry be forced to enlist after all (after days of deliberation, no), and, above all, how could all this be made into a positive? The solution had been one Bea and Henry came up with together, twin philanthropic efforts under their own names. Bea's, a charity fund supporting addiction recovery programs all over the UK, and Henry's, an LGBT rights foundation.

To their right, the lighting trusses are going up quickly over the stage where Bea will be playing an £8,000-a-ticket concert with a live band and celebrity guests tonight, her first solo fund-raiser.

"Man, I wish I could stay for the show," Alex says.

Bea beams. "It's a shame Henry here was too busy signing papers with Auntie Pezza all week to learn some sheet music or we could have fired our pianist."

"Papers?" Alex says, cocking an eyebrow.

Henry shoots Bea a silencing glare. "Bea—"

"For the youth shelters," she says.

"*Beatrice,*" Henry admonishes. "It was going to be a *surprise.*"

"Oh," Bea says, busying herself with her phone. "Oops."

Alex looks at Henry. "What's going on?"

Henry sighs. "Well. We were going to wait to announce it— and to tell you, obviously—until after the election, so as not to step on your moment. But . . ." He puts his hands in his pockets, in that way he does when he's feeling proud of something but trying not to act like it. "Mum and I agreed the foundation shouldn't just be national, that there was work to be done all over the world, and I specifically wanted to focus on homeless queer youth. So, Pez signed all our Okonjo Foundation youth shelters over." He bounces on his heels a little, visibly tamping down a broad smile. "You're looking at the proud father of four worldwide soon-to-be shelters for disenfranchised queer teenagers."

"Oh my God, you *bastard,*" Alex practically yells, lunging at Henry and throwing his arms around his neck. "That's amazing. I *stupid* love you. *Wow.*" He yanks back suddenly, stricken. "Wait, oh my God, this means the one in Brooklyn too? Right?"

"Yes, it does."

"Didn't you tell me you wanted to be hands-on with the foundation?" Alex says, his pulse jumping. "Don't you think maybe *direct supervision* might be helpful while it gets off the ground?"

"Alex," Henry tells him, "I can't *move* to New York."

Bea looks up. "Why not?"

"Because I'm the prince of—" Henry looks over at her and gestures at the Orangery, at Kensington, sputtering. "*Here!*"

Bea shrugs, unmoved. "And? It doesn't have to be permanent. You spent a month of your gap year talking to yaks in Mongolia, H. It's hardly unprecedented."

Henry moves his mouth a couple times, ever the skeptic, and swivels back to Alex. "Well, I'd still hardly see you, would I?" he reasons. "If you're in DC for work all the time, beginning your meteoric rise to the political stratosphere?"

And this, Alex has to admit, is a point. A point that after the year he's had, after everything, after the finally opened and perfectly passable LSAT scores sitting expectantly on his desk back home, feels less and less concrete every day.

He thinks about opening his mouth to say as much.

"Hello," says a polished voice from behind them, and they all turn to see Philip, starched and well groomed, striding across the lawn.

Alex feels the slight flutter through the air of Henry's spine automatically straightening beside him. Philip came to Kensington two weeks ago to apologize to both Henry and Bea for the years since their father's death, the harsh words, the domineeringness, the intense scrutiny. For basically growing from an uptight people-pleaser into an abusive, self-righteous twat under the pressure of his position and the manipulation of the queen. "He's fallen out with Gran," Henry had told Alex over the phone. "That's the only reason I actually believe anything he says."

Yet, there's blood that can't be unshed. Alex wants to throw a punch every time he sees Philip's stupid face, but it's Henry's family, not his, so he doesn't get to make that call.

"Philip," Bea says coolly. "To what do we owe the pleasure?"

"Just had a meeting at Buckingham," Philip says. The meaning hangs in the air between them: a meeting with the queen because he's the only one still willing. "Wanted to come by to see if I could help with anything." He looks down at Bea's Wellington boots next to his shiny dress shoes in the grass. "You know, you don't have to be out here—we've got plenty of staff who can do the grunt work for you."

"I know," Bea says haughtily, every inch a princess. "I want to do it."

"Right," Philip says. "Of course. Well, er. Is there anything I can help with?"

"Not really, Philip."

"All right." Philip clears his throat. "Henry, Alex. Portraits go all right?"

Henry blinks, clearly startled Philip would ask. Alex has enough diplomatic instincts to keep his mouth shut.

"Yeah," Henry says. "Er, yes. It was all right. A bit awkward, you know, just having to sit there for ages."

"Oh, I remember," Philip says. "When Mazzy and I did our first ones, I had this horrible rash on my arse from some idiotic poison-oak prank one of my uni friends had played on me that week, and it was all I could do to hold still and not rip my trousers off in the middle of Buckingham, much less try to take a nice photo. I thought she was going to murder me. Here's hoping yours turn out better."

He chuckles a little awkwardly, clearly trying to bond with them. Alex scratches his nose.

"Well, anyway, good luck, Bea."

Philip walks off, hands in his pockets, and all three of them watch his retreating back until it starts to disappear behind the tall hedges.

Bea sighs. "D'you think I should have let him have a go at the cullen skink man for me?"

"Not yet," Henry says. "Give him another six months. He hasn't earned it yet."

Blue or gray? Gray or blue?

Alex has never been so torn between two equally innocuous blazers in his entire life.

"This is stupid," Nora says. "They're both boring."

"Will you please just help me pick?" Alex tells her. He holds up a hanger in each hand, ignoring her judgmental look from where she's perched atop his dresser. The pictures from election night tomorrow, win or lose, will follow him for the rest of his life.

"Alex, seriously. I hate them both. You need something killer. This could be your fucking *swan song*."

"Okay, let's not—"

"Yes, okay, you're right, if the projections hold, we're fine," she says, hopping down. "So, do you want to talk about why you're choosing to punt so hard on this particular moment in your career as a risk-taking fashion plate?"

"Nope," Alex says. He waves the hangers at her. "Blue or gray?"

"Okay, so." She's ignoring him. "I'll say it, then. You're nervous."

He rolls his eyes. "Of course I'm nervous, Nora, it's a presidential election and the president gave birth to me."

"Try again."

She's giving him that look. The "I've already analyzed all the data on how much shit you're full of" look. He releases a hiss of a sigh.

"Fine," he says. "Fine, yeah, I'm nervous about going back to Texas."

He tosses both the blazers at the bed. Shit.

"I always felt like Texas claiming me as their son was, you know, kind of conditional." He paces, rubbing the back of his neck. "The whole half-Mexican, all Democrat thing. There's a very loud contingent there that does not like me and does not want me to represent them. And now, it's just. Not being straight. Having a boyfriend. Having a *gay sex scandal* with a *European prince*. I don't know anymore."

He loves Texas—he *believes* in Texas. But he doesn't know if Texas still loves him.

He's paced all the way to the opposite side of the room from her, and she watches him and cocks her head to one side.

"So . . . you're afraid of wearing anything too flashy for your first post-coming-out trip home, on account of Texans' delicate hetero sensibilities?"

"Basically."

She's looking at him now more like he's a very complex problem set. "Have you looked at our polling on you in Texas? Since September?"

Alex swallows.

"No. I, uh." He scrubs his face with one hand. "The thought, like . . . stresses me out? Like, I keep meaning to go look at the numbers, and then I just. Shut down."

Nora's face softens, but she doesn't move closer yet, giving him space. "Alex. You could have asked me. They're . . . not bad."

He bites his lip. "They're not?"

"Alex, our base in Texas hasn't shifted on you since September, at all. If anything, they like you more. And a lot of the undecideds are pissed Richards came after a Texas kid. You're really fine."

Oh.

Alex exhales a shaky breath, running one hand through his hair. He starts to pace back, away from the door, which he realizes he's gravitated near as some fight-or-flight reflex.

"Okay."

He sits down heavily on the bed.

Nora sits gingerly next to him, and when he looks at her, she's got that sharpness to her eyes like she does when she's practically reading his mind.

"Look. You know I'm not good at the whole, like, tactful emotional communication thing, but, uh, June's not here, so. I'm gonna. Fuckin'. Give it a go." She presses on. "I don't think this is just about Texas. You were recently fucking traumatized in a big way, and now you're scared of doing or saying the kind of stuff you actually like and want to because you don't want to draw any more attention to yourself."

Alex almost wants to laugh.

Nora is like Henry sometimes, in that she can cut right down to the truth of things, but Henry deals in heart and Nora deals in facts. It takes her razor's edge, sometimes, to get him to pull his head out of his ass.

"Uh, well, yeah. That's. Probably part of it," he agrees. "I know I need to start rehabilitating my image if I want any chance in politics, but part of me is like . . . really? Right now? Why? It's weird. My whole life, I was hanging on to this imaginary future person I was gonna be. Like, the plan— graduation, campaigns, staffer, Congress. That was it. Straight into the game. I was gonna be the person who could do that . . . who *wanted* that. And now here I am, and the person I've become is . . . not that person."

Nora nudges their shoulders together. "But do you like him?"

Alex thinks; he's different, for sure, maybe a little darker. More neurotic, but more honest. Sharper head, wilder heart. Someone who doesn't always want to be married to work, but who has more reasons to fight than ever.

"Yeah," he says finally. Firmly. "Yeah, I do."

"Cool," she says, and he looks over to see her grinning at him. "So do I. You're Alex. In all this stupid shit, that's all you ever needed to be." She grabs his face in both hands and squishes it, and he groans but doesn't push her off. "So, like. You want to throw out some contingency plans? You want me to run some projections?"

"Actually, uh," Alex says, slightly muffled from how Nora's still squishing his face between her hands. "Did I tell you that I kind of . . . snuck off and took the LSAT this summer?"

"Oh! Oh . . . *law school,*" she says, as simply as she said *dick you down* all those months ago, the simple answer to where he's been unknowingly headed all along. She releases his face, shoving his shoulders instead, instantly excited. "That's *it,* Alex. Wait—yes! I'm about to start applying for my master's; we can do it together!"

"Yeah?" he says. "You think I can hack it?"

"Alex. Yes. Alex." She's on her knees on the bed now, bouncing up and down. "Alex, this is genius. Okay—listen. You go to law school, I go to grad school, June becomes a speechwriter-slash-author Rebecca Traister–Roxane Gay voice of a generation, I become the data scientist who saves the world, and you—"

"—become a badass civil rights attorney with an illustrious Captain America-esque career of curb-stomping discriminatory laws and fighting for the disenfranchised—"

"—and you and Henry become the world's favorite geopolitical power couple—"

"—and by the time I'm Rafael Luna's age—"

"—people are going to be *begging* you to run for Senate," she finishes, breathless. "Yeah. So, like, a lot slower than planned. But."

"Yeah," Alex says, swallowing. "It sounds good."

And there it is. He's been teetering on the edge of letting go of this specific dream for months now, terrified of it, but the relief is startling, a mountain off his back.

He blinks in the face of it, thinks of June's words, and has to laugh. "Fire under my ass for no good goddamn reason."

Nora pulls a face. She recognizes the June-ism. "You are . . . passionate, to a fault. If June were here, she would say taking your time is going to help you figure out how best to use that. But I'm here, so, I'm gonna say: You are great at hustling, and at policy, and at leading and rallying people. You are so fucking smart that most people want to punch you. Those are all skills that will only improve over time. So, like, you are gonna crush it."

She jumps to her feet and ducks into his closet, and he can hear hangers sliding around. "Most importantly," she goes on, "you have become an icon of something, which is, like, a very big deal."

She emerges with a hanger in her hand: a jacket he's never worn out before, one she convinced him to buy online for an obscene price the night they got drunk and watched *The West Wing* in a hotel in New York and let the tabloids think they were screwing. It's fucking *Gucci,* a midnight-blue bomber jacket with red, white, and blue stripes at the waistband and cuffs.

"I know it's a lot, but"—she slaps the jacket against his chest—"you give people hope. So, get back out there and be Alex."

He takes the jacket from her and tries it on, checks his reflection in the mirror. It's perfect.

The moment is split with a half scream from the hallway outside of his bedroom, and he and Nora both run to the door.

It's June, tumbling into Alex's bedroom with her phone in one hand, jumping up and down, her hair bouncing on her shoulders. She's clearly come straight from one of her runs to the newsstand because her other arm is laden with tabloids, but she dumps them unceremoniously on the floor.

"I got the book deal!" she shrieks, waving her phone in their faces. "I was checking my email and—the memoir—*I got the fucking deal!*"

Alex and Nora both scream too, and they haul her into a six-armed hug, whooping and laughing and stomping on one another's feet and not caring. They all end up kicking off their shoes and jumping on the bed, and Nora FaceTimes Bea, who finds Henry and Pez in one of Henry's rooms, and they all celebrate together. It feels complete, the gang, as Cash once called them. They've earned their own media nickname in the wake of everything: The Super Six. Alex doesn't mind it.

Hours later, Nora and June fall asleep against Alex's headboard, June's head in Nora's lap and Nora's fingers in her hair, and Alex sneaks off to the en suite to brush his teeth. He nearly slips on something on the way back, and when he looks down, he has to do a double take. It's an issue of *HELLO! US* from June's abandoned stack of magazines, and the image dominating the cover is one of the shots from his and Henry's portrait session.

He bends down to pick it up. It's not one of the posed shots—it's one he didn't even realize had been taken, one he definitely didn't think would be released. He should have given the photographer more credit. He managed to capture the moment right when Henry cracked a joke, a candid, genuine photo, completely caught up in each other, Henry's arm around him and his own hand reaching up to grasp for Henry's on his shoulder.

The way Henry's looking at him in the picture is so affectionate, so openly loving, that seeing it from a third person's perspective almost makes Alex want to look away, like he's staring into the sun. He called Henry the North Star once. That wasn't bright enough.

He thinks again about Brooklyn, about Henry's youth shelter there. His mom knows someone at NYU Law, right?

He brushes his teeth and climbs into bed. Tomorrow they find out, win or lose. A year ago—six months ago—it would have meant no sleep tonight. But he's a new kind of icon now, someone who laughs on even footing with his royal boyfriend on the cover of a magazine, someone willing to accept the years stretching ahead of him, to give himself time. He's trying new things.

He props a pillow up on June's knees, stretches his feet out over Nora's legs, and goes to sleep.

Alex tugs his bottom lip between his teeth. Scuffs the heel of his boot against the linoleum floor. Looks down at his ballot.

PRESIDENT and VICE PRESIDENT of the UNITED STATES
Vote for One

He picks up the stylus chained to the machine, his heart behind his molars, and selects: CLAREMONT, ELLEN *and* HOLLERAN, MICHAEL.

The machine chirps its approval, and to its gently humming mechanisms, he could be anybody. One of millions, a single tally mark, worth no more or less than any of the others. Just pressing a button.

It's a risk, doing election night in their hometown. There's no *rule,* technically, saying that the sitting president can't host their rally in DC, but it is customary to do it at home. Still, though.

2016 was bittersweet. Austin is blue, deep blue, and Ellen won Travis County by 76 percent, but no amount of fireworks and champagne corks in the streets changed the fact that they lost the state they stood in to make the victory speech. Still, the Lometa Longshot wanted to come home again.

There's been progress in the past year: a few court victories Alex has kept track of in his trusty binder, registration drives for young voters, the Houston rally, the shifting polls. Alex needed a distraction after the whole tabloid nightmare, so he threw himself into an after-hours committee with a bunch of the campaign's Texas organizers, Skyping in to figure out logistics of a massive election day shuttle service throughout Texas. It's 2020, and Texas is a battleground state for the first time in years.

His last election night was on the wide-open stretch of Zilker Park, against the backdrop of the Austin skyline. He remembers everything.

He was eighteen years old in his first custom-made suit, corralled into a hotel around the corner with his family to watch the results while the crowd swelled outside, running with his arms open down the hallway when they called 270.

He remembers it felt like his moment, because it was his mom and his family, but also realizing it was, in a way, not his moment at all, when he turned around and saw Zahra's mascara running down her face.

He stood next to the stage set into the hillside of Zilker and looked into eyes upon eyes upon eyes of women who were old enough to have marched on Congress for the VRA in '65 and girls young enough never to have known a president who was a white man. All of them looking at their first Madam President. And he turned and looked at June at his right side and Nora at his left, and he distinctly remembers pushing them out onto the stage ahead of him, giving them a full thirty seconds of soaking it in before following them into the spotlight.

The soles of his boots hit brown grass behind the Palmer Events Center like he's coming down from a much greater altitude than the back seat of a limo.

"It's early," Nora is saying, thumbing through her phone as she climbs out behind him in a plunging black jumpsuit and killer heels. "Like, really early for these exit polls, but I'm pretty sure we have Illinois."

"Cool, that was projected," Alex says. "We're on target so far."

"I wouldn't go that far," Nora tells him. "I don't like how Pennsylvania looks."

"Hey," June says. Her own dress is carefully selected, off-the-rack J. Crew, white lace, girl-next-door. Her hair is braided down one shoulder. "Can't we, like, have *one* drink before y'all start doing this? I heard there are mojitos."

"Yeah, yeah," Nora says, but she's still staring down at her phone, brow furrowed.

HRH Prince Dickhead 💩

Nov 3, 2020, 6:37 PM

HRH Prince Dickhead 💩

Pilot says we're having visibility problems? May have to reroute and land elsewhere.

HRH Prince Dickhead 💩

Landing in Dallas? Is that far?? I've no bloody clue about American geography.

HRH Prince Dickhead 💩

Shaan has informed me this is, in fact, far. Landing soon. Will try to take off again once the weather clears.

HRH Prince Dickhead 💩

I'm sorry, I'm so sorry. How are things on your end?

things are shit

please get your ass here asap
i'm stressing tf out

Oliver Westbrook ✔ @BillsBillsBills
Any GOPers still backing Richards after
his actions toward a member of the First
Family—and, now, this week's rumors of
sexual predation—are going to have to
reckon with their Protestant God tomorrow
morning.
7:32 PM · 3 Nov 2020

538 politics ✔ @538politics
Our projections had Michigan, Ohio,
Pennsylvania, and Wisconsin all at a 70%
or higher chance of going blue, but latest
returns have them too close to call. Yeah,
we're confused too.
8:04 PM · 3 Nov 2020

The New York Times ✔ @nytimes
#Election2020 latest: a bruising round
of calls for Pres. Claremont brings the
electoral tally up to 178 for Sen. Richards.
Claremont lags behind at 113.
9:15 PM · 3 Nov 2020

They've partitioned off the smaller exhibit hall for VIPs
only—campaign staff, friends and family, congresspeople. On
the other side of the event center is the crowd of supporters
with their signs, their CLAREMONT 2020 and HISTORY,

HUH? T-shirts, overflowing under the architectural canopies and into the surrounding hills. It's supposed to be a party.

Alex has been trying not to stress. He knows how presidential elections go. When he was a kid, this was his Super Bowl. He used to sit in front of the living room TV and color each state in with red and blue magic markers as the night went on, allowed to stay up hours past his bedtime for one blessed night at age ten to watch Obama beat McCain. He watches his dad's jaw in profile now, trying to remember the triumph in the set of it that night.

There was a magic, then. Now, it's personal.

And they're losing.

The sight of Leo coming in through a side door isn't entirely unexpected, and June rises from her chair and meets them both in a quiet corner of the room on the same instinct. He's holding his phone in one hand.

"Your mother wants to talk to you," Leo says, and Alex automatically reaches out until Leo holds out a hand to stop him. "No, sorry, Alex, not you. June."

June blinks. "Oh." She steps forward, pushes her hair away from her ear. "Mom?"

"June," says the sound of their mother's voice over the little speaker. On the other end, she's in one of the arena's meeting rooms, a makeshift office with her core team. "Baby. I need you to, uh. I need you to come in here."

"Okay, Mom," she says, her voice measured and calm. "What's going on?"

"I just. I need you to help me rewrite this speech for, uh." There's a considerable pause. "Well. Just in case of concession."

June's face goes utterly blank for a second, and suddenly, vividly *furious*.

"No," she says, and she grabs Leo by the forearm so she can talk directly into the speaker. "*No,* I'm not gonna do that, because you're not gonna lose. Do you hear me? You're not losing. We're gonna fucking do this for four more years, *all of us.* I am not writing you a *goddamn concession speech,* ever."

There's another pause across the line, and Alex can picture their mother in her little makeshift Situation Room upstairs, glasses on, high heels still in the suitcase, staring at the screens, hoping and trying and praying. President Mom.

"Okay," she says evenly. "Okay. Alex. Do you think you could get up and say something for the crowd?"

"Yeah, yeah, sure, Mom," he says. He clears his throat, and it comes out as strong as hers the second time. "Of course."

A third pause, then. "God, I love you both so much."

Leo leaves, and he's quickly replaced by Zahra, whose sleek red dress and ever-present coffee thermos are the biggest comfort Alex has seen all night. Her ring flashes at him, and he thinks of Shaan and wishes desperately Henry was *here* already.

"Fix your face," she says, straightening his collar as she shepherds him and June through to the main exhibit hall and into the back of the stage area. "Big smiles, high energy, confidence."

He turns helplessly to June. "What do I say?"

"Little bit, ain't no time for me to write you anything," she tells him. "You're a leader. Go lead. You got this."

Oh God.

Confidence. He looks down at the cuffs of his jacket again, the red, white, and blue. *Be Alex,* Nora said when she handed it to him. *Be Alex.*

Alex is—two words that told a few million kids across America they weren't alone. A letterman jacket in APUSH. Secret loose panels in White House windows. Ruining something because you wanted it too badly and still getting back up and trying again. Not a prince. Something bigger, maybe.

"Zahra," he asks. "Did they call Texas yet?"

"No," she says. "Still too close."

"Still?"

Her smile is knowing. *"Still."*

The spotlight is almost blinding when he walks out, but he knows something. Deep down in his heart. They still haven't called Texas.

"Hey, y'all," he says to the crowd. His hand squeezes the microphone, but it's steady. "I'm Alex, your First Son." The hometown crowd goes wild, and Alex grins and means it, leans into it. When he says what he says next, he intends to believe it.

"You know what's crazy? Right now, Anderson Cooper is on CNN saying Texas is too close to call. *Too close to call.* Y'all may not know this about me, but I'm kind of a history nerd. So I can tell you, the last time Texas was *too close to call* was in 1976. In 1976, we went blue. It was Jimmy Carter, in the wake of Watergate. He just barely squeezed out fifty-one percent of our vote, and we helped him beat Gerald Ford for the presidency.

"Now, I'm standing here, and I'm thinking about it . . . A reliable, hardworking, honest, Southern Democrat versus corruption, and maliciousness, and hate. And one big state full of honest people, sick as hell of being lied to."

The crowd absolutely loses it, and Alex almost laughs. He raises his voice into the microphone, speaks up over the sound of cheers and applause and boots stomping on the floor of the hall. "Well, it sounds a little familiar to me, is all. So, what do y'all think, Texas? ¿Se repetirá la historia? Are we gonna make history repeat itself tonight?"

The roar says it all, and Alex yells with them, lets the sound carry him off the stage, lets it wrap around his heart and squeeze back in the blood that's drained out of it all night. The second he steps backstage, there's a hand on his back, the achingly familiar gravity of someone else's body reentering his space before it even touches his, a clean, familiar scent light in the air between.

"That was *brilliant,*" Henry says, smiling, in the flesh, *finally.* He's gorgeous in a navy-blue suit and a tie that, upon closer inspection, is patterned with little yellow roses.

"Your tie—"

"Oh, yes," he says, "yellow rose of Texas, is it? I read that was a thing. Thought it might be good luck."

All at once, Alex is in love all over again. He wraps the tie once around the back of his hand and reels Henry in and kisses him like he never has to stop. Which—he remembers, and laughs into Henry's mouth—he doesn't.

If he's talking about who he is, he wishes he'd been someone smart enough to have done this last year. He wouldn't have made Henry banish himself to a bunch of frozen shrubbery, and he wouldn't have just stood there while Henry gave him the most important kiss of his life. It would have been like this. He would have taken Henry's face in both hands and kissed him hard and deep and on purpose and said, "Take anything you want and know you deserve to have it."

He pulls back and says, "You're late, Your Highness."

Henry laughs. "Actually, I'm just in time for the upswing, it would seem."

He's talking about the latest round of calls, which apparently came in while Alex was onstage. Out in their VIP area, everyone's out of their seat, watching Anderson Cooper and Wolf Blitzer parse the returns on the big screens. Virginia: Claremont. Colorado: Claremont. Michigan: Claremont. Pennsylvania: Claremont. It almost fully makes up the difference in votes, with the West Coast still to go.

Shaan is here too, in one corner with Zahra, huddled with Luna and Amy and Cash, and Alex's head almost spins at the thought of how many nations could be brought to their knees by this particular gang. He grabs Henry's hand and pulls him into it all.

The magic comes in a nervous trickle—Henry's tie, hopeful lilts in voices, a few stray bits of confetti that escape the nets laced through the rafters and get stuck in Nora's hair—and then, all at once.

10:30 brings the big rush: Richards steals Iowa, yes, and sews up Utah and Montana, but the West Coast comes storming in with California's fifty-five fucking electoral votes. "Big damn heroes," Oscar crows when it's called to raucous cheers and nobody's surprise, and he and Luna slap their palms together. *West Side Bastardos.*

By midnight, they've taken the lead, and it does, finally, feel like a party, even if they're not out of the woods yet. Drinks are flowing, voices are loud, the crowd on the other side of the partition is electric. Gloria Estefan wailing through the sound system feels fitting again, not a stabbing, sick irony at a funeral. Across the room, Henry's with June, making a gesture at her hair, and she turns and lets him fix a piece of her braid that came loose earlier in a fit of anxiety.

Alex is so busy watching them, his two favorite people, he doesn't notice another person in his path until he collides with them headfirst, spilling their drink and almost sending them both stumbling into the massive victory cake on the buffet table.

"Jesus, sorry," he says, immediately reaching for a pile of napkins.

"If you knock over another expensive cake," says an extremely familiar whiskey-warm drawl, "I'm pretty sure your mom is gonna disinherit you."

He turns to see Liam, almost the same as he remembers— tall, broad-shouldered, sweet-faced, scruffy.

He's so mad he has such a specific type of dude and never even noticed it for so long.

"Oh my God, you came!"

"Of course I did," Liam says, grinning. Beside him, there's a cute guy grinning too. "I mean, it kind of seemed like the Secret Service were gonna come requisition me from my apartment if I didn't come."

Alex laughs. "Look, the presidency hasn't changed me *that* much. I'm still as aggressive a party instigator as I ever was."

"I'd be disappointed if you weren't, man."

They both grin, and God, on tonight of all nights it's good to see him, good to clear the air, good to stand next to someone outside of family who knew him before all this.

A week after he got outed, Liam texted him: 1. I wish we hadn't been such dumb assholes back then so we both could have helped each other out with stuff. 2. Jsyk, a reporter from some right-wing website called me yesterday to ask me about my history with you. I told him to go fuck himself, but I thought you'd want to know.

So yeah, of course he got a personal invitation.

"Listen, I," Alex starts, "I wanted to thank you—"

"Do not," Liam interrupts him. "Seriously. Okay? We're cool. We'll always be cool." He makes a dismissive gesture with one hand and nudges the cute, dark-eyed guy at his side. "Anyway, this is Spencer, my boyfriend."

"Alex," Alex introduces himself. Spencer's handshake is strong, all farmboy. "Good to meet you, man."

"It's an honor," Spencer says earnestly. "My mom canvassed for your mom when she ran for Congress back in the day, so like, we go way back. She's the first president I ever voted for."

"Okay, Spence, be cool," Liam says, putting an arm around Spencer's shoulders. A beam of pride cuts through Alex; if Spencer's parents were Claremont volunteers, they're definitely more open-minded than he remembers Liam's being. "This guy shit his pants on the bus on the way back from the aquarium in fourth grade, so like, he's not that big of a deal."

"For the *last time,* you douchebag," Alex huffs, "that was Adam Villanueva, not me!"

"Yeah, I know what I saw," Liam says.

Alex is just opening his mouth to argue when someone shouts his name—a photo op or interview or something for *BuzzFeed.* "Shit. I gotta go, but Liam, we have, like, a shitload to catch up on. Can we hang this weekend? Let's hang this weekend. I'm in town all weekend. Let's hang this weekend."

He's already walking away backward, and Liam is rolling his eyes in an annoyed but fond way, not in a this-is-why-I-stopped-talking-to-you way, so he keeps going. The interview is quick, cut off mid-sentence: Anderson Cooper's face looms on the screen overhead like a disgustingly handsome Hunger Games cannon, announcing they're ready to call Florida.

"Come on, you backyard-shooting-range motherfuckers," Zahra is muttering under her breath beside him when he falls in with his people.

"Did she just say backyard shooting range?" Henry asks, leaning into Alex's ear. "Is that a real thing a person can have?"

"You really have a lot to learn about America, mijo," Oscar tells him, not unkindly.

The screen flashes red—*RICHARDS*—and a collective groan grinds through the room.

"Nora, what's the math?" June says, rounding on her, a slightly frantic look in her eyes. "I majored in nouns."

"Okay," Nora says, "at this point we just need to get over 270 or make it impossible for Richards to get over 270—"

"Yes," June cuts in impatiently, "I am familiar with how the electoral college works—"

"You asked!"

"I didn't mean to remediate me!"

"You're kinda hot when you get all indignant."

"Can we *focus*?" Alex puts in.

"Okay," Nora says. She shakes out her hands. "So, right now we can get over 270 with Texas or Nevada *and* Alaska combined. Richards has to get all three of those. So nobody is out of the game yet."

"So, we *have* to get Texas now?"

"Not unless they call Nevada," Nora says, "which never happens this early."

She barely has time to finish before Anderson Cooper is back onscreen with breaking news. Alex wonders briefly what it's going to be like to have future Anderson Cooper stress hallucinations. *NEVADA: RICHARDS.*

"Are you *fucking* kidding me?"

"So, now it's essentially—"

"Whoever wins Texas," Alex says, "wins the presidency."

There's a heavy pause, and June says, "I'm gonna go stress

eat the cold pizza the polling people have. Sound good? Cool."
And she's gone.

By 12:30, nobody can believe it's down to this.

Texas has never in history gone this long without being
called. If it were any other state, Richards probably would have
called to concede by now.

Luna is pacing. Alex's dad is sweating through his suit.
June is going to smell like pizza for a week. Zahra is on the
phone, yelling into someone's voicemail, and when she hangs
up, she explains that her sister is having trouble getting into a
good daycare and agreed to put Zahra on the job as an outlet
for her stress. Ellen, too tense to stay upstairs, is stalking
through it all like a hungry lioness.

And that's when June comes charging up to them, her hand
on the arm of a girl Alex recognizes—her college roommate,
his brain supplies. She's got on a poll volunteer shirt and a
broad smile.

"Y'all—" June says, breathless. "Molly just—she just came
from—fuck, just, tell them!"

And Molly opens her blessed mouth and says, "We think
you have the votes."

Nora drops her phone. Ellen steps over it to grab Molly's
other arm. "You think or you know?"

"I mean, we're pretty sure—"

"How sure?"

"Well, they just counted another 10,000 ballots from Har-
ris County—"

"Oh my God—"

"Wait, *look*—"

It's on the projection screen now. They're calling it. *Anderson
Cooper, you handsome bastard.*

Texas is gray for five more seconds, before flooding beautiful, beautiful, unmistakable Lake LBJ blue.

Thirty-eight votes for Claremont, for a grand total of 301. And the presidency.

"*Four more years!*" Alex's mom outright screams, louder than he's heard her scream in *years.*

The cheers come in a hum, in a rumble, and finally, in a storm, pressing from the other side of the partition, from the hills surrounding the arena and the city surrounding the streets, from the country itself. From, maybe, a few sleepy allies in London.

From his side, Henry, whose eyes are wet, seizes Alex's face roughly in both hands and kisses him like the end of the movie, whoops, and shoves him at his family.

The nets are cut loose from the ceiling, and down come the balloons, and Alex staggers into a press of bodies and his father's chest, a delirious hug, into June, who is a crying disaster, and Leo, who is somehow crying *more.* Nora is sandwiched between both beaming, proud parents, screaming at the top of her lungs, and Luna is throwing Claremont campaign pamphlets in the air like a mafioso with hundred dollar bills. He sees Cash, severely testing the weight limits of the venue's chairs by dancing on one, and Amy, waving around her phone so her wife can see it all over FaceTime, and Zahra and Shaan, aggressively making out against a giant stack of CLAREMONT/HOLLERAN 2020 yard signs. WASPy Hunter hoisting another staffer up on his shoulders, Liam and Spencer raising their beers in a toast, a hundred campaign staffers and volunteers crying and shouting in disbelief and joy. They did it. They *did* it. The Lometa Longshot and a long-awaited blue Texas.

The crowd pushes him back into Henry's chest, and after absolutely everything, all the emails and texts and months on the road and secret rendezvous and nights of wanting, the whole accidentally-falling-in-love-with-your-sworn-enemy-at-the-absolute-worst-possible-time thing, they made it. Alex said they would—he *promised*. Henry's smiling so wide and bright that Alex thinks his heart's going to break trying to hold the size of this entire moment, the completeness of it, a thousand years of history swelling inside his rib cage.

"I need to tell you something," Henry says, breathless, when Alex pulls back. "I bought a brownstone. In Brooklyn."

Alex's mouth falls open. "You *didn't*!"

"I did."

And for a fraction of a second, a whole crystallized life flashes into view, a next term and no elections left to win, a schedule packed with classes and Henry smiling from the pillow next to him in the gray light of a Brooklyn morning. It drops right into the well of his chest and spreads, like how hope spreads. It's a good thing everyone else is already crying.

"Okay, people," says Zahra's voice through the rush of blood and love and adrenaline and noise in his ears. Her mascara is streaming, her lipstick smeared across her chin. Beside her, he can hear his mother on the phone with one finger jammed into her ear, taking Richards's concession call. "Victory speech in fifteen. Places, let's go!"

Alex finds himself shuffled sideways, through the crowd and over to a little corral near the stage, behind the curtains, and then his mother's on stage, and Leo, and Mike and his wife, and Nora and her parents and June and their dad. Alex strides out after them, waving into the white glow of the spotlight, shouting a jumble of languages into the noise. He's so caught up that he doesn't realize at first Henry isn't at his side, and he turns back to see him hovering in the wings, just behind a curtain. Always hesitant to step on anyone's moment.

That's not going to fly anymore. He's family. He's part of it all now, headlines and oil paintings and pages in the Library of Congress, etched right alongside. And he's part of *them.* Goddamn forever.

"Come on!" Alex yells, waving him over, and Henry spares a second to look panicked before he's tipping his chin up and buttoning his suit jacket and stepping out onto the stage. He gravitates to Alex's side, beaming. Alex throws one arm around him and the other around June. Nora presses in at June's other side.

And President Ellen Claremont steps up to the podium.

EXCERPT: PRESIDENT ELLEN CLAREMONT'S VICTORY
ADDRESS FROM AUSTIN, TEXAS, NOVEMBER 3, 2020

Four years ago, in 2016, we stood at a
precipice as a nation. There were those
who would have seen us stumble backward
into hatred and vitriol and prejudice, who
wanted to reignite old embers of division
within our country's very soul. You looked
them square in the eye and said, "No. We
won't."

You voted instead for a woman and a
family with Texas dirt under their shoes,
who would lead you into four years of
progress, of carrying on a legacy of

hope and change. And tonight, you did it
again. You chose me. And I humbly, humbly
thank you.

   And my family—my family thanks you
too. My family, made up of the children of
immigrants, of people who love in defiance
of expectations or condemnation, of women
determined never to back down from what's
right, a braid of histories that stands
for the future of America. My family. Your
First Family. We intend to do everything we
can, for the next four years and the years
beyond, to continue making you proud.

The second round of confetti is still falling when Alex grabs
Henry by the hand and says, "Follow me."

   Everyone's too busy celebrating or doing interviews to see
them slip out the back door. He trades Liam and Spencer the
promise of a six-pack for their bikes, and Henry doesn't ask
questions, just kicks the stand out and disappears into the
night behind him.

   Austin feels different somehow, but it hasn't changed, not
really. Austin is dried flowers from a homecoming corsage in
a bowl by the cordless phone, the washed-out bricks of the rec
center where he tutored kids after school, a beer bummed off
a stranger on the spill of the Barton Creek Greenbelt. The no-
pales, the hipster cold brews. It's a weird, singular constant,
the hook in his heart that's kept tugging him back to earth his
whole life.

   Maybe it's just that *he's* different.

They cross the bridge into downtown, the gray grids intersecting Lavaca, the bars overflowing with people yelling his mother's name, wearing his own face on their chests, waving Texas flags, American flags, Mexican flags, pride flags. There's music echoing through the streets, loudest when they reach the Capitol, where someone has climbed up the front steps and erected a set of loudspeakers blasting Starship's "Nothing's Gonna Stop Us Now." Somewhere above, against the thick clouds: fireworks.

Alex takes his feet off the pedals and glides past the massive, Italian Renaissance Revival façade of the Capitol, the building where his mom went to work every day when he was a kid. It's taller than the one back in DC. Everything's bigger, after all.

It takes twenty minutes to reach Pemberton Heights, and Alex leads the Prince of England up onto the high curb of a neighborhood in Old West Austin and shows him where to throw his bike in the yard, spokes still spinning little shadow lines across the grass. The sounds of expensive leather soles on the cracked front steps of the old house on Westover don't sound any stranger than his own boots. Like coming home.

He steps back and watches Henry take it all in—the butter-yellow siding, the big bay window, the handprints in the sidewalk. Alex hasn't been inside this house since he was twenty. They pay a family friend to look after it, wrap the pipes, run the water. They can't bear to let it go. Nothing's changed inside, just been boxed up.

There are no fireworks out here, no music, no confetti. Just sleeping, single-family homes, TVs finally switched off. Just a house where Alex grew up, where he saw Henry's picture in a magazine and felt a flicker of something, a start.

"Hey," Alex says. Henry turns back to him, his eyes silver in the wash of the streetlight. "We *won*."

Henry takes his hand, one corner of his mouth tugging gently upward. "Yeah. We won."

Alex reaches down into the front of his dress shirt and finds the chain with his fingers, pulls it out carefully. The ring, the key.

Under winter clouds, victorious, he unlocks the door.

ACKNOWLEDGMENTS

I came up with the idea for this book on an I-10 off-ramp in early 2016, and I never imagined what it would turn out to be. I mean, at that point I couldn't imagine what *2016 itself* would turn out to be. Yikes. For months after November, I gave up on writing this book. Suddenly what was supposed to be a tongue-in-cheek parallel universe needed to be escapist, trauma-soothing, alternate-but-realistic reality. Not a perfect world—one still believably fucked up, just a little better, a little more optimistic. I wasn't sure I was up to the task. I hoped I was.

What I hoped to do, and what I hope I have done with this book by the time you've finished it, my dear reader, is to be a spark of joy and hope you needed.

I couldn't have done any of this without the help of so many. To my angel of an agent, Sara Megibow, thank you for driving this crazy bus. I went into this whole experience hoping to find one person who felt even half of what I feel for this book, and you matched me from the first moment we spoke. Thank you for being the champion this book needed and the reassurance always at my back. To Vicki Lame, my editor, the Texas girl who fought for this book and always saw in it what it could mean to people. Thank you for giving this your all, for forever being the person in the corner of the ring with the water bottle. You and the team at St. Martin's Griffin have literally made dreams come true. Thank you to my publicity team, DJ DeSmyter and Meghan Harrington, and to everyone else who threw themselves behind this book.

More thanks: Elizabeth Freeburg, who taught me more than I can ever give back to her, without whom I'd be half the writer I am today. Lena Barsky, who doula'd this entire novel, who was the first to love these characters as much as I do. Sasha Smith, my literary sherpa who believed in me most, without whom I would have been drowning before I was even out of the slip. Shanicka Anderson, the beta reader of my dreams, who loved this book even when it was 40,000 words too long. Lauren Heffker, the person who sat with me in a Taco Bell while I untangled this plot, who never didn't want to hear what I was thinking. Season Vining, who poured my wine and told me that my dream wasn't so unattainable. Leah Romero, my number-one fan and political inspiration, the reader I was always writing to impress. Tiffany Martinez, who read this book with care and love and gave it to me straight. Laura Marquez, who helped with translations. CJSR, who knows it all, whose sleepless nights this book happened in spite of. My FoCo fam, my new home.

To my family, who have done more for me over the years

than any person deserves: You had no idea what you were signing on for when I told you I wrote a book, but y'all still
cheered me on. Thank you for loving me as I am. Thank you
for letting me be your weirdo baby. To Dad, my original sto-
ryteller: I know you always knew I had this in me. Thank you
for helping me believe it. Big as the universe, over the clouds,
forever. This is my best work to date.

To the sources that helped me with the mountains of research I did for this: WhiteHouseMuseum.org, the Royal
Collection Online, *My Dear Boy* by Rictor Norton, the V&A's
extremely helpful website, countless others. To the country of
Norway, literally, for the week that broke me out of the slump
and made 110,000 words of the first draft happen. To "Texas
Reznikoff" by Mitski.

To every person in search of somewhere to belong who happened to pick up this book, I hope you found a place in here,
even if just for a few pages. You are loved. I wrote this for you.

Keep fighting, keep making history, keep looking after one
another.

Affectionately yrs. Have a Shiner on me.

Read on for an excerpt from Casey
McQuiston's next novel

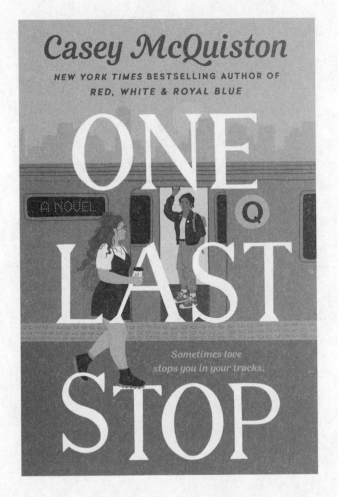

Available June 1, 2021, from St. Martin's Griffin

1

Taped to a trash can inside the Popeyes
Louisiana Kitchen at the corner of Parkside
and Flatbush Avenues.

SEEKING YOUNG SINGLE ROOMMATE FOR 3BR APARTMENT
UPSTAIRS, 6TH FLOOR. $700/MO. MUST BE QUEER & TRANS
FRIENDLY. MUST NOT BE AFRAID OF FIRE OR DOGS. NO
LIBRAS, WE ALREADY HAVE ONE. CALL NIKO.

"Can I touch you?"

That's the first thing the guy with the tattoos says when August settles onto the rubbed-off center cushion of the brown leather couch—a flaking hand-me-down number that's been a recurring character the past four and a half years of college. The type you crash on, bury under textbooks, or sit on while sipping flat Coke and speaking to no one at a party. The quintessential early twenties trash couch.

Most of the furniture is as trash as the trash couch, mismatched and thrifted and hauled in off the street. But when Tattoo Boy—Niko, the flyer said his name was Niko—sits across from her, it's in a startlingly high-end Eames chair.

The place is like that: a mix of familiar and very much not familiar. Small and cramped, offensive shades of green and yellow on the walls. Plants dangling off almost every surface, spindly arms reaching across shelves, a faint smell of soil. The windows are the same painted-shut frames of old apartments in New Orleans, but these are half covered with pages of drawings, afternoon light filtering through, muted and waxy.

There's a five-foot-tall sculpture of Judy Garland made from bicycle parts and marshmallow Peeps in the corner. It's not recognizable as Judy, except for the sign that says: HELLO MY NAME IS JUDY GARLAND.

Niko looks at August, hand held out, blurry in the steam from his tea. He's got this black-on-black greaser thing going on, a dark undercut against light brown skin and a confident jaw, a single crystal dangling from one ear. Tattoos spill down both his arms and lick up his throat from beneath his buttoned-up collar. His voice is a little croaky, like the back end of a cold, and he's got a toothpick in one corner of his mouth.

Okay, Danny Zuko, calm down.

"Sorry, uh." August stares, stuck on his question. "What?"

"Not in a weird way," he says. The tattoo on the back of his hand is a Ouija planchette. His knuckles say FULL MOON. Good lord. "Just want to get your vibe. Sometimes physical contact helps."

"What, are you a—?"

"A psychic, yeah," he says matter-of-factly. The toothpick rolls down the white line of his teeth when he grins, wide and disarming. "Or that's one word for it. Clairvoyant, gifted, spiritist, whatever."

Jesus. Of course. There was no way a $700-a-month room in Brooklyn was going to come without a catch, and the catch is marshmallow Judy Garland and this refurbished Springsteen who's probably about to tell her she's got her aura on inside out and backward like Dollar Tree pantyhose.

But she's got nowhere to go, and there's a Popeyes on the first floor of the building. August Landry does not trust people, but she trusts fried chicken.

She lets Niko touch her hand.

"Cool," he says tonelessly, like he's stuck his head out the window to check the weather. He taps two fingers on the back of her knuckles and sits back. "Oh. Oh wow, okay. That's interesting."

August blinks. "What?"

He takes the toothpick out of his mouth and sets it on the steamer trunk between them, next to a bowl of gumballs. He's got a constipated look on his face.

"You like lilies?" he says. "Yeah, I'll get some lilies for your move-in day. Does Thursday work for you? Myla's gonna need some time to clear her stuff out. She has a lot of bones."

"I—what, like, in her body?"

"No, frog bones. Really tiny. Hard to pick up. Gotta use tweezers." He must notice the look on August's face. "Oh, she's a sculptor. It's for a piece. It's her room you're taking. Don't worry, I'll sage it."

"Uh, I wasn't worried about . . . frog ghosts?" Should she be worried about frog ghosts? Maybe this Myla person is a ritualistic frog murderer.

"Niko, stop telling people about frog ghosts," says a voice down the hall. A pretty Black girl with a friendly, round face and eyelashes for miles is leaning out of a doorway, a pair of goggles shoved up into her dark curls. She smiles when she sees August. "Hi, I'm Myla."

"August."

"We found our girl," Niko says. "She likes lilies."

August hates when people like him do things like that. Lucky guesses. She *does* like lilies. She can pull up a whole Wikipedia page in her head: *lilium candidum*. Grows two to six feet tall. Studied diligently from the window of her mom's two-bedroom apartment.

There's no way Niko should know—no way he *does*. Just like she does with palm readers under beach umbrellas back home in Jackson Square, she holds her breath and brushes straight past.

"So that's it?" she says. "I got the room? You, uh, you didn't even ask me any questions."

He leans his head on his hand. "What time were you born?"

"I . . . don't know?" Remembering the flyer, she adds, "I think I'm a Virgo, if that helps."

"Oh, yeah, definitely a Virgo."

She manages to keep her face impartial. "Are you . . . a professional psychic? Like people pay you?"

"He's part-time," Myla says. She floats into the room, graceful for someone with a blowtorch in one hand, and drops into the chair next to his. The wad of pink bubblegum she's chewing explains the bowl of gumballs. "And part-time very terrible bartender."

"I'm not that bad."

"Sure you're not," she says, planting a kiss on his cheek. She stage-whispers to August, "He thought a paloma was a kind of tumor."

While they're bickering about Niko's bartending skills, August sneaks a gumball out of the bowl and drops it to test a theory about the floor. As suspected, it rolls off through the kitchen and into the hallway.

She clears her throat. "So y'all are—?"

"Together, yeah," Myla says. "Four years. It was nice to have our own rooms, but none of us are doing so hot financially, so I'm moving into his."

"And the third roommate is?"

"Wes. That's his room at the end of the hall," she says. "He's mostly nocturnal."

"Those are his," Niko says, pointing at the drawings in the windows. "He's a tattoo artist."

"Okay," August says. "So it's $2,800 total? $700 each?"

"Yep."

"And the flyer said something about . . . fire?"

Myla gives her blowtorch a friendly squeeze. "Controlled fire."

"And dogs?"

"Wes has one," Niko puts in. "A little poodle named Noodles."

"Noodles the poodle?"

"He's on Wes's sleep schedule, though. So, a ghost in the night."

"Anything else I should know?"

Myla and Niko exchange a look.

"Like three times a day the fridge makes this noise like a skeleton trying to eat a bag of quarters, but we're pretty sure it's fine," Niko says.

"One of the laminate tiles in the kitchen isn't really stuck down anymore, so we all just kind of kick it around the room," Myla adds.

"The guy across the hall is a drag queen, and sometimes he practices his numbers in the middle of the night, so if you hear Patti LaBelle, that's why."

"The hot water takes twenty minutes to get going, but ten if you're nice."

"It's not haunted, but it's like, not *not* haunted."

Myla smacks her gum. "That's it."

August swallows. "Okay."

She weighs her options, watching Niko slip his fingers into the pocket of Myla's paint-stained overalls, and wonders what Niko saw when he touched the back of her hand, or thought he saw. *Pretended* to see.

And does she want to live with a couple? A couple that is one half fake psychic who looks like he fronts an Arctic Monkeys cover band and one half firestarter with a room full of dead frogs? No.

But Brooklyn College's spring semester starts in a week, and she can't deal with trying to find a place *and* a job once classes pick up.

Turns out, for a girl who carries a knife because she'd rather be anything but unprepared, August did not plan her move to New York very well.

"Okay?" Myla says. "Okay what?"

"Okay," August repeats. "I'm in."

In the end, August was always going to say yes to this apartment, because she grew up in one smaller and uglier and filled with even weirder things.

"It looks nice!" her mom says over FaceTime, propped on the windowsill.

"You're only saying that because this one has wood floors and not that nightmare carpet from the Idlewild place."

"That place wasn't so bad!" she says, buried in a box of files.

Her buggy glasses slide down her nose, and she pushes them up with the business end of a highlighter, leaving a yellow streak. "It gave us nine great years. And carpet can hide a multitude of sins."

August rolls her eyes, pushing a box across the room. The Idlewild apartment was a two-bedroom shithole half an hour outside of New Orleans, the kind of suburban built-in-the-'70s dump that doesn't even have the charm or character of being in the city.

She can still picture the carpet in the tiny gaps of the obstacle course of towering piles of old magazines and teetering file boxes. *Double Dare 2000: Single Mom Edition.* It was an unforgivable shade of grimy beige, just like the walls, in the spaces that weren't plastered with maps and bulletin boards and ripped-out phonebook pages, and—

Yeah, this place isn't so bad.

"Did you talk to Detective Primeaux today?" August asks. It's the first Friday of the month, so she knows the answer.

"Yeah, nothing new," she says. "He doesn't even try to act like he's gonna open the case back up anymore. Goddamn shame."

August pushes another box into a different corner, this one near the radiator puffing warmth into the January freeze. Closer to the windowsill, she can see her mom better, their shared mousy-brown hair frizzing into her face. Under it, the same round face and big green bush baby eyes as August's, the same angular hands as she thumbs through papers. Her mom looks exhausted. She always looks exhausted.

"Well," August says. "He's a shit."

"He's a shit," her mom agrees, nodding gravely. "How 'bout the new roommates?"

"Fine. I mean, kind of weird. One of them claims to be a psychic. But I don't think they're, like, serial killers."

She hums, only half-listening. "Remember the rules. Number one—"

"Us versus everyone."

"And number two—"

"If they're gonna kill you, get their DNA under your fingernails."

"Thatta girl," she says. "Listen, I gotta go, I just opened this shipment of public records, and it's gonna take me all weekend. Be safe, okay? And call me tomorrow."

The moment they hang up, the room is unbearably quiet.

If August's life were a movie, the soundtrack would be the low sounds of her mom, the clickity-clacking of her keyboard, or quiet mumbling as she searches for a document. Even when August quit helping with the case, when she moved out and mostly heard it over the phone, it was constant. A couple of thousand miles away, it's like someone finally cut the score.

There's a lot they have in common—maxed-out library cards, perpetual singlehood, affinity for Crystal Hot Sauce, encyclopedic knowledge of NOPD missing persons protocol. But the big difference between August and her mother? Suzette Landry hoards like nuclear winter is coming, and August very intentionally owns almost nothing.

She has five boxes. Five entire cardboard boxes to show for her life at twenty-three. Living like she's on the run from the fucking FBI. Normal stuff.

She slides the last one into an empty corner, so they're not cluttered together.

At the bottom of her purse, past her wallet and notepads and spare phone battery, is her pocketknife. The handle's shaped like a fish, with a faded pink sticker in the shape of a heart, stuck on when she was seven—around the time she learned how to use it. Once she's slashed the boxes open, her things settle into neat little stacks.

By the radiator: two pairs of boots, three pairs of socks. Six shirts, two sweaters, three pairs of jeans, two skirts. One pair of white Vans—those are special, a reward she bought herself last year, buzzed off adrenaline and mozzarella sticks from the Applebee's where she came out to her mom.

By the wall with the crack down the middle: the one physical book she owns—a vintage crime novel—beside her tablet containing her hundreds of other books. Maybe thousands. She's not sure. It stresses her out to think about having that many of anything.

In the corner that smells of sage and maybe, faintly, a hundred frogs she's been assured died of natural causes: one framed photo of an old washateria on Chartres, one Bic lighter, and an accompanying candle. She folds her knife up, sets it down, and places a sign that says PERSONAL EFFECTS over it in her head.

She's shaking out her air mattress when she hears someone unsticking the front door from the jamb, a violent skittering following like somebody's bowled an enormous furry spider down the hallway. It crashes into a wall, and then what can only be described as a soot sprite from *Spirited Away* comes shooting into August's room.

"Noodles!" calls Niko, and then he's in the doorway. There's a leash hanging from his hand and an apologetic expression from his angular features.

"I thought you said he was a ghost in the night," August says. Noodles is snuffling through her socks, tail a blur, until he realizes there's a new person and launches himself at her.

"He is," Niko says with a wince. "I mean, kind of. Sometimes, I feel bad and take him to work with me at the shop during the day. I guess we didn't mention his, uh—" Noodles takes this moment to place both paws on August's shoulders and try to force his tongue into her mouth. "Personality."

Myla appears behind Niko, a skateboard under one arm. "Oh, you met Noodles!"

"Oh yeah," August says. "Intimately."

"You need help with the rest of your stuff?"

She blinks. "This is it."

"That's . . . that's it?" Myla says. "That's everything?"

"Yeah."

"You don't, uh." Myla's giving her this look, like she's realizing she didn't actually know anything about August before agreeing to let her store her veggies alongside theirs in the crisper. It's a look August gives herself in the mirror a lot. "You don't have any furniture."

"I'm kind of a minimalist," August tells her. If she tried, August could get her five boxes down to four. Maybe something to do over the weekend.

"Oh, I wish I could be more like you. Niko's gonna start throwing my yarn out the window while I'm sleeping." Myla smiles, reassured that August is not, in fact, in the Witness Protection Program. "Anyway, we're gonna go get dinner pancakes. You in?"

August would rather let Niko throw *her* out the window than split shortstacks with people she barely knows.

"I can't really afford to eat out," she says. "I don't have a job yet."

"I got you. Call it a welcome home dinner," Myla says.

"Oh," August says. That's . . . generous. A warning light flashes somewhere in August's brain. Her mental field guide to making friends is a two-page pamphlet that just says: *DON'T*.

"Pancake Billy's House of Pancakes," Myla says. "It's a Flatbush institution."

"Open since 1976," Niko chimes in.

August arches a brow. "Forty-four years and nobody wanted to take another run at that name?"

"It's part of the charm," Myla says. "It's like, our place. You're from the South, right? You'll like it. Very unpretentious."

They hover there, staring at one another. A pancake standoff.

August wants to stay in the safety of her crappy bedroom with the comfortable misery of a Pop-Tarts dinner and a silent truce with her brain. But she looks at Niko and realizes, even if he was faking it when he touched her, he saw something in her. And that's more than anyone's done in a long time.

Ugh.

"Okay," she says, clambering to her feet, and Myla's smile bursts across her face like starlight.

Ten minutes later, August is tucked into a corner booth of Pancake Billy's House of Pancakes, where every waiter seems to know Niko and Myla by name. The server is a man with a beard, a broad smile, and a faded name tag that says WINFIELD pinned to his red Pancake Billy's T-shirt. He doesn't even ask Niko or Myla's order—just sets down a mug of coffee and a pink lemonade.

She can see what they meant about Pancake Billy's legendary status. It has a particular type of New Yorkness to it, something she's seen in an Edward Hopper painting or the diner from *Seinfeld,* but with a lot more seasoning. It's a corner unit, big windows facing the street on both sides, dinged-up Formica tables and red vinyl seats slowly being rotated out of the busiest sections as they crack. There's a soda shop bar down the length of one wall, old photos and Mets front pages from floor to ceiling.

And it's got a potency of smell, a straight-up unadulterated olfactory turpitude that August can feel sinking into her being.

"Anyway, Wes's dad gave them to him," Myla says, explaining how a set of leather Eames chairs wound up in their apartment. "A 'good job fulfilling familial expectations' gift when he started architecture school at Pratt."

"I thought he was a tattoo artist?"

"He is," Niko says. "He dropped out after one semester. Bit of a . . . well, a mental breakdown."

"He sat on a fire escape in his underwear for fourteen hours, and they had to call the fire department," Myla adds.

"Only because of the arson," Niko tacks on.

"Jesus," August says. "How did y'all meet him?"

Myla pushes one of Niko's sleeves up past his elbow, showing off the weirdly hot Virgin Mary wrapped around his forearm. "He did this. Half-price, since he was apprenticing back then."

"Wow." August's fingers fidget on the sticky menu, itching to write it all down. Her least charming instinct when meeting new people: take field notes. "Architecture to tattoos. Hell of a leap."

"He decorated cakes for a minute in between, if you can believe it," Myla says. "Sometimes, when he's having a good day, you come home and the whole place smells like vanilla, and he'll have just left a dozen cupcakes on the counter and dipped."

"That little twink contains multitudes," Niko observes.

Myla laughs and turns back to August. "So, what brought you to New York?"

August hates this question. It's too big. What could possess someone like August, a suburban girl with a swimming pool of student loan debt and the social skills of a Pringles can, to move to New York with no friends and no plan?

Truth is, when you spend your whole life alone, it's incredibly appealing to move somewhere big enough to get lost in, where being alone looks like a choice.

"Always wanted to try it," August says instead. "New York, it's . . . I don't know, I tried a couple of cities. I went to UNO in New Orleans, then U of M in Memphis, and they all felt . . . too small, I guess. I wanted somewhere bigger. So I transferred to BC."

Niko's looking at her serenely, swilling his coffee. She thinks he's mostly harmless, but she doesn't like the way he looks at her like he knows things.

"They weren't enough of a challenge," he says. Another gentle observation. "You wanted a better puzzle."

August folds her arms. "That's . . . not completely wrong."

Winfield appears with their food, and Myla asks him, "Hey, where's Marty? He's always on this shift."

"Quit," Winfield says, depositing a syrup dispenser on the table.

"No."

"Moved back to Nebraska."

"Bleak."

"Yep."

"So that means," Myla says, leaning over her plate, "you're hiring."

"Yeah, why? You know somebody?"

"Have you met August?" She gestures dramatically to August like she's a vowel on *Wheel of Fortune.*

Winfield turns his attention to August, and she freezes, bottle in her hand still dribbling hot sauce onto her hashbrowns.

"You waited tables before?"

"I—"

"Tons," Myla cuts in. "Born in an apron."

Winfield squints at August, looking doubtful.

"You'd have to apply. It'll be up to Lucie."

He jerks his chin toward the bar, where a severe-looking young white woman with unnaturally red hair and heavy eyeliner is glaring at the cash register. If she's the one August has to scam, it looks like she's more likely to get an acrylic nail to the jugular.

"Lucie loves me," Myla says.

"She really doesn't."

"She loves me as much as she loves anyone else."

"Not the bar you want to clear."

"Tell her I can vouch for August."

"Actually, I—" August attempts, but Myla stomps on her foot. She's wearing combat boots—it's hard to miss.

The thing is, August gets the sense that this isn't exactly a normal diner. There's something shiny and bright about it that curls, warm and inviting, around the sagging booths and waiters spinning table to table. A busboy brushes past with a tub of dishes and a mug topples from the pile. Winfield reaches blindly behind himself and catches it midair.

It's something adjacent to magic.

August doesn't *do* magic.

"Come on, Win," Myla says as Winfield smoothly deposits

the mug back in the tub. "We've been your Thursday nighters
for how long? Three years? I wouldn't bring you someone who
couldn't cut it."

He rolls his eyes, but he's smiling. "I'll get an app."

"I've never waited a table in my *life*," August says, when they're
walking back to the apartment.

"You'll be fine," Myla says. "Niko, tell her she'll be fine."

"I'm not a psychic reading ATM."

"Oh, but you were last week when I wanted Thai, but you
were sensing that basil had *bad energy for us.* . . ."

August listens to the sound of their voices playing off
each other and three sets of footsteps on the sidewalk. The
city is darkening, a flat brownish orange almost like a New
Orleans night, and familiar enough to make her think that
maybe . . . maybe she's got a chance.

At the top of the stairs, Myla unlocks the door, and they kick
off their shoes into one pile.

Niko gestures toward the kitchen sink and says, "Welcome
home."

And August notices for the first time, beside the faucet: lilies,
fresh, stuck in a jar.

Home.

Well. It's *their* home, not hers. Those are *their* childhood
photos on the fridge, *their* smells of paint and soot and lavender
threaded through the patchy rugs, *their* pancake dinner routine,
all of it settled years before August even got to New York. But
it's nice to look at. A comforting still life to be enjoyed from
across the room.

August has lived in a dozen rooms without ever knowing

how to make a space into a home, how to expand to fill it like Niko or Myla or even Wes with his drawings in the windows. She doesn't know, really, what it would take at this point. It's been twenty-three years of passing through, touching brick after brick, never once feeling a permanent tug.

It feels stupid to say it, but maybe. Maybe it could be this. Maybe a new major. Maybe a new job. Maybe a place that could want her to belong in it.

Maybe a person, she guesses. She can't imagine who.

ABOUT THE AUTHOR

Valerie Mosley

Casey McQuiston is the *New York Times* bestselling author of *Red, White & Royal Blue,* as well as a pie enthusiast. She writes books about smart people with bad manners falling in love. Born and raised in southern Louisiana, she now lives in New York City with her poodle mix and personal assistant, Pepper.